Fic Farm
Farmer, W. Michael.
The Iliad of Geronimo : a
song of blood and fire

THE ILIAD OF GERONIMO: A SONG OF BLOOD AND FIRE

THE ILIAD
OF GERONIMO:
A SONG OF
BLOOD AND FIRE
A Novel

W. MICHAEL FARMER

FIVE STAR
A part of Gale, a Cengage Company

GALE
A Cengage Company

LIBRARY OF CONGRESS CATALOGING-IN-PUBLICATION DATA

Names: Farmer, W. Michael, 1944– author.
Title: The Iliad of Geronimo: a song of blood and fire : a novel / W. Michael Farmer.
Description: First edition. | [Waterville] : Five Star, a part of Gale, a Cengage Company, 2022. | Series: Five Star frontier fiction | Identifiers: LCCN 2021039503 | ISBN 9781432888060 (hardcover)
Subjects: LCSH: Geronimo, 1829-1909—Fiction. | Apache Indians—Wars—Fiction. | LCGFT: Biographical fiction. | Historical fiction. | Novels.
Classification: LCC PS3606.A725 I45 2022 | DDC 813/.6—dc23
LC record available at https://lccn.loc.gov/2021039503

First Edition. First Printing: March 2022
Find us on Facebook—https://www.facebook.com/FiveStarCengage
Visit our website—http://www.gale.cengage.com/fivestar
Contact Five Star Publishing at FiveStar@cengage.com

Printed in Mexico
Print Number: 01   Print Year: 2022

For Corky, my best friend and wife
The wind beneath my wings

For the Iliad of Geronimo, the epic warrior

Rage—Child of the Water, sing the rage of Taklishim's son, Goyale,
Murderous, doomed, that cost White-eyed and *Nakai-yi* enemies countless losses,
Hurling to the ghost pony so many sturdy souls,
Great fighters' souls, but made their bodies food for fire and iron, coyotes and vultures,
And the will of *Ussen* was moving towards its end. Begin, Child of the Water, when the two
First broke and clashed, a lord of the White-Eyes and the brilliant Geronimo.

—A paraphrase from *The Iliad* by Homer
as translated from the Greek by Robert Fagles

TABLE OF CONTENTS

ACKNOWLEDGMENTS 11
MAP OF THE GERONIMO
   ILIAD PLACES OF WAR 12
HISTORICAL CHARACTERS . . . 15
WORDS AND PHRASES 19
APACHE RECKONING OF
   TIME AND SEASONS 21
CHIRICAHUA APACHE BANDS . . 23
PREFACE 25
THE ILIAD OF GERONIMO . . . 29
ADDITIONAL READING 397
ABOUT THE AUTHOR 401

ACKNOWLEDGMENTS

There have been many friends and professionals who have supported me in this work and to whom I owe a special debt of gratitude for their help and many kindnesses.

My longtime personal editor, Melissa Watkins Starr, provided independent eyes, valuable technical suggestions and corrections, and light on passages that needed clarification.

Lynda Sánchez's insights into Apache culture and their voices are a major point of reference in understanding the times and personalities covered in this work.

Pat and Mike Alexander, good friends, a rare and a true gift, opened their home to me during numerous visits to New Mexico allowing me time and a place from which to do research that otherwise would not have been possible.

Among the histories listed in Additional Reading that provided particularly helpful insights were those by Angie Debo; Eve Ball, Nora Henn, and Lynda Sánchez; Alicia Delgadillo with Miriam Perrett; Lynda Sánchez; Sherry Robinson; Edwin Sweeney; Paul Andrew Hutton; and Robert Utley.

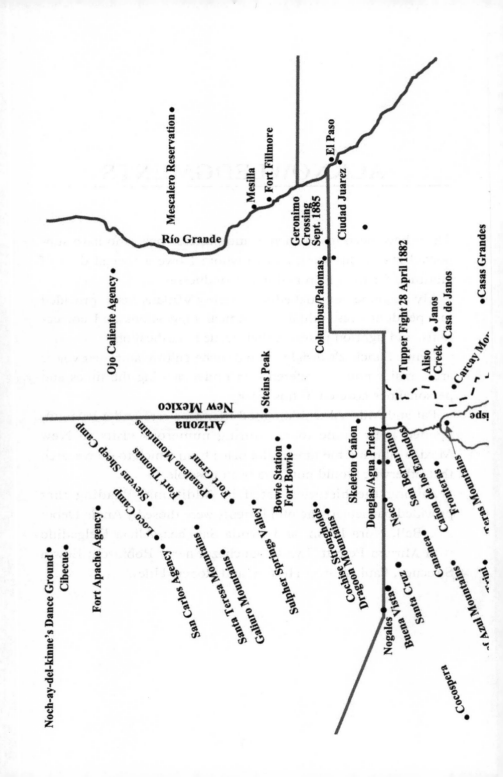

Noch-ay-del-kinne's Dance Ground ●
Cibecue ●

Fort Apache Agency ●

San Carlos Agency ●
Loco Camp ●
Stevens Sheep Camp ●
Fort Thomas ●
Fort Grant ●
Peñaleno Mountains ●
Santa Teresa Mountains
Galiuro Mountains
Sulpher Springs Valley
Bowie Station ●
Fort Bowie ●
Dragoon Mountains
Cochise Strongholds ●
Skeleton Cañon ●
Douglas/Agua Prieta ●
Naco ●
San Bernardino ●
Cañon de los Embudos ●
Nogales ●
Buena Vista ●
Santa Cruz ●
Cananea ●
Fronteras ●
Cocospera ●
Azul Mountains ●

Arizona
New Mexico

Steins Peak ●

Ojo Caliente Agency ●

Río Grande

Mescalero Reservation ●
Mesilla ●
Fort Fillmore ●
Geronimo Crossing Sept. 1885 ●
Columbus/Palomas ●
El Paso ●
Ciudad Juarez ●
Tupper Fight 28 April 1882 ●
Aliso Creek ●
Janos ●
Casa de Janos ●
Carcay Mo●
Casas Grandes ●

spe
teras Mountains

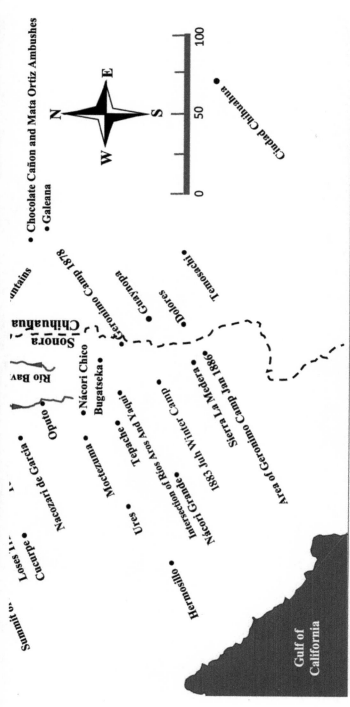

The map shows the approximate locations for points of interest in the Iliad of Geronimo and the Chiricahua Apaches: events that began at the Ojo Caliente Reservation, New Mexico, in 1877 and ended with the Trojan Horse of lies in General Nelson Miles's surrender terms at Skeleton Canyon, Arizona, September 4, 1886, when the Geronimo-Naiche band of Chiricahua Apaches surrendered to become prisoners of war. Modern locations are provided for common reference.

HISTORICAL CHARACTERS

APACHES

Geronimo's Family:
Goyale—Apache spelling of Geronimo's given Apache name
Taklishim—Geronimo's father
Chee-hash-kish—Wife to Geronimo, mother of Chappo and
  Dohn-say
She-gha—Wife to Geronimo
Shtsha-she—Wife to Geromino
Zi-yeh—Wife to Geronimo
Fenton—Son of Geronimo, mother was Zi-yeh
Eva—Daughter of Geronimo, mother was Zi-yeh
Ih-tedda—Mescalero wife to Geronimo, taken in 1885,
  divorced in 1889
Lenna—Daughter of Geronimo, mother was Ih-tedda
Robert—Unknown son of Geronimo until 1904, mother was
  Ih-tedda
Chappo—Son of Geronimo, mother was Chee-hash-kish
Dohn-say—Daughter of Geronimo, full sister of Chappo,
  mother was Chee-hash-kish
Thomas Dahkeya—Grandson of Geronimo, mother Dohn-
  say, father Mike Dahkeya
Ishton—"Sister" wife of Juh, mother of Daklugie
Daklugie—"Nephew" of Geronimo, married Ramona Chihua-
  hua at Fort Sill

15

Jason Betzinez—Geronimo's cousin and an acolyte

Fun—"Brother of Geronimo" (second cousin), *segundo* in Naiche-Geronimo Band

Perico—"Brother of Geronimo" (second cousin), major warrior in Naiche-Geronimo Band

Jelikinne—Father-in-law (Zi-yeh's father) to Geronimo

Geronimo's Warriors:

Jasper Kanseah—Youngest warrior in Naiche-Geronimo Band

Yahnozha—Major warrior in Naiche-Geronimo Band and training warrior for Kanseah

Jason Betzinez—Geronimo's cousin and an acolyte of Geronimo

Fun—"Brother of Geronimo" (second cousin), *segundo* in Naiche-Geronimo Band

Tsisnah—"Brother of Geronimo" (second cousin), (full brother of Fun) in Naiche-Geronimo Band

Perico—"Brother of Geronimo" (second cousin), major warrior in Naiche-Geronimo Band

Ahnandia—Geronimo war leader and close friend of White Eye interpreter George Wratten

Naiche—Chief of Chokonen Apaches, youngest son of Cochise

Nat-cul-baye—Geronimo war leader, also known as Jose Maria Elias

Atelnietze—Geronimo war leader, who with Nat-cul-baye, refused to surrender to General Miles

CHIRICAHUA LEADERS

Ah-dis—Nednhi Apache warrior who survived an attack by the Nakai-yes in which Nolgee was murdered

Ahnandia—Geronimo war leader and close friend of White Eye interpreter George Wratten

Chato—a chief of Chokonen Apaches who rode with Geronimo, great warrior who became a First Sergeant of Scouts during the last three years of the Geronimo wars

Cathla—a chief of Chokonen Apaches who rode with Geronimo

Chihuahua—a chief of Chokonen Apaches, protégé of Cochise

Gordo—Friend of Geronimo and famous war leader

Juh—Chief of Nednhi Apaches

Kayihtah—Scout who talked to Geronimo about surrender

Kaytennae—Second in command to Nana and later leader of the Mimbreño Apaches

Loco—Chief of the Mimbreños

Mangas—Mimbreño chief, son of Mangas Coloradas, named Carl Mangas by the army

Martine—Scout with Kayihtah who talked to Geronimo about surrender

Naiche—Chief of Chokonen Apaches, youngest son of Cochise

Nana—Married to Geronimo's sister, Nah-dos-te, leader of the Mimbreño Apaches, Victorio's segundo

Noch-ay-del-kinne—The prophet who brought the "Ghost Dance" to the Apaches

Nolgee—A *segundo* of Juh, murdered by federal Mexican soldiers during peace negotiations

Victorio—Great war chief and leader of the Mimbreños

ANGLOS

General Orlando Bolivar Willcox—Commander of the military department of Arizona

Captain Harry L. Haskell—Emissary from General Willcox to Juh and Geronimo

Tom Jeffords—Former Agent to Cochise and Advisor to Commanders of New Mexico

Captain Adna R. Chaffee—Army officer acting as San Carlos Agent in July 1879 to July 1880

Lieutenant Marion P. Maus—Second in command to Captain Crawford, who after Crawford's murder by Tarahumara Mexican paramilitary, negotiated Geronimo's March 1886 meeting with General Crook

General George Crook—Directed the war against Chiricahuas from 1882 until 1886

General Nelson Appleton Miles—Replaced General Crook and made surrender terms to the Chiricahuas that were never kept

John Clum—San Carlos Agent 1874–1877

Clay Beauford—John Clum's Chief of Apache Police

Lyman Hart—San Carlos Agent 1877–1879; freed Geronimo and his war leaders from the guardhouse upon arrival at San Carlos in 1877

Joseph C. Tiffany—Agent at San Carlos 1880–1882

George Wratten—Trusted interpreter for Apaches

Colonel Eugene Asa Carr—Commander at Fort Apache who arrested Noch-ay-del-kinne in 1881

WORDS AND PHRASES

APACHE

Be'idest'íné—binoculars
Di-yen—medicine woman or man
Enjuh—good or all right
Googé—whip-poor-will
Haheh—puberty ceremony
Hoddentin—sacred pollen
Isdzán—woman
Ish-kay-neh—boy
Ish-tia-neh—woman
Iyah—mesquite bean pods
Nakai-yes—Mexicans
Nakai-yi—Mexican
Nant'an—leader
Nant'an Lpah—(Gray Leader) the Apache name for General
  George Crook
Nish'ii'—I see you
Pesh—iron
Pesh-lickoyee—white iron (silver)
Pesh-klitso—yellow iron (gold)
Pindah-lickoyee—White-eyed enemies
Shi'aa—wife
Shida'á—uncle
Shik'a'á—nephew

19

Shiyé—son
Tobaho—tobacco
Tsach—cradleboard
Tulapai—(literally "gray water") corn beer, also known as *tizwin*
Ussen—the Apache god of creation and life

SPANISH

Alcalde—mayor or head man in a village
Arroyo—a small steep-sided waterway with a flat floor and usually dry except during heavy rain
Bosque—brush and trees lining a waterway
Casa—house
Hacendado—wealthy landowner
Jefe—chief or leader
Llano—dry prairie
Patrones—bosses or captains
Playa—the flat sandy, salty, or mud-caked flat floor of a desert basin usually covered by shallow water during or after prolonged heavy rain
Por favor—please
Río—river
Río Grande—Great River
Teniente—lieutenant

APACHE RECKONING OF TIME & SEASONS

Harvest—a year when used in the context of time
Handwidth (against the horizon sky)—about an hour
Season of Little Eagles—early spring
Season of Many Leaves—late spring, early summer
Season of Large Leaves—midsummer
Season of Large Fruit—late summer, early fall
Season of Earth Is Reddish Brown—late fall
Season of Ghost Face—lifeless winter

CHIRICAHUA APACHE BANDS

Bedonkohe—Located in eastern central Arizona and western central New Mexico. Originally Geronimo's band as a young man. Eventually merged with Mimbreños and other bands.

Chokonen—Located in southern Arizona. Band of Cochise and later his son Naiche, Chihuahua, and Chato.

Chihenne (also known as "Warm Springs" or Mimbreños)—Located in the Mimbreño Mountains of New Mexico. Band of Victorio, Loco, Kaytennae, and Nana.

Nednhi—Located primarily in the mountains of Sonora and Chihuahua in northern Mexico. Band of Juh.

PREFACE

The word *iliad* means a long series of woes, trials, or events. *The Iliad* is an epic poem said to have been told by Homer describing the ten-year Trojan War, a clash of heroes and gods during the siege of the fortress Troy by the Greeks. It is a story of many woes and trials suffered by the Greeks who, in self-righteous anger, attacked Trojans in their impregnable fortress. The Greeks finally won the Trojan War using a famous deception. They hid soldiers in a huge wooden horse outside Troy's gates, loaded up their ships, and appeared to sail away. The Trojans falling for the trick, believed the Greeks, giving up and going home, had left the horse as an offering to the gods. The Trojans, overjoyed that ten years of war were over, pulled the horse inside Troy to celebrate their victory with the consumption of many jars of wine. With the Trojans sleeping in a drunken stupor, the hidden Greeks left the horse to open the city gates for their soldiers on the hidden ships returning for Troy's destruction.

The story of Geronimo's wars in the last ten years before his surrender, and the way General Nelson Miles finally deceived him into surrendering in his Sierra Madre stronghold with false promises, is an epic story that often mirrors the rage, battles, and deception told in *The Iliad*. After his surrender, Geronimo was a prisoner of war for twenty-three years. Those years were Geronimo's Odyssey, the story told earlier as *The Odyssey of Geronimo*, also an epic story that reveals the strength and character of Geronimo and the Chiricahua Apaches through a long series of woes and trials ending with his death. Geronimo's death was the key that unlocked the door for the Chiricahua Apaches to escape their captivity four years later and continue as a People, but the memory of Geronimo and his spirit continue to this day.

The Iliad of Geronimo begins, like the story of the Trojan War, about ten years before the Naiche-Geronimo band surrendered to General Nelson Appleton Miles at Skeleton Canyon, Arizona, September 4, 1886, under terms that ultimately proved, at best, promises that could not be kept, and, at worst, carefully crafted lies that brought the Apaches into the hands of an army determined to end their freedom once and for all.

Geronimo and his followers escaped San Carlos Reservation twice and Fort Apache Reservation once during the nearly ten years that followed his one and only capture. After those escapes, Geronimo and other Chiricahuas retreated to and made war from their great Troy-like fortress, the Mexican Sierra Madre Mountains. Chiricahua Apache heroes in those days were great warriors, their names filling the White Eyes and Mexicans with terror—Naiche, Loco, Chihuahua, Nana, Jelikinne, Ulzana, Kaytennae, Chato—and the most feared—Geronimo.

The White Eye soldiers, those the Apaches called "Blue Coats," had overwhelming numerical superiority and advanced weapons. The Apaches had only their bodies (they were among the best athletes in the world), an extraordinary knowledge of the land—its layout, water sources, locations of food, and places to hide—weapons they made or stole, and a burning thirst for freedom and independence.

In the last five months before Geronimo's band of eighteen warriors and twenty-two women and children surrendered, they were hunted by 5,000 Blue Coats (one quarter of the U.S. Army), 3,000 Mexican soldiers, and hundreds of civilian posses. During that time, Geronimo didn't lose a single member of his band from capture or death in a fight. Only after General Miles offered terms that allowed Geronimo and his warriors to see their families were the ten years of blood and fire ended. The terms General Miles offered were a Trojan horse of lies, which, once accepted, allowed no escape.

Nearly every event that appears in this story happened in a historical sense. Where there are differences in who told the story, be it via Apache oral history or written military records, I have attempted to use the version that would more nearly match how the Apaches saw it, consistent with all the known facts.

For over eighty years there have been a variety of spellings for Apache names and terms by various historians and ethnologists. To the Apache many of these pronunciations are incorrect. For example, General George Crook, a major player in the events in this book, is often said, to have been called, *Nantan Lupan*, meaning *Chief Gray Wolf*, in other stories about this time in history. Apaches such as Geronimo's nephew, Daklugie, have long said this is incorrect, that Apaches actually referred to Crook as *Nant'an Lpah* meaning *Gray Leader*. I have used Nant'an Lpah for General Crook in this story rather than Nantan Lupan. In most other cases I've used names for Apaches, usually given to them by their Mexican victims, that the warriors used as a badge of honor and that are commonly found in historical references, in order to avoid reader confusion.

To give the reader some sense of Apache life during these ten years of war, I've used their terms for hours, days, seasons, and years, how they lived their lifeways as the tsunami of White Eye settlers roared over them, and why they fought their battles as they did.

The Iliad of Geronimo is the story, told through his eyes, of the ten years of blood and fire he wrought on his enemies when most of his people wanted peace with the White Eyes and the Mexicans. It is an epic story of men who did not suffer fools gladly and could not be broken as warriors or as prisoners of war.

W. Michael Farmer
Smithfield, Virginia
December 2019

CHAPTER 1
CAPTURED

Ojo Caliente Apache Reservation, South Central New Mexico,
April 21, 1877

The sun was pouring *pesh-klitso* (gold) on the mountains and turning the morning sky many colors—reds, oranges, and purples. I made my morning prayer to *Ussen* and then sat with my son Chappo on a blanket near the door of my wives' *wickiup*. We bathed ourselves in the warmth of their fire and a little smoke from the sage I had sprinkled on it. My women, with the help of Dohn-say, my daughter, pretty and quickly growing to womanhood, worked well together cooking our meal of baked mescal, juniper berries, and horse meat. I was a blessed man. I had good, strong children, and I had good women who worked hard to keep us in comfort and pleasured me often that we might have more children.

I thought of my last raid, how productive it was, and where we should raid next as I stared out across creosotes, mesquite, and slowly opening gourd flowers of blue and yellow. The dark outline of a nearly grown boy appeared, running on the trail to our camp from the agency. At the first *wickiup*, he stopped to talk a moment with a grandfather of many harvests who watched his woman make him a morning meal. I squinted at the runner's dark outline against the bright blue sky and wondered what business he had in our camp. Nearly toothless, grandfather smiled and nodded at the runner's words and pointed in our direction. The runner came on. He was a Chihenne boy about novitiate age, with the big chest of one who often runs long distances.

When he reached my blanket, he was not breathing hard and said in the soft *Nakai-yi* (Mexican) filled accent of a Chihenne, "Jeronimo?"

"Who asks?"

"I carry a message for Jeronimo and his leaders from the Ojo Caliente agent."

"I am Geronimo. Speak. I listen."

"The agent asks that you and your leaders come in this morning to talk with the agent from San Carlos, who came in late last sun."

I studied the boy a moment but saw no signs of Coyote, no guile in his eyes.

"Do you know why the San Carlos agent wants to talk?"

"No, I know only that he wants to talk with you and your leaders first, and then he says he will speak to Victorio."

"Hmmph." I could think of no reason why we should not speak to the San Carlos agent. "We eat and then all come. It is the day for giving us our rations, and my women will be pleased to look at things in the agency trading post while we talk. We come to the agency in two hands above the horizon (about two hours)."

The boy nodded. "*Enjuh* (good). I tell the agent you come."

I wondered why the San Carlos agent wanted to talk to us. I remembered when I spoke with him last harvest. He had wanted Juh and me to move to San Carlos with the Chiricahuas led by Cochise's son, Taza. Juh and I had said we would come, but then changed our minds on the way back to our camp and left for Mexico that day to stay out of the way of the White Eyes. I thought, *Maybe the agent wants to ask us again to come to San Carlos. I won't go. It's too hot and filled with many enemies, rattlesnakes, heat, and biting insects that are hard to see. No, I will not go.*

Most of the women and children in the band came with us. After the Pima raid, we had plenty of horses. It was good to ride listening to women chattering and the children laughing and playing in the cool morning air, the sun fast warming us and casting shadows across our path from mesquite and creosotes. When we reached the dusty ground in front of the agency, the agent named Clum from San Carlos came out the agency door carrying his rifle in the crook of his arm and sat down on a porch chair facing us as we dismounted and walked toward the porch. We also carried our rifles in the crooks of our arms. I thought, *Is this supposed to be a peaceful talk? If it isn't, then we're ready.*

Three White Eyes who worked at Ojo Caliente Agency came out to stand behind Clum. Clay Beauford, who I learned later was in charge of the scouts at San Carlos, stood with them. Lastly, six armed scouts filed out the agency door to stand three to Clum's right and three to his left on the ground in front of the porch.

When I saw this, I frowned. I thought, *Why does Clum think he needs the scouts?* They quietly watched us advance toward them while our women and children joined the crowd of Chihenne who had gathered on the south side of the agency to watch our meeting. Our warriors walked to within thirty paces of the porch and stopped while I and my warrior leaders walked on another twenty paces so we could hear easily and watch Clum's eyes to know he spoke true. I was to be speaker for us in reply to whatever the agent from San Carlos had to say. Squinting because the morning sun was in his face, he nodded toward us.

He said, "I've waited a long time to speak to you and your

people, Geronimo. You and Juh told me you would gather your people and come to join Taza and the Chokonen Chiricahua at San Carlos. But you never returned." He leaned forward and pointed a finger at me. "You and Juh lied. You took your people off the Chiricahua reservation the same day we talked and disappeared into Mexico."

I nodded and said, "You speak true about our going to Mexico. But we did not lie. We changed our minds and decided we could live better in Mexico than crowded together at San Carlos."

Clum's face turned red in the bright sunlight and he said in a loud, arrogant voice, "You broke your promise to me to settle at San Carlos. During the seasons of the harvest since you went to Mexico, you and your warriors have killed peaceful people, burned their *casas,* and stolen their livestock. You have broken the treaty promise Cochise and you gave to General Howard to make war no more."

I thought, growing angrier at each word from this White Eye, *I have broken no promise, Clum. I promised General Howard not to kill White Eyes, but I said nothing about Mexicans and other Indians.*

"Your raids and your lies will not be tolerated by the Great Father who lives far to the East. I've come to take you to San Carlos to stand trial for your crimes. Put down your rifles. Submit to arrest by my Apache Police."

There was silence as I stared in disbelief at the fool, Clum, slowly shook my head, and smiled. "We're not going to San Carlos with you, and unless you're very careful, you and your Apache Police won't go back to San Carlos either. Your bodies will stay here at Ojo Caliente to make food for coyotes."

I heard the clicks of hammers pulled back on rifles held by his scouts and my war leaders. I saw Clum's face grow redder at my words. He pulled off his big-brimmed, black hat and fanned his face with it. The doors on the commissary house just south of the agency house burst open. A long line of armed Apache Police came running out in their blue jackets with bright, yellow buttons. They carried gleaming, well-oiled rifles. They formed a straight line an arm-length apart, south of us, headed by big Clay Beauford who raised his rifle and pointed it at me.

My wife, Chee-hash-kish, didn't hesitate. She ran from the crowd and jumped on Beauford, throwing her arms around his neck and shoulders and pulling down his rifle. He growled like an angry bear as he wrestled with her, and some in the crowd laughed and clapped their hands that such a small woman had the fire to attack him and could make him growl. I didn't laugh. I knew the fire Chee-hash-kish carried. She was from strong blood. By the time he threw her off and raised his rifle again, all the police, including the ones standing by Clum, had their rifles at the ready.

We stood in the middle of a possible cross fire. If the scouts fired, it would be certain death for all of us. Clum's trickery gave him the upper hand. It took all my willpower not to fight, and the hatred I felt for Clum grew like a roaring fire burning in my soul, making my eyes burn and my head feel hot. While my woman fought against the police chief, my thumb instinctively reached for my rifle's hammer. But I knew we had no chance and relaxed, knowing it was best to fight another time and in another place of my choosing.

Clum handed his rifle to the Apache policeman standing to his left and said to my leaders and me, "Lay your rifles on the ground. No harm will come to you if you do."

I thought, *Fool! Do you think my warriors and I are crazy?* We looked at each other but did not lay down our rifles, shuffling our feet to get in position for a fight. I tilted my jaw up in defiance as if to say, *Come and take it, fool.*

The man named Beauford raised his rifle, pointed it straight at me, and pulled the hammer back. Clum stood, stepped off the porch, and walked toward me, the barest hint of a smile on his lips that made my mind roar with fury, and he knew it. When he reached me, he jerked my rifle from my hands. With narrowed eyes, I burned his image in my mind and prayed to *Ussen* that one day Clum would pay for this insult.

When Clum returned to the porch, Beaufort gave a signal to his police, and we heard hammers cocked on all the police rifles as Beaufort leaned his rifle against the agency wall, walked out to the leaders standing around me, and took their rifles as Clum had taken mine. He backed up to the porch and then yelled for all the warriors standing behind us to lay their rifles on the ground. They moved slowly, but did as he told them. Clum then told the leaders and me to come to the porch for a talk.

We squatted on the porch, smoking cigarettes made with oak leaves and White Eye *tobaho,* and listened as Clum said what a liar I was for leaving the Chiricahua Reservation after telling him I would go to San Carlos. He crossed his arms, frowned his worst, and tried to look like a fearful warrior, but to us he was no warrior, only Coyote the trickster. Then he said, "You are all prisoners." He ordered Beaufort to put us in the guardhouse. It galled us more that he was Coyote pretending to be a great warrior than him ordering us to prison.

Rage boiled up in my guts, and I jumped to my feet, the others behind me quick to do the same. I reached for my knife, intending to cut Clum from his man parts to his chin and watch his guts fall out, but a voice in my head asked, *Is this the best thing for the people?* I hesitated for a heartbeat.

One of his Apache policemen, faster than a striking rattlesnake, jerked my knife away from its sheath, and the other policemen cocked their rifles, aiming them at the others on the porch. I took a last look a Clum, Beaufort, and the scouts who held guns on us. We had no chance, even though *Ussen* had said

I would not die by a bullet. We must live to fight another day. I nodded my head at my leaders and said, *"Enjuh."* I thought, *We will wait for our revenge. Now we must live.*

The policemen surrounded us and, with shoves of their rifle butts, they guided us to the man who worked *pesh* (iron) with a hot fire and put shaped pesh on horses' feet or made broken wagons roll again. *So,* I thought, *they will put fire on our bodies to hear us beg, but we won't beg for mercy or let them hear our suffering. We have the courage Ussen gave us. This they will see.*

But they didn't brand or burn us. The pesh-working-man made pesh bracelets that clamped around our ankles. He locked them on us by hammering a piece of pesh through a hole on the outside. They couldn't be opened except with pesh tools, and hot fire. Then he put chains between the leg bracelets. We couldn't run or move anywhere except to wash, eat, or do our personal business. Clum kept us shackled in the corral under the watch of many scout policeman eyes. They gave us straw and blankets to sleep on, and they fed us while we waited for Clum and his scouts to talk Victorio and Loco into bringing the Chihennes to San Carlos with him when he returned.

Our women could not come to us. We could not escape. We were truly prisoners, a new experience I hated. I expected that, if *Ussen* didn't help me, I would dance on air while the White Eyes watched and laughed. *Help us, Ussen,* I prayed under my breath. *Help us.*

CHAPTER 2
THE SAN CARLOS GUARDHOUSE

My war leaders and I rode to San Carlos shackled in a wagon over trails with stones that rocked and shook us for nearly a moon. The White Eyes gave us food on the way; we did not starve. They let us do our personal business, as men should, so we did not make the wagon nasty with our dirt and water, but we couldn't run far or fast in chains.

We rode during the Season of Many Leaves, days when the brilliant, yellow sun, from its coming in the east to its disappearing in the west, burned on our skin. Some days Wind, moaning and screaming, carried great, brown clouds of dust that whipped us like mesquite switches and left every valley and wrinkle on our bodies filled with dirt. We often smelled as bad as the White Eyes. There was no water in which to bathe every day, as we would have wanted, but we did not give the White Eyes the pleasure of hearing us complain. Every day when the sun came, I vowed to *Ussen* that, if I escaped through his Power, the White Eyes would surely know the price of my freedom.

After splashing across the rippling waters of the *Río* San Carlos, our wagon stopped at an adobe building with a covered walkway running between two rooms. On the left side of the walkway, the room was a sleeping place for guards; on the right side was a bigger room with a locked door for prisoners. The door, made from heavy, wood planks spaced two or three fingers apart, let light and air in and gave guards a view of the prisoners. Near that door, another small board door covered a hole too small to crawl through that let the guards pass us food and water. There was also another hole too small for even a small man to wiggle through where we passed the bucket that we used to catch our dirt and water.

Before the guards pulled us off the wagon, I studied the outside of the guardhouse, remembering its every detail. I would need a clear memory of the guardhouse outside and the surrounding land for when I escaped. It would be a long dash across the hot, bare ground to the brush and trees in the *bosque* along the *río.* If I got a head start on the guards, I knew I could outrun any of those fat dogs, and doubted any among them was good enough with his rifle to hit a running man. They were all soft and looked like it. Their slow-moving reservation life had made them fat and lazy.

The guards pushed us into the prisoners' room, three already there before us. The room stank of unwashed men, rotting food scraps, and the bucket holding their dirt and water. The only light came through the wide spaces in the door. Guards kept their rifles ready and left our shackles on as the door creaked closed and a key scraped and rattled in its lock. The guard watching us grunted, sweating in the heat, as he sat down, clicked his rifle back to full cock, and watched us through the door slats. He watched as though looking for an excuse he could use to settle some long-forgotten grievance.

We Chiricahuas knew none of the guards or their families, but one never knew what a turncoat scout or policeman might be thinking. At night, the only light came from the golden glow of an oil lantern the guard kept hanging on the post beside him while he watched the door, his rifle fully cocked and ready, while we tried to sleep in the dirt, stink, and rattle of chains as we got up to make water or tried to find a comfortable position in which to sleep.

Three suns after we arrived at the guardhouse, the key rattled in the lock, and the door squeaked open. Two guards, black outlines in the frame of bright light, each armed with a rifle pointed in the room and a pistol hanging on his hip, stood at the doorway. One said, "Geronimo! Come out!" Their eyes nervously swept every knuckle length of space where we slept, and they looked ready to use their weapons. I wished I had a knife. Then those guards would have had reason to be nervous.

In the blinding glare of the sunlight, I held my hand before my eyes as they walked with me between them to the agency house where Clum made many black tracks on paper. He worked sitting behind a table. When the guards brought me to the door, he glanced up, but said nothing as he curled his fingers toward us to come in and motioned me to sit in a chair in front of his table. My guards stood behind him, their rifles ready, while I sat in the chair, stared at him, and waited while he made more tracks on the paper.

Soon he laid down the little spear he dipped often in the black water to make the tracks on paper. To his left sat a stack of paper about a knuckle-length high, the top paper covered with many black tracks. In a stack on his right were many papers with the White Eye talking-wire sign across the top.

Clum crossed his arms, leaned back in his chair, and grinning, said to me in the *Nakai-yi* tongue, "So, Geronimo, you come to San Carlos. I hope you and the others are enjoying your time in the guardhouse." He wrinkled his nose. "It doesn't smell like it. I'll have the guards take you and the others down to the *río* so you can bathe. I don't think you've washed since we left Ojo Caliente. No need to die unwashed, is there?"

I said, "*Ussen* decides if I ride the ghost pony, Clum, not you.

Maybe I live. Maybe you die."

Clum laughed and slapped the table. "I think *Ussen* will let the good people of Tucson decide that, Geronimo. This stack of paper has the stories of the people who speak with straight tongues that you and your boys committed murder and livestock theft. It's more than enough proof for a jury in Tucson to make you do a jig on air while you choke, waiting on the ghost pony. I've sent word to the sheriff in Tucson to come get you. I don't expect him to waste any time, as bad as they must want you. I just wanted you to know he's coming. He ought to be here in a few suns, and then you're on the way to Tucson and out of that dark room they have for you in the guardhouse. It might go easier on you in Tucson if you confessed to all these charges." He lifted the stack of paper to his left and dropped it. "Then they might actually hang you, rather than just let you choke to death kicking in the air."

I stared into Clum's eyes. "*Ussen* decides, Clum. Only *Ussen* will decide if I live or die."

Clum shook his head and rubbed his forefinger in the great bush of hair under his nose. "Believe what you want, Geronimo. Before the next moon, you'll be swinging by the neck and kicking at the end of a rope. Get him out of here, boys. Tell the guards I said to take all the prisoners down to the *río* for a bath. My nose has had about all it can stand of that unwashed stink from the guardhouse. I'll see you when you leave, Geronimo."

The tribe of little biting insects attacked us when we bathed in the *río*. I didn't care. The dirt and stink we wore like White Eyes since Ojo Caliente had to go. Ponce, my brother, moved close enough for me to tell him what Clum had said. He made a face and asked when we would break out. I answered, "Watch and be ready."

After I spoke to Clum, the suns we spent in the guardhouse

continued without change. Every sunrise, I stood at my sleeping place, faced the light through the door cracks, and, spreading my arms wide, prayed to *Ussen,* asking that he deliver us. The guards swapped the night buckets with empty ones, gave us Blue Coat trail rations, a tin cup of coffee, and a fresh bucket of water with a drinking cup. For the rest of the sun, we paced about, the chain links between our ankle bracelets clinking against each other, while we prayed for the freedom of a fast horse across the *llano* (dry prairie) or a run up a hidden trail through the mountains.

I often sat watching the shafts of light pour through the door and the occasional flecks of *pesh-klitso* drifting through them. I thought of why *Ussen* had brought me here, the women I had taken for wives, the children we had, and the good and hard times we had suffered. I never forgot how the *Nakai-yes* (Mexicans) murdered my first family: my wife Alope, our children, and my mother all left lying together facedown in a pool of their black, drying blood. I remembered my rage, shock, despair, and the great pool of water waiting to overflow from my eyes and the ball of mesquite thorns in my throat.

In a later time, *Ussen* spoke to me, gave me the Power to avenge my family, and said that I would die a natural death. No bullet or arrow would kill me. He would make my arrows fly true. Sitting in the dark, I smiled to myself at the memories of leading the killing of many *Nakai-yi* soldiers in revenge for the deaths of my family and of leading raids with Juh all over northern Mexico. Juh taught me much in those days. I thought, *Ussen will free us yet from this black hole. I will make the Nakai-yes pay fifty times, even a hundred times over, for the deaths in my family.*

A moon passed. I counted the number of suns passing since we had come to this place of darkness. No sheriff came from Tucson to take us to the trial and hanging ceremonies in that ugly, dusty town of White Eyes and *Nakai-yes.*

There were stories across the reservation that Clum and the Blue Coats were arguing over who was supposed to be in charge. We heard the guards speak of this gossip. Some said Clum was angry enough at the great chief far to the East that he talked about leaving the reservation. *Ha,* I thought, *maybe Clum is part Apache. He won't bow to a White Eye chief, either.*

Another half a moon passed, and then one afternoon while we slumped against our prison walls panting like dogs in the hot still air, we heard the guards talking among themselves, wondering what would happen to them now that Clum had left. I smiled and thought, *No sheriff, no Clum. Maybe soon we are free.* But the suns drifted on. The stink of our bodies and buckets of our dirt and water tore at our noses like the claws of some unnamed monster as we shuffled about in the darkness all day, watching the bright lines of light filling the open places in the door and sweeping across the dark floor.

From listening to the guards talk, we learned a new agent, a White Eye named Lyman Hart, was coming soon. *Perhaps,* I thought, *he will let us go.* We had never heard of Lyman Hart. Maybe he didn't know that the White Eyes in Tucson wanted to hang us and watch us dance on the air.

We often heard the guards speak of Victorio's growing fury at the lies Clum and the scouts told about life at San Carlos. Many Chihenne people from Ojo Caliente now suffered from the shaking sickness (malaria). Rations were slow to come. Some even developed smallpox and had to live away from their families and friends. They all lived with the deadly snakes in the terrific heat near the rushing waters of the Gila and San Carlos *ríos.* I knew that Victorio must be planning a breakout.

We had lived in the guardhouse for nearly three moons before

Lyman Hart came. He told the guards to open the door and bring us out. The bright glare of the sun after many suns in that dark room made us squint our eyes nearly closed. Hart watched us, his face wrinkling into a frown, and waited to speak until we had all staggered into the light. We looked weak and ragged after those moons locked away in the guardhouse darkness. The guards had not taken us to bathe since Clum had ordered it. I saw Hart turning his mouth down and shaking his head in disgust. I knew we didn't look like the fierce warriors the great chief in the East must have told him we were.

When we were able to see in the bright glare, Hart sat down with us in the shade of the guardhouse porch. He said through a scout interpreter, "I am Lyman Hart, who comes to replace Agent Clum. Which one of you is Geronimo?"

I stepped in front of my leaders to face him. "I am."

"Has the Tucson sheriff ever come to take you away?"

"No. Over three moons ago, Clum told me he comes in less than a moon. We wait. He never comes here."

"Well, do you boys want to go with the sheriff?"

We all shook our heads. I said, "We want to be with our families, not in this stinking, dark hole. Set us free. We harm no one."

Hart stared at us and scratched and rubbed his chin whiskers. A breeze blew heat like that from a bread oven over us, and I noticed a great, black bird circling and seeming to float on the air far above us while the wind curled little, twisting demons out of the dusty ground around us. Finally, Hart nodded and said, "All right, Geronimo, if you and your men will keep your word that you do no harm and live in peace here at San Carlos. I'm letting you go."

I nodded. "This we do, Lyman Hart."

Lyman Hart nodded and smiled, saying the only word in Apache I guessed he might know. "*Enjuh*. Guard, take these men to the blacksmith and remove their shackles. They're free to go."

Those were the best words I remember hearing in my life. Truly, *Ussen* had saved us. *Ussen, I vowed, never again will White Eyes capture me and keep me in a place of stinking darkness away from my family. No, never again. I will die before they take me. Many White Eyes will suffer because of what they did to us in this place of dirt and stench.*

CHAPTER 3
IN THE CAMP OF NAICHE

The worker of hot pesh swung his big, heavy club against the bracelets holding the chains and ankle bracelets together. The bracelets falling from my ankles made my blood rush in anticipation and my legs eager to run, free at last to find my family. We bathed in the *Río* Gila, its headwaters to the northeast, the place of my birth. Rather than take time to make our own, we washed with soap the White Eyes gave us and used it with sand to scrub our skins free of guardhouse stink and dirt. We dried ourselves sitting on rocks in the sun. Our strength returned as our skins grew warm and prickly while we squinted against the sun's brightness and felt its light drive away the darkness, even in our minds, in which we had lived the past four moons. Our clothes dry, we dressed and ran down the wagon road that wound its way beside the Gila toward Taza's village, where my family and others had placed their *wickiups*.

The sun lit the sky with streaks of purples, oranges, and reds. We first saw smoke, floating like an early morning mist above the *río*'s *bosque* from fires in Taza's camp. The shadows were growing long, but we could see places planted in corn, its stalks already turning yellow; beans; bright green and red chilies; green-striped yellow pumpkins; and women and children carrying water to some of the plants. After the long days and nights of nothing but silence in the guardhouse, we delighted to hear the yells of children and the chatter and laughter of women as they finished their work in the growing darkness among the

44

songs of frogs, tree peepers, and insects.

Being in chains four moons had made us weak and slow. It took us longer to run to Taza's camp than I expected, but I knew a moon of daily running would bring our strength back. We stopped for a short time to regain our wind and then followed the trail leading to the camp's *wickiups*. At the edge of the camp, men who had been talking together heard the women and children grow quiet and turned to see what had disturbed the camp's normal rhythm. Silence spread across the camp like a ripple in still water as all the people turned to watch us. I nodded toward them, some signaling they recognized us, as we walked toward Taza's big *wickiup*. In the dim light, I saw a *wickiup* on the edge of the village where Chee-hash-kish looked up from stirring a pot hanging over her fire, her hand covering her mouth, as she pointed at us for She-gha and Shtsha-she to see.

Chappo and Dohn-say, my son and daughter with Chee-hash-kish, saw us, too, and ran to join the crowd following us. At last, I saw my women and children in the flesh and not just behind the lids of my closed eyes watching my memories. This night, my wives would know their husband was free and, unlike a young man a long time away from women, not shy.

I wound my way past many family lodges to Chief Taza's large *wickiup* and cleared my throat to signal I stood at the door. In the space of a breath, the blanket over the door flew back and out stepped the tall, handsome, youngest son of Cochise, Naiche. I raised my brows in confusion. I saw no other *wickiups* larger than this one, the size a chief might use. Perhaps Naiche was visiting his brother. He smiled and waved his hand parallel to ground.

"Ho, Geronimo. You and your leaders are no longer in the chains of the White Eyes. *Enjuh.* Your women camp safely with us. You are as welcome as family."

I, too, waved parallel to the ground that all was well. "Na-iche, my eyes are happy to see you. Yes, my leaders and I are free of the White Eye chains and come to find our families. Is Taza in the camp? I wish to thank your chief that he took us into his village during a hard time."

Like a dove disappearing into the brush, the smile flew from Naiche's face, replaced by a frown filled with sadness. "My brother has gone to the Happy Place. My people say I am chief now. I know I have much to learn about being a chief, but it is what they want."

I stared at Naiche's face and knew he spoke true. My thoughts were like a flock of little juniper tits scattering from the brush. *Had Clum killed Taza? Why was Naiche chief—he liked to dance, drink, and fight, but he had no Power, no gift from Ussen, to help the people. Who should lead these people? Why wasn't Juh chief?* At last, I asked, "What happened to your brother?"

"Last harvest in the Season of Large Fruit, my brother went to the place of the Great Father with Clum and nineteen other Apaches. Clum said he wanted to show the White Eyes our customs as true Apaches do them. This they did many times in the East for the White Eyes, but at the *casa* of the Great Father, Taza became sick and died. Clum buried him there with a big ceremony. Some among us say Clum poisoned Taza. I don't think Clum did this. It makes no sense. *Ussen* took Taza. That is all we know. Now Clum has left, but we're still here, with nothing to do, and surrounded by Blue Coats on land holding many old Chiricahua enemies and few friends. I welcome your counsel, Geronimo, if you choose to stay among us. All your leaders are welcome. Their wives, led by your woman Chee-hash-kish, are here."

When my leaders knew they were welcome, they spoke their gratitude and left us to find their *wickiups* and wives.

Naiche was right. He had much to learn. "In memory of your

father and brother, I will stay with you and give you my counsel as you ask."

Naiche nodded and then looked toward the sky, fast turning a dark blue to black and showing a few points of light. "*Enjuh. Go now. Your wives await your coming.*"

"Naiche will be a strong chief. Soon I see you again." I waved parallel to the ground and walked with dignity to the *wickiup* of my wives and children and the comfort I knew they would give me.

It was a happy time in Naiche's camp. My women fixed fine things to eat and lay with me often. I began the work of regaining my strength and ran long distances every day and practiced with my bow and arrows. I wanted to practice shooting with my rifle, but Clum had kept it. I would have to find another and a good supply of ammunition.

A few days after our release, Victorio and Loco, furious at the sorry life their people led at San Carlos, had had all they could stomach of disease, insects, snakes, and strong, hot winds at San Carlos. They led over three hundred Chihenne off the reservation in a fast run east toward their mountains. They took over a hundred White Mountain horses and mules when they left, making those people angry. The White Mountains joined scouts and Blue Coats to form what the White Eyes call a "posse" to chase the escaping Chihenne people.

The San Carlos posse caught up with Victorio and Loco and their people. They trapped them against a cliff wall of the mountains the White Eyes call Natanes. The Chihenne fought well but lost the horses and mules they had taken and their own stock. After taking all the Chihenne livestock, the posse returned to San Carlos, and the Chihenne continued their escape, but the posse returned to pick up their trail again. Victorio and Loco, smart war leaders, scattered their people in the mountains until they gathered in a meeting with the White Eyes at Fort Wingate during the Ghost Face. They asked to return to Ojo Caliente, or any place other than San Carlos. Nana took his group to Mescalero and asked to stay there. The agent was happy to have him.

Victorio's breakout left the San Carlos Apaches in turmoil. Just before the breakout, Poinsenay had come up from Mexico loaded with loot and bragging about how easy it was to steal from the Nakai-yes. He wanted the Chiricahuas to return to the Sierra Madre, and a few left with him. I counseled Naiche to stay calm and peaceful with the Chokonens. If he did, then the Blue Coats and agents would trust him to lead his people in a good way. Naiche stayed at San Carlos as I advised.

One night, a little less than a moon after Victorio and the Chihenne left, the agent, Lyman Hart, held a council with the Chiricahua leaders and me around a big fire next to Naiche's *wickiup*. First, we smoked to the four directions, and I prayed that *Ussen* would give us good hearts and clear eyes to hear what Lyman Hart had to say.

Hart was quiet for a few breaths as he stared at the snapping and popping fire. He finally looked up and said through an interpreter, so all understood what was said, "Geronimo, I've heard how you counseled Naiche and his Chokonens to stay calm and not run with Victorio and Loco. That was a smart move, and I'm glad Naiche listened to you. I think you were very wise with that advice."

I thought, *We'll see, Lyman Hart. Maybe the day comes when we'll have to run, too, but not now. Coyote waits.* I said, "Hmmph. Lyman Hart is a good man. Speaks with straight tongue."

Hart grinned and nodded. "I'm pleased you think so, Geronimo. I want to ask you to be the captain for the Chihenne people who didn't go out with Victorio and Loco. I want you to use your wisdom in counseling these people, so they don't finally decide to run with Victorio and Loco and leave the reservation. I want you to report back to me, so I know what they're thinking and planning. I know you can do this. Will you?"

I stared at the fire as it burned down and considered what to do. Hart wanted me to spy on the Chihenne, which I didn't think was right. But then I thought, *I don't have to tell him everything I hear, and I won't.*

I said, "Yes, Lyman Hart, I'll be your Chihenne captain as long as I'm needed. I won't leave San Carlos, and I'll tell you of any who even think about leaving."

The Chiricahua leaders sitting around the fire with us all nodded and grunted they would do the same thing.

Our men had nothing to do except play cards or hoops and poles or watch the women work. Watching the warriors lose their fighting edge, while all they did was gamble, made me sorry the White Eyes brought me to this place, even if my wives were here.

We heard many stories about how the Chihenne had surrendered at Fort Wingate and General Hatch had told them that if they "behaved" while the great chiefs in the East decided where they must live, they could stay at Ojo Caliente, which was where they wanted to live.

The agents at San Carlos kept part of what the great chiefs in the East said we should have for rations and sold it to make themselves money, leaving the people to forage and hunt for enough to eat. Even the cattle the White Eyes supplied us for food were too thin to feed us well. I soon had enough of the thievery of the White Eye agents.

I began speaking to the people, telling them what they could see with their own eyes and asking them obvious questions. Usually, a few warriors and even some novitiates like Chappo and his friends, Fun, Tsisnah, and Yahnozha, gathered around a small fire in a little open space in the brush but hidden from sight of the camp. When it looked like they were ready to talk, a warrior called me out of the brush, and I appeared and sang to *Ussen* that he would hear us and give us power as we needed it.

Then I said, "Brothers, let us smoke to the four directions. We have serious business to discuss." They all looked at each other, their eyes shining in the firelight, and murmured, "*Enjuh.*" We smoked and were still. I remember the glow of orange and yellow flames flickering dim and soft on their faces as they all stared at me. I had passed the call for a meeting. Now they waited for my words. Off to the south, a milk *río* of stars filled the night sky as I slowly stood and looked at each face, young and old, each one filled with curiosity.

I said, "Brothers, I've been freed from the guardhouse where Clum put me in chains. I expected to die escaping from there. Clum told us the sheriff from the place the White Eyes call Tucson would come for me and make me dance in the air while I choked to death. They would do this because they said I killed many White Eyes, Nakai-yes, Tontos, and Pimas. I killed no White Eyes. I stole from no White Eyes, but I took horses and mules from the farming tribes as I have always done. I killed any *Nakai-yi* I could for the murders of my first wife, children, and mother. I will never have enough *Nakai-yi* blood for those of mine they murdered."

I saw the frowns on their faces and knew they listened to me. Someone stood and got more brush for the fire. I waited to say more until he had fed the fire and sat down.

"The sheriff from Tucson never came to our prison in the guardhouse, and Clum left San Carlos. I don't think he'll ever return." I shook my fist in thanks. "*Enjuh. Ussen* saved us. I prayed many times in the guardhouse for him to do this. Some say Clum's chiefs wanted him to go. Others say the Blue Coats must be chiefs and agents for the reservation. But they never became chiefs. Clum's chiefs sent the man Lyman Hart. He set us free because *Ussen* wanted it so. Lyman Hart asked that I be captain of the Chihenne people who stayed at San Carlos after Victorio and Loco led the others away. I agreed to be a captain for Lyman Hart, but I don't spy for him and tell him all I know. There are spies among us who will be quick to tell the Blue Coats or Lyman Hart anything they hear. Be careful what you say and where you say it."

There were nods and grunts of understanding all around the circle.

"Times are not good here at San Carlos. Many enemy people surround us. They won't hesitate to kill us. They'll use anything they can—lies, bullets, or arrows. The agents steal our rations to make gold for themselves. They let White Eye settlers take our land."

All the warriors had angry faces.

"There is nothing for a man to do here but gamble or watch the women work. Warriors grow soft and lose their fighting edge. Soon, even the Pimas will be able to overpower us in a fight, for there are many of them. Even Nakai-yes will no longer run from us to tell lies about how they whipped us, for truly they will whip us."

Now the warriors were shaking their fists and saying in angry whispers, "No, no, no. We fight. We always beat the Nakai-yes, best the Pimas. Tell us what to do, Geronimo. We had rather die than become the little dogs of the White Eyes."

I waited until they were ready to listen. When they grew quiet, I said, "A time soon comes when we must leave San Carlos and take what we want from the White Eyes who steal land and food from our family's mouths. We can live in Mexico where the Blue Coats can't come. We'll live in Mexico and raid the White Eyes in the north and then return to our camps in the Blue

Mountains (Sierra Madre) where they can't touch us. If you want to leave San Carlos, then your women must begin saving food, and you should steal rifles and as many bullets as you can and hide them. Hunt often with your bows so your women can build up a big supply of meat and hides."

They nodded agreement with me as they murmured, *"Enjuh, Enjuh."*

A warrior stood, looked around the circle of faces, and said, "Tell us, Geronimo. How will we know when it's time to go?"

"I have many groups I must tell of our need. Every day I pray to *Ussen* about this. When the time to leave is good, he will tell me, and I will tell you. But to leave, you must be ready. Save food, rifles, and bullets for that time. Run every day and no longer grow soft."

I paused and looked at each one, making certain they heard and understood my words.

"I have said all I have to say."

I saw their shining eyes and knew they would be ready to leave; all, that is, except Naiche, who sat back and listened and studied the faces of the others as I talked. I knew Cochise made Naiche and Taza promise to avoid war with the White Eyes. Naiche would have to think hard about leaving San Carlos and fighting the White Eyes.

During the time I talked to other groups of Chiricahuas, Juh often came to San Carlos from his camps in Mexico and urged the warriors in these meetings to think about joining him in Mexico. The warriors' urge to leave San Carlos grew strong. I believed then I would leave before the next Ghost Face.

CHAPTER 4
THE FIRST SAN CARLOS ESCAPE

In the harvest time the White Eyes named 1878, in the Season of the Ghost Face, my war leaders, my brother-in-law, Juh, and I spoke often about leaving San Carlos. The warriors crowded in *wickiups* to hear us as the dust-filled wind moaned, whispering that we needed to go as it tore against the grass, canvas, and blankets covering our *wickiups*. I often spoke alone with Naiche and, though he understood the truth of my words, he hesitated to break the promise he had made to his father Cochise to avoid war with the White Eyes. Even as we talked, the women continued to save as much food as they could, and the men stole rifles and bullets to hide away where the White Eyes and Blue Coats or their scouts couldn't find them.

As the days began to warm, I saw some of Naiche's people get the shaking sickness (malaria). No *di-yen* (medicine man or woman), including me or any White Eye, knew what caused it. I tried medicines and ceremonies, but they didn't work. I prayed every day for *Ussen's* help and guidance, but I learned nothing new. I knew enough about shaking sickness to know that we needed to move the camp from its bad ground of sickness. To keep the White Eyes from seeing too much of our business, I decided my family should camp in the mountains north of the agency from Naiche's camp. Lyman Hart let us go there.

Near the middle of the Season of Little Eagles, our women received bags of corn for planting in the Season of Many Leaves as part of our rations. The women had more corn than they thought they could plant and decided to make *tulapai* (also known to the White Eyes as *tizwin* [corn beer]) with what they didn't need. I agreed. With the long days coming, it would be good to have a good drink and get drunk. I thought the women were smart. Living on the San Carlos reservation was enough to make anyone drink.

When he left with Victorio and Loco, Nana left my sister Nah-dos-te, his first *shi'aa* (wife), and their son, in my care. They camped with us, along with Ponce, and about twenty of my other relatives and their families. We waited patiently for our drink until the moon hid and the *tulapai* had stopped bubbling in its big pitch-lined basket jars and was ready to drink. We made a big fire to give us plenty of light and to warm us on the outside while the *tulapai* warmed us on the inside.

This *tulapai* we drank then was stronger than usual and good on the lips. I sat with my back to a juniper tree and watched our children playing hide and find at the edges of the big circle of firelight, smelled the sharp odor of pine sap and burning piñon and juniper, heard the coo and whistle of doves and night birds in the trees, and felt pride in my women as they helped fill jugs and large cups with *tulapai*. I drank slowly after feeling the sides of my face growing numb, telling me I was getting drunk. I watched the boys who sat together having their first drinks, wanting to start their novitiate to prove they were ready to raid and make war as warriors and as men provide for their families. A way to prove his manhood was a problem for any boy living on a reservation. A boy needed to go on four raids, serving as a novitiate for the warriors, before being accepted as a warrior, becoming a man, and taking a woman. But warriors couldn't raid off the reservation.

The son of Nah-dos-te and Nana, close to the age of Chappo, sat among those drinking *tulapai* for the first time. They were ready, along with two or three others, to become novitiates, but there would be no novitiate for anyone as long as we let the White Eyes tell us what we could do. It made me angry to think about my people chained to the reservation like some White Eye dog to a post.

I thought more about what those boys could do to prove they had a place among the warriors while we stayed on the reservation. It was a hard question. I had talked about it with other warriors and chiefs. I had even asked Chappo what he thought, but there were no good answers.

The more I drank, and the drunker I became, the harder it was to think clearly about it, and the angrier I grew. I waved my nephew to come join me. Maybe he had an idea about what to do. He flashed a big smile and came; as the others in his group watched him go, their eyes filled with envy that a powerful *di-yen* wanted to speak with him.

He came walking slowly, planting his feet carefully, the *tulapai* already making his brain fill with clouds. He stopped a couple of bow lengths from me, and lowering his eyes, said, "You called me, *Shida'á* (uncle)?"

"I did, *Shik'a'á* (nephew). I'm trying to think how you'll ever become a warrior."

His eyes grew wide and filled with hurt, but I wasn't paying any attention, and was too drunk to notice. I see now that he must have felt I was trying to insult him.

"The White Eyes won't let us raid anymore. I spent four moons in the guardhouse last harvest because they planned to hang me for raiding, but *Ussen* freed me instead. You can't go on raids from San Carlos. You stayed with your mother when your father, Nana, went out with Victorio and Loco." I wasn't even looking at the boy, talking more to myself than him. "How do you plan to become a man? Maybe you'll never be recognized as a warrior . . . you should think about that . . . no manhood for you . . . go away. I must think on this some more."

My nephew squinted at me with his head cocked to one side, his hands balled into fists. As he turned to go, he said, "I will be a man, *Shida'á.*"

I nodded. "*Enjuh.* I think on this some more."

I took another long swallow of *tulapai* and watched him wobble past the group of boys he came from and off into the darkness beyond. *Enjuh,* I thought. *Go think about this problem, nephew. Maybe you find an answer.*

Chee-hash-kish had Dohn-say bring me several large cups of *tulapai,* and I drank them all. As the fire was dying into orange and black coals in the blackest night I had seen in a long time, clouds from the *tulapai* filled my mind, and I fell asleep under the juniper tree.

The sound of women wailing filled my dream. I wondered for whom they cried. But their cries didn't vanish when I cracked an eye open to the bright sunlight and felt the throbbing in my head like someone keeping time on a stiff hide with a looped willow stick. Someone had covered me with a blanket, which I pushed off as I staggered up, drank a long time from the water jug left for me, and then splashed cold water on my face. It was three or four hands (hours) after the sun had come, bright and throwing shafts of its light through the tops of the pines.

I saw the people of the camp gathered at the farthermost *wickiup* set back in the trees. I stared at the place. Through the thick fog in my brain, the realization came slowly that they stood around Nah-dos-te's lodge. I ran, staggering and stumbling, for it, thinking that my sister had ridden the ghost pony to the Happy Place. The crowd parted to let me into the inner circle. Nah-dos-te was on her knees keening beside a blanket on which the body of my nephew lay. An angry, raw rope burn was around his neck. He had made himself dance on air and ridden the ghost pony to the Happy Place. I shook my head in disbelief. Why would a young man near the prime of his life kill himself?

I turned to the group around us. "Why did he do this? Why?"

Chappo spoke up and said, "After he spoke with you, Father, he walked past us and into the darkness saying over and over, 'I will be a man. I will be a man.' "

Nah-dos-te stopped her crying and said, "What did you say to him, brother?"

"I was thinking of what we should do now that boys cannot go on raids as novitiates in order that they be recognized as warriors and men. I asked him how he thought he might prove himself a man if he couldn't be a novitiate. He said he would be a man, and I said, '*Enjuh.*' "

Nah-dos-te buried her face in her hands and wailed.

I said, "Come, sister. I will help you with the burial ceremonies for your *shiyé* (son) and my *shik'a'á*. He was a good boy. *Ussen* will hurry his journey to the Happy Place."

This is the White Eyes' fault, I thought. *They won't let our sons become men.* But as I thought of the last time I spoke with my nephew, I realized it was my fault. My nephew had thought I had said he could never be a man and had killed himself to prove he was a man. It was time to leave this place where no good comes to those who stay under the watch of the Blue Coats and White Eyes and they would blame me for the *tulapai* drink.

After burying my *shik'a'á* high in the rocks on the mountain, I spoke with my women and children as we warmed by the fire. I said, "My *shik'a'á* went to the Happy Place because I didn't speak plain to him about a problem our people must solve. How do we recognize boys as men and warriors if they cannot be novitiates for raiders? Soon Chappo will need to begin his novitiate, but he can't have one here at San Carlos. We must go.

We'll leave tomorrow night. The moon hides its face, and there will be little light in the night sky. Juh waits for us up the Gila."

Chee-hash-kish nodded. "We'll be ready, husband. Where will we go? To Juh in Mexico, or a place in the Blue Mountains of our own?"

"Hmmph. Chee-hash-kish is a wise *isdzán* (woman). We go to the camp of Juh at his flattop mountain stronghold not far from Casas Grandes and Janos. We'll be safe there. No Blue Coat can follow us across the line where the White Eyes say the other side is Mexico. The Mexicans have quit trying to drive Juh out of his stronghold. In the village of Janos, they trade for what Juh takes in Sonora. The Mexicans don't like it when the Americans come. Ponce and my other leaders and their families will come with us. We must leave soon and travel fast for the Blue Mountains, or the Blue Coats and their scouts will catch us and force us return to San Carlos. We'll travel light and raid as we go. I won't come to Juh's camp empty-handed. As the sun falls, I'll speak with Naiche and tell him we're going while you make ready. His medicine still says he is bound by the promise he and Taza gave their father not to fight the White Eyes if they could avoid it. Someday, I think he'll change his mind and come to us."

Chee-hash-kish looked at She-gha and Shtsha-she, who nodded. She said, "We'll be ready, husband." The children were smiling, their glittering eyes filled with excitement about moving south to see their uncles and cousins with Juh's band.

The new moon was easy to see, but it gave little light for the ground. I hated to ride at night, but anything to leave this hated place was worth the risk. To avoid making noise, we led our ponies from the corral and covered their feet with rawhide, but waited to put food supplies and ammunition on them until we were well east along the road to Camp Thomas that we had followed from the guardhouse to Naiche's camp. This would make the scouts who followed us think we had no supplies.

We had ridden down the road for a time when I heard the snort of a pony and felt more than saw dim shadows drifting through the night gloom toward us. Juh, with the few warriors who had come north with him, rode out of the dark to join us on the road. The warriors fell back behind us as Juh rode up beside me, his size making his big pony look small. "At last you leave this miserable place, Geronimo. Your sister Ishton will be happy to see you and your family join us. There is food and ammunition for the taking soon before us."

I smiled. "Speak plain, brother. Your words are full of mystery."

"My scouts say we will meet a White Eye wagon train about three hands (three hours) after the sun comes. Four wagons, filled with supplies headed this way. They go to the mining camp the White Eyes call *Globe*. Food and ammunition are what we need, brother."

My smile grew bigger. "Hmmph. Four wagons will be easy to ambush. Already the White Eyes give us what we need. We have enough lead time over the Blue Coats and scouts sent after us to take our time and do what needs to be done." The big, heavy man riding beside me was already making life better for us.

"Geronimo speaks true. Hurry and be quick. I know a good spot to take them."

Juh chose a wide place between a high and a low hill after a long pull up a steep grade for the ambush. The wagon drivers often stopped to rest their mules there before continuing on the down slope. Juh and I watched the warriors with the women and children hidden below us on the far side of the hill from the wagons. The wagons were slower coming than we expected and made us more likely to face the Blue Coats and scouts before we crossed the border. It couldn't be helped. We would fight our way through if we had to, but we needed the supplies, especially bullets that must be on those wagons.

We waited. With the sun three hands above the horizon, mules pulling the first wagon appeared at the top of the long pull, went a little further, and then stopped as others came in sight. The warriors were ready with bow and arrows. We wanted to save the ammunition for long-range fights.

The first wagon driver climbed down from the driver's box and began to fill a bucket from a barrel to water his team. The other drivers had reached the top and had also climbed off their wagons to water their mules. They faced into the bright sun and squinted. The first driver carried the water bucket to his team, sat it down in front of the first mule, and, pulling his big, floppy hat off, slowly fanned himself and wiped the sweat from his head with a bandana. An arrow pinned his hand to his head and passed through his ear on the other side. He flopped into the trail dust without a sound.

I heard the thuds of arrows in the drivers' backs, and the last driver had an arrow tear through his chest. He fell pulling at the arrow and gagging and spitting blood. The warriors didn't even have to use a rock to crush a head to finish any of them off. Taking personal effects from their clothes, they left the bodies alone.

Not a shot had been fired, not a sound uttered on the wind carrying us away. I motioned for the women and children from the far side of the high hill to come and help us take supplies from the wagons. They came running, leading their horses and mules. We had guessed right. Divided among the four wagons, there were several heavy boxes of ammunition that would fit our rifles, in addition to four new rifles carried by the drivers. There was also enough food to feed us all well until we came to Juh's camp in Mexico.

We ate White Eye food from the wagons without building a fire, took all the food and cloth we could, in addition to the ammunition, and loaded it on the mules. A warrior asked about burning what was left, but I said no. Smoke would be a sure sign of an attack and draw soldiers and scouts anywhere near us to this place. A sentinel watching our back trail with soldier glasses saw a tiny plume of dust three or four hands (hours) away. Blue Coats and scouts from San Carlos were coming for us.

We turned south. We were a long day's fast ride from Mexico, maybe more, depending on how fast the women and children could travel. Our outriders kept a close watch on the Blue Coats and their scouts. They were gaining on us.

Juh and I rode side by side side and talked for a while about how to escape those who chased us.

Juh said, "Hmmph, Geronimo. Soon we come to the canyons around the mountain the White Eyes call Steins Peak. There is a canyon we can pass the women and children through and keep them heading south until they cross the border. A spring isn't far from the line on the Mexican side where they can drink and rest. It will be hard on them to run all day and into the night, but they can do it. I'll take my warriors who are good shots at long ranges and hold the Blue Coats and scouts in the canyon while Ponce leads the women and children and continues running for the border. You take your warriors and hide yourselves in the canyon for an ambush. When the night is black, your warriors and mine will head for the border, too, but on different trails to make the Blue Coats and scouts split up to follow all of us. We'll meet you and your families at the spring. There we rest, and then go on to the stronghold near Janos. What do you think?"

I nodded my head in respect for his tactical planning. Juh

was the best war leader the Apaches had. As we neared Steins Peak, we stopped for a short rest at a little hidden spring. I told Chee-hash-kish what we planned and for her to tell the other women. Juh picked the warriors he wanted with him to hold the Blue Coats in the canyon. We now had plenty of ammunition and no reluctance to use it.

The shadows of the yucca and mesquite were growing long when the first scouts came to the little spring we had used. We watched them from the canyon with our soldier glasses. They stopped to study our trail. One talked and pointed toward us and possible hiding spots riflemen might take for an ambush, the other nodding. Another scout came up, and they talked with him. He, too, studied the canyon places for shooters and made no move to go farther.

The Blue Coat commander, a *teniente* (lieutenant), I think, arrived, dismounted, and spoke with the scouts after lighting his pipe. He waited while his Blue Coats watered their horses and mules and then took a drink themselves. His pipe finished, he knocked the ashes from its bowl, pulled his rifle from its saddle scabbard, barked orders to his soldiers, and, mounting his horse, started for the canyon. I smiled. It would be good to shoot a few Blue Coats.

We waited. Soon they passed the mouth of the canyon and advanced a long rifle shot (about 300 yards) following the scouts. I thought, *You follow me no more,* Teniente. I sighted on his head and fired. His hat flew off, tumbling in the air, while he and the others ran for cover among the rocks beside the trail, wildly firing down the canyon as they ran. After the initial exchange of gunfire, no one on either side wanted to shoot for fear the flash from their rifles would give away their location in the nightfall. We stayed where we were long enough to hold the Blue Coats and scouts in place with a few random shots until there were long shadows and low twilight.

Without sound, we ran down the canyon to our horses, mounted, and rode different trails to join our families. Now, with the help and leadership of Juh, the other warriors and I could live as we should in Mexico, free at last to be Apaches and not chained like dogs to a post by the White Eyes.

CHAPTER 5
FREE AT LAST

It had been a long hard ride from where we had taken the supplies and ammunition to the Steins Peak Canyon fight to Juh's stronghold. Juh told us to rest a few suns, and then we would have a council to talk of his plans for trading in Janos. The women made our *wickiups* under tall pines near Juh's big tipis on the east side of the Blue Mountains. The stronghold overlooked brown and light-green hills that soon flattened into *llano* speckled with groves of light green mesquite and forest green, feather-leafed creosotes that stretched beyond the Janos and Casas Grandes *Ríos* east and to the gray horizon. On the flattop mountain, there was good water, grass for livestock, and plenty of wood for fires. Many Mexicans had died trying to attack it and had failed. We were safe and lived in comfort at Juh's stronghold.

Each morning before the sunrise, I left my blankets and the warmth of my wives to go stand at the edge of the eastern cliffs and sing to *Ussen* as he sent the sun to bring us light and drive the darkness away. I sang, holding out my hands to gather in the growing light, praying to *Ussen:*

> *Ussen* watch over me
> At the east where mountains of the earth lie
> At the south where all kinds of fruit lie
> At the west where I hear singing
> At the north where wind comes cold

Ussen hold your hand before me in protection
Ussen arise before me as my protector
As I do your bidding, arise before the people as
    their protector
Let no harm befall me from weapons
From wind and rain and lightning arrows as they
    strike
From water as it flows
Great sky and stars may I enjoy
Let yellow pollen fall upon me and be beautiful
    before me
Restore me to the day
Restore all in beauty.

When I returned from welcoming the morning, Chee-hash-kish, as first wife, gave me coffee and a morning meal of beef, cooked on a stick, its fat dripping in the fire, baked mescal, acorn bread, and steamed tips of yucca. It was the best food I had eaten since Clum captured me at Ojo Caliente. My women knew how to make the fire bring forth good things to eat.

I and the warriors and leaders who left San Carlos with me rested four days. On the fifth day, Juh invited us to sit in council with him and his leaders. We met at his council place in a small grove of big juniper trees and waited for him. Soon he appeared, walking in the shade of the tall pine trees. He was tall and big chested, his long hair woven into a single braid that reached to his knees. He held a well-oiled, shiny Winchester rifle in the crook of his left arm, and he had a hard face that, when angry, made any enemy fear for his life.

One of Juh's wives was my sister, Ishton. I had prayed for her last harvest as she struggled, nearly dying, to push Juh's big baby from her body. Upon the mountain where I prayed for

Ishton, *Ussen* spoke to me and said, *Don't be afraid. Return to your sister, for both she and her child will survive. And you will live to be an old man. No bullet will kill you. No arrow will strike you, and you will die a natural death.* In all the war years after *Ussen* spoke, I knew I would live. Wounded many times, I always recovered. When I returned from the mountain, Ishton's big, strong baby had been born, and she lived to have another child.

Juh spread his fine Navajo blanket and sat down beside me to my right. A good breeze kept us cool as it lightly shook the tops of the junipers. Sunlight fell through the branches over us and made pools of gold at our feet. I smelled the sweet scent of cactus flowers on the edge of the cliffs mixed with the tart scent of pine sap and I heard the *Jeet! Jeet!* of a canyon wren in a place near our council. It was a fine day to be free.

Reaching in a fine, fawn skin bag he carried with him, Juh brought out papers and *tobaho* to make a cigarette. His other leaders made one, too. The cigarettes were lighted, smoked to the four directions, and passed to my warriors and me. After we smoked, we burned the remains of the cigarettes and were ready to speak and listen.

Juh looked around the circle, pausing to gaze at the face of each warrior for a short time before going to the next. Juh stuttered. I could tell he was ready to speak when he began rhythmically moving his foot, which helped him keep his stuttering manageable.

He said, "Brothers from San Carlos, welcome to the camp of Juh. Let this be your camp as you join me in our raids. Live well with us. You did well taking the four wagons headed for the village the White Eyes call Globe. You did well holding the Blue Coats near the place they call Steins Peak. Now we're ready to form our own way and to go on the attack if need be.

"My brother-in-law, Geronimo, is a great war chief. When we ride together, I want him as my *segundo* (number two). He will lead us well if I cannot be with you. Will you serve as my *se-gundo*, Geronimo?"

Juh surprised me with his request. I thought he would want Nolgee as his *segundo*, but Nolgee was not the warrior with great experience I was. Curious faces and squinting eyes studied me for any sign of reluctance. Juh was the best war chief the Chiricahuas had in those days. I had known him since before we were novitiates, had even fought with him once when he and his friends who were visiting my mother's camp tried to steal nuts and berries my sisters were collecting. When we trained, he was always a worthy opponent. Sometimes he beat me; sometimes, I him. We had been friends for a long time, and he always treated my sister Ishton well after I fought him for teasing her by stealing her nuts and berries.

I smiled and said, "Juh honors me. I will be his *segundo.*"

Juh nodded and smiled. The council said together, *"Enjuh!"*

Juh said, "Nolgee, you have your own band, but you often ride with us under my leadership when we raid and make war. Do you accept Geronimo as my *segundo*?"

Nolgee stared at me almost to the point of rudeness and challenge, and I stared back before he said, "Yes, I accept Geronimo as your *segundo*. There is no one else. He is a great warrior and will lead us well when you're not with us."

Juh, his stutter under control, said, "Nolgee is a great and wise warrior. Now hear my words. In past harvests, I've made treaties with the Mexican leaders in the land on the east side of the Blue Mountains, the land the Mexicans call Chihuahua. The treaties usually say we Nednhis will leave them alone in our raiding as long as they give us what we need to live—food, blankets, and ammunition."

A breeze sighed through the trees shifting the pools of yellow sunlight at our feet as their limbs danced. I wondered if this was a message from *Ussen*—a warning of shifting loyalty or a sign all things are new. Juh paused a moment, and the rhythm of his foot became faster. He continued, "The *Nakai-yes* on the west side of the Blue Mountains in the land they call Sonora, they want no treaty. They want to fight. They want to kill us all, making certain we raid no more. To this I say, *'Enjuh.'* Soon we will make their land fit for nothing, a barren place of rocks, weeds, and cactus where even the dogs starve. Soon they will be afraid to walk on their land even at the time of shortest shadows, for they will know we are watching and ready to strike. We will take much plunder from them, more plunder than even we or our women can use or can store for hungry times.

"I've talked with the Mexican chiefs at Janos and Casas Grandes. They say their trading posts will take our plunder from Sonora and the American side—horses, mules, cattle, wagons, guns, and tools—in fair trade for other things we need or that our women want. To this I also say, *'Enjuh.'* "

All around the council circle, heads were nodding to everything Juh had said.

"In four suns, Nolgee, Geronimo, Nat-cul-baye, Jelikinne, and I go to Janos. Their chiefs wanted time to think over what I wanted in rations, how we traded, and where we could ride without fighting. Still, the treaty only says give us rations, and we will leave you alone. I think they will do this. Soon we see. Who among you will support me in this?"

All the council agreed with Juh. He knew how to deal with the *Nakai-yes.* He knew how to lead his warriors so that few, if any, died in his raids and wars of revenge.

Juh led us through tall brush and across arroyos I had never seen before as we rode for his treaty meeting at Janos. We were at ease and in no hurry. Once we reached the edges of the *llano,* we passed and paid no attention to a few *Nakai-yes* driving their creaking carts pulled by cattle or leading brown burros carrying big bags of supplies. Their eyes grew wide and filled with fear when we appeared, but then relief and smiles came when we left them alone.

I thought, *Enjoy your lives now. One day I come to take them.*

Near Janos, we passed ten lightly guarded freight wagons. Still we attacked no one. After the treaty agreement, we would be at peace in Chihuahua but at war in Sonora.

At the place of meeting, beside a large spring surrounded by tall cottonwood trees, we waited a day, two days, and then on the third day, when even the sky seemed to be on fire in the hard sunlight, we saw a dust plume growing large coming from the direction of Janos. It approached where we waited, and we saw many riders spread out against the plume's brown background.

Juh crossed his arms and watched them come. "Hmmph. The Chihuahua chiefs come with a few soldiers to make a good show and maybe a few pack animals with presents. If they had waited another day, I would have been gone. Enough of these games."

But there were no presents, and the *alcalde* Juh had spoken to at his last meeting was now *segundo* to a young *hombre* who wore a big, fancy hat and clean pants only *Nakai-yes* and White Eyes would wear in the desert heat. He also wore a fancy revolver with shiny, white handles, so we all could see it. I knew he thought he was a mighty warrior and wanted us to see his fine *pistola*. He was always smiling, showing bright, white teeth, and he spoke in a voice like a big chief to the old *alcalde*. A voice in my head said, *Don't trust this one. One day I'll enjoy taking that fancy pistola and killing him with it as he begs for mercy.*

We sat in a shaded circle and smoked a *cigarro* to the four directions by the big stone tank holding the spring's water before it leaked out into the desert. The *alcalde*, since he had first talked of the treaty with Juh, began to speak after asking

Juh's approval. With many hand motions, he told how the Mexicans in Chihuahua always suffered when they fought with Juh and prospered when they traded with him. He noted that the first treaty worked well, but both sides wanted some things changed, and both sides had talked about them in their councils. The chiefs in Janos asked the big chiefs over the land to sit in their council. They thought all the chiefs must understand what the treaty meant and speak of other things they wanted included.

After speaking about these things in the warm, still air with the sound of gurgling water from the overflowing spring tank, the *alcalde* folded his hands together, leaned forward to rest his elbows on his knees, and stared at the ground for a moment. Then, with sad eyes, he nodded toward the young chief with the big hat and said, "*Señor* Comacho represents the big chiefs of the state of Chihuahua and speaks for them. He will tell you the terms of the treaty they say they must have with you. This is all I have to say."

Señor Comacho nodded and, with a big smile, looked at us like we were ignorant children. He said, "*Gracias, Alcalde. Buenas tardes, amigos.* It is a good place and time to meet and sit with our *amigos,* the Nednhis. *Amigos,* my *patrónes* offer a new treaty with you, one that is much better than what our friends at Janos offered."

The *Nakai-yes* were fools. After listening to the *alcalde,* I already knew what he would say, just not the details. Juh knew, too, but he kept his growing anger under control as he crossed his arms, his jaw muscles rippling, and stared at Comacho.

"*Mis patrónes* say they will give your people rations—flour, corn, meat, cloth—but your people must move and stay where we say, at Ojinaga in the *Río Grande* country, six days' ride east of Janos. There, near the great *río,* you'll always have enough water, and the land, with water from the *río,* will grow anything. It will be yours to use. What do you think, *amigos?*"

Juh leaned over and whispered in my ear, "You talk. You know what I think of this. I feel anger's fire. I will stutter more than usual. They can't understand me. Say we will go away and think on this offer for a moon and listen to what our leaders say. Then we return."

I said, "Chief Juh asks me to speak for him. There must be no misunderstanding. Today he stutters much. He says he did not expect this offer. There is much to consider. We will go away, think, and talk with our leaders. In a moon, we return with our answer."

Comacho's eyes suddenly grew nervous and quickly moved from face to face when he saw the dark thundercloud filling Juh's face. His lips barely moving, he said, *"Bueno, señores.* It is good your people understand what my people offer you. Return in a moon with your answer and your people. Then we will accompany you to Ojinaga. *Adios."*

As Comacho spoke, I knew Juh's rage was growing hot, his brown skin growing red. But as we left, I gave the Mexican and White Eye wave for *adios* and said no more.

CHAPTER 6
CHOCOLATE PASS

Juh led us from the meeting place. We rode out into the tall creosote bushes, mesquites, and cholla on the *llano* and disappeared from the sight of Comacho and his soldiers. Juh rode his pony at a walk for a while, but then he applied his quirt, and his pony broke into a gallop down a twisting trail through the brush. As the light began to dim, we turned off the main trail into a deep canyon against a high ridge. We climbed to the top of the canyon on a narrow trail up the western side only Apaches would know. Near the top of the ridge, the trail widened to a flat place where we stopped by a spring filling a natural tank surrounded by junipers of great age. We could still see far out on the *llano* and saw no dust plumes from anyone following us. The shadows in the canyon made it look like a great black hole.

We built a small fire deep in the boulders that hid it from the *llano*. After eating and resting, confident neither the *Nakai-yi* soldiers with Comacho nor others had followed us, Juh motioned for us to gather close for a smoke. He was calm, and I was glad. I was angry with Comacho and his false warmth toward us. I wanted to wipe him and his *Nakai-yi* soldiers out, but I knew we had to be crafty in thinking about what to do.

As we smoked, the night sky closed around us, filled with soft colors of orange and purple and red fading into soft black. Juh, his face wrinkled by a frown, said, "Brothers, I didn't expect what this *Nakai-yi*, Comacho, wanted us to do for the treaty. I don't like it. Geronimo tells us what San Carlos Reservation is like—the people nearly starving and some with the shaking sickness. Will this place the *Nakai-yes* call Ojinaga be any better than nasty San Carlos? Will there be more food and no shaking sickness? I have learned from friendly *Nakai-yi* traders at Janos that the Sonoran and Chihuahuan chiefs talk of joining forces and marching their armies into the Blue Mountains to destroy us."

Juh raised his war club and swung it down hard against a long dead juniper blown over by the wind. Broken wood pieces flew in all directions, and we laughed and ducked the chips. "I say, let their armies come. We can destroy them." He tapped his temple with his forefinger. "But we may lose too many warriors for such battles to be of value to us."

This did not sound like the great warrior, Juh, we all followed. I said, "Then what should we do? Tell us your plan."

"We must agree within twenty-four suns to Comacho's demands for our living at Ojinaga, or the armies of Chihuahua and Sonora come after us. I count each sun as a scratch on my war club. Now, hear me. Between the villages the *Nakai-yes* call Casas Grandes and Galeana is the pass they call Chocolate. We have raided and ambushed there many times, but the *Nakai-yes* seem to forget this. When the last day for us to surrender is past, we will be waiting there for a good ambush, so they will know the destruction we will give them if the treaty is not on our terms."

Juh fell silent and for a little while stared at the points of light filling the night sky while he rolled another cigarette. At first, he didn't light it, holding it in his fingers, frozen in place as if seeing a vision from *Ussen*. At last he spoke.

"After the ambush we separate into three bands. This will make it harder for the soldiers *Nakai-yi* to find us. Nolgee talks good with the *Nakai-yes*. He'll camp in a stronghold near Janos and try more talk with its *alcalde* and, by then, maybe Comacho will be ready to listen and want to change his chiefs' minds. I doubt it. Let Nolgee tell Comacho that Geronimo and I wait in different strongholds in the Blue Mountains to learn what they'll do. This makes the *Nakai-yes* divide their forces into three parts if they decide to come after us. Makes them much weaker. They know this. They'll wait to attack us. They've tried the strongholds before and lost many soldiers without getting to the top of the mountains. They'll wait and try to catch us when we leave the strongholds—if they can find the ones farther south.

"Three days south of the Janos stronghold is another stronghold. Geronimo takes his people and part of mine to stay there. Three days south of Geronimo's stronghold is another. I take this one with the rest of the warriors and their families.

"Before we split after Chocolate Pass, Geronimo sends two men to San Carlos to learn if shaking sickness is no more and White Eyes have more rations. If it is so, then maybe we go there. In any case, we will wait for the coming of the next bright moon and then move north."

The ridges of Chocolate Pass were a dark-brown color like that of the sweet the *Nakai-yes* and Americans like so much. Juh had raided *Nakai-yi* freight there often, yet still the *Nakai-yes* liked the wagon road there so well, they continued to use it.

I let Chappo, Yahnozha, and Fun, all strong and eager to prove themselves warriors, serve as novitiates to the warriors waiting in Chocolate Pass where Juh and I had decided to ambush a freighter and make the Chihuahua chiefs reconsider the treaty terms we didn't want. I watched these boys with interest to learn how they performed when the bullets and arrows flew.

There was much more for novitiates to do this time than during our raid on the four wagons. While the warriors made their weapons ready, sharpening their pesh, barrel-hoop arrow points and trade-store knives and cleaning and oiling their rifles, the novitiates took care of the warriors' horses, cooked, and carried water, all under our rules and customs I prescribed to them that had been learned over many harvests.

There is a high ridge above Chocolate Pass where Juh and I, using soldier glasses, watched for something more impressive to take than a few riders or two or three freight wagons. When we struck, we wanted to show the *Nakai-yes* our power and make Comacho and his *amigos* want what Juh offered in the treaty.

On the last day we had to sign the Chihuahuan treaty, Juh and I waited until the shadows were long, saw no one coming, and came down from the ridge to look over the places the warriors planned to use. Our grunts of approval told the warriors they were ready.

The next day, with the sun rising high, we signaled for the war leaders to come to the top of the ridge and told them a large wagon train was following the road through Chocolate Pass. Juh planned to wait, let all the wagons get in the pass and then kill the mules on the lead and rearmost wagons, so the other wagons couldn't back up or turn around. Then we'd use the best rifle shots to kill the guards and anyone else with rifles, and the rest of the warriors would finish off everyone else with bows and arrows, knives, slings, and rocks—any weapon that didn't require precious ammunition.

The warriors watched the pass road and saw the dust from the wagons. There were many wagons making a great dust plume behind them, and they moved slowly without extra outriders. I knew they must think no one would want their cargo if they didn't have extra guards. There were fifteen wagons pulled by teams of four mules. The mules alone would be a prize worth taking, even forgetting about all the other possibilities of tools, clothes, blankets, food, guns, and ammunition.

The sun passed the time of no shadows, and the wagon drivers stopped for a while to rest, eat, and water their animals. They were not far from the pass. We could see women and children among them. Juh signaled to take no prisoners or slaves.

Good, I thought. *Kill them all. My mother, children, and Alope beg from the Happy Place for spilling Nakai-yi blood.*

We waited. A dust devil whirled across the road behind the wagon train and disappeared into the *llano,* twisting the thorn trees and creosote bushes, some into broken pieces, a prophecy for the wagon train. But they didn't see it, or if they did, they didn't believe it.

After a meal and a smoke, the freighters tightened and checked harnesses and then started moving again. In the pass the warriors, silent like great, black birds waiting for a carcass, watched them come. The wagons started up the gradual incline through the pass, the freighters whistling to their mules, snapping whips, and yelling, "Git on there, Clyde! Move it Brownie!" to make them lean into the harness for the long pull through the pass. Women and children got off the wagons and walked to ease the load. The women in bonnets or with cloths over their hair walked up the road holding the hands of young children while the older children ran ahead alone. The warriors waited.

The lead wagon was nearly through the pass when there were four quick shots followed by yells and screams, and then more shots at the end of the train. I saw a young woman throw her hand over her mouth, look up and down the wagon road, and then start to run for a nearby boulder after snatching up the child with her. A long arrow passed through the child held against her breast and thrust through her back. Her eyes grew wide with surprise as the child screamed and went silent and limp. She stumbled forward coughing blood and collapsed.

More wildly fired shots buzzed down the line of wagons or ricocheted off boulders, striking nothing before arrows and stones knocked the freighters from their wagons. Some spooked mules reared into the path of stones and arrows and brayed in fear or pain, contributing to the confusion. Warriors sprang from the brush or from behind boulders with rocks to smash the heads of women and children running to hide. Not one escaped. I wasn't sorry to see them die. This was war. The Mexicans had done the same thing to my family. We had no choice, if we wanted to live.

Suddenly there was an eerie silence in the heat and dust. All the freighters were dead or dying. There were no more women and children. There were only the sounds of running feet as the warriors ran forward to take anything of value and those mules snorting and stamping their feet wanting to get away from the smell of death.

The wagons held sacks of beans. We took some of the bean sacks, all the pesh tools and pots, clothes, rope, leather off harness lines, and blankets. The novitiates packed all the plunder and loaded it on the mules freed from their harnesses and strung together. We were gone from Chocolate Pass in less than half a hand against the horizon. We left some freighters near their death, Juh telling us not to finish them.

He said, "Let them suffer. There are more *Nakai-yes* coming. Soon they'll learn to take my treaty offers."

CHAPTER 7
IN THE BLUE MOUNTAINS

After destroying the wagon train, I led my people to the Juh stronghold, about three days' ride south of Janos. Nolgee went to a stronghold within half a day's ride from Janos, from where he would try talking to the Chihuahua chiefs about the treaty Juh wanted. Juh took his people south about three days' ride from my camp.

Chappo and his friends saw the wagon train taken with ease. Like all novitiates after their first raid, they already felt as if they were warriors, and nothing could hurt or stop them. They asked why Juh broke up his warriors into three different strongholds far apart. I told them that if we were in smaller groups, the Mexicans were less likely to find us and, even if they did, many would die trying to fight their way into a stronghold. Juh and Nolgee could come to help us. In harvests past, they had killed many Mexicans who had tried to break into a stronghold. Juh and a few of his warriors had rolled big stones down on them. Besides, Ghost Face was coming. Mexican soldiers would stay out of the mountains. Fighting in the mountains during the Ghost Face was too hard.

My women made a strong *wickiup* to stand against the coming Ghost Face winds and cold. Covered with hides and wagon cover cloth, it kept us warm during the cold nights high on the flattop mountain stronghold. The warriors and novitiates who were part of the ambush did well hunting to keep meat in the camp. My war leaders and warriors met often to talk about the best places for big raids we might do during the Season of Little Eagles. The women made clothes and baskets and cooked many good meals. We were content.

One bright day at the time of no shadows, less than a moon after the Chocolate Pass ambush, Yahnozha, Tsisnah, Fun, and Chappo sat on a stronghold cliff edge overlooking the *río* running in the deep canyon below them. Yahnozha suddenly grabbed Chappo's arm and pointed into the canyon. Riders, barely more than specks in the distance, were coming down the *río*.

I sat warming myself in the sun and saw their sudden excitement. Chappo ran to tell me what they had seen and asked to use my Blue Coat glasses. When I gave him the glasses, I told him to come back quickly and tell me what he saw.

I smiled and made the all-good sign after Chappo told me the scouts I had sent to talk with the People at San Carlos and Victorio with some of his warriors were coming. The scouts later told me they were returning from San Carlos when they crossed trails with Victorio and his warriors. Victorio had refused to consider returning to San Carlos with Loco, who was still waiting to learn what the White Eye chiefs would do with them. Victorio told the scouts he wanted to ride with them to meet and council with Juh and me. The scouts, having learned where we camped, had agreed to show Victorio the way. I was pleased to see the scouts return with Victorio. I sent riders to tell Juh and Nolgee the scouts from San Carlos had returned and that Victorio wanted a council.

Within seven suns, Juh and Nolgee arrived with their war leaders. We held a big council under tall pines near the cliff edges of the stronghold. Chappo asked if he and his novitiate friends, Yahnozha and Fun, could listen to the council. Because they did well in the Chocolate Pass attack, I let them listen, but I warned them, "You say nothing." I swept my hand parallel to the ground in the all-is-good sign and, after looking at each of them with a stern eye, nodded and walked away. They would be good warriors someday.

The night before the council, we had a big feast for the many guests in camp. The women and girls dressed in their finest dresses and served the warriors beef, yucca tips, cooked and steamed mescal, mesquite beans and bread, acorn bread, and honey. The men were hungry and cut big chunks of beef from pieces on wooden boards with their knives. The brown-red juice from the meat ran from the corners of their mouths and down their chins. Conscious of good manners, they quickly wiped the juice off their faces with their hands and rubbed their long-shaft moccasins to keep them soft and comfortable.

After the meal, we sat around the big fire slowly dying into a big heap of orange and red coals, and we smoked and told stories of hunts, battles, and raids. There was no dancing that night, but I said there would be when the council concluded.

I served as the *di-yen* for the council and sat in the circle of war leaders with Juh, Victorio, and Nolgee. I saw the novitiates perched on boulders or by a tree where they could see who was speaking. Juh and Victorio didn't like each other, but they had put aside their personal feelings to gain success against the Mexicans and Blue Coats. Knowing this, I began the council by singing to *Ussen* and asking that we have ears to hear, eyes to see, and wisdom to make good choices. I made a cigarette rolling *tobaho* in an oak leaf and, lighting it with a White Eye match, smoked to the four directions before passing it around. The bright sun on the high, flattop mountain made pools of *pesh-klitso* on the ground around us as it splashed through trees. The air, still for a breath or two, held our smoke until a puff of breeze came and took it away.

I first looked at each man around the circle before I spoke.

"Juh asks that I, as his *segundo,* first speak for him. Juh, Nolgee, and I tried to make a treaty with the Chihuahua chiefs. But they wanted to put us on a reservation at Ojinaga. This is not what Juh expected when he offered peace for rations. We knew that if bad things happened at the San Carlos Reservation where the White Eyes kept us on, then *Nakai-yes* would do no better, maybe worse. If rations increased to what the White Eyes promised and the shaking sickness went away at San Carlos, then we thought it might be better for us to return there rather than to live life fighting wars all the time. Wars are always harder on the women and children than on warriors." Victorio snorted and slowly shook his head. Juh, his forehead pinched in frown, looked at him.

"We decided to make the Chihuahua chiefs rethink their treaty terms by showing them how bad our raids can be, so we wiped out all on a wagon train in Chocolate Pass between Casas Grandes and Galeana. The *Nakai-yes* chased us until we were in the mountains and then decided we were too powerful to attack there. We know more *Nakai-yi* soldiers will come after us in the Season of Little Eagles. But, if things are better at San Carlos, then maybe we can cross the border for a while and live there again to avoid war with the *Nakai-yes* until they decide to trade us rations for peace. If things are still the same as when we left San Carlos, then I say we must raid against the *Nakai-yes* until they learn the best policy is to give us rations. Make them give us what we ask.

"Martine, you went with the scouts to San Carlos. Tell us if it's better or worse than when we left."

Martine crossed his arms and looked around the circle.

"The people still don't get their rations. Some say they only get about half of what they should. The shaking sickness attacks more of those living near the *río*. It does not seem to be so bad

---

up in the mountains. We went to Naiche's camp, where we lived when we were there, and spoke to Naiche. His camp is no better. Food is scarce, and the shaking sickness does not stop. He has already moved his camp once. In the Season of Little Eagles, he plans to move up into the mountains away from the *río*. We went to other camps. Still the people have to hunt to survive, and the agents take Apache food rations to sell to other White Eyes."

His face grew dark and angry like afternoon rain clouds in our country.

"We should stay in the Blue Mountains, even if we have to fight the *Nakai-yes* every sun. That is all I have to say."

There were grunts, nods, and shaking fists around the circle.

Nolgee said, "Ojinaga will be as bad as, if not worse than, San Carlos. We must stay in the mountains. I'll continue talking to the Chihuahuan chiefs while you raid. Maybe soon they listen."

There were grunts and nods of agreement again.

Juh looked around the circle and saw none holding back. His foot tapped a slow drum rhythm. "I see . . . I see all are ready to . . . to fight the *Nakai-yes. Enjuh.* I . . . I will bring my people north to join . . . to join with Geronimo. From this . . . this stronghold, we will raid far and do . . . do much to the *Nakai-yes* until they give us . . . give us the treaty we want."

I lifted my hands and sang again to *Ussen*. I never thought that rations would improve at San Carlos or that shaking sickness would go away. I knew we would not leave the Blue Mountains.

When I finished singing, I said, "Our brother, Victorio, comes to speak to us. We welcome him. Speak, Victorio. We will listen."

Victorio, nodding, looked around the circle.

"Your scouts speak true. Clum and the tribal police lied to us at Ojo Caliente. They told us San Carlos was a fine place to

82

live. I and my people could only stand to live there three months before we returned to Ojo Caliente. There was no food, nothing to do, and much shaking sickness at San Carlos. But the White Eyes won't let us stay at Ojo Caliente. The big chiefs in the East will probably say we must return. I don't understand why. Loco and some of the women and children will have to march back to San Carlos. Nana stays in the mountains and camps away from Loco. I think one sun soon Nana goes to Mescalero to wait and see where I go, but maybe not. I and my warriors stay free. Maybe we go to Mescalero, but maybe not. You plan to raid. I ask to join you. Maybe the Chihuahua chiefs will listen to you quicker if the raids are bigger and more often."

Once more there were grunts and nods around the circle. Juh again slowly tapped his foot, a sign he would speak.

Juh said, "Victorio is a great warrior. I am . . . I am glad he and his warriors come . . . come to help us. I will . . . I will speak with him, Geronimo, and Nolgee about . . . about when and how we raid. We must use our warriors . . . use our warriors well . . . make the *Nakai-yes* suffer the most . . . the most when we . . . when we raid and attack their soldiers."

There were nods of agreement around the circle. Victorio frowned but said nothing. Soon the council ended. Juh, Nolgee, Victorio, and I spoke together privately.

That night, the women had a big feast with dancing and *tulapai* drinking. Victorio's warriors were unexpected and left little *tulapai* to go around. Chappo and the other novitiates didn't get any and, although they were just novitiates, it still made them feel cheated out of their share. They had worked hard during the ambush and deserved a good drink with the rest of us. I began to understand why Juh cared little for Victorio.

After Victorio and his warriors left, Juh went back to his

southern camp. Chappo and I ate together at our morning meal. I said, "Chappo, you didn't look happy at the great feast. Why did you have a long face?"

"My friends, Yahnozha, Tsisnah, Fun, and I had no drinks of *tulapai* at the feast. We worked hard at the ambush in Chocolate Pass. I think we should have gotten some, but Victorio's warriors drank it up before we were offered any."

I smiled. "Novitiates serve all warriors. Patience. Your turn will come. But you aren't alone. Juh doesn't like Victorio and his warriors either, and Victorio doesn't like Juh."

"Then why would they ride together?"

"You have heard the wisdom, 'the enemy of my enemy is my friend'?"

Chappo nodded.

"That's the way it is between Juh and Victorio. Victorio is the enemy of Juh's enemies. Juh thinks Victorio is too impulsive and doesn't think ahead far enough to understand the risks for what he wants to do. Victorio thinks Juh is too cautious for quick decisions. They'll work together for a time, but then they'll go separate ways. Watch. You'll see."

CHAPTER 8
DISASTERS

In the moon following the council meeting, Nolgee returned to his stronghold near Janos with the intent of talking to the Mexican chiefs about a treaty Juh would accept to stop the raids. The longer the raids continued, the more they talked.

Juh and I, sometimes with Victorio, raided north in the villages across Chihuahua and Sonora, but not often across the border. The soldiers from Sonora and Chihuahua chased us long days after the raids with no success, and the Blue Coats always stopped their chases at the border. Victorio stayed mostly south of the border except for an occasional raid for ammunition and horses in the land the White Eyes claimed. In these raids, he told his warriors to kill as few White Eyes as possible, believing the White Eye reservation chiefs in the East might still let his people stay at Ojo Caliente Reservation.

A moon after the council meeting, the raids I made against haciendas and trading posts around Nácori Chico and other small villages brought much plunder to our camp. Chappo and his friends, Tsisnah, Fun, and Yahnozha, begged me to let them serve as novitiates during these raids, but I said no. There were too many soldiers looking for me and our warriors, and I needed them to help guard the camp while we were gone. They took turns guarding the camp every night, each taking a third of the cold darkness to watch for any soldiers trying to come up the trail into the stronghold, but they saw nothing.

A runner from Juh's camp to the south of us came to tell me

that Juh wanted to meet in ten suns at the place called Guaynopa on the edge of the Great Canyon. The moon growing brighter during this time, I sent the runner back to Juh with a message saying I would bring my band to a meeting place we had in the mountains near Guaynopa, and that we would be there at the sun Juh wanted to meet me.

In the meantime, I also planned to raid the village of Bacadéhuachi northwest of Nácori Chico. A raid during this time would let me take advantage of the moon coming to its full circle, since with the new moon it would be dark enough to give us the opportunity to travel unseen across the mountains.

Chappo and his friends again asked to go on this raid as novitiates but, to their great disappointment, I said no. They didn't yet know the customs for night rides and raiding. Night raids were hard and dangerous, and it was difficult for the warriors to protect the novitiates during a night raid. I told Chappo and his friends I needed them to help move the women, children, and old ones to a new camp on a high, flattop mountain to the southeast of the village of Nácori Chico, where the warriors and I could meet them on our return from the Bacadéhuachi raid. Then we would all together go on to where I planned to meet with Juh.

My people easily reached the flattop mountain southeast of Nacorí Chico, but it was a long, hard run up and down steep mountain ridges. Chee-hash-kish told me the women and children moved slowly and were tired, as they worked to set up camp while waiting for our return, and the novitiates had acted well. She said they were promising men. This I was happy to hear.

My warriors and I came to the camp late in the night two days later, but the novitiates were watching for us and weren't surprised. The Bacadéhuachi raid had been a good one. We returned without casualties and a good string of pack mules carrying corn in bags, a case of ammunition and, for the women, cloth.

I planned to rest my warriors two suns and two nights and leave on the third day after our return. I thought our flattop mountain camp safe and told the novitiates to continue guarding it. Their chests swelled with pride when asked to do such important work. We forgot to remember the old saying, *Coyote waits.*

The moon was bright and the shadows dark in the cold while the novitiates watched for enemies. On that first night, they heard only the calls of night birds and animals passing through the brush, and all they saw moving was the steam from their breath floating out of the shadows. It was a battle to stay awake during that quiet, cold time when everyone else was sleeping.

The next day the novitiates tried to sleep to prepare for watching the next night, but there was too much activity around the camp getting ready for the hard run to Guaynopa and the meeting with Juh and his band. As the sun cast long shadows across the mountains toward the east, I ate with my family. Chee-hash-kish told Chappo that he should eat all he could hold because rations on the trail would be quick and spare. It would be two or three suns before she and my other wives would have a big, hot meal for us. He did as she suggested, but later that night, his full belly and no sleep during the day made him doze off.

Our camp on the flattop mountain sat in a grove of juniper trees surrounding a large, natural water tank, almost full from the rains coming in the Season of Earth Is Reddish Brown. A trail to this camp, one of two trails usable with horses to access the stronghold, came up from a deep canyon. The other access trail came down from the eastern ridges, forming the canyon we used. The ridges were accessible from another canyon on the east side of the canyon we used to enter our camp. Both trails split off the same trail from Nácori Chico I had followed to reach the camp.

Chappo later told me he had jerked awake to realize he had been asleep for much of the night. There was a golden glow behind the high eastern mountains. He sat up, ashamed he had fallen asleep and, shivering, wrapped his blanket over his shoulders and went to make water. He hoped the other novitiates had not fallen asleep. Something didn't seem right. The birds weren't calling. The women were getting up to gather firewood and feed their families. He stared through the low light of dawn down through the trees to the canyon floor but saw nothing. As the light came, driving away the eastern shadows, he continued to stare down at the brush around the camp but still saw nothing to make him raise the alarm.

Off to Chappo's right, he saw a grandfather warrior, Stiff Leg, come out of the brush behind the camp, limping toward his woman's fire. A shot from just below him sent thunder rattling down sides of the canyon and knocked Stiff Leg backwards. He lay unmoving, a bright red spot appearing on his chest centered perfectly between his nipples and gushing squirts of bright, red blood.

Reflexively, Chappo shot toward the gun flash. There was a scream of pain and brush shaking for a moment just before a rain of thunder and lead fell on us. Stiff Leg's wife, looking up from her fire, ran toward him. A hail of bullets killed her before she took three steps. Warriors sprang out of their blankets, grabbed their rifles, and ran toward the cliff where they could get a clear shot at those across from the camp.

I was on the edge of the cliffs for my morning prayer to *Ussen* when I heard the first shots. Many bullets whined like tiny death stones through the air and killed some before I reached my *wickiup.* The women were in a scramble. I told them to get under the trees and lie as close to the ground as they could, and that I would be back for them.

From behind a big boulder, Chappo reloaded, while bullets whined off the rock, sounding like angry hornets or striking the ground, raised little geysers of dirt all around him. I looked for muzzle flashes and fired where I thought the shooters' bodies ought to be. A soldier jerked erect and then fell into the bush in front of him. Two more women fell, one into her fire. Her little daughter ran to her. Many bullets ripped the child to pieces. The warriors reached the cliff and fired into the trees and brush below them. Soldiers screamed in pain and whooped in anger. Angry, whining bullets found two more women and a child. Another warrior fell. My women and daughter stayed flat on the ground under the juniper trees, nearly impossible to see or to hit.

To see better where the *Nakai-yes* hid, I ran a little way up the trail that led down into the camp and called to the warriors, pointing to where they should shoot. More *Nakai-yes* fell. They juked and jerked between boulders and trees, firing as they went. I could tell as the shots became few that we had killed many who had attacked us.

Chappo leaned out around his protecting boulder to shoot at the next muzzle flash. A bullet grazed the rock, making sand that hit his face. He was lucky the spray of sand didn't blind him. Chappo, his face bleeding from a hundred small scratches, killed the soldier who fired the shot.

An unsteady calm settled over the camp, as the gunfire grew more sporadic. The warriors continued to watch and fire when they saw any movement in the brush hiding the soldiers. A few horses screamed in pain and ran off down the canyon. I led the warriors, dodging left and right, toward the place where I thought the soldiers had taken cover. There was a roar of gunfire from both sides. A warrior fell and was still. The warriors flew into the brush where the soldiers had taken cover. There were yells of victory and screams of anger and pain. I saw three soldiers running down the path to the canyon below. I shot but missed them. Then they were on horses, charging down the canyon too far away to hit with my old rifle.

I claimed not to know how the Mexicans were able to surprise us like they did, and I never told anyone else. Chappo told me how he and the others had dozed off and were ashamed. He promised to never sleep again when he was a guardian of the camp and to take his revenge against all the *Nakai-yes* he could.

The novitiates were lucky. Chappo was the only one remotely wounded. I had taught my son well. I understood why he and his friends had fallen asleep. It was my fault for not choosing guards who had had more rest. I saw how well the novitiates fought. They were ready to fight as warriors.

Out of forty in my band, we had lost ten—four women, two children, and four warriors. Several of our people had bullet wounds, but they all lived, thanks to my medicine and *Ussen*'s blessings.

That afternoon, we buried those who had fallen, along with their things, in the cracks of the cliffs. I sang songs to *Ussen* for them all and prayed for their fast journey to the Happy Place.

The moon created a bright, white glow behind the eastern ridges when we left our camp. I led the people across the mountains to the meeting place with Juh and his people. Juh arrived a day after we did. The number of his people and ours made for many lodges in the camp.

That evening, Juh came to our *wickiup*. I told him then what had happened. Juh was shocked and angered and said we would make the *Nakai-yes* pay for their attack. I knew Chappo sat back in the dark of the *wickiup,* listening and hoping Juh didn't see the shame on his face. While we talked, I heard people outside talking in surprise and anger. Juh and I looked at each other across the fire and frowned.

A throat was cleared outside my *wickiup* door, and I said, "Come! You are welcome." A short, muscular man, who looked weary beyond recognition, his face sagging like he hadn't slept in days, the salt from dried sweat covering his body, pulled back the door blanket and entered. I recognized him as Martine, who rode with Nolgee. Juh and I stared at him and knew something was wrong.

I said, "Ho, Martine! We see you are weary from many days of running. Let us give you food. Then tell us your story." I motioned for Chee-hash-kish to bring Martine a gourd filled with food from her cook pot, but Martine shook his head. "I have very bad news to tell you. Food can wait."

Juh and I nodded. "Tell us."

"The chiefs in Janos finally sent word to Nolgee that our war with them must end and they were ready to agree to the treaty he had been asking for. They invited him to bring his people and come to a feast in celebration at Janos."

Martine clenched his teeth and hammered his thigh with a fist.

"We believed them. Nolgee believed them. He thanked *Ussen* for this blessing and said peace was ours around Janos. He brought everyone in his camp, all forty-four men, women, and children to the feast. All in Janos said they were glad to see us. Peace was good. But I saw Mexican army soldiers standing around with the Janos people watching us. Nolgee didn't seem to see them or, if he did, he didn't pay them any attention. After all, we were at a feast to celebrate no more fighting and killing.

"Much food was there. The chiefs in Janos gave us mescal. They said they knew how much we liked strong drink, and they were giving us their best mescal with the feast to honor us. Nolgee paused for a moment, looking at them as if to say, 'I'm not sure I believe you.' Then he put the jug to his mouth and drank two great swallows before laughing and passing it along to the next person."

Juh's face grew darker than a thundercloud. He shook his head in disbelief.

"But Juh, I remembered what had happened to you and your warriors a few harvests before. I passed the jug on without drinking. I said I had to see about my pony first. The Janos chiefs grinned and nodded. They knew I meant I had to take care of personal business. I never returned to the feast. I watched, waiting in the shadows of the great *casa*.

"Nolgee and the people ate until their bellies were big and round. They drank much mescal. They had a good time, and I wanted to join them. Still, I waited. Soon they said they could eat no more, but the Mexicans continued to offer them mescal. Some became so drunk they went to sleep where they sat and slumped forward, snoring. When the Mexicans saw how drunk they were, the soldiers came out of the crowd around them, calmly loaded their rifles, and began to murder them. In a rage, I fired at the soldiers, and they came after me, but I managed to get away. Those who weren't too drunk to stand also ran."

Juh said through clenched teeth, "How many got away?"

"Counting myself, ten or eleven. Maybe three or four warriors. I learned from a woman who got away that a few women and children with Ah-dis were running for San Carlos. The rest came here with me."

Juh looked at me and crossed his arms, his face a blank mask, but fury burned in his eyes. He said to Martine, "You have traveled far and hard to bring this news, Martine. Rest. Soon we will have our revenge. We go in two days."

Martine nodded his understanding and left the council. Juh

stared into the fire. I rolled a cigarette and thought how best to avenge Nolgee and his people. *We must kill many in Chihuahua to make this outrage smooth.*

CHAPTER 9
A HARVEST OF BLOOD AND FIRE

A moon after news of the Janos massacre and the attack on our camp outside of Nácori Chico, the Season of the Ghost Face grew out of the Season the Earth Is Reddish Brown.

Juh decided the safest place for our People to endure the Ghost Face cold and snow was at the Guaynopa stronghold near where he had met us. I agreed Guaynopa was the best place for defense against Mexican soldiers and from which to hunt or to sit by warm, yellow, and orange fires and plan raids beginning in the Season of Little Eagles. I knew Chappo and his novitiate friends listened to the war leaders plan raids and revenge. The novitiates hoped and dreamed to be acknowledged as warriors in the coming harvest. They wanted recognition as warriors who could defend the People and attack our enemies. For a time, I thought about asking the warriors to offer them council entry but decided to wait a little longer.

A handful of suns after we settled in Guaynopa, a rider came from San Carlos. He told Juh and me that the Blue Coats had forced Loco and his Chihennes back to San Carlos after they believed they would stay at Ojo Caliente. Jason Betzinez, a nephew about the age of Chappo, who had stayed with us often at San Carlos, and Sam Haozous, three or four harvests younger, were among them.

The rider, his face a dark thundercloud of anger, said that when Victorio learned they were to be sent back to San Carlos, he told the White Eye agent at Ojo Caliente, "This is my country. I don't want to go. We have done nothing wrong. I'd rather die fighting than return to San Carlos." He and about ninety of the People, half of them warriors, disappeared into the mountains.

With him were many whose names I recognized and admired from my time at Ojo Caliente. They included Victorio's sons-in-law, Turivio and Mangas; Lopez and Tomaso, two sons of Mangas Coloradas; Nana and his two sons-in-law, Horache and Jatu; the great warrior Sánchez; and the war chief Showano and his brother, Choneska. Victorio had the warriors with which to do serious damage to the White Eyes, but he told them to kill only when they had to, thereby hoping not to stir White Eye anger too much so they might find a place to stay that made them and the White Eyes smooth again with each other.

Victorio visited us with a few warriors a time or two and held long councils with Juh and me. We had a good laugh when he told us how Nana had taken the old men, women, and children with him and asked the agent to let them camp on the Mescalero Reservation. The agent seemed glad to have them, registered them, gave them rations, and let them camp up in a Rinconada side canyon. Nana had been sly and told the warriors with him to wait and come over the western ridge of the Rinconada once his camp lodges were up. In that way, the warriors with him weren't registered, so they could come and go as they pleased without the agent knowing they were there.

It was a hard Ghost Face with many storms and much rain to the north in the mountains of the land the Americans claimed as theirs, which we all knew had belonged to Cochise, Mangas Coloradas, and Victorio. Another rider came with news. Victorio so hated separation from his people, he began talks with the Blue Coat chief at Ojo Caliente. He asked to settle anywhere but San Carlos. I asked the messenger if he thought the Blue Coats would let him do that. I knew the answer before I asked the question.

He lifted his shoulders, shook his head, and said, "I don't know, but Victorio is fast losing patience with the White Eyes. If they try to force him back to San Carlos, there will be a hard war."

The Season of Little Eagles came with strong winds from the northwest down on the *llano* but not so much across Juh's stronghold at Guaynopa. The first raid for Juh and me in the Season of Little Eagles was for ammunition after a hard winter of hunting. We ambushed several Sonoran military patrols and found arms and bullets we could use, but as usual, there was never enough ammunition. As the Season of Little Eagles bloomed into the Season of Many Leaves, we kept most of our raids south of the border to keep the Blue Coats calm, so Victorio might get what he wanted and not have to fight in order to stay away from San Carlos.

One sun in the Season of Large Leaves, three or four Mescaleros slipped off the reservation and came to join us. They spoke with Juh and me and told us the White Eyes had agreed to let Victorio and the Chihennes move to where Nana camped at Mescalero. But the agent there, a White Eye named Russell, with face hair like an old male goat, was slow to give them rations, and Victorio was losing patience. When I heard that news, I looked at Juh and smiled.

Juh nodded and said, "Victorio won't stay at Mescalero. He will leave."

Later, Chappo asked me why Juh had said that. I answered, "Victorio thinks the White Eyes will not keep his People in a good way. He thinks they cheat on rations and make the Chihennes weak and sick at Mescalero. When he knows they do this, he will leave and go on the warpath. Many White Eyes and Blue Coats will die."

Victorio left the Mescalero Reservation during the moon the White Eyes call August. His people and a few Mescalero warriors went with him. In a few days, the land north of the border and east of the Mimbres Mountains blazed with his anger. He killed everyone in his path unless they were Apache.

When Juh and I learned this, we took a few war leaders and headed north up the Animas Valley in the land the White Eyes call New Mexico. Juh did not like Victorio. They didn't agree about anything often, but he went anyway, hoping he might find opportunities for good raids. We found Victorio three suns later approaching the Mimbres Mountains to pass unseen a string of lookout points the Blue Coats made to catch him going north.

It was easy to get around the lookout points if you knew the trails and passes. We traveled at night if we couldn't avoid the lookouts during the day. We had to be careful to avoid Apache scouts who might also know the trails and passes and wait for us in an ambush, but we never saw any scouts on that trip.

I again disappointed Chappo and his novitiate friends. I was concerned about their safety, and what Victorio would try against the White Eye ranches and Blue Coat camps now that he had his people off the Mescalero Reservation. It would be a time of many White Eye and Apache ambushes. I told them to wait until I returned from the raiding north of the border. Juh and I planned many raids in Sonora. While I was across the border with Juh, I told them to help move the camp north to the stronghold near Janos and Casas Grandes where Nolgee had stayed.

Juh and I returned a moon later from our raids with Victorio. We had taken some plunder and many horses and mules.

Convinced our people were well-hidden, Juh and I took our warriors and returned back across the border for more raids before Ghost Face limited our range.

A handful of suns after Juh and I left, two warriors rode into our camp. One was Ah-dis. He had escaped to San Carlos from Janos after the massacre of Nolgee and most of his band by Mexican soldiers. Gordo, a respected chief and warrior from Naiche's band, was with him. They said they had important business to discuss with Juh and me. In a council with all present, Ah-dis told our people that the Chokonens of Naiche and the Blue Coat big chief, Nant'an Willcox, wanted Juh's band to come back to San Carlos and not join Victorio's raiding. He said the Blue Coats had made things right with the rations on the reservation and had let the Chiricahuas move their camp up out of the *río* valley where the shaking sickness had started and had become worse. Ah-dis and Gordo talked long into the night, telling the people it would be good for them all to go to San Carlos.

Most of those in the camp thought Ah-dis and Gordo made sense, but they would not go to San Carlos until Juh said so. Every night Ah-dis and Gordo spoke about the need to reach San Carlos before the Blue Coats and Mexicans chasing Victorio attacked the people in the camp.

In a few suns, two men, five women, and some children decided they wanted to see for themselves how San Carlos life was now and would head north to meet Atzebee, a Blue Coat chief's sergeant of police. Atzebee would escort them to San Carlos and protect them from Blue Coats and Mexicans chasing Victorio. The rest of the people would not leave until Juh and I returned from raiding north of the border and decided what to do.

Juh and I returned to the stronghold with our warriors about a moon after Ah-dis and Gordo had come. Our raids had been good. We drove a nice herd of horses before us and had many mules packed with plunder. Before he slid from his pony, Juh looked over the faces in the crowd and then shouted, "Ho, Gordo, my great, fat friend! I see you and Ah-dis. You come to join us? Raiding is good."

Gordo laughed. "It is good to see my old friend at last. Raiding makes you fat, too. Ah-dis and I come to speak of an important matter when you are rested and ready to talk."

Juh's laugh turned to a smile as he slapped his belly. "Raiding makes a good appetite. I wash and eat, visit with my women and children, and then we sit by the fire and talk together, eh?"

Gordo nodded. "When you are ready, my friend, we will speak of the long-ago times and the words I've brought you."

Juh nodded and headed for the tipis of his three wives.

My family was very happy to see me return safely. I had a pack mule loaded with much plunder. After I dismounted, I gave the pack mule lead rope and my pony to Chappo to care for. He led them to a corral where he rubbed them down and looked for any injuries or wounds but found none. It took four trips to carry all the plunder to his mother's *wickiup*.

I had bathed and was finishing my gourd of meat stew, juniper berries, and acorn bread when Chappo finished moving the plunder and caring for animals. Chee-hash-kish, smiling in approval, also gave him his meal in a gourd. After she looked through the plunder, we gave most of it away.

I looked Chappo over and said, "My son looks more like a grown man each time I return. *Enjuh.* Soon you will be a novitiate no more. Your mother tells me you've done well in helping the family cross the mountains to this stronghold."

"I'm happy my father is pleased."

"Hmmph. Why are Gordo and Ah-dis here?"

"They bring word from Naiche and the Blue Coat, Nant'an

Willcox. They want you and Juh to return to San Carlos. Gordo says things are much better at San Carlos now. The rations are as they should be. They let people camp up high where the shaking sickness doesn't come."

I raised my brows, feeling many little valleys on my forehead. "Does Nant'an Willcox think we are fools? They either want to put us in the guardhouse or make us dance in the air while hanging by our necks. They know we've been raiding with Victorio. They want to punish us. Gordo and Ah-dis are fools!"

Chappo shook his head. "I'm not even a warrior yet, Father, so I don't yet know how to read the hearts of men, but Gordo says Nant'an Willcox won't hold your raiding against you, and no one will hang you. I believe him."

I stared in the fire a moment. "Hmmph. I don't believe it. Maybe Juh will. Juh is my chief. I'll do what he says."

CHAPTER 10
DECISION TO RETURN TO SAN CARLOS

Juh, Gordo, Ah-dis, and I sat by the fire outside Juh's tipi and smoked to the four directions and swallowed a little whiskey from Juh's brown bottle. Up on the ridge, coyotes yipped. I knew Chappo and his novitiate friends sat back in the darkness listening to us. I let them stay as long as they kept quiet in the cold, black shadows made by yellow moon rising above the eastern mountains.

We enjoyed the warmth from the whiskey and the low flickering flames a while, and then Juh said, "So, old friend, what words do you bring me? Speak. I will listen."

Gordo looked up from the flames and said, "The Blue Coat, Nant'an Willcox, sends these words to you: 'I will be your friend if you and Geronimo return to San Carlos. All memory of raiding and fighting on the warpath is no more. There is no guardhouse, no hanging ropes for you and your warriors. The Blue Coats are chiefs at the reservation now. They make sure the People receive their fair share of rations. The People can camp far from the places of shaking sickness. Victorio ranges far, murders and robs many. Great numbers of Blue Coats, White Eyes, and Mexican soldiers chase him. One sun there will be no place for him to run. He must surrender or die. Save yourselves or you, too, will die. Comeback to San Carlos where the Blue Coats can protect you.' "

Before Gordo could finish, Juh was shaking his head, but waited to speak. When Gordo finished, Juh said, shaking his rifle just over his shoulder, "I'm not going in . . . if they get me, they kill me."

Gordo held up his hands palms out and said, "Wait, wait. Listen to me, my friend. Your band has many children. I don't understand why you run like a wild man without food, sleep, or water. On the reservation, you have a peaceful time. You have a chance to see your children grow up, not get run to death or shot in their beds by the Blue Coats. On the reservation, they give you rations. You don't have to raid for food and warm clothes anymore."

I said to those around the fire what I had told Chappo at our meal. "Nant'an Willcox wants to punish us for our raids and killing White Eyes. He wants us in the guardhouse so he can give us to a sheriff. The White Eyes will come get us and make us dance on air while we choke on the end of rope. We aren't fools, Gordo."

Gordo shook his head. "Nobody is going to hang you. The little chief Blue Coat, Haskell, sent by Nant'an Willcox, says nobody will hang you. No guardhouse or separation from your families for you."

I looked at Gordo, said nothing, raised my chin, and shook my head.

Gordo took a swallow of Juh's whiskey as he stared in the fire. "Remember when the Blue Coat Chief West killed Mangas Coloradas when he brought his people in for talks? The Blue Coats have red faces about this. They drove Chief West away. Remember all the good raids we had in the days of Cochise? We killed many White Eyes and Blue Coats. Made them pay for how they treated us. Now there are too many to fight, and more come every day. There is no more war between the White Eye tribes in the East. Juh, you and Geronimo both know this. The line of Blue Coat soldiers never ends. They always have all the ammunition they need. The old days when we could raid when and where we wanted without losing warriors fast goes away."

Juh took the whiskey bottle back from Gordo, took a big swallow, and handed it to me. I took a big drink and smacked my lips. I said with a sigh, "White Eyes know how to make good whiskey."

Juh said, "Yes, I remember all these things, Gordo. I know times are different. Even south of the border, there are many more Mexicans. Now they want us to go to their reservation and send their soldiers after us in the mountains. Soon we'll have no place for our people to hide—even in the Blue Mountains."

I frowned and shook my head. "At least in the Blue Mountains the White Eyes can't follow us over the border. I fear one day that will change. Now, our People are safe from the Blue Coats there. That is something of value."

We talked and drank together long into the night as old friends and warriors. When the gray light was coming on the far eastern mountains, Juh looked at Gordo and said, "All right. You speak good words, Gordo. They make sense. Tell Haskell I'll talk about San Carlos."

Before they left the next sun, Gordo and Ah-dis talked with Juh and me about a meeting place with Haskell in half a moon to talk about our bands living at San Carlos. I later told my family that we were going to meet Haskell at a spring we often used, but few knew about, in the mountains the White Eyes called Guadalupe, a little north of the border with Mexico, and that we would be leaving in two days. My women and children began making ready to travel with the rise of the next sun.

The spring where we planned to meet Haskell was in a deep canyon and a good place to camp. We moved there in a few days and made ready for Haskell to come. Before Juh talked to Haskell, he held a council with his war leaders and warriors to discuss the offer brought by Gordo and Ah-dis. Again, I let Chappo and his novitiate friends listen.

Juh told the council what Gordo and he had discussed and said if Haskell did make those terms, he favored staying at San Carlos until conditions there proved him wrong. He asked the council what the warriors favored doing. Nearly all of the council was in favor of going to San Carlos if Juh decided the Blue Coats were honest and the terms were what Gordo said. But there was one, a chief, third behind me in leadership, the third chief, who objected. Tall and muscular, he stood near the fire with his arms crossed, a black, angry scowl on his face, shaking his head.

He said, "This is the work of fools. How are Juh and Geronimo gulled by lying fools? It makes them as foolish as those dogs, Gordo and Ah-dis. We should have killed them to shut them up and make their noise go away. We must not go to San Carlos, place of lies and disease. Regardless of what the rest of you do, I won't go."

Juh leaned back on an elbow, casually stared at the third chief, who stood on the other side of the fire, and, with a calm wave of his free hand, said, "Gordo has been a great warrior for a long time. He's no fool, and neither is Ah-dis. All your brothers here think what I say about listening to Haskell is a wise move. Geronimo and me, we don't listen to lying fools. I'm your chief. I think you need to do what we all agree to."

"No! This can't happen. I won't let it happen. We Nednhis are not fools—"

Cold, clear anger at this churlish fool curled my fingers around the handle of my revolver. Without thinking, I pulled back the hammer as its barrel cleared my holster. In the still night, the thunder of the gunshot echoed down the canyon. The third chief stood for a moment, staring with big eyes at the bright red lake growing in the middle of his chest and streaming down his belly. He looked in surprise at me holding my revolver with smoke twisting out of the barrel like a snake leaving a hole in the earth. The light went out of his eyes, and he rocked back on his heels to land on his back with a light crunch on the sand next to the fire.

I winced and nodded. "Most Nednhis are not fools, but those who overrule their chief are. Drag that fool from my sight. He shames us no more."

Juh sent a messenger to Teniente Haskell to come without soldiers to the canyon the messenger would show him. He brought only his interpreter, one who could speak our language and his. When they arrived in our camp, Gordo led them to Juh's lodge, where we spoke of the terms for our return to San Carlos.

We asked Teniente Haskell a simple question but one of the greatest concern to us: "Will our people have to go jail if we surrender?"

His interpreter answered that the agent would treat them well if they lived in peace, and that Haskell would escort them to the reservation and stay until Juh was satisfied with the arrangements. Juh and I decided Teniente Haskell spoke straight and told him we would think on his terms and let him know our decision in a few days. I sat and smoked a long time, thinking about going back to San Carlos. It was not something I wanted to do. I risked the darkness in the guardhouse again, but I told my family the next evening over a meal that I would do whatever Juh wanted.

The following morning, as sunlight filled the western wall of the canyon, painting bright places filled with sparkling morning ice on the plants, and the birds began their songs, Juh, followed by Ishton and their young sons went to Haskell's tent. He told the soldier cooking the morning meal that Chief Juh wanted to speak Teniente Haskell.

Haskell strode from the tent before the cook could answer and, looking past Juh, saw the woman and children. He nodded at Juh and waved parallel to the ground. Juh nodded to him and, swinging his hand back toward his family, said, "Here are my wife and little boys. It's too cold in the mountains. I will stay with my friend."

A big smile filled Teniente Haskell's face when his interpreter told him what Juh said, and Haskell replied, *"Enjuh."*

CHAPTER 11
PEACE IN A TIME OF BLOOD AND FIRE

When Juh and I agreed with Teniente Haskell to return to San Carlos, there was ice on the still places of the streams at sunrise, and some suns Wind shook the mesquite and creosote bushes hard. It was the Season of the Ghost Face. Haskell rode with us to the place called Fort Bowie where Blue Coats lived in stone and *adobe casas* and had a trading post.

We stopped there to hold a council between Teniente Haskell, Tom Jeffords, Captain Chaffee, Juh, and me. We all wanted certainty that we knew and understood everything the White Eyes expected of us. Juh stuttered at big councils and sometimes didn't say the right words for what he meant. He asked that I do most of the talking for the People.

Juh told me to say he wanted a stable treaty. The White Eyes promised there would be one.

We wanted assurance that the Blue Coats wouldn't put our people in the guardhouse for what they had done fighting the White Eyes, and that White Eyes would leave us alone.

Teniente Haskell waved the flat of his hand parallel to the ground and said, "Chiefs, as long as your people are good Indians and keep the peace at San Carlos, Captain Chaffee will take good care of you." I watched the face of Teniente Haskell as he spoke and saw no lies.

Juh and I later spoke with Jeffords in private. We asked if he believed the words of Teniente Haskell. Jeffords said, "Yes, I believe Haskell. I think it's good for your people to go on to

San Carlos." Jeffords's belief in the words of Haskell led Juh and me to decide to move on and stay at San Carlos. We did as the White Eyes like to do after a bargain and shook hands with everybody. We gave two good pumps with each one as Jeffords said we should to make the White Eyes believe us. Pumping hands is another White Eyes custom I think is foolish, but the White Eyes must also think some of our customs are strange.

After the council, Juh, other Nednhis, and I visited, ate, and bet on hoop and pole games with the White Mountain scouts who camped near Fort Bowie. It was a good time. Then we rode on through the wind to San Carlos, where Captain Chaffee let us camp with Naiche's Chokonen People as Juh had asked.

The Chokonens camped in the trees close to the Gila where we had stayed after I got out of the guardhouse. Many of our friends from that camp had died from the shaking sickness, and the water had a bad taste. We complained about this. Soon the agent let us move to the mountains where the spring water was good, and there was no shaking sickness. It was colder up in the mountains than by the Gila, but life was better high above the *río*.

Every morning, Chappo and I ran along deer paths through the junipers and then bathed in the streams, even when there were thin sheets of ice floating on the deep slow pools. Chappo was growing tall and strong. Soon I would have to give him my approval that he become a warrior.

Often stories came to us about Victorio's raids and his fights with the Blue Coats. The stories told how he and his warriors won many battles with the Blue Coats and spread fire and spilled blood at many White Eye ranches and mines. I often smiled when I told my family these stories. At least Victorio was teaching the White Eyes they shouldn't trifle with us.

As the Season of Little Eagles warmed into the Season of

Many Leaves, whispers across San Carlos said Victorio planned to return. He wanted revenge against the White Mountain scouts who chased him and his people when they left San Carlos for Ojo Caliente. At the Natanes Mountain cliffs fight, the White Mountain scouts took back all their animals and Chihenne ponies. Victorio also wanted to free his people who had stayed with Loco. The White Eyes had forced them to return to San Carlos from Ojo Caliente, where they had begged to stay. A moon went by. We heard nothing of Victorio. The silence during those suns reminded me of the stillness before Wind and Thunder speak and lightning arrows fly. We all wondered what was about to happen.

In the Season of Little Leaves, Captain Chaffee sent a messenger with tracks on paper to Naiche and his people. The tracks said the Chokonens and Nednhis had to come down out of the mountains and camp close to the subagency. The Blue Coats wanted to protect them from Victorio. This, despite the water tasting bad, shaking sickness in the warm and hot seasons, and Naiche never making a move to leave San Carlos.

Naiche did as Chaffee ordered. He said to me, "Uncle, I'm so disgusted with the White Eyes that I'm ready to leave the reservation. We should be able to live in the Blue Mountains where there is no shaking sickness."

I nodded but said, "Wait a little while, my son. *Ussen* has not told me the time is right. Maybe Victorio's days before he rides the ghost pony are few. I don't know if this is true, but *Ussen* does many things that make no sense at the time, but later we see they were for our own good. When Victorio is gone, the agent will let us go again to the mountains, and life will be better at San Carlos."

Naiche looked at me with an eyebrow raised for a few moments before turning to walk away along the winding path to his *wickiup*.

Blue Coats, seemingly without number, continued to fill the land, some waiting at San Carlos for Victorio to come, others always chasing and following him in the country where the White Eyes claimed to have last seen him. Others stayed at camps in the mountains along the border where they also watched for him. Who could know where a ghost such as Victorio might appear or what harm he might do?

Many White Mountain scouts came east to our side of the reservation and rode long days on many trails, staring east toward the gray mountains and across the *llano* for some sign of Victorio, who might take revenge against the White Mountains, steal back Loco and the people, or speak to Juh and Naiche to convince them to ride with him.

Victorio and his warriors came quietly and unseen as shadows during a fingernail moon. They slipped past scouts watching for them and crossed the land to San Carlos. Victorio found some of his White Mountain enemies and killed nineteen, including the great scout Bylas and those of his family, but the Blue Coats kept Victorio's family too close to the agency for him even to creep close enough to see them. He sent messengers to Juh and me saying we should leave our camp and join him. We decided to stay where we were. When we didn't come, he returned east back to the mountains of New Mexico.

The Blue Coats continued to chase Victorio, but they couldn't catch him. One sun, word came that Blue Coat Major Morrow, who had been chasing Victorio since he had left the Mescalero Reservation, had won a big battle against him. With his big gun (a cannon shooting exploding shells) and his Blue Coat soldiers with dark skins, Major Morrow killed thirty of Victorio's People.

I told my family what had happened to Victorio while we ate our evening meal. My women stared at me with sad faces. Chappo exchanged glances with Dohn-say, and then they both looked at the ground, knowing they might never leave San Carlos if the Blue Coats could defeat a warrior as great as Victorio. Off in the distance I heard coyotes howl and thought, *Don't worry, my wives and my children. Coyote, the trickster, waits. One day soon, we will go quietly into the Blue Mountains. The Blue Coats will never find us there. We must always be ready.*

His chief sent Captain Chaffee to another place. Until the new agent came, we had to continue living where Chaffee left us. Victorio might come back. Chaffee had stopped the ration-stealing from us. We didn't starve, but we were hungry. We needed to get to where our women could collect good things from the land to eat. We needed to get away from the shaking sickness and bad water. All the chiefs knew we had to move away from there before all our People died. Jeffords talked us out of moving until the new agent, Tiffany, came. Coyote waits.

Within two moons, Tiffany saw how bad the shaking sickness was in our camps and told us to leave for camps in the mountains where we were away from the shaking sickness, and we could gather food from the land to help feed ourselves. Life on the reservation was soon much better as Jeffords told us.

Every ration day, we went to the main San Carlos office to collect what we were due. Then we visited the trading post at San Carlos where the women found things they needed from sharp, steel axes, to cook pots, to cloth. The men usually bought *tobaho* and papers and even something sweet.

A young White Eye named George Wratten, who looked about the age of Chappo, worked at the trading post. Unlike other White Eyes, he wanted to learn our words and speak them clearly. I watched him for a while and saw that he worked hard to get our words right and made friends with several of our young warriors who helped him. They joked and teased with him in a good way when he didn't speak our words as he should.

He laughed with them. Although he was several harvests younger, he was taller and bigger across the shoulders than my cousin Ahnandia, who had become his good friend and spent many hours helping the young White Eye speak our words correctly.

One day while we were watching a hoop and pole game, I asked Ahnandia how he came to be friends with Wratten. Ahnandia looked across his shoulder at me and grinned like a sly coyote. "I am friends with Wratten since last harvest soon after we are forced to return with Loco back here. I had picked up a few words of the White Eye tongue at Ojo Caliente, but the White Eyes made funny faces or rolled their eyes when I tried to use what I knew."

I laughed. "I know what you mean. I understand their tongue, but I won't speak it around the White Eyes. I won't have them make faces or roll their eyes at me if I say the wrong words. Besides, they might think I'm saying something dangerous and try to kill me."

Ahnandia smiled and nodded. "I'm not a *di-yen* and war chief like you, Uncle. White Eyes don't care what I say and only laugh at how I say it. I don't care if they do laugh. They think I'm simpleminded, but I'm a lot smarter than they think. I proved my friendship with Wratten one day at the trading post, and we're very close now. We first came to know each other when I couldn't make the trader understand that I wanted something sweet. Wratten, who had learned a few of our words, helped me make the trader understand what I wanted, and soon we are friends. He teaches me White Eye tongue, and I teach him mine.

"One day, the warrior we call Always Angry comes in the trading post while I swap words with Wratten as he works behind the table. Always Angry asks for *tobaho*. Wratten lays the *tobaho* on table and holds up two fingers and says, 'two coin.'

Always Angry reaches in vest and throws one coin on table and reaches for *tobaho*. Wratten puts hand over *tobaho* and shakes head. 'No. Two coin. Then you have.'

"Always Angry, faster than a rattlesnake with his knife, has it against Wratten's throat. He says, 'No, I say one coin, and I think maybe you die.' Wratten's face has no fear. He said, 'No, two coin. You leave now.' I see little trickle of blood on Wratten's shirt.

"Then Always Angry feels my knife on his neck, and a little trickle of blood flows on his shirt. I say, 'No, Always Angry, you leave now. I pay two coin, you pay two coin, all pay two coin for *tobaho*. This man Wratten is fair with us. You go now, or maybe you die. What you say?'

"Always Angry puts knife back in sheath, reaches in his vest, and puts another coin down. Wratten smiles and hands Angry the *tobaho*. Always Angry doesn't look angry; he looks scared with my knife still close to his neck. He backs away and leaves. Wratten's cheeks fill with air, and he blows and grins. All there laugh. We have good time. He still helps me with the White Eye tongue, but now he speaks good Apache words. Even the way words are different between the bands, he understands good what they mean. That is all I have to say."

After hearing Ahnandia's story, I went to the trading post and spoke to Wratten to buy a pot for my women. He spoke my tongue good. He was easy to know. I liked him. He was one of the few White Eyes I thought spoke straight. I went to the trading post many times that summer to visit with Wratten, talk with friends in the porch shade, and hear new stories about Victorio.

Victorio lost more battles in the Season of Large Fruit, and he had fewer and fewer warriors to fight against the Blue Coats. He stopped to rest with his band at a place of water and grass near three small mountains, Tres Castillos, in Chihuahua. They had few bullets left. He sent Nana out with a few others to find ammunition and to hunt. But, before Nana returned, the *Nakai-yi* Army Chief, Joaquin Terrazas, came with many men. The battle was soon over, the warriors killed and scalped, some women killed, other women and children taken as slaves and sold in the City of Mules, Ciudad Chihuahua.

Nana returned with ammunition too late and found the band wiped out. He told me Victorio had fired his last bullet and then stabbed himself in the heart. Nana buried what the *Nakai-yes* left, including a scalped Victorio. One day, I will take vengeance against *Nakai-yi* soldiers for what Terrazas did to Victorio and his people.

Nana vanished. Some said he went to the Blue Mountains to recover and gain strength for his own revenge; others, that he was hiding in the mountains of New Mexico. No one knew where Nana was hiding until, like a bear sleeping in his cave all Ghost Face, he reappeared in the spring. I heard stories from scouts that in the Season of Many Leaves, he had sent emissaries four times to Mescalero to learn if the agent there would accept him and his people back, but the emissaries never got to talk to the Mescalero agent because soldiers were still watching the reservation for trouble and blocked their path. Nana again disappeared, but this time I was sure that he must be near Mescalero waiting for a time to strike or get the agent to accept them.

In the dark of the moon the White Eyes call July, stories came to us that Nana was raiding all along the border with his warriors and maybe fifteen Mescaleros out for a good time. He was avenging Victorio with blood and fire. For many, his long, hard raid was difficult to believe. Old, stiff Nana killed many White Eyes and *Nakai-yes,* took their animals, and burned their ranches. Even experienced scouts couldn't catch him. He raided for nearly two moons and then suddenly disappeared into the Blue Mountains. My people could only shake their heads in disbelief at the power the old man had. But I didn't shake my head. I knew his power.

CHAPTER 12
NOCH-AY-DEL-KINNE
CALLS THE DEAD CHIEFS

One evening on Cibecue Creek, a long day's ride north from the San Carlos Agent's house, Juh and I watched the *di-yen* Noch-ay-del-kinne sing and sprinkle golden pollen on his followers. They danced in ecstasy, aligned liked spokes of a wheel and facing him at the hub, circling around and drawing Power from him. They believed he could speak with the spirits of the dead and had the power to bring the dead chiefs back to help the people. There were many people and even scouts sent there by Agent Tiffany from all over the reservation. Juh and I planned to see if the *di-yen* could call Mangas Coloradas, Cochise, or even Victorio back from the spirit world. I didn't believe he could do it, but I was willing to watch and see the truth for myself. Juh thought maybe Noch-ay-del-kinne had the Power, but he also wanted to see it firsthand.

We Apaches believe there is a life after this one in the Happy Place. Maybe it is the same place the White Eyes call heaven. I don't know. No one ever told me what part of a man lived after death. I have seen many men die. I have seen many human bodies decayed, but I have never seen the part called spirit. I don't know what it is. I thought by watching the Power of Noch-ay-del-kinne I might see the spirit of a man, and maybe the best spirits, which were parts of the great chiefs. He said that when he called the great chiefs, and they came again, the White Eyes would leave, and the game would come back.

Tiffany had made him come to the agency for a talk about

116

this. After the talk with Tiffany, Noch-ay-del-Kinne changed his story a little and said his followers had misunderstood him. He said he couldn't call the great chiefs back until all the White Eyes had left. I laughed. I knew unless *Ussen* shook the earth, the White Eyes would never leave our country, and the Apaches were too few to drive them out. Still I wanted to see if this *di-yen* truly had Power or just talked to have the people follow him.

Noch-ay-del-kinne's camp stood among the cottonwood and oak trees on one side of Cibecue Creek in a canyon that narrowed as it climbed into the hills. On the east side of the creek beyond the camp was a large place free of brush, and there he held his dances.

The day we arrived to see his dance, we found many people on the wagon road to his camp. The sun was beginning to touch the western mountains when we first looked down on the place for his dance. There was enough light to see four places in the field where wood was piled for fires at the corners of a large square, each corner on a cardinal direction, and there was a place in the center of the square where the dirt was plainly packed. Near the east corner of the square were drums or hides used to keep the dance rhythm. To the north were barrels of water for the crowds to drink from, maybe one or two holding *tulapai.*

I wanted a good drink. It had been a long ride up from San Carlos, but I settled for water because I wanted a clear head if the spirits of the great chiefs came. Juh, his alert black eyes taking it all in, said nothing as he watched people gather outside the corners of the four places of fire stacked with great piles of wood.

We tied our ponies off in a little canyon that led northeast off the road and walked down to the field to get something to eat and a little water. We saw many who were friendly with us, but we just nodded at them with a smile. There was little talking by anyone. We approached the camp, and some Chihenne women there with their families offered us bread and roasted meat, for which we were grateful. We ate quickly, thanked our hosts, drank some water, and crossed the dancing field back to the edge of the wagon road to climb up on some boulders. We watched and waited for the ceremonies to begin. I sensed a strange Power in the air. The air crackled like the times before Wind and Thunder with their lightning arrows came.

All the people grew quiet as they waited in the growing darkness. I had never been to a dance where there was such silence at its beginning. The darkness was complete except for the milk *río* of stars filling the sky. Even in the camp, there was no light, no fires. We waited.

Then from the place of the drums, came a single, slow, steady beat. A low sigh of happiness and anticipation floated through the people waiting below us. Toward the east, a torch flared, revealing the clown dancer, and the deep thump of the pot drums began. The clown advanced, whirling and dancing, to light the fire on the east point of the square. Then he whirled to light the south fire, then moved west and, finally, north.

A crown dancer in elaborate headdress seemed to appear from each of the fires, and they danced together around the center of the great circle, as if a fire were there, while the clown danced on the edges. Still, there was no singing, only the drums. The drumbeats were powerful and raised my expectations of things to come.

The drums suddenly stopped, and out of the silence a high, single voice singing to *Ussen* came from the dark beyond the eastern fire. Noch-ay-del-kinne, the prophet, came walking to the eastern light, singing, to stand in the center of the crown dancers, who circled him, led by the clown, and then backed away and disappeared into the darkness. A deep thumping began from a pot drum and, with its rhythm, he sang four songs facing each direction as he turned east to south and ended where he began, facing east.

The drums stopped and, holding his arms out, Noch-ay-del-kinne began to speak of his vision and Power, saying he had been shown that when the White Eyes leave the land, the great chiefs have told him they would rise from their graves and come to help the people reclaim the land over which they once freely roamed. The wild game the White Eyes had driven away would return, and our days would be like those of our grandfathers. To call the spirits, he showed the people a new dance to follow and said they had to keep its rhythm in their hearts to help him call the great chiefs that they might help all the people.

Holding his arms out like wings, Noch-ay-del-kinne called all the people to come to him and dance as he had taught them and to receive a blessing as he sprinkled golden pollen on them. All the drums began the rhythm for the dance.

Young and old streamed out of the crowd gathered around the square. The dancers first grouped in a circle around Noch-ay-del-kinne. Then, as if by some unseen power, they naturally formed spokes facing him. At a change in the drumbeat, he began a new song. Those who were first to dance circled around him, the hub of a wheel, to receive their scattering of the sacred, golden pollen. People new to Noch-ay-del-kinne's dance watched the dancers a while to learn the steps and rotational moves and then joined as spoke members of the wheel.

I glanced at Juh, who seemed to be having his own vision as he focused all his attention on Noch-ay-del-kinne. A hand pressed on my shoulder. I glanced up to see Nana sitting down with a bone-weary groan beside me. He, too, had come to see this *di-yen* and hear his message. Nana leaned forward a little and, smiling, looked around me to study the transfixed face of

Juh watching the prophet speak.

I said in a low voice, "Grandfather, I thought you were avenging Victorio with blood and fire. Now you're here. Aren't you worried the Blue Coats might catch you here?"

"No, my son, I'm not worried the Blue Coats will catch me. I see scouts the Blue Coats have sent here to watch, and they smile and nod when they see me. They won't try to arrest me. These people would kill them if they did. My little band rests in the mountains to the east, and a few sell our plunder in Mexico before we strike again." Nana rubbed his chin and stretched his wrinkled lips over his teeth. "I wanted to hear Noch-ay-del-kinne's own words, not as someone else has heard him, and maybe see his Power in raising someone from the dead. This may be the path we need to free our country from the White Eyes who have swarmed over us and taken our land. I wait and watch. I thought I saw you from up the wagon road where I waited. I came to sit on your rock so we can speak privately. What do you think of this *di-yen*? Can he call the spirits or not?"

I shrugged. "I don't know. If I see him call the spirits and they appear, then I will believe. Now I can only wait and hope he speaks true."

Nana nodded. "We think the same. I hope to see Noch-ay-del-kinne's Power before the dawn, when I must truly disappear and return to my people."

"Hmmph, Nana. I, too, want to ride free and punish our enemies, but I have given my word to stay on the reservation. This agent, Tiffany, tries to give us what we need, but not all I think we are due. I don't trust the White Eyes. If they try to put us in the guardhouse again, Juh and I will leave. Maybe this prophet has true visions. I hope so. It will save many of our lives and much spilled blood."

"*Enjuh,* Geronimo. When will you leave this place?"

"We need to turn for our camps tomorrow. We leave at first light. Travel safely, Grandfather."

Nana nodded, and we said no more.

The dancing went on until the color of gold lighted the eastern horizon. The dancers appeared happy and in their own trances as they moved together all dusted with the golden pollen in the spokes of Noch-ay-del-kinne's wheel. It was inspiring to watch such unity of Apaches who sometimes fought each other. Perhaps the prophet could call the spirits of the great chiefs back to help us and it would happen soon. Still, neither Juh nor I knew for sure.

Near the time of coming light, a mist came creeping down the creek's canyon. Without warning, Noch-ay-del-kinne raised arms, the drums beat no more, and the dancing stopped. It was strange how quiet it was as the mist filled the square. I felt my heart beat faster as though I was running. I looked at Nana. He stared as though in a trance, unmoving, barely breathing, at a place in front of Noch-ay-del-kinne where the mist seemed to rise in three separate places. The prophet waved his hands upward as though urging someone to stand. Then some pointed into the mists and shouted, "The spirits come!" I stared across the field, but saw nothing but the bumps in the mist. As the morning light increased the mist began to disappear and a sigh rippled through the crowd as Noch-ay-del-kinne lowered his arms and began to back out of the square with his head bowed. The dancers seemed to awake and began to speak with each other.

Nana said, "It's time for me to go."

"What did you see, Grandfather?"

He pointed toward where the bumps in the mist had been. "There in the mists in front of Noch-ay-del-kinne I saw Mangas Coloradas, Cochise, and Victorio rising out of the earth, but they came only to their knees before they stopped. They said, 'Why do you call us? You are not ready. Leave us alone.' Then they were gone. Truly, Noch-ay-del-kinne has shown his great Power to call them, but he still can't call them back into this life. This prophet has great Power. Perhaps he uses it soon to help us all. We will see."

Nana groaned as he stood up on his arthritic knees, tottered over to Juh, said something in his ear to which Juh nodded, and then went hobbling up the stones to where horses were tied in the brush nearby. I saw him tighten his pony's cinch, then pull himself up to mount slowly, throw a leg over his saddle, and turn, leaving the wagon road to ride up the narrow canyon east where we had our ponies tied.

When the dawn grew bright, Juh and I saddled our ponies after the drums below stopped, and the exhausted but ecstatic dancers, as if drunk, sat down on the ground. In the surprising quiet that followed, we heard the chatter of birds in the brush and saw the golden light falling like waterfalls over the mountains and into the canyons as we headed back down the wagon road south and across many juniper-covered ridges for our camp high above the Gila.

We stopped to rest our ponies in the middle of the morning by a small fast-running stream still in the shadows, and with good brush cover that would make us hard to see even as the sunlight drove away the shadows. We ate while our hobbled ponies drank and then grazed on the good green grama grass.

Juh, taking a bite of mescal cake his women made for him, said, "So what do you think of this prophet, Noch-ay-del-kinne, Geronimo? Can he really call the great chiefs back to help us?"

"Maybe he can," I said as I poured some dried juniper berries into my hand from the pouch of food my women had fixed for this journey. "We haven't yet seen him raise spirits as he says

he can. Nana told me, and I have heard others say, they have
seen his spirits—seen Mangas Coloradas and Cochise and Victorio come from their graves. Nana said that in his visions in
the morning mists, he saw them come up to their knees and tell
the Prophet to leave them alone. I've seen many made happy
with his dance. These are good signs the prophet has the Power
of the vision he claims. Maybe in another moon we come back.
Maybe then we see a true show of his Power. I want to see that
before I believe in him. What do you think? You're the chief."

Juh chewed and thought for a while before he said, "I don't
know for sure, either. I want to think he's not just imagining
what he says his vision showed him, but his dances could get us
attacked by the Blue Coats if they think he's trying to start an
uprising. There are more soldiers at San Carlos than usual, but
I think that's because of Nana's raiding. I worry some that the
soldiers might change their minds about us and think they
should put us on trial now that Teniente Haskell has gone away.
I don't like this agent, Tiffany. I don't trust him. We have to be
smarter than the White Eyes in everything we do, from believing
in Noch-ay-del-kinne's Power, to staying out of the guardhouse
if they change their minds about us."

In this I thought Juh was wise. It was best to wait and listen
and outmaneuver the Blue Coats if they acted about anything.

CHAPTER 13
MORE BLUE COATS COME AFTER NOCH-AY-DEL-KINNE IS KILLED

The Blue Coats were afraid of Noch-ay-del-kinne. It was as if they believed he had the Power he claimed while, at the same time, they denied any such thing existed. Scouts we knew said Agent Tiffany feared all Noch-ay-del-kinne's talk about the White Eyes leaving the country would cause an uprising across the reservation and lead to the murder of many White Eyes.

Tiffany told the Blue Coats to arrest Noch-ay-del-kinne and to bring him to the main agency. Noch-ay-del-kinne surrendered when the Blue Coats came, but his followers in and around his camp didn't tolerate his arrest. I heard the fight with the prophet's followers killed eight Blue Coats, Noch-ay-del-kinne, and about eighteen others. The followers, very angry at the killing of the prophet, chased the Blue Coat chief in charge of the arrest all the way back to Fort Apache. They even attacked the fort for a while. Small bands scattered around the reservation killed any White Eyes and Blue Coats they found.

Juh and I stayed calm and did nothing. It was clear to me that Noch-ay-del-kinne was not the prophet many had thought. He couldn't bring back the great chiefs to fight for him or protect himself. Most of the people across the reservation thought the same thing. They swallowed their bitter disappointment like a ball of thorns and went on with their lives. There was no uprising, as Agent Tiffany thought there might be. But the White Eyes still shook in fear of us, believing that maybe all the tribes on the reservation would leave to take their revenge for the prophet's death.

Many Blue Coats came to the reservation, some pulling their big guns on wheels, to ensure there was no uprising. No Blue Coats had come near the Chokonen camps since the time my war leaders and I were in the guardhouse waiting for the Tucson sheriff. Now the Blue Coats were everywhere. A man couldn't do his personal business in the brush without seeing a Blue Coat pass by.

Juh and I watched the dust clouds of riding and marching soldiers on the reservation grow bigger by the day, too many for killing a false prophet. We thought maybe they planned to take all the Chiricahua leaders captive and lock them up to keep the peace, even though we had done nothing. After all, that's the way Clum did me and my chiefs. If the sheriff had come for us, we would have danced on air hanging from a rope while the White Eyes laughed. I would never risk that again.

One night, under a soft, black sky filled with a *río* of stars while many coyotes yipped on the ridge above us, I sat with Juh by his fire. We smoked to the four directions and then talked as brothers about why all the Blue Coats were riding around San Carlos.

Juh, his hands folded together and his elbows resting on his knees, leaned forward, staring at the fire. He said, "Today I saw Blue Coats with eight of the big guns on wheels like the one Blue Coat Major Morrow used to win a battle with Victorio. In a head-to-head fight with Blue Coats using those things, we have no chance. One time, I saw *Nakai-yes* using them on some Yaquis who tried to attack them. The Mexicans wiped them out. I'm not even sure the Mexicans had a man wounded. The Yaquis couldn't see the guns. They were far away. I worry about all these Blue Coats coming around. The agents say they come to arrest those who made war when the prophet died. But why are there so many? They don't need all these soldiers to arrest a few White Mountains."

The night was cold. I pulled my blanket up over my shoulders. "Hmmph. We do well to stay alert to the danger. I tell you, I will never go back to the guardhouse. The Blue Coats will kill me first. When we see any signs that they're coming to arrest us, we must take our families and disappear into the Blue Mountains, maybe far into Mexico to your stronghold on the rim of the Great Canyon, to Guaynopa. I wish we were there now."

Juh nodded. "Maybe the *Nakai-yes* have talked the Americans into arresting us for all the raids we did in Mexico like the ones in Chocolate Pass, or for all the soldiers we killed in ambushes when they came after us. I don't know if they're here to arrest us and hold us for the *Nakai-yes*, but I worry about the White Eyes working with *Nakai-yi* soldiers against us."

I raised my brows and stared at the features of his strong face in the flickering firelight. The White Eyes had little to say about how good, strong, or powerful *Nakai-yi* army soldiers were. Maybe the *Nakai-yes* were trying to get us through the Americans now that we were easy to find at San Carlos.

"I had not thought of this. They haven't done it before, but there's always a first time. If the Blue Coats plan on doing this, Tiffany would know. He seems fair. Maybe he would tell us."

Juh stared into the fire as the wood popped and crackled in the flames. He held his palms out to catch some heat and rubbed his hands and arms. "Maybe he would. I think we ought to at least ask him and watch him to learn if he speaks the truth."

I nodded and pulled my blanket closer.

In the middle of the moon the White Eyes call September, Juh and I rode to the San Carlos Agency. We told the man guarding

Tiffany's door, the one White Eyes called "Clerk" who worked for Tiffany as interpreter and keeper of White Eye word tracks on paper, we wanted to speak with Tiffany. He asked what we wanted to talk about so he could tell Tiffany in advance. The White Eyes have strange customs and ideas. I said, "Blue Coats." Clerk's eyebrows raised, and he walked quickly into Tiffany's place. I heard a mumble of White Eye words I didn't understand, and then Tiffany said, "Of course, show them in."

Clerk came to the doorway and motioned for us to come. Tiffany made a big smile and motioned for us to sit in chairs in front of where he worked. He said through the interpreter, "Welcome, chiefs. Please sit down. My clerk will stay to interpret for us." He slid a box of *cigarros* toward us. "Will you smoke?"

Juh picked up a *cigarro*, ran it under his nose, and nodded. Clerk made fire with a little fire stick, and Juh lighted it. While Clerk and Tiffany watched, Juh smoked to the four directions and passed it around. Tiffany had been an agent long enough to understand that smoking to the four directions meant we had come on serious business.

He said, "What can I do for you?"

Juh looked first at Tiffany and then Clerk. "Geronimo and I have come to ask why the Blue Coats are everywhere. What's going on? What does so many here at one time mean? Will they become part of the agencies?"

As the interpreter spoke our words in the White Eye tongue, Tiffany began to shake his head. He answered, "I understand your worry. It has been quiet here at San Carlos with few soldiers for a long time. Now there are many. They won't be here a long time, and they aren't looking for you or any of your people. If you've been peaceful, they won't bother you in any way. They're supposed to arrest those who made trouble for Colonel Carr when he tried to arrest Noch-ay-del-kinne."

Both Juh and I smiled and nodded. I said, "*Enjuh.* You know when we returned to San Carlos in the Season of the Ghost Face, we were on the warpath in Mexico. Teniente Haskell said there is no memory of our past war. We came to San Carlos trusting Teniente Haskell. We are content here. We don't want war or fighting. Do the Blue Coats here have anything to do with what we did in Mexico?"

Tiffany shook his head and said, in a loud voice, "No." It was the kind of answer we wanted to hear. Juh and I made big grins. We were relieved. If Tiffany was a liar, he was a very good one.

We stood and each pumped his hand twice and said, *"Enjuh."* He stood there smiling and nodding and gave us the White Eye wave of see-you-again as we left. We mounted our ponies and rode back to our camps.

One day about ten suns after we had spoken to Tiffany, Juh and I smoked. He said, "Tiffany said the Blue Coats would not bother us if we had not been in the fighting over Noch-ay-del-kinne. We Chiricahuas were not in the prophet's fight. The Blue Coats took the White Mountain bands of Bonito and George who surrendered to the agent, but then let them go like they really didn't want them. If they're the only ones they were after, then why didn't they keep them? And if they aren't keeping them, why are the Blue Coats still here? I smell a trick."

Again, Juh was thinking ahead of me. Wise Juh. *Why are the Blue Coats still here?* I could only shrug and say, "I don't know. Maybe Tiffany lies. Maybe it's a trick, and the Blue Coats are after us. We must watch and be ready for whatever they do."

Two suns after Juh and I talked, our women and children went to the place for getting our rations. It was a good sun, the air cool. A softness in the light spread like a blanket on the far mountains and valleys below us. I worked on my medicine hat. Others made dolls for their little daughters or bows and arrows for their sons or cleaned their rifles and made ready for the next hunt. Then we heard the pounding rumble of many horses coming toward our camp. We were quick to put away our work and find a weapon we might use. George and Bonito came riding with their bands but stopped in a whirling cloud of dust before they swung down from their ponies to speak.

George, breathing hard, spoke in a rush of words as we gathered around him. "The Blue Coats sent many more soldiers to ration day. We surrendered before. They let us go. Now they come to arrest us again. Bonito and I rode here with our warriors. We didn't know what else to do. We came here to warn you. The Blue Coats want to put us in the stinking guardhouse. The Blue Coats rode for our village. Our women and children are prisoners because we ran. I think the Blue Coats want to arrest us all for fighting over the taking of Noch-ay-del-kinne. We won't let them take us. We fight them. They say they will put the Chiricahua chiefs in chains. Carry them off to a far country. They will murder our women and children. Help us fight them!"

I felt the grip of despair and anger squeeze my guts. *Betrayed! Tiffany lied. The Blue Coats planned to put us all in the guardhouse.* I bellowed to the blue, peaceful sky like a howling wolf. I shook my fist. "No! The Blue Coats will fail. They can't have my family! I'll kill every Blue Coat I can first."

Juh grabbed me by shoulder and shook me. "Calm yourself, brother." He turned to the others and said, "Call a council of the chiefs and leaders. Let us decide what we will do together."

CHAPTER 14
THE COUNCIL

I sent Chappo and his novitiate brothers, Tsisnah, Fun, and Yahnozha, out to watch the trails for signs of Blue Coats coming as Naiche, Chato, Juh, and leaders from other camps gathered in council. I said to my women, "The Blue Coats might be coming for us. A council gathers to talk about what to do. I want you ready to move quickly, if the council decides we must leave for Mexico."

Chee-hash-kish tilted her head to one side and, looking at me with her large, dark eyes, said with the unyielding strength of a warrior, "My sisters, your children, and I will be ready to follow wherever you go, Husband."

Her words and look filled my heart. I said, *"Enjuh,"* and headed for the council fire.

The fire was not a large one. We didn't want the Blue Coats and White Eye agents to think we were in council about anything. We gathered in a flat place surrounded by junipers, their tart smell filling the air along with the songs of insects and the far yips of coyotes. More men were there than I thought might come—even a few White Mountains sat with us to listen and to consider what to do now that their prophet and their dream of seeing the White Eyes disappear had died.

The most powerful warriors, now in their prime, were there—Naiche, Chihuahua, Kaytennae, Chato. The bravest, most fearsome of us all, Jelikinne sat back a little from the fire next to the older chiefs, Juh, Mangas, George, and Bonito, those oldest, most experienced warriors, their faces flat, unyielding to their inner feelings, the fire's soft, flickering shadows painting neither excitement nor anger in their eyes. They had lived through many fights with the Blue Coats and White Eyes.

When no more appeared for the council, Naiche looked at me and nodded. I stood and spread my arms singing to *Ussen* and for the council, asking that he give us wisdom and show us the right way. After we smoked to the four directions, Naiche, as chief of the Chokonens, spoke first. He stood where all could see him.

"Warriors. Friends. Brothers. George, a chief of the White Mountains, brings us hard-to-hear news. The Blue Coats released him and Bonito after they surrendered for their part in the fighting over the death of the prophet. Now the Blue Coat chiefs have decided George and Bonito will not be free. They tried to take them again today during ration distribution. These chiefs with their warriors disappeared after learning the White Eye plans. The Blue Coats went to their villages and, when they couldn't find them, took their families and children. Now George tells us the Blue Coats plan to attack those who have done nothing. They will murder our women and children and put our chiefs in the guardhouse to get who they want. This may be so. But then maybe the Blue Coats change their minds. Who can know the mind of a Blue Coat? Who can trust a Blue Coat?"

The fire snapped and crackled, the only sounds, as Naiche's question hung in the air like a black cloud filled with lightning arrows. Even the coyotes, insects, and night birds were listening to Naiche.

"I was only a few harvests off the *tsach* when Teniente Bascom called my father, Cochise, to a meeting at his tent in Apache Pass. Cochise had no quarrel with the Blue Coats. He had nothing to hide. He brought his family with him while he spoke in peace with the Blue Coats. Teniente Bascom demanded my father return a rancher boy my father had not taken and knew nothing about, but Cochise offered to find him among the other bands if that's what the Blue Coats wanted. Teniente Bascom didn't listen. He said Cochise must return the boy. He ordered my father taken to the guardhouse. Cochise cut the tent and escaped, but he lost brothers and other family to Teniente Bascom's disbelief in his words. My father's war against the White Eyes and Blue Coats began with Bascom's disbelieving ears. It ended ten harvests later when General Howard gave him the reservation and agent he wanted. Then he believed he could live in peace with the White Eyes.

"My brother and I foolishly left our father's reservation for this awful place after listening to Clum's lies, trying to avoid fighting with the White Eyes and Blue Coats, as Cochise made my brother and me promise. Now it seems, even at San Carlos where we have lived in peace five harvests, suffered many deaths from the shaking sickness, and tried to survive on the few rations the agents do not cheat us out of, that the Blue Coats will destroy most of us and put our chiefs in the guardhouse. This is beyond any promise I made to my father. My patience is gone. This will not stand. I'll take my family and go if the Blue Coats come."

There were hoots of approval and men slapping the ground in agreement with Naiche. Some yelled, "Ho!" and shook their fists. Then Naiche said, "My counselor, the great *di-yen* Geronimo, knows I was ready to leave when the agent forced us to live where shaking sickness comes to many, but before I did this, the new agents have let us live up high, away from that place, and our life is better. No more shaking sickness comes, but agents still steal our rations. I now ask Geronimo's wisdom in this time of trouble with the Blue Coats."

Standing back in the shadows as Naiche spoke, I saw Juh's

right foot begin to tap and his eyes shine in excitement. Je-likinne sat with crossed arms and nodded. George wore a little crooked smile.

I stepped out of the shadows and stood where Naiche had stood as he moved to the shadows. "Warriors! Naiche speaks with a straight tongue. Juh and I were at the reservation when Clum came to speak with Naiche and his brother. He wanted us to move to San Carlos, too. We said we would, but then changed our minds. We knew San Carlos was not a good place to live, and enemies already lived there. We decided it was bet-ter to live in Mexico. A harvest later, I came north. My people and I camped with Victorio's people at Ojo Caliente. We did nothing to the White Eyes north of the border. We just took a few horses and mules from the tame Indians. That's all.

"But Clum came and took me and my war leaders captive by trickery, chained our legs, and brought us to the San Carlos guardhouse, where we waited in the dark and stink for a White Eye sheriff to take us where the White Eyes could laugh watch-ing us dance on air while we choked hanging from a rope. *Ussen* freed us. But life here was too hard. The White Eyes cheated us every ration day. We prepared to leave and waited for when *Us-sen* told us to go. He spoke to me. My people and I left. We went to live with Juh's people in the Blue Mountains. It was a hard life, but it was better than living in the heat, dust and bit-ing insects, avoiding snakes, being cheated and counted like sheep, or getting the shaking sickness like we did at San Carlos."

Juh sat listening but, unable to stay still, crossed and uncrossed his arms, rubbed a hand over his hair, and made faces with frowns and half smiles at what I said. His eyes, like two black coals of fire, glittered with excitement.

"The Blue Coat Nant'an sent us emissaries and word from Naiche who told us life was better at San Carlos and wanted us to come back. We saw the changes at San Carlos since we had left, and we talked with Teniente Haskell. For our raids and war in Mexico, the Blue Coat Nant'an promised no memory, no punishment. We believed he spoke straight. We returned to San Carlos. There were no punishments for our raids and war in Mexico. We lived for a time where there was no shaking sickness. From the land, we gathered food we liked to eat. All our rations came. The agents didn't cheat us. Life was better.

"Now the agents steal from us again. Many Blue Coats ride the reservation trembling in fear that Nana will come. We know he has gone to the Blue Mountains and stays in its strongholds. Most White Eyes do not keep their promises. Fearful men often act without thinking. George tells us the Blue Coats will come for us. I believe him. Who else speaks?"

I saw a tall, dark form rise from among the leaders near the fire and step near me into the light. It was Mangas, son of Mangas Coloradas, great chief of the Chihenne people.

Mangas looked at the faces glowing in the firelight and said, "Brothers! My father fought Mexicans and White Eyes for many harvests. He married his daughters to the other great chiefs, Cochise and Victorio, binding our families together by blood. He decided to talk with the Blue Coats after they offered peace. He went to talk, but they took him prisoner. They murdered him, buried him, and then dug him up, cut off his head, boiled it, and kept his skull."

The insects made no more noise. Even the fire made no pops and crackles. Far up on a ridge, Wolf called his brothers, and every man in the council sighed at what happened to Mangas.

"Victorio became chief of the Chihenne. He wanted peace, wanted to live in peace at Ojo Caliente. Clum said San Carlos was a better place, and Victorio led his people and followed Clum there. Clum lied. Victorio left San Carlos in three moons and went back to Ojo Caliente, but the White Eyes said they would not let him stay there. He tried to stay with the Mescaleros, but the agent would not give him rations. The White Eyes paid in blood for their treatment of Victorio. We here at San Carlos did nothing to help Victorio. We did as the White Eyes wanted us to do. Now George says the White Eyes come for us. We are fools to believe White Eye lies. We are fools to wait for them to come and kill us and throw us in the guardhouse. That is all I have to say."

Again, the men were slapping the ground and agreeing with shouts of, "Ho!" Juh could stand it no longer. He came to stand next to me. He said in my ear, "Tell them for me. I'm leaving. They can come with me or stay." When the warriors saw Juh standing with me, they grew quiet again. Off in the distance, Wolf howled again.

I stepped into the light with my arms raised. "Juh is leaving. I say to Naiche, Mangas, and all of you, it's time to leave this place of enemies, snakes, heat, and insects. Let us go to the Blue Mountains."

As if with one voice, they all said, *"Enjuh!"*

Naiche and the other leaders asked that Juh and I lead the people to the Blue Mountains. This we agreed to do. Juh with his warriors would protect the rear. I and my war leaders would stay to the front while other warriors stayed to the sides. Juh and I decided to follow nearly the same path I had followed the first time I left San Carlos two harvests earlier.

CHAPTER 15
ESCAPE

Most of the people—women and children and a few old men and teenaged boys—had no horses, but there were plenty of wagon trains and *ranchos* along the way where we could get all we needed. It was a good night to run. The air was cool. The half moon, not yet at the top of its ride across the stars, shone with enough soft, white light to see the trail, and the pregnant, moody clouds of the rainy season were gone.

Chiefs and leaders left the council to tell their people they had decided to leave for Mexico. Seeing the faces of my family, I laughed as I told them we would soon leave this place of White Eyes with two tongues; this hot, miserable place full of biting insects; this place where there were never enough rations. My women smiled, but mostly they had solemn faces. They knew hard times were coming. They were ready.

Chappo and Dohn-say tried to act like they were grown. They remembered the lonely, hard trails we rode after we left two harvests ago. Now it seemed most of the Chiricahuas, a great crowd, over three hundred and fifty by my count, were leaving with us, and excitement showed in my children's eyes. Once more the people would live free.

My women and children had horses. They loaded them with a few things they wanted from our *wickiup,* and then put little children, two to a horse, to ride with our baggage. They led the horses and ran with the others down from the hills, like many little streams after a rain quietly rippling through the junipers and brush to gather in a *río* of human beings on the Gila wagon road from the house of the White Eye agent for Naiche to Fort Thomas. The White Eyes and Blue Coats did not hear us leave.

As we moved down the wagon road, warriors and chiefs arranged themselves in the usual way when Apache bands moved. I and three or four other war leaders led the march, a few warriors rode along the flanks of the main group to ensure we weren't ambushed, and Juh and the rest of the warriors and war leaders rode behind to fight off attacks from where they would most likely come.

The moon began riding south for about a hand width against the horizon when we turned south off the wagon road and soon divided into four groups under the leadership of Juh, Naiche, Chato, and Bonito. This was to confuse and slow down the Blue Coats and their scouts, who were sure to follow us. The groups were to meet later that morning at a place we called Black Rock, near the hills on the east side of the mountains the White Eyes call Santa Teresa.

While the groups ran toward Black Rock, I took some warriors to get horses and mules from two groups of freighters our scouts had seen camped near the place where the people turned from the road. We also took horses from a *rancho* farther along the road toward Fort Thomas. We left a clear trail for the cowboys and ranch chief, who were sure to follow us. I had warriors wait in ambush for them near where we turned south. The stars were dimming, and the night sky turning gray as the moon disappeared in the west.

At Black Rock, the people rested in the cool of the morning light until my warriors and I came with the horses and mules, so the slowest ones could ride. From Black Rock, the people rode and ran on until the sun was falling into the mountains. We camped in the hills near the Santa Teresa Mountains as the sky grew streaked with high red, yellow, orange, and purple

137

clouds. It had been a long, hard day with heat, but a good day without trouble and with the taste of freedom.

I rested that evening with my family. My women had prepared well for our run to the Blue Mountains. They made some good White Eye coffee to warm our bellies and then gave us dried meat, acorn bread, juniper berries, and slices of mescal they carried in their sacks.

Before we lay down and wrapped in our blankets, I spoke with Chee-hash-kish privately to learn how the others in our family were holding up.

"We are all good, Husband. You made us run often at San Carlos. We are strong. Our children, although nearly grown, think this running in a big band is play. I feel much pride for them. My sister wives run easy. We stay near the front to serve you. What will we do tomorrow? When do you think the Blue Coats will come?"

"It's hard to say. I'm surprised we haven't already seen sign of them. Tomorrow, I think. Yes, tomorrow they will come at us. We think the Blue Coats will come down the road from the camp they call Thomas and join with any from San Carlos. Warriors will lead them away from the women and children. It's important that babies and little ones don't cry and that the women keep silence. You understand this?"

She nodded. "We all understand this. We know this is a time of war, and we must do what is right. We won't expose you to danger. Your wives miss you, Husband. We wait patiently until we have you to ourselves again in our *wickiup* in Mexico."

Chee-hash-kish smiled, the soft shadows from the low light filling her face and stirring my passion, but I dared not touch her. It was not proper to lay with your wife in war times like these. I was very proud of this fine woman who led my wives and children.

Before the morning star disappeared in the dawn's light, our people were running. The extra horses and mules let us move a little faster with the older, slower people riding rather than running. Juh and Naiche led most of the warriors south. The women and children and a few warriors helping them were about three rifle shots away to the east in the hills of the mountains called Pinaleños.

The warriors with Juh and Naiche found a Nakai-yi hunting in the mountains. Seeing them, he ran for the house the White Eyes called "stagecoach station" with some of the warriors hard after him. Lucky for him, he outran them and made it. I thought, *Those warriors are getting soft. They need to train more if a Nakai-yi can outrun them.* Several of the warriors, good shots, wounded him. They stopped firing before killing him. A freight train with many mules was coming. The sound of shots would alert them to their danger before our ambush could surprise the freighters.

The men driving the freight train were brave and fought us well, but we killed them all. We killed six mules in the fight, but took over a hundred after we cut them from their harness. The drivers we killed had eight good lever rifles and eight pistols and plenty of ammunition. The warriors were taking all the good things from the wagons they could carry, when a sentinel on the other side of the hill fired warning shots to hurry, and they all left.

We stayed on the road to Fort Grant and took four horses and supplies a White Eye was carrying to the place where the Nakai-yi was hiding from us. Then we found four soldiers trying to fix the talking wire Chihuahua had cut. They never knew we were near until our arrows flew from the brush. We killed them quickly and took their horses and guns.

A sentry from down the road came riding fast and said more soldiers were coming. We knew that, if they continued down the road, they would probably find the women and children and massacre every one. Juh said we should ambush the soldiers when they stopped to help the ones we had just killed. I agreed, and so did Naiche. We hid in ambush on a hillside to the east of the road.

The Blue Coats, more than a hundred of them with half as many scouts, came jogging down the wagon road on their horses. When their chief saw one of the soldiers we had killed lying in a blackening pool of blood in the road, he put spurs to his horse and led the soldiers in a gallop up to the body. The arrows in the soldier's chest and his throat cut made the Blue Coat chief yell many loud words in the White Eye tongue and beat his thigh with his fist.

I laughed when I saw his scouts move back and let the soldiers move forward. The scouts knew what was coming and wanted to get to cover as the Blue Coats moved forward to see the bodies. The Blue Coat chief dismounted, called forward scouts and soldiers with three yellow stripes on their shirtsleeves, and began to look over the bodies.

Juh gave the signal to fire. In the swarm of bullets, the Blue Coats kept their heads. Our bullets killed or wounded a few soldiers or scouts, but because they were up the hill, many warriors shot too high. The battle settled into a long day of occasional shots. Thirsty warriors and soldiers, eyes sighted down their rifles, sweated in the heat and waited for someone on the other side to make a mistake and show themselves.

The women and children came up behind the hill where we were and waited for us to tell them what to do. We fought this way for six hands against the horizon. The day was long and hot, and dust mixed with a little gun smoke to fill the air, making a golden haze as the sun began falling in the west. The Blue Coats didn't run, and neither did we.

Jelikinne counseled with Juh, Naiche, and me. He said we had to get the women and children across the road without the Blue Coats seeing and massacring them. He thought the best way to do that was to charge the line of soldiers below us to our right when it got dark. We knew that some warriors wouldn't want to fight at night, but they would if Jelikinne and Juh, fierce and respected war leaders, led them. While we had the soldiers' attention with the fight on our right, the women and children could cross the road farther down to our left. The Blue Coats and scouts wouldn't notice them. Then the women and children could run west toward the Galiuro Mountains. It was a good trick, and we used it.

While some warriors occasionally fired their rifles to hold the Blue Coats in place, a large group of us crept toward those on our right side. Fearless Jelikinne lead us. The women and children moved down close to the road and waited for the warriors with them to tell them when to cross.

It was dark, as the moon had not yet risen, when Jelikinne and his warriors began shooting and advancing on the Blue Coats. From higher up, we could see the flash of rifles turned toward the place Jelikinne attacked. Soon all the soldiers were trying to shoot Apaches they couldn't see except for their rifle flashes. Jelikinne and some of the warriors got within two or three rifle lengths of the Blue Coats—almost close enough to lunge and touch them—before they began to move back up the hill.

Some warriors, scattered across the hillside, continued firing occasional shots until a *googé* (whip-poor-will) called three times, the signal that the women and children were safely across the road. Then we slipped off the mountainside to join our women and children. We suffered no warriors killed, and none even wounded in this fight. I learned later that the Blue Coats had two wounded and one killed. We should have killed more Blue Coats than we did, but their cover across the road was too good, and it was hard to see.

As we ran south, we took more horses and mules for riding and for carrying loads. From one ranch, we took one hundred thirty-five horses. Later, we took another fifty-one horses and mules from a ranch and a freight train. Now we had enough horses and mules so everyone could ride and carry a few supplies. We camped in a place the next night where we could see the light from the village the White Eyes called Willcox, where the iron wagons stopped for wood and water to feed the demons pulling them.

By the middle of the next day, we had made a camp near Cochise's east stronghold in a canyon the White Eyes call Grapevine. The warriors found some cattle and were making meat to carry south with us when the Blue Coat scouts surprised and attacked us. They had come in from the north from behind a mountain where we couldn't see and were only a good rifle shot away from us when they attacked.

We dropped everything and ran. They chased us, and it was a continuous fight until the warriors stopped in the place called South Pass and held the soldiers and scouts back while the rest ran across the Sulphur Springs Valley to a pass that took us across the border and into the Blue Mountains.

CHAPTER 16
FREE AGAIN

Juh led us through the mountains and across the *llano* toward his great flattop mountain stronghold west and a little south of Casas Grandes. He let the people rest and camp at its base. He kept sentinels on the mountaintop who could signal any danger they saw far out on the *llano* and give the people plenty of time to reach safety following the winding trail to the top. It had taken seven days for the people to cross the border, and then two more days' riding to Juh's stronghold.

The people needed rest. Our warriors had done well, taking more than four hundred horses and mules with us across the border, even after leaving or losing nearly a hundred when they could run no more, and fighting the Blue Coats twice so the women and children could get away. My chest grew big with pride for our people.

At the foot of Juh's stronghold, we made meat from cattle the warriors took from nearby *ranchos,* and the women made *wicki-ups* by the little stream that ran at the foot of the mountain. At night, we celebrated with dances around great, leaping fires, rhythms kept from the time of the grandfathers by old men singing and beating on dry hides. Life after living under the thumb of the White Eyes and escaping their lies began to fill us like rain falling on a thirsty land making it bloom again.

The leaders gathered in council around a nice little fire in a bare spot among the juniper trees. The shadows were long, and the skies to the west filled with the many shades of red, orange, gold, and purple as the sun ended its ride west. Three suns had passed since we had come to the stronghold, and we were all rested, ready to get on with living among the *Nakai-yes* and taking what we needed when we needed it. We smoked, and then Naiche spoke.

"At last we're free of the White Eyes, free of San Carlos, free of shaking sickness. We have all raided in the Blue Mountains, but we haven't spent as much time here or dealt with the *Nakai-yi* soldiers and their chiefs as Juh and his *segundo*, Geronimo, have. We're like strangers here."

Naiche looked at the circle of great warriors and leaders sitting around the fire as the sky grew dark and filled with points of bright white light.

"I say we should ask Juh to lead us so we can stay together as one powerful band, rather than going off on our own with small bands of warriors."

Chihuahua, Chato, Bonito, and Jelikinne were slowly nodding their heads, but not all the leaders nodded. Some crossed their arms and waited to hear the rest of what Naiche had to say.

"Then I say to Juh, we ask you to lead us."

Juh stood and slowly looked at every face around the circle before he nodded and then said, "Yes, I will lead you. I ask that you accept Geronimo as my *segundo*. He has power and great medicine. Before we went to San Carlos with Teniente Haskell two harvests ago, he was my *segundo* and showed his power and wisdom many times."

There were grunts and nods of approval around the circle. I saw no one shaking his head. I saw no future enemies.

"It will be so. Riding through the mountains to come here, we crossed a trail a few days old. I looked at the signs and recognized tracks made by some ponies Nana and his warriors use. I don't know where Nana is now, but I'm sure he will appear again to us. When he does, I will ask him to work with us while we raid and talk peace with the *Nakai-yes*."

I saw frowns of disbelief on faces around the fire circle, and Juh smiled. "For many harvests now, I make peace with the *jefes* of villages like Janos and Casas Grandes. In these villages, I trade them the plunder and animals we take on the other side of the mountains for supplies. The *Nakai-yes* in the villages on the east side of the mountains don't care where our plunder comes from, as long as it's not from them, but they know where we take it. We have to be careful when we do this. If the *Nakai-yes* offer you whiskey as a gesture of friendship, turn it down. When you're drunk, they may try to kill you, even though they know if they do, I'll come slaughter them with men who aren't drunk. They'll consider this a long time before they try to kill us. You'll be safe as long as you aren't drunk. Listen to me and live."

I looked around the council. Frowns of disbelief had disappeared. All the leaders were carefully listening to Juh. *Listen carefully, my brothers.*

"In a moon, during the Season of Earth Is Reddish Brown, I'll meet with the soldier *jefe* for the *Nakai-yes* in Chihuahua to talk about a peace treaty for all of Chihuahua, not for just a few villages. With this treaty, we can move about in Chihuahua without worry of attack. I'll take all of you and maybe a few others to this meeting. A big crowd of known warriors will show the soldier *jefe* how powerful we are now. Geronimo will speak for me. Geronimo, Nolgee, and I tried this before with the soldier *jefe,* but he insisted we live on a reservation outside Ojinaga. We said no.

"The *Nakai-yes* paid with blood for wanting to pen us up on a reservation. Nolgee later tried to make peace with them. They asked for peace and then gave him whiskey. Like fools, Nolgee and his people drank the *Nakai-yi* whiskey. The *Nakai-yes* killed them where they sat after they grew drunk. Again, we took our revenge against the *Nakai-yes* for the death of Nolgee. We killed many *Nakai-yes* and sent them burned and cut to pieces to their Happy Place. I hope the *jefe* speaks to us with a straight tongue. I want no more blood spilled between us. We will see.

"In a few suns, let us take some of our plunder from across the border and trade in the villages. You'll see how I do it. Then maybe we talk some more before we see the soldier *jefe* in council. I have said all I have to say."

As if with one voice, the warriors said, *"Enjuh!"*

Two suns later, Nana and his people rode into the camp. Learning Juh, others, and I would soon return from scouting ranches for supplies and cattle, Nana, with a few warriors, rode down the trail lined with junipers and blooming plants out of camp to meet us. Juh and his men returned before I did.

I was told that when Juh saw Nana warming himself by a small fire beside the trail, he laughed and said, "Ho, Old Man. *Nish'ii'* (I see you)."

Nana stood up slowly, tottering on his stiff leg joints, but he, too, smiled and said, "Ho, Juh. *Nish'ii'*. You have returned from the land the White Eyes claim but is still ours. *Enjuh.* Where is your brother, Geronimo?"

"He comes not far behind me. I saw his dust on the *llano*. Cover your fire, and we'll have a little fun with him."

One of Nana's warriors covered the fire, and then Nana and Juh and their men all hid in the brush on both sides of the trail to surprise us. There was nothing at all for us to fear riding for our camp a bowshot away under the dark-green juniper trees. We gave little attention to the trail. We passed Nana. Then he and three or four of his men stepped out from behind a big creosote bush. He called, "Ho, Geronimo. If I had been a Nakai-yi, you would be dead and scalped by now." My pony reared in surprise at the voice coming out from the brush, but I held him easily, as Juh and his warriors appeared, laughing, from the other side.

They had surprised me. I could only grin and say, "I knew all the time you were here."

Laughing and patting his belly, Nana said, "You did not. You, the sly fox of the Apaches! Ha! *Nish'ii'*, Geronimo and Naiche. This is a good day."

Juh, looking like a giant compared to Nana, who was not a small man, came up to us laughing. "Come, friends. Let's go to the camp and enjoy the night with good food and dancing. At last our brother, Nana, and his people have come to us."

After a fine meal from our women, Juh and I spoke with Nana, and we agreed to help each other.

In the Season of Earth Is Reddish Brown, Juh, thirty warriors, and I met with the Mexican soldier *jefe,* Joaquin Terrazas, who had led the Mexicans against Victorio, destroyed him, took slaves, and scalped the warriors, women, and children fallen with him. Nana refused to go to the meeting, saying that if he went, he would try to kill that *jefe* for Victorio. It would end whatever Juh wanted to do with the Mexicans. Yes, Nana needed to stay in camp. I didn't doubt, and neither did he, that his chance for revenge would come one day.

The meeting place was a nice, flat spot beside a big *arroyo* half a handwidth against the horizon ride from Casas Grandes. Our chiefs and recognized leaders sat with the Mexican leaders in a small circle near the *arroyo.* Our shade came from a tall cottonwood tree still holding brown with speckled green leaves trembling in the breeze. The other warriors sat behind us, facing east on the west side of the circle. Mexican soldiers stood relaxed on the east side behind their *jefe* and faced west.

I sang to *Ussen* for help and guidance, and then we smoked with Terrazas. After our smoke drifted away, Juh swung his arm toward the Nakai-yi side in a gesture of welcome. He spoke in the tongue of the Nakai-yes. "*Jefe*, it is good we speak with you. We hope our words bear fruit that falls on fertile ground. My *segundo*, Geronimo, will speak for us. Sometimes my words are not clear. Geronimo speaks clearly."

Terrazas, a little twisted smile on his lips, nodded at me. "*Bueno*. We will hear Juh's words from the mouth of Geronimo."

I said, "We speak straight words. Our life is hard. For a long time, we wanted peace with the people of Chihuahua. We tried to make a peace three harvests ago. The *jefes* said we must stay on land at Ojinaga. We did not want this land. We didn't believe the promises to give us rations there. We returned to the land where the White Eyes said we must live. The White Eyes treated us fairly for a while until they killed the Cibecue prophet. Then many Blue Coats came to our land. We knew they planned to put us in the guardhouse, even though we had done nothing wrong. We left and returned to the Blue Mountains two moons ago."

The *jefe* sat with his arms crossed, nodding he understood me. Even the breeze, waiting to hear what I had to say, seemed to pause.

"Our people are tired of war with the *Nakai-yes*. We have no reason to fight with you except to live. We ask that you set aside land for us. If there is land for us, there will be peace. If there is no land, there will be war never-ending."

Terrazas said, "I understand you want war no more. Your words are ones our people have waited a long time to hear. Where do you want land for your people, so there is peace between us?"

"We ask for the little mountains you name Carcay and the plains and valleys on both sides. There are few *Nakai-yes* there, and our people can raise horses and cattle, even sheep and goats. There we can gather good food—mescal, yucca tips, piñon nuts, juniper berries, and acorn nuts—from the land. We can grow our own food on that land. We can hunt deer and mountain sheep and other animals to fill our women's stew pots or make roasts for their men. This is all we ask. Give it to us, and there will be peace. This is all we have to say."

Terrazas nodded and thought a while before he said, "You have spoken well for your people. We hear you. What you ask is beyond my power to give. But today I send what you ask to the governor of Chihuahua. He has the power to grant your request. I think we'll have his answer within half a moon. I ask that you come with me to Casas Grandes, have some good food and whiskey, while we speak of how this land you want as yours will be marked as yours."

I glanced at Juh and knew exactly what he was thinking. I said, "We know the *jefe* is a man of generosity. But we think it is wise not to frighten the people of Casas Grandes with too many of us there. We'll wait in our own camp."

Terrazas smiled and shrugged. "*Bueno.* As you wish, *Señores. Por favor,* return here tomorrow while we wait for the governor's answer, and I'll provide you gifts of rations to show our good faith in these talks."

I looked at Juh who nodded. "We'll return next sun and receive your gift of rations."

The *jefe* looked over all of us and said, "Bueno. *Mañana* (tomorrow) we will bring you rations. Until then, *adios.*"

Juh led us to a blind canyon nearby that would be easy to defend if Terrazas decided to turn his men loose on us, but the *Nakai-yes* returned to Casas Grandes, leaving us in peace. The next day, Terrazas brought us cattle, sugar, flour, blankets, and coffee, which we were glad to have. He spoke again of our coming to Casas Grandes to have a drink and talking of the limits of our land. I and others wanted some of that good whiskey, but we knew better than to drink with him. To do so was an invitation to death or slavery if we drank too much, which we usually did.

Over the next half moon, Terrazas came two more times with rations, and we took them. He kept asking us to return to Casas Grandes with him to drink a little whiskey and to talk more about the details of the land. We continued to say no, we would stay in our own camp. Some warriors visited Casa Grandes to trade their plunder, and they returned unharmed. Juh and I began to think that maybe it would be all right for us to have some whiskey with the *jefe*. Still no word had come from the governor.

Another half moon passed, and still there was no answer from the governor, but Terrazas gave us more rations and continued to invite us into Casas Grandes for a drink of whiskey. One evening, a few days after we had last spoken with him, as the sun began hiding behind the mountains and filling the sky with golds the color of old gourds, a White Eye who lived near the border, and with whom we often traded horses and cattle for coffee, sugar, and good iron cooking pots, came to our camp and said he wanted to speak with Juh and me alone. This we did.

After we smoked, Juh said, "Speak, we listen."

The White Eye said, "Boys, I been hearin' some stories about your new friend, ol' Terrazas. He's got big groups of soldiers scattered all over this country, and they's more on the way. They's about three hundert and fifty in Casas Grandes, a hundert at Janos, and a hundert at Carrizal, and they's a general comin' from Durango with two hundert more that Terrazas is a-waitin' for. That there general is out to get you anyway he can. Terrazas don't wanna go chasin' you again up in them mountains." At this the White Eye grinned. "You know he always comes back empty-handed."

It was the first time I had seen Juh laugh out loud in a long time. Juh's women appeared out of the dark with cups and a pot of hot coffee for us. The White Eye took a long, noisy swallow of the coffee, almost too hot to drink, and continued, "The story is Terrazas and that general wants to clamp all of you in chains and take you to guardhouses far to the south. They's also a story that the governor made up his mind, and he ain't about to give you no land. You been good traders. I enjoy doin' business with you. But if I was you boys, I'd hit the trail *pronto* and get away from them lying Mexican soldiers."

We talked more, and then he left. Juh decided to leave that night for the stronghold at Guaynopa where we had stayed during the last Ghost Face. I was glad to go. I had grown tired of the smiling faces of Joaquin Terrazas and his *segundo,* Juan Mata Ortiz. I wished Nana had them under his knife and fire.

CHAPTER 17
A PLAN TO SAVE LOCO

We left the *Nakai-yes* at Casas Grandes. Terrazas had thought that with just a few more suns, they'd have us. Our White Eye friend had given weight to what Juh and I had thought after Terrazas invited us to Casas Grandes for some whiskey. Moving all the people and taking care to avoid *Nakai-yes* soldiers, so they wouldn't know where we were, took us five suns to reach the Guaynopa stronghold near the rim of the Great Canyon. The stronghold had plenty of water in natural tanks, a good supply of firewood, much game, enough space for each band to have its own village, and clear views from the ridges in every direction of the surrounding mountains. We would be safe and comfortable during Ghost Face while we talked and thought about raids in the coming spring.

The women and young children spent a day making lodges and *wickiups* ready for Ghost Face. The older boys and novitiates spread across the country to learn the best places to hunt. We left the *Nakai-yes* alone. We wanted peace in the Ghost Face before we raided again in the Season of Little Eagles. After the women finished their *wickiups*, we danced every night for three days with a big fire. It was good to come back to the Guaynopa stronghold.

After the days of dancing, the war leaders, Juh, and I often sat together in Juh's big tipi and spoke of raids to make when the cold winds and snow left in the Season of Little Eagles. Some wanted to raid packtrains to the west of the *Río* Bavispe—maybe even going as far as the village Ures. I thought this was a good place to go and said so. The *Nakai-yi* traders did much business on the trail to Ures. We could take many pack animals and the good plunder they carried. Others, led mostly by Chato and Bonito, wanted to go north across the border to find ammunition and guns. We had fine guns, rifles that shot many times without reloading, but few bullets for them. Juh listened to the arguments about where and when to raid, studying each speaker with his narrow slit-like eyes, but he said nothing.

One sun, while wind carrying snow whistled across the tops of the mountains and we sat wrapped in our blankets around Juh's fire, Kaytennae, a young war leader, spoke as one old and experienced.

He said, "All these raids of which you speak are good. We always need plunder, good mules, and much ammunition, but I think men are what we need most."

There was only the sound of the fire crackling in the center of the tipi as all heads turned to stare at Kaytennae. Some leaders frowned, and others looked around at each other as though they didn't know what he was talking about, but I knew, and the other warriors should have known, too.

Juh nodded and said to Kaytennae, "Why do you say this, Kaytennae? Speak. We will listen."

Kaytennae crossed his arms and looked around the fire. "Juh and Geronimo told us the White Eye trader friend said that in the time we waited to hear the governor answer us and give us land of our own, this *Nakai-yi jefe* had over five hundred fifty men in the villages of Janos and Casas Grandes, and that he was waiting for two hundred more to come up from the south. That's why we left. This Terrazas and his *jefe* want us in chains far from our mountains. That's why he has so many soldiers. When the soldiers from the south arrive in Casas Grandes, there will be seven soldiers for every Apache warrior. In a fight with these *Nakai-yes*, we could probably still win, but we would lose many and become much weaker as a band. We need all the warriors we can find.

"Nana has joined us after escaping a *Nakai-yi* attack on a camp of Mescaleros. I know he will fight against this Terrazas, the *jefe* whose men killed Victorio and his army. But even with Nana, there are not nearly enough warriors for us to fight the *Nakai-yes* and keep our women and children protected."

The wind whistled and moaned through the tall pines and sounded like the rush of falling water. We pulled our blankets close around us, but the wind didn't make us cold. Kaytennae's words were true. They made us shiver.

I said, "Kaytennae speaks wise words. When does he think the *jefe* will come to fight and enslave us?"

"I don't know when he will come or how he will attack us, but Loco must have close to four hundred people in his band now. I know many of his warriors. There must be nearly as many still at San Carlos as here. We should ask him to come. It would make us much stronger."

Chato, always rude in council, spoke uninvited as he shook his head. "No! Loco's warriors who wanted to leave San Carlos left with us. You're one of them, Kaytennae. There're probably not more than fifty to seventy-five warriors with Loco at San Carlos, and they stayed behind when we left. We gave Loco his name because he's crazy. He thinks not fighting the White Eyes is the best thing for the Chihenne people. We're wasting our time asking Loco to join us. It never happens."

Kaytennae stared at Chato and frowned. I could tell he was angry. I would have been, too, but we didn't need to fight among ourselves. I looked at Juh and ignored what Chato had said. "I think Kaytennae is right. We must ask Loco to come to us in the Season of Little Eagles." I smiled. "We must save him from the hot, miserable life the Chihenne people have at San Carlos. The warriors taken with Loco will have to come here with the rest of Loco's people anyway, and they can help us fight the *Nakai-yes.*"

Chato snarled, "But what if Loco won't come to us?"

"If Loco won't come on his own, then we'll go to San Carlos and take them with us back to strongholds here, whether they want to go or not."

Again, the only sounds in the tipi came from the wind and crackling fire as the warriors looked at each other and then stared at the orange glow of the coals in the fire. Kaytennae's face held a crooked smile, but Chato shook his head. Juh stared at the fire a little while, pulled his bag of *tobaho* and fine cigarette papers he had taken off a White Eye freighter. He sprinkled *tobaho* in a paper, rolled it closed, and with a splinter from the fire lighted it, smoked to the four directions, and then passed it to me. Soon we had all smoked around the circle.

Then Juh said, "I hear you, Kaytennae, Geronimo, and Chato. My medicine says this is what we should do. I ask Bonito, our great war leader, to take who he wants, only a few; no more than seven. Go to San Carlos, speak to Loco and listen to his words and those he trusts. Tell him why he should come here in the next Season of Little Eagles. Tell him of the life we live here. It is for their own good we ask them to come."

Bonito nodded and said, "This I will do. We'll leave tomorrow, give Loco your words, listen to those around him, and scout the reservation. We'll return as soon as we can slip past the Blue Coats."

Juh grunted, "*Enjuh.* This is the time the White Eyes say their God was born. They won't be ready for raids. While you're gone, I'll take about forty warriors south. Geronimo will take about forty warriors west. We may find little in the Season of the Ghost Face, but we'll learn the best trails to use in the

Season of Little Eagles. What do the war leaders say?"

All slapped the ground and said, *"Ho."* Most smiled. Raids in the Ghost Face were uncommon but not unheard of.

The raids Juh and I led south and west didn't produce much, just a few sacks of food. We saw no packtrains at all, and the *Nakai-yes* stayed with their doors barred inside their *casas*, their guns ready for us. We lost no warriors, but the trail was cold and hard. We returned in half a moon, and Bonito soon followed us. He said Loco told them he wanted nothing to do with joining us.

We talked in council again, and, after hearing all Bonito had to tell us, Juh asked that he go again and emphasize to Loco that living was much better in Mexico, and that there was plenty to eat, warm clothes, and no shaking sickness for him and his people if they joined us in Mexico.

Again, Loco said to Bonito, "No. What Geronimo and Juh wanted for the Chihenne people is no good. The Blue Coats and *Nakai-yes* would be chasing them all the time. No. Not good. No go to the Blue Mountains."

After Bonito returned the second time with Loco's refusal, Juh sent him again a third time, and this time he told Bonito to tell Loco if he refused this last call to come to the camps in the Blue Mountains, our warriors would return in forty days to force him and his people to come to us. When Bonito returned the third time, he told us Loco had warned him not to return again or there might be trouble.

Juh smiled and said, "Yes, Loco. There will be trouble—for you."

Juh and I talked a long time with the war leaders. We decided that first we would send a few warriors to retrieve ammunition we had hidden across the border in the mountains near Fort

Cummings. After they returned, I would lead most of the warriors through the Blue Coat line of watchers and scouting parties near the border, go to San Carlos, cut the talking wire to the main post, and surround Loco's camp before the people awoke to the sun coming over the mountains. We would let the people take a few of their things, threaten them if they moved too slowly, and then lead them east over a different trail than the one we had followed when we had escaped six or seven moons earlier. Juh and Nana would stay behind with about thirty warriors and fifteen young men who were able to shoot well enough to protect the women and children.

Our White Eye trader friend told us we needed to be very careful with the *Nakai-yes.* He had learned from a drunk *jefe* who worked with Terrazas that they planned to wipe us all out, down to the last child.

When he heard this, Juh laughed and said, "We're grateful for your warning, brother. I think we need to take more rations from this *jefe* before Geronimo rides north, and then the rest of us will disappear."

We loaded our rifles and pistols and, taking our bows and arrows, rode as one big group to meet with Terrazas at the place called Casa de Janos near the land we had asked for in the Carcay Mountains. Terrazas had a big camp of men but when the warriors, Juh, and I seemed to appear in front of him out of nowhere one morning, he decided it was not time to fight. Instead, he offered to give us rations—flour, meat, sugar, *tobaho*, and even mescal if we wanted it—at Janos. Juh told Terrazas we would come to claim them in a few days. Terrazas, with a big grin, said we would be welcome.

The next sun as dawn crept into the mountains, my warriors and I headed for San Carlos. Juh and Nana, with their warriors and near-warrior boys, returned to Juh's stronghold on the great flattop mountain west of Casas Grandes, where my family and many others awaited them. The moon for freeing Loco and his people had come.

CHAPTER 18
ASH FLAT

All the great war leaders—Naiche, Chihuahua, Kaytennae, Chato, Mangas, Sánchez, and Jelikinne; and our best fighting men, altogether seventy-two warriors—rode with me to San Carlos. Each fighting man was deadly and, in a group this size, very powerful. I felt good about going to San Carlos. I knew we would set Loco and his people free from their misery and grow even stronger together.

After a long day of riding west of the Carcay Mountains through canyons and *arroyos* across the dry, thirsty Sierra San Luis covered with yucca blooming with white, sweet smelling flowers and cholla with purple blooms, we crossed the border on the east side of the Animas Valley. The sun was nearly gone, casting long shadows from the Guadalupe Mountains on us and across the great, white *playa* on the valley floor. We stayed in the foothills on the west side of the Animas Mountains and then rode across the valley to the east side of the Guadalupe Mountains until we came to a natural tank at the opening of a small canyon. We watered our ponies, drank our fill, ate from sacks of war food, and then rested until the moon began to fall toward the southern mountains.

Warriors don't like riding at night, but it was the safest path for us, and my Power told me it was the best way. We kept the great *playa* on our right and passed up the valley until we reached the end of the *playa* near the White Eye village of Lordsburg, and then we turned west, following a trail across the Pel-

159

oncillo Mountains and into the San Simon Valley.

Ridden hard all night, our horses needed rest. We found a well-hidden place in the *bosque* by the *Río* San Simon, drank from its trickle of water, ate, put out guards, and rested until the sun had fallen two hands past the time of no shadows. Then we were up and riding again.

We rode north up the San Simon Valley until the moon began falling into the southern mountains, and we stopped to rest. Riding before dawn, we heard and then saw the flow of the *Río* Gila. Just listening to the water reminded me of my days as a child living with my father. I felt at home again. We rode up the Gila to Eagle Creek and followed it north most of that sun toward a ranch where we might be able to take fresh horses if we returned this way.

When the sun began falling into the mountains and shadows filled the canyon where Eagle Creek ran, we found a place in the tall trees to rest. There was little moonlight that night, not enough to see by, so we stayed where we were until the gray light of dawn began the next day. We followed Eagle Creek Canyon until we found the trail going down the side of the Nantanes Mountains cliffs on the northern edge of Ash Flat. It had been an easy ride most of the day because the shade from pine, oak, and willow trees by the creek kept us cool. The ride down the trail to Ash Flat was easy. But I was glad we rode it in the sunlight. The chances of a slip on that trail down those cliffs were higher than on many other canyon trails in the Blue Mountains.

Off the cliff trail and out on the grass, we rode west across the Ash Flat Valley, planning to cross the Saddle Mountains into San Carlos. There Chihuahua would first cut the talking wire and tie it together with a rawhide strap, so the agent near Loco's camp couldn't signal the agent chief who had scouts and soldiers at the place the White Eyes called "headquarters."

The sun was near the western horizon when we were ready to turn toward the Saddle Mountains, but then we smelled sheep and heard them and herder dogs in the falling light. My warriors were hungry. This was a good time to stop and eat. We turned and rode toward the sheep. The sky was aflame with a deep, blood red on clouds tinted in dappled orange and whites when we rode up to the big wagon used by the chief of the sheep men. I counted nine *Nakai-yes* and three White Mountain Apaches working the sheep. The Apaches camped in tents with their women up the creek a short way from the *Nakai-yi* wagons and tents.

I smiled to myself as I realized here was a chance to take more *Nakai-yi* blood for the murder of my family more than thirty harvests ago, a long time to carry the stones of hate and anger burning in my guts, stones that never cooled. *This night, the Nakai-yes must pay once more for the murder of my family.*

I rode with Naiche, Chato, and Chihuahua up to the big wagon of the *jefe,* whose woman cooked the evening meal at a fire nearby. Three young boys played and chased each other, and I saw two of the other *Nakai-yi* women, but there were no children playing near where they cooked.

We approached the big wagon in silence. The *Nakai-yes* didn't know we were there until the woman cooking near the big wagon looked up from her fire, saw us, covered her mouth with a hand, ran to the open door, and called inside, breathless and desperate, "Apaches! Apaches! Come quick."

A tall *Nakai-yi* man about my size, an ugly, hairy spreading bush growing under his nose, appeared at the wagon door. His rifle was cocked, ready for use. The woman ran from the door calling the young boys and telling them to get under the wagon. She told them to stay there until she called them.

The man frowned as he looked at us, cocked his head to one side, and said, "Geronimo, is that you?"

He looked familiar. I realized it was Bes-das, a *Nakai-yi* boy now grown whom I had taken ten or fifteen harvests ago in a raid. He had light behind his eyes, quickly learning to speak Apache and working hard around the camp. I treated him well. I gave him a spotted pony, a saddle trimmed in silver, and shirts to keep the sun from burning his skin, but he wasn't happy living with us. I think he was too old when we took him. It would have been better if I had killed him and been done with him. I had known I couldn't trust him to stay with us, so I'd traded him to a White Eye rancher for a pistola, a box of cartridges, and two ponies. The rancher said the boy's *Nakai-yi* name was Victoriano Mestas, which he'd never told me, even though I spoke good Spanish and could have easily pronounced his name.

I hadn't seen Bes-das since I'd traded him. He had grown into a big, strong man. His woman had made fancy designs with colored thread on his shirt. It was a very nice shirt. I liked it. Bes-das walked up to us as we sat quietly on our ponies, looking over his camp and deciding what we wanted, but he didn't seem to have much. He waved his arm parallel to the ground and said, *"Nish'ii'*, Geronimo. Welcome to my camp. Do you remember me?"

I swung down from my pony and walked over to him as he cradled his cocked rifle in the crook of his arm. I had to be careful, or I might lose men here when it wasn't worth it for the lives of a few *Nakai-yes*. Every *Nakai-yi* stood still and watched us while the sheep milled about nearby making bleating noises as the dogs barked and herded them in close bunches, and the children gathered around the white and blue colored skirts of their mothers, who held fingers over their mouths to keep from screaming in fear of us.

"I know you, Bes-das. Don't be afraid. We just want something to eat. We won't harm you. You know that. I took you from the *Nakai-yes* to raise myself when you were small. You grew into a big *Nakai-yi* after I traded you to the White Eye rancher, and I see you have a woman and three children playing around her. You're the chief of the *Nakai-yes* here? They do what you tell them?"

Bes-das cocked his head to one side and nodded. "*Sí*, I am the *jefe* here."

I waved my arm toward the *Nakai-yes* who had come to see the riders talking to their *jefe*. Warriors pushed the sheepherders over by a wagon, where they made them sit down, and then tied their hands together with rope they found on a wagon, but they left the women free to work.

"We don't want anyone hurt here, Bes-das. We tie your men, so they do nothing foolish."

I saw fear flicker for a blink in the brown eyes of Bes-das. "There is no need to do that, but if it makes you feel safe to do it, then I accept it."

"I see another little camp of *wickiups* just over there." I pointed toward them with my nose. "They look like Apaches, and they have their women with them. Who are they?"

"That's Bylas and three other men. They're White Mountains helping wether lambs."

"Hmmph. I've lived in the White Mountains. I think I know this man Bylas. My warriors have ridden far. They're hungry." I swung back up on my pony and smiled down at Bes-das. "We can have a few of your sheep?"

Bes-das smiled back, but I saw the fear in his eyes grow as he turned toward the sheep and spread his arms wide. "*Sí, sí,* Geronimo. Take all you need."

I turned to the warriors and told them to take sheep they needed for a meal and then turned back toward Bes-das. I saw a fine, sorrel pony grazing near his wagon. "That's a nice pony that grazes near your wagon."

The smile left his face. He said, "That pony belongs to *Señor*

Jimmie Stevens, whose father owns the sheep. I just ride him once in a while. It's not mine."

"*Enjuh.* I like horsemeat better than sheep." Still mounted, I killed the pony with an easy shot to its head not fifty yards away. The rifle's report made the tied *Nakai-yes* jerk in surprise and look around in fear to see who was shooting. I laughed at them. It was always good to see *Nakai-yes* flinch in fear. "Tell your women to prepare the meal. Is that Bylas's *wickiup* over by those trees?"

Bes-das's fear was leaking out of his eyes and onto his face now. He nodded. I said, "I know White Mountains. I know Bylas probably has some whiskey. I'm thirsty. Maybe he'll give me a drink. Let's go over to see Bylas."

Bes-das told the women to fix whatever the warriors wanted and followed me on foot as I rode over to Bylas's *wickiup* and dismounted. I sat down by his fire and waited for him to come out of his *wickiup*. Soon he came. He smelled of good whiskey and could not walk straight. *Yes, I remember you always had whiskey for your amigos, Bylas. Now you can give me some.* I said, "I know you. You lived in the White Mountains when I did. You always have some whiskey around. Give me a bottle."

Bylas shook his head as he dropped down in front of me. The whiskey stains on his shirt were still damp, their smell fresh and powerful, making me thirsty for it. "I don't have any more. I drank it all when I saw you and your war party ride out of the brush."

"Hmmph. Not another bottle you have? None you can give me?"

"Whiskey all gone."

"That's too bad. I was hoping for a drink of good whiskey. You come eat with us. You know Naiche and Chato from their San Carlos days. The women cook sheep and horse now. Maybe you remember where another bottle is after you eat."

Bylas and his White Mountains walked behind me as I slowly walked my pony back to Bes-das's wagons, where the women cooked beans and tortillas along with the meat.

I sat with Bylas and his men, one a grown son of one of them, while we ate. I said to Bylas, "You still don't remember having any more whiskey?" He looked at his moccasins and shook his head. I spoke of old times with Bes-das, who relaxed a little. I asked Bylas to tell me if things were any better on the reservation while the warriors filled their bellies. After he said not much, that the White Eye agents were still thieves, and there was still much shaking sickness among the *Ríos* San Carlos and Gila villages, I said, narrowing my eyes like I didn't believe his earlier answer, "Still you don't remember having any more whiskey?"

That grown son of one of Bylas's men had not grown enough to control his tongue. He said, "This man, Bylas, is not a boy for you to talk to this way and keep on asking for whiskey. He won't give you any whiskey."

I didn't need a boy to tell me how to act. His disrespect blew on the flames of my anger at not having any whiskey. He didn't look like an Apache to me. He looked like a *Nakai-yi.*

"This boy is a full-blooded *Nakai-yi.*" I cocked my rifle. I was ready to kill him, but one of the White Mountains said, "No, he's not a *Nakai-yi.* He's a full-blooded White Mountain, and his mother is of the Black Water clan, so he's of that clan also."

I looked at Bylas and then at my rifle, cocked and lying in my lap. "What is he?"

Bylas swallowed hard and then said in a croaking whisper, "He is White Mountain."

My anger grew. I didn't want to kill a White Mountain. They had many scouts who worked for Nant'an Crook. My anger at all *Nakai-yes* grew hotter.

I said to Bes-das in a soft, flat voice, "That's a fine shirt you wear your woman decorates for you. I think I would like to have it. Why don't you take it off and give it to me, so I can keep it clean?"

Bes-das's face froze. He stood, and his fingers trembled as he unbuttoned the shirt and pulled it off his shoulders. I saw him glance at his woman, his head making a tiny shake most did not see. She spoke to her children, and they climbed back under the wagon, squatted there, and watched their father give me his shirt.

I laid it over my knees, taking my time to fold it carefully. I knew Bes-das was trembling inside. He knew what was coming. Most of the warriors had eaten and were leaning back on their elbows enjoying their meal, but a group near us sat on their heels with their rifles cocked, wondering what we would do next. I looked at Bes-das and grinned. Then I said to the waiting warriors, "Tie these *Nakai-yes* together with the others and kill them all."

Bylas, who sat near Naiche and Chato while they ate, said, "Why do you want to kill these people after they fed you? You promised Bes-das you would harm no one."

Bylas's words cooled my heat some, and I held up my hand to stop warriors as Naiche said, "Be straight with these people, Geronimo. They've done nothing to us. They fed us as you wanted. You even took a fine pony to eat. Why don't you pay the women for cooking for you?"

Chato said, "Why would you kill these people? They've done all we asked and nothing at all to harm us. We could have lost many men if we had attacked this camp."

The words of Bylas, Naiche, and Chato had poured cool water on my heat, and my anger was going away when Chihuahua said, "These people are *Nakai-yes,* and they're our enemies. Always the *Nakai-yes* have lied to us and killed our people. You told me what the *Nakai-yes* did to your own family. Remember what Terrazas is trying to do to us now."

Despite what the others had said, the stones in my guts grew hot again. I waved the warriors on. They jumped Bes-das before he could take a step toward me. They dragged him and the women, screaming and begging for their lives, over to the men already tied together. Bes-das's woman screamed at the children under the wagon and told them to run. They ran quickly, like rabbits leaving a hole taken by a rattlesnake.

Warriors looked at me, and I said, "Yes, even the little ones. They must die like all my children did." They caught two of the three and threw the smallest one on the thorns of a big cactus. It wailed for a long time. It was a strong child, like my children were. The other child they tied over the coals of a fire to roast. It, too, screamed a long time.

The warriors smashed the heads of the screaming women with rocks and bashed some of the men with their war clubs. They had knife-throwing contests at the bodies of the other men, and two or three of the throws went straight and true. Those men didn't last long. They brought me Bes-das's loaded rifle. I tried it out on Bes-das, shooting him in his man parts. He screamed and groaned only a little while because he bled so much, and then I put a bullet in his heart. I was merciful to him. After all, I had raised him for a while.

The warriors found the third child, a boy, hiding under the skirts of Bylas's wife. They dragged him away from her while she pleaded for his life. When they looked at me, I nodded and said, "Yes, all must die. Die good in pain."

Jelikinne was squatting nearby watching and leaning against his spear. He shook his head and said, "No good. No good."

Naiche said, "No! There's been enough killing here. Let the boy live."

"He dies! All *Nakai-yes* die like my children died. Kill the woman, too. She protected him."

I felt the point of Jelikinne's spear push against my chest. He said through clenched teeth, "Kill that boy, and you die, Geronimo."

I heard the hammer click back on Naiche's rifle and saw the barrel pointed at me, not two bow lengths from my belly. "Kill that child and woman, and you'll die with them, Geronimo." Naiche was a good warrior, just soft sometimes.

Perhaps my thirst for *Nakai-yi* blood was satisfied by now. I was not afraid of Jelikinne and Naiche, but I thought, *This is enough for now*, nodded, and lifted my hands. "Naiche is chief. I obey Naiche. Let them go."

We took all the supplies we could from the camp. We would need them for Loco's people. Bylas went with us on to Dewey Flat and the Old Wagon Road. I left two warriors behind to keep watch on his people, so they couldn't run off and warn the White Eyes we had come. It was an unexpected gift to eat so well before we raided the reservation to take Loco and his people back to their freedom.

CHAPTER 19
FREEING LOCO AND
THE CHIHENNE PEOPLE

We left the sheep camp and rode south across Ash Flat. At the foothills of the Gila Mountains, we stopped in a small canyon while I made medicine to learn if we did well to continue across the mountains to free Loco and his Chihenne people. Some warriors rested, but others gathered around while I sang four songs and listened to my Power.

I saw, as though seeing dimly in early morning mists, people roused from deep sleep and running, laughing, from their *wickiups,* and splashing through water. I saw women running with full baskets and children beside them and many warriors on ponies with rifles raised high. I saw Blue Coats wandering blind in the night. I saw familiar high mountains and deep canyons with slow water. I saw many people welcoming others with their arms wide.

It was a good sing. Its guidance was clear. We would do well helping Loco and the Chihennes escape. I learned all was well, and that Power put the Chihennes in a deep sleep so our coming didn't make them afraid. These and other things I told the warriors, and we mounted to follow a canyon pass across the mountains to the *río.*

We reached the *Río* Gila deep in the night. Chihuahua rode down the wagon road. He found a good place in the *bosque* and cut the talking wire, tied it together with rawhide, and then cut it again farther on and tied it again, so the agent chief couldn't

169

call for help from the miners at the village they called Globe and they couldn't talk to the Blue Coats at Fort Apache. I sent the men, who had been with Bonito when he went to talk to Loco in the Season of the Ghost Face, to the people they knew in Loco's camp to tell them we were nearby, coming to free them, and not to be afraid. This day we would free them from White Eye control. This day they would go with us to the Blue Mountains.

Some scouts called "tribal police" in the camps worked only for the agents. I wanted to send men to kill them all in their sleep, but I decided not to risk it. We wanted to take Loco and his people without alarm to give us time for a good getaway.

I sent men across the *río* to form a barrier between the camp and the agency, so no one could run to warn the agent. The rest of our men and I waited with our horses across the *río* for dawn's light. It was quiet and still, the only sounds the quiet gurgle of the *río* and the occasional snort of a horse. Mists grew from the slowly flowing water and drifted downstream. A bird made the first call of the morning.

A warrior near where I squatted tossed a stone high in the air, and we could see it at the top of its arc. Soon there would be enough light to see by. I swung up on my pony, and those waiting with me made a line on their ponies up and down the *río*. We began splashing across the Gila. I saw men from the line blocking the Loco people from the agency, run into the village, and begin to throw back blankets on the camp *wickiups* and tell the people it was time to go. The people crawled out of their *wickiups*, wiping sleep from their eyes and looking dazed. Some started to run for the agency, but stopped when they saw the line of warriors blocking their path.

I yelled, "Take them all! Shoot anyone who refuses to go with us!" We were risking everything for these foolish people who let the White Eyes tell them where and how to live. We had to get them moving while we had time. "Some of you men lead them out." No one tried to fight. They did as we told them.

Chato confronted Loco, as he appeared coming out his *wickiup* with his women. He said, "Ho! Loco! We come to take you from this place of heat, snakes, White Eyes, and shaking sickness. Lead your people down the Gila. Follow Geronimo on the spotted pony."

Loco had no fear as his people left their *wickiups* to gather around his. His craggy face with a drooping eye, torn by a bear, stared at Chato in the dim light. He crossed his arms while he slowly shook his head. "No, you tell Geronimo, as I told Bonito every time he came to threaten us, I told the White Eyes I'd stay here. Here I stay."

I knew if Loco didn't lead them, most would not go with us. Chato saved the day. He cocked his rifle, pointed it at Loco's heart, and said with his lips drawn back in a snarl, "You'll lead them, following Geronimo, or you'll die now."

Loco stared at Chato for a couple of breaths, uncrossed his arms, and lifted his hands in resignation.

I understood how he felt. The agent Clum had me cornered the same way before he brought me to San Carlos in chains. I nodded and waved him forward. "Lead them down the wagon road toward Fort Thomas. Soon I'll join you."

Loco swung his arm in a big arc and said with a bellow so all could hear in the confusion, "Come, my people, follow me." His wives ran inside their *wickiup* and gathered what they could of their camp supplies in baskets as he moved off toward the *rio* and, without looking back, waded across to walk in the ruts of the wagon road to Fort Thomas.

All the Chihenne had left their camp and were beginning to move at a faster pace as the warriors behind them prodded them along. We all heard two shots back at Loco's camp. Chihuahua and two or three warriors had fired the shots and waited for the tribal police to come investigate the cause of trouble. Chihuahua had a score to settle with the chief of police, a White Eye named Stirling. Stirling had accidentally killed a child when he fired on a *tulapai* drunk the year before. Chihuahua knew Stirling would come as soon as he heard the shots, and he did come with a scout sergeant named Sagotal. Chihuahua and the warriors killed them both and cut them up good, so they would have a hard time getting to the Happy Place. Then Chihuahua rode to join us. Chihuahua and his brother, Ulzana, were tough men. I was glad they were on my side and not that of the scouts.

I led Loco and his people in a line that stretched far down the wagon road along the Gila, but I soon turned up a twisting, nearly treeless canyon north into the Gila Mountains toward Ash Flat. It was a long climb to Ash Flat. The sun had nearly completed its ride into orange and black feathered clouds when I stopped at a large tank fed by a spring to let the people rest while the leaders held a council.

We asked Loco to sit with us as we considered what to do. Still angry at being forced to leave San Carlos, he sat with crossed arms but had little to say except that his people had been climbing up the canyon to Ash Flat nearly all that sun with little or nothing to eat and now would have to run into the night before we came another spring near the trail up the cliffs on the eastern side of Ash Flat. They needed rest and food.

Loco was right. Their men were doing all right, but the women and children, even the nearly grown ones, had become soft while staying in their camp at the reservation with nothing to do. We knew the sheep camp where Bes-das had been *jefe* was not too far from us. It should be easy to travel over the land of Ash Flat until we came to the cliffs on the north side. We sent the warriors to collect a few hundred sheep and drive them east along the cliffs of the Nantanes Mountains to a spring where the people could rest and eat. They would need their strength to make it to the border when the Blue Coats came out against us.

We ran the rest of the night, stopping to rest only once in the high, cool air, near the middle of the night at another tank fed by a cold-water spring. As the sun brought the dawn and light began to spread out over the valley, we came to the spring near the eastern end of Ash Flat and the trail up the Nantanes Mountains cliffs. The people drank, rested, and wished they had something to eat. Soon we saw in the distance warriors, not much bigger than specks, looking like they were driving snow before them. The hungry people wasted no time slaughtering and roasting those sheep. I didn't like the meat, but I ate it anyway. I was hungry.

We let the Chihenne people rest and eat all that day and the next. The second night, we began our run up the cliff trail and then over to a trail south through junipers. There was good water on this part of the trail and, because it was dark and cool, we rested only once, and that near the middle of the night.

We followed Eagle Creek down to the *Río* Gila. Even though the trail was easy, Loco's people moved too slowly. If we didn't pick up the pace, the Blue Coats would catch us. I had believed Loco's people were as fit as the ones in our camps in the Blue Mountains when I planned taking Loco's people. But the Chihenne women were very slow, and even the adolescent boys couldn't run too long or too hard without getting sick, like they had eaten bad meat. I thought it bad that Loco's people had grown soft living on the reservation. We had to get them animals to ride if we wanted to beat the Blue Coats to the border.

I sent warriors up the *Río* San Francisco to raid ranches for horses and mules. On the *Río* Gila, a handwidth on the horizon ride past the *Río* San Francisco, was a flattop ridge where we made camp. There the people could rest. Sentinels could see from any direction, and the warriors I sent out could bring the ponies and mules to the green grass and cool trees on the *río* at the foot of the ridge. After the warriors arrived, driving the herd of horses and mules splashing down the *río* side, we spent the rest of the day breaking them to ride bareback or with saddles the women made from bundles of reeds they had gathered from the *río*.

We left the flattop ridge and moved up the Gila, taking mounts and killing White Eyes as we went. Some we found on the trail near the Gila. Others were on *ranchos,* but everyone we found, we killed to keep the Blue Coats from learning about us. As we rode and the warriors took time to raid the ranches, one of the Chihenne girls reached womanhood. We held a short ceremony for her within the sound of gunfire as the warriors raided a nearby ranch. I promised to sing her the usual four-day ceremony when we were safe in the Blue Mountains.

Not far from the village of Duncan, we waited for the warriors to return with more animals from their raids. After they returned, we held a council and decided to ride that night, cross the ridges into the San Simon Valley, and try to make camp by dawn near the place the White Eyes called Steins.

Early the next morning, we made camp about a handwidth's ride north of Steins. We climbed a high flattop mountain after a hard night's ride. The tired people worked hard to get to the top in the dim light of dawn. There was a spring at the top, and there they could safely rest. Our scouts had told us to watch for Blue Coats on our trail from Fort Thomas.

The Blue Coat chief chasing us sent his scouts to look for our camp, but we saw them first and ambushed them while the people watched the exchange of gunfire from the cliffs. The Blue Coat chief raced to the fight with his soldiers to save his scouts. The hot fight lasted for most of the afternoon until the Blue Coats pulled back. We had no men wounded or killed. The

Blue Coats might have lost two or three soldiers, but I don't know for certain.

Before the moon came, we moved down the mountain, broke into small groups to move across the foothills, and then crossed the San Simon Valley. We watered at the *Río* San Simon, and the people and animals rested a little while.

I sang to my Power and asked that the night be long enough for us to reach the *arroyo* in the Chiricahua Mountains where there was water and the people could rest for the day. I was the last to reach the resting place in the long, winding *arroyo*. The sun's *pesh-klitso* was just reaching the twin peaks to the east, and the stars in the black velvet night above us were fast disappearing. I sent warriors to the top of the mountains rising above us. They were high enough so they could watch Fort Bowie with Blue Coat glasses. When the soldier chief sent out any Blue Coats to look for us, the warriors could signal us with their mirrors to move on. But it was quiet all day at Fort Bowie, and I was glad for the people to rest.

That night we moved south along the edge of the mountains and then east across the valley until we came to large spring and natural tank of water, good for our animals and the people to drink. We rested again as the sun came. Grass was thin there, but it was enough for the animals to graze all that sun, gathering strength to carry us another night south across the border into the Sierra San Luis.

When the night came, we rode at a good, even pace to save the horses and mules and by morning, we found water and rested in the Sierra San Luis, where the Blue Coats would not come and the *Nakai-yi* soldiers were weak and ineffective. We had saved Loco's people despite Loco's unwillingness to leave San Carlos. We rested again.

As soft as they were, the Chihennes escaping from San Carlos had done well. I was glad we had taken them.

CHAPTER 20
BLUE COATS IN MEXICO

The people slept easy, no longer fearing attacks by the Blue Coats. I wondered what had happened to those Blue Coats we had fought near Steins and why they weren't after us. But then, the Blue Coats did many things that made no sense. That night we began to move in an easy way toward the camp of Juh. The people would soon meet their friends and family members who had left San Carlos with Juh and me.

Happy and excited to escape San Carlos and expecting soon to see their families, the younger ones sang bits of love songs, called to each other, and made bets on short races. I made a race bet with Chihuahua on a young man in a race who looked like he had a fine pony. He couldn't ride well, and I lost, but I didn't care. It was a small price to free the Chihenne people.

We stopped several times at springs to rest and then crossed the *llano* to the little mountains sitting all alone the *Nakai-yes* called Sierra Enmedio.

On the northern end of Sierra Enmedio, we made camp by wet ground pooled with water fed by a good spring. For two days, we rested and relaxed playing games, gambling, and danc-ing by a big fire at night. Some of the women who gathered mescal bolls got the young men to dig a pit to roast the mescal with hot, covered stones, which usually took three days, and then they, too, rested. The White Eyes would not let them go far enough on the reservation to find all the mescal they needed to make pit cooking worthwhile. This was the first mescal, one of their favorite foods, they had eaten in a long time.

On the third night at Sierra Enmedio, some were still dancing around the dying fire as the dawn light grew among the stars to the east. If the mescal had finished cooking, we could pack it up and leave for Juh's camp that day. As the dawn grew brighter, Beyihtsun, the mother of Gooday, grandson of Loco, called him and two young women to go with her to check the mescal cooking pit. Some of the people were beginning to stir, getting ready to move on. It was quiet and peaceful in the camp, and the smoke from the dying fire rose straight into the sky, where it soon bent and crawled along in a column following the ground.

Soon after Beyihtsun disappeared into the rocks with the young ones, a rifle shot cracked and echoed off the little mountains beside us. I was near to napping when the first shot jerked me awake. A volley of bullets, singing their deadly songs, thumped into the camp. A woman and then another flopped to the ground, blood covering their shirts. Men and women kicked dirt on their fires and ran toward a little, round, rock-covered hill about a thousand yards south from our camp. Some more men and women fell while running in the hail of bullets.

Off toward the west, I heard a Blue Coat bugle sound their call to charge and the distant yells of men. Charging soldier horses raised a cloud of dust coming toward us. I counted the bodies of six men fallen around us and maybe twice that many women. Our only chance was to get to the little rocky hill, and I yelled to all those in confusion and pointed for them to go there. It was a long run, but the shooters were on a little ridge behind us, maybe three or four hundred yards. If we could get to the little hill, our best shots could keep them from advancing and doing more damage.

Our men reached the hill and got behind cover to use their long rifles to cover those still running and to stop the Blue Coat charge. I yelled for them to wait for a sure shot. They waited. The charging troopers came on. Three hundred, two hundred, one hundred yards, and our warriors fired. It was like thunder bouncing off the mountains, and, for an instant, our hill appeared bathed in fire and smoke. I expected many Blue Coat saddles to be empty, but the warriors had misjudged the distance in the changing light and shot too high. The Blue Coats emptied out of their saddles and took cover on the ground to return our fire. Our warriors, having found the right range, were deadly with their shots and killed and wounded a few as they made the Blue Coats back up.

Loco called to the scouts who had fired the first shots to come over to our side, but they laughed at him and fired many shots in the direction of his voice. I called to our men, urging them to be careful not to waste their bullets but to kill any Blue Coat or scout they could when they had a clear shot.

A fearless old woman, thinking that her son, Toclanny, was with the scouts stood on top of the little stone hill and called for him to come to her. He wasn't with those scouts, and one of them shot her in the head. She was dead before she hit the ground.

I called the young warriors, all anxious to make names for themselves, and told them a few needed to get behind the soldiers hiding in the rocks and keeping us pinned down. If they could turn the scouts' fire away from our hill, then the rest could run for the mountains behind us.

Chato had revenge coming against those Yavapai scouts. They had killed one of his relatives in forcing the move of Loco's band to San Carlos from Ojo Caliente. He wanted to lead the four young men, who included Fun and Kaytennae, and they all agreed. They worked their way around behind the scouts and began to fire on them. They showed great skill and courage going after the scouts. Soon the scouts, like ants out of a fire hole, climbed out of the rocks and rushed to join the Blue Coats. It was about a handwidth past the time of shortest shadows when the Blue Coats and scouts began moving north and away from us.

Loco had led many from our hill into the hills at the foot of the Sierra Enmedio when the Yavapai scouts firing on them turned away to fight our warriors attacking them from behind. Loco and those with him waited until they saw the Blue Coat dust disappearing in the falling light before returning to our camp by the big spring water. It was a bad day, with fourteen men killed, many horses taken, and maybe fifteen men wounded.

Before we began another long night of walking toward Juh's camp, we shared what food we had and filled ourselves with water from the spring. As we began our walk, warriors brought in maybe forty horses they had stolen back from the Blue Coats. We put the wounded on these ponies. Now the Chihenne women and children were on foot again, making it easy for the Blue Coats to catch us if they decided to follow.

I kept most of the fighting men behind the Chihenne women and children with Chihuahua and me, in case the Blue Coats decided to try and attack us again. A small group led by Mangas scouted far in front. Another fifteen warriors led by Chato, Kaytennae, and Naiche rode in the front of the column directly in front of a long stretch of women and children.

The country was flat and grassy. The only hard walking came when we had to cross washes or walk around big thickets of sotol that looked ready for harvest, like the maguey. One woman even said to me that maybe, if the White Eyes didn't return, we could harvest it.

I told her, "No. We can't risk being attacked again. It's best to find Juh first." She smiled, shrugged, and walked on.

The night was cool, the moon bright, and the land, mostly

flat. We stopped several times to rest and look after the wounded. As we worked our way south toward the Blue Mountains, I tried to understand why we had done well getting away from the Blue Coats on the American side of the border, but they had caught us on the *Nakai-yi* side.

Were the Blue Coats breaking their chief's rules? Was there some new understanding between the Americans and *Nakai-yes* that let them follow us into Mexico? I planned to ask Juh about this. If he didn't know, he would know whom to ask. We might have to begin living farther south than I had thought, or change how and when we raided. Always there was the possibility we had to change, or the *Nakai-yes* and White Eyes would wipe us out.

CHAPTER 21
ALISO CREEK

The women and children were walking down the valley stretched out in a line maybe a long rifle shot long. Dawn was driving the stars away, and cold air softly blew down from the mountains. It was very quiet—not even the brush sparrows were awake yet. We were close to the place where we would all gather. I noticed the women in front were moving faster. I smiled. Maybe they smelled coffee made by the group of warriors leading them who might have already camped.

The roar of shots snapped us all out of our dream walk and cut down women, children, and a few men at the head of the line like a sharp knife swung against green grass. Among those who had walked into the storm of bullets were Tzoe, his two wives, and their child. Only Tzoe lived to tell me what happened. It's too bad he lived to betray us within a harvest.

I yelled, "Men! Gather around me! We go to protect the women and children." I charged forward with Chihuahua while deciding what to do.

We galloped down the line of our confused and frightened people toward the slaughter of screaming women and crying children trying to get away. The light was not good, but I could see many bodies on the ground; a few of the women and men were still standing, waving at the others, and yelling, "Go back!"

Nakai-yi soldiers in uniform—long knives on the ends of their rifles—yelled and screamed for courage as they rushed out of the wash from which they took their first shots. They ran among the women and children, stabbing and slashing anyone they could reach. Men died trying to stop the soldiers with nothing but a knife. The young men riding with Chihuahua and me were swept into the confusion, killing anyone they could see in a *Nakai-yi* uniform.

My revolver filled my hand. I killed a *Nakai-yi,* charging me with his long knife on his rifle, and then another, who was about to stab a woman and her baby. The *Nakai-yes,* seeing the warriors among them on horses, pulled back to their wash.

The men and I gathered and hurried the women and children up a deep wash draining into the *arroyo* where we had been walking and riding. I learned later the *Nakai-yes* called it Aliso Creek. We made ready to fight off another *Nakai-yi* charge, the women desperately scooping out places in the bank to crawl into out of reach of humming bullets, the men digging footholds in the opposite bank so they could step up to see and fire their rifles before stepping back down into the wash to reload. The place where the women dug soon gave us water seeping into the draw from just below its sandy surface.

Two of our best shots, young men not long warriors, took up a place at the edge of the wash under a tree and made good use of the coming light to pick off *Nakai-yes* with each of their shots. Chappo, not long a warrior, made me proud of his courage and skill as he joined the sharpshooters with my brothers, Tsisnah, Fun, and Perico, and my father-in-law, Jelikinne.

Chihuahua and his nephew Espida, and Loco, who had a slight wound from the fight the day before, were there, too. They made the *Nakai-yi* soldiers pay in blood for this attack. I stayed in the dugout places with the women and children to protect them in case the soldiers tried to come up the wash from the big *arroyo.* We were lucky the wash had many twists and turns to get where we were. The soldiers couldn't see us, and their bullets hit the dirt well before they arrived where we were.

We began to run low on ammunition. Loco had carried a sack of five hundred bullets, but when the heavy firing had started, he had dodged and juked his way, running along the top of the wash, so he wouldn't slow the women and children running to take cover. The sack had slipped from his hand when he had tripped to his knees fifty feet away from the edge of the wash where we had taken cover and started returning fire. Loco scrambled on his hands and knees like an old gray wolf to the edge of the wash and dived in as bullets whined around him or spattered in the sand and dirt, raising little dust plumes that together created a little dust cloud, making him hard to see and probably saving his life.

If it wasn't a matter of life and death, we would have laughed. He looked funny crawling for us, his mouth gasping for air, his old scared faced distorted in pain, his good eye wide in the expectation of a *Nakai-yi* bullet hitting him at any time.

We needed that ammunition in the bag he'd dropped. All were running out of bullets, but Loco had to rest before he was strong enough to run and drag it back to us. An ancient, gray-headed woman said she would get it. Chihuahua rolled up on the edge of the bank and began to lay down a withering fire as the old woman of great courage used the footholds to crawl up the bank, over the edge of the wash, and run for the sack. Fun ran in front of her as she left the wash's cover. He charged the *Nakai-yes* in a zigzag pattern with shells between his fingers, loading, firing, and killing soldiers to draw *Nakai-yi* attention away from her as he ran. Hit and disabled or killed, she couldn't have retrieved the ammunition, and we would probably all have died that morning.

Fun's courage was a thrill to watch. I knew he would be a legendary warrior one day, the kind of man I'd always want with me. Fun and Chihuahua were the reasons Gray Hair reached the sack of ammunition. She grabbed the sack, which I knew must be heavy, and dragged it back toward our wash.

When she was a couple of bow lengths from the edge of the *arroyo* she fell, tried to crawl on, and then called to Fun and Chihuahua, "Help me! I have no more strength." They grabbed her ankles and pulled her and the sack in her grip back into cover in the wash.

Scratched and bruised, Gray Hair modestly pulled her torn and ragged dress down over her knees from above her skinny old thighs, shook her fist in victory, and shouted, *"Hey-yeh!"*

Chihuahua's face was covered with little blood spots from flying sand raised by bullets hitting near him, and he had two or three grazes on his arms and body. Fun, probably in the best physical shape of his life, gasped for breath after his bullets left four *Nakai-yi* soldiers twisted in death on their backs, blindly staring at the morning sky. Men with rifles took turns coming to fill their vest pockets and bags with bullets from the sack Gray Hair brought us.

The wash where the *Nakai-yes* hid was quiet for a short time. Men and boys came to the scooped-out places in the back bank to get water that was quickly turning red from blood. I took a quick count of the men. Thirty-two men and a few boys who could handle a rifle were with me. Where were the other warriors? Why didn't they come to help us?

Soon we heard a *Nakai-yi* yelling as the soldiers began firing and charged us. Their *jefes* yelled, "Geronimo is in that ditch. It's his last day. Go in and get him!"

Yes, I thought. *Come and get me. We'll cut you down like horse grass.* And we did, charge after charge. It was not my last day, but it was the last day for many *Nakai-yi* soldiers and their *jefes*.

Fun made more daring runs during the day and cut down many. The people had begun calling him, *Llt'i'bil'ikhaltii'*

185

(Smoke Comes Out) because the end of his rifle barrel that day was always filled with smoke drifting out its end.

Two hands on the horizon before the time of shortest shadows, the *Nakai-yi jefes* again screamed at their men to go kill me. "Go kill El Diablo," they said. A captain led them yelling, "Geronimo, this is your last day!"

Ha! There was no shooting down the wash from the big *arroyo*. I left the women's dugout, looking down the wash toward the big *arroyo*, then I peered over the bank edge at the soldiers running toward us. Fun was already up and running his zigzag pattern toward them, bullets between his fingers, shooting his Springfield carbine rifle, firing almost as fast as a man could with a good lever gun and dropping a soldier every time he fired.

Perico, my other brother, was also out running with Fun, but in a different direction, as they fired at the soldiers. Fun had so inspired all the warriors that others ran with them. The *Nakai-yes* were halfway from their wash to ours and drawing close to Fun, who had started back toward us.

I found the captain leading the *Nakai-yes* in my rifle sights, and I killed him. What satisfaction! It was the most and best I felt all day.

Our ammunition was getting low again, but the *Nakai-yes* weren't firing much, either. When the sun was halfway from the time of shortest shadows to disappearing behind the mountains, a mounted patrol of *Nakai-yes* came from the direction of Janos. We knew, if all the *Nakai-yes* charged us, we would die. However, after a short time, only the cavalry came galloping toward us firing their revolvers with much yelling for courage. Our men, with their long guns shooting fast, took many down, and soon the *Nakai-yes* turned tail and went back to their *jefe*. There were no more horse charges that day.

As the shadows grew long and night birds began to call, I

and the other leaders made plans to escape from where we waited for the next *Nakai-yi* charge. We decided to fire the grass just before dark, so we could slip out behind the smoke, leave a few at a time, and keep strict silence. To do this, warriors asked the women to let them strangle their babies so there would be no noise. They all agreed, except for one woman, who said she would do it herself. She had rather the baby die than be a *Nakai-yi* slave all its life.

As darkness came and smoke from the burning grass filled the air, small groups left as we planned, but I worried that a woman or a child would give us away just from coughing in the smoke or from being seen because they were too slow and not as skilled as warriors in disappearing.

I called out, "If we leave the women and children, we can escape." After all, we could always bargain them back, and warriors were more important than women and children to fight any *Nakai-yes* attacking Juh's main camps. Leaders had to think of the most good for everyone in times of war.

Fun, who stood nearby taking quick looks over the edge of our *arroyo* to be sure there was not another *Nakai-yi* charge, frowned and looked in my direction.

"What did you just say?"

I repeated my recommendation to leave the women and children. Fun raised his rifle to his shoulder and pointed it at me.

He said, "Say that again, and I'll shoot."

I stared at my brave brother and was tempted to use my pistol on him, but the people needed him. His wisdom needed to catch up with his bravery. I spoke no more. A few more warriors and I now left for the gathering place where we planned to all head for Juh's stronghold a day's run across the mountains.

Fun and a few other sharpshooters would stay longer, occasionally shooting to make the *Nakai-yes* think we were still there, before they slipped away. We left many ponies and mules behind in this last battle. Many of the surviving women and children would have to go across the mountains on foot.

As I ran for the gathering place, I wondered why all this evil had fallen on us in the land of *Nakai-yes*. Loco had not wanted to leave San Carlos, but we'd made him go. We had few losses getting across the border. But the Americans broke the word their chiefs had given to the *Nakai-yes* and each other. They had followed us into the land the *Nakai-yes* claimed.

Those Apache scouts who fired on us yesterday, one day I would kill them all, for they had betrayed us and would again. They would betray us until we killed them all. That needed to come soon. I didn't understand how the *Nakai-yes* knew where we were and the path we would take. Someone who knew what we planned must have told them, but why?

I knew that now, Loco's people would not like me. Maybe they'd even hate me, and even some of my own people, whose husbands and sons had died in the fighting, would also hate me. *Let them hate me. I don't care. I do only what I think Ussen wants me to do.*

CHAPTER 22
GATHERING IN JUH'S CAMP

We left many dead, nearly all women and children, in the *arroyo*. Crawling through the grass flames and smoke, we found the pathway we needed toward our mountainside gathering point and ran into the cold, smoke-filled darkness. The firelight behind us gave the smoke along the wash a soft, orange, ghost-like glow.

I led those who missed the *Nakai-yi* bullets and long knives to the group waiting with Naiche, Chato, and Kaytennae. They were ready to protect us at the gathering place near a mountain-side spring where the women wailed their sorrow for the many dead. I estimated we had lost nearly half of Loco's people, mostly women and children, during the two days we had spent fighting Blue Coats and *Nakai-yi* soldiers. I promised *Ussen* that one day I would leave the bodies of many *Nakai-yes* to the coyotes and buzzards for this. Now we had to care for those who still lived, especially the wounded.

In the cold, black night air filled with the steam of our breaths, the women tore cloth from their skirts to bind wounds, and I told them what plants to look for that would help healing. Many already had dried plants of their own and used peeled prickly pear over the wounds under the bandages so the flesh healed and didn't rot. I had two or three little wounds from the fighting in the wash, but they weren't serious and didn't bleed much, so I ignored them.

Our people suffered much that night. We couldn't make any

fires. It was cold, and blankets were few. Many slept together in one place to share body warmth and pulled juniper leaves or grass over and around them to help keep the cold out. We shared what little food we had and were lucky a few of the warriors still had their ponies to help us find food and fight *Nakai-yes* and Blue Coats. Most of the people, even the wounded, would have to walk to the next gathering point. It would be very dangerous, with the *Nakai-yes* ready to attack at any time.

Terrors filled the night. People shook from the cold. Bellies cramped from hunger. The wails of women who had lost family members never ceased, and the wounded moaned in pain. Our terror faded when we finally saw the sun's fiery glow below a soft blue horizon sky beginning to hide the stars in the smooth blackness above us. I scanned the *llano,* using my soldier glasses, and saw the streaking dust cloud raised by a great army of Blue Coats that must have been five or six times the size of the one we fought. I knew the Blue Coat army shouldn't be there. Then I saw the *Nakai-yi* soldiers marching out from the valley below us and straight toward the Blue Coats.

Naiche stood beside me as we watched the sun come. I nudged him with my elbow and pointed at the two dust plumes approaching a common point. He took my glasses and watched the tiny plumes grow.

"Ha. The *Nakai-yes* come out to meet the Blue Coats! Now maybe we see our enemies spill each other's blood on the *llano.* The Blue Coat soldiers are many more than the ones we fought."

Grinning, Naiche handed me back my soldier glasses.

"Yes, many more Blue Coats, a great many more. I hope they destroy the *Nakai-yi* chief who tried to wipe us out. This will be fun to watch."

But there was no battle between the Blue Coats and the *Nakai-yes.* Their leaders dismounted and talked for a time, then mounted, and the Blue Coats followed *Nakai-yes* back to the place where we fought them. The *Nakai-yi* leader strutted around like a White Eye chicken chief, what they call "rooster," as he pointed out all the Chiricahua bodies of our people they had murdered. We had wounded many *Nakai-yi* soldiers during the fight in the last sun. The Blue Coat leader motioned for his *di-yens* to help the *Nakai-yi* wounded. This was a bad sign for us. *Nakai-yi* soldiers and Blue Coats working together.

After the Blue Coats ate a morning meal with the *Nakai-yes*, they rode north toward the border up the valley we had followed. Soon the *Nakai-yes*, with our women and children they had taken prisoner, rode east for Casas Grandes.

Maybe, I thought, *Juh will know how to get them back.*

When the *Nakai-yes* were out of sight, I told some warriors to go looking for cattle to take and to drive them to our next camping place, *Bent-ci-iye* (Plentiful Pine Trees), near a fine spring of cold water. Some of the people had not eaten in three days. They were weak, hungry, and needed rest.

Warriors I sent out found a small herd of cattle and drove them into a nearby canyon at *Bent-ci-iye* where we could make meat. I decided it was best we stay there for a couple of days.

In two days, we moved again, but two of the wounded men and a woman, still too weak from their wounds to move on over the mountains, stayed where we camped. We left them a little food and some blankets. Those were two good warriors we left behind. I didn't want to lose them. I sent a warrior back to carry them more food and to help them survive.

The warrior returned the next day. He said *Nakai-yes* had camped where we left the warriors and woman, but he saw no sign of our people. In a moon, all three appeared at Juh's stronghold, their wounds nearly healed. I never talked to them to learn how they got away from the *Nakai-yes*. A time came when I regretted helping those men, Kayitah and Tzoe, survive. I've forgotten the name of the woman.

With the wounded walking slowly, it took three or four days before we reached our big camp at the foot of the great flattop mountain Juh used as his stronghold. Many happy reunions happened when the long line of ragged, weary people, with nothing except the clothes they wore, reached the camp. All in the camp showed even strangers kindness and respect, giving them all blankets and food and invitations to eat at cooking fires all over the camp.

Before we went to our family, Chappo and I went to the stream and bathed the stink of many days of travel and war from our bodies. My wives, Chee-hash-kish, She-gha, and Shtsha-she, and my daughter, Dohn-say, had a fine meal of beef, mesquite bread, wild potatoes, yucca tips, and juniper berries waiting for us. I was happy to see all my wives and my beautiful daughter but, most of all, I was glad to see Chee-hash-kish, my number one wife. It seemed this raid had lasted a very long time. Through the long days of running and riding, I had longed to hear her voice, see her, and feel her beside me in our blankets. Her eyes told me she felt the same way.

My women told us to sit so they could serve us. I ate until my shrunken belly swelled like that of a thirsty horse that had drunk water too fast. I could eat no more. As Chappo and I ate, we told the women the stories of our escape, how well things had gone until we came to the land of the *Nakai-yes,* and of the hard fights we had with the Blue Coats and *Nakai-yi* soldiers. They stared at us with wide eyes, as though they didn't believe us, but I knew they did.

I slept that night with Chee-hash-kish. When I pulled off my shirt, she saw the little wounds and scrapes I had from the fights at Enmedio and Aliso Creek. She insisted, before she would lie with me, on tending the wounds, although they had already begun healing. A good wife she was and, in the days and nights to follow, I realized She-gha and Shtsha-she were fine women, too. *Ussen* had been good to me with my fine wives.

The next morning, I smoked with Nana and Juh in Juh's tipi and told them the story of our raid on San Carlos. I finished my story by saying, "I have sorrow we lost all the Loco people we did. I don't understand what kind of agreement the Blue Coats have now with the *Nakai-yes,* but it is unexpected and will hurt us in the future. Before this season, the Blue Coats never followed us across the border. Will they always follow us now? I also want to know how the *Nakai-yi* chief knew the trail where we were when they attacked us."

Juh nodded, the lines in his face highlighted by the yellow flickering fire in the middle of his tipi. "Yes, we must be more careful in what we expect the Blue Coats will do at the border. My friends in Janos say the White Eyes talk with Terrazas, so they can follow us across the border after we raid. I sent two men to warn you in the White Eye country that the *Nakai-yi jefe,* García, and his *segundo,* Mata Ortiz, were prowling the *llano* like Cougar. But after those men crossed the border, they found and took some fine ponies and decided to bring them back first before they went to find and warn you. Fools and traitors. García was lucky and caught them. He promised them if they told him your way back, he would free them. They betrayed us, and he still killed them. This I didn't know until two days ago when another captive slipped away and found me, but it was too late to help you."

Old Nana drank from his blue-speckled coffee cup and sighed, his face wrinkled like mountain foothills cut with canyons and arroyos. "It's a hard thing to see so many of my people ride the ghost pony so soon. I talked to Loco last night.

He grieves for our people. He lost many, even his beautiful daughter and a grandson, in escaping San Carlos. But he said it makes no difference. Shaking sickness or other diseases in the hot seasons would have taken them anyway. This running from the reservation for freedom is a hard thing, but he says he would do it again. Better to die free, than shaking in blankets while the sun burns the ground."

I took little comfort from Juh and Nana's words. Many had died because I pushed them to run, but unless an Apache is free, he is not much of an Apache.

Juh stared at the fire and then said, "I have a treaty now with the *Nakai-yes* in Casas Grandes. Let's move from this camp. We should camp a hand or two's ride from Casas Grandes on the *Río* San Miguel, relax a few days, and then go on for some trading and a little of the good whiskey the *Nakai-yes* have. Then we will be ready to take what we want in Sonora and other places in Chihuahua. What do you say, brothers?"

The memory of good whiskey tasted sweet on my tongue. "*Enjuh.* I need a good drink, and there are things I know Chee-hash-kish and my other women want. I'll take them with me. When will we leave the stronghold on the San Miguel?"

Juh glanced at Nana, who raised his cup and said, "*Enjuh.*"

Juh smiled. "Then we leave tomorrow."

Chee-hash-kish laughed and said my women would be ready after I told her we were going to camp on the *Río* San Miguel a hand or two away from Casas Grandes and then to do some trading and drinking. Dohn-say, ready for marriage, also wanted to go trading at Casas Grandes, and I agreed.

After a long time of running and being apart, it was time we all celebrated together and had a good time with a drink of the good whiskey like the *Nakai-yes* and White Eyes made. It had been a long time since we traded with the *Nakai-yes* in Casas

Grandes or Janos. There would be much to trade and to enjoy in the villages of the *Nakai-yes*.

CHAPTER 23
CASAS GRANDES

Many of Loco's people still suffered from their wounds. We took four or five days to travel what we normally covered in one day to reach the camp on *Río* San Miguel. We made our camp up on a mountainside close to its eastern bank. On the western side of the *río* was a wide fertile valley and then more mountains. If the *Nakai-yes* attacked—Juh didn't believe they would—we planned to run for the mountains above where we camped to defend ourselves.

Before we went into Casas Grandes, one of Juh's raiding parties returned, and we celebrated their success with the Dance of Triumph. From the looks of surprise on the faces of some of the children from San Carlos, I guessed they had never seen such a dance. It was good that they learned how warriors celebrate, even after Victorio had ridden the ghost pony to the Happy Place.

I told my family that even though Juh had a treaty with the people in Casas Grandes, we would follow Juh's drinking rule for a *Nakai-yi* village. The rule said that only half could drink on any one day, and that the rest must remain sober. Knowing sober Apaches would attack them kept the *Nakai-yes* from trying to slaughter those who were drunk. Juh had learned this trick many harvests before, and I think it saved many lives in his camp.

My women were eager to find new cloth, clothes, cooking pots, axes, and sweets to trade for the plunder I had gathered in

Sonoran raids. I was eager for the taste of good whiskey and wanted to fill sacks with ammunition for more raids in the Season of Many Leaves. About one in three of the people in camp left for Casas Grandes early with the coming of the sun. Juh led the way following the *Río* San Miguel on an easy trail north for two hands above the horizon. The air was cool. Many birds sang in the *bosque* along the *río,* and the people were quietly content.

We reached the wide wagon road stretching toward the center of Casas Grandes and waited while Juh rode into town alone. He soon returned with the *alcalde* (mayor) and other village *jefes* who, with smiling faces, welcomed us and asked that we come into the town and enjoy ourselves. We waved parallel to the ground and rode down the wide road between the village buildings, keeping a wary eye out for any betrayals.

We had a good day trading. I traded a black and white pony and two rifles once belonging to Blue Coat soldiers for two bottles of mescal and two big sacks of bullets. Thirsty for the whiskey, I decided that Chee-hash-kish and I would drink that day, and She-gha and Shtsha-she could drink the next day. I told Dohn-say and Chappo that they must stay sober and serve their parents a little longer.

Chee-hash-kish and I had a good time first eating and then drinking with the *Nakai-yi* friends of Juh. Near the end of the day, we mounted our ponies and, after a short ride to the *Río* San Miguel, we made a quick camp in the *bosque* while Dohn-say and Chappo packed away the things for which Chee-hash-kish and I had traded. I shared another bottle of mescal with Chee-hash-kish before we fell into our blankets and slept.

She-gha and Shtsha-she, with Chappo and Dohn-say to help, rode into Casas Grandes the next morning. They planned to trade more plunder for things they wanted, including a bottle of mescal. When Chee-hash-kish and I awoke, the sun was already high, and our heads throbbed with a feeling like war clubs had struck them. The mescal demons left after hot cups of coffee in the weak light of the tipi drove them away.

We slept again. Chee-hash-kish and I were together in the blankets two or three times that day with the rest of my family out trading. It was good to be with her often after the long march from San Carlos and the fights with the Blue Coats and *Nakai-yi* soldiers. Her sweet body pulled the sorrow of great loss from my spirit, but I never forgot the dead and dying from Enmedio and Aliso Creek.

As the sun approached the edge of the western mountains, filling the sky with much purple and red, Chee-hash-kish made a pot of beef, wild potatoes, onions and chilies, and fried mesquite bread for her sister wives and our children soon to return from their day of trading and drinking in Casas Grandes. Then she sat with the warm sunlight softly covering and warming her face and making her more desirable every time I looked at her.

In the sun's falling light, Dohn-say and Chappo came leading packhorses loaded with trade goods. There was no sign of She-gha and Shtsha-she, who had done much trading. When I asked about them, Chappo smiled and said they had drunk all of a bottle of mescal and were not far behind if they could keep from falling off their horses. I laughed when I saw them not far down the trail holding on to their reins with one hand and their saddle horns with the other as they swayed from one side to the other. We all laughed when they rode up to the tipi and nearly fell in the fire as they dismounted. Chappo took their horses, brushed them down, and hobbled them to graze with the camp herd.

I had never seen She-gha and Shtsha-she have trouble with their balance from drinking too much mescal. They must have found a bottle stronger than usual. Eating the evening meal Chee-hash-kish had made drove away most of their mescal demons.

She-gha, looking first at Shtsha-she, who nodded, rubbed her forehead and then, looking at me, said, "I think we have all the whiskey we need from this one sun. We won't go back again. Husband, you drink all you want. We watch your back for enemies."

I smiled and nodded. *"Enjuh."*

With the coming of the next sun Juh, most of the other leaders, Chee-hash-kish, and I rode to Casas Grandes from our little nearby camp for another day of trading and a good drink. Our people had been in Casas Grandes two days, and the *Nakai-yes* had kept their bargains. They were polite and gave us all the mescal we could use. It was a good visit. By the time the sun was two hands off the western mountains, Chee-hash-kish had drunk all she wanted and returned back to the little camp next to the village to rest and sleep off the effects of the mescal and be ready to leave the next sun.

As the shadows grew long, I was squatting against the side of a store with nearly a full bottle of that good, fiery mescal in my belly as the clouds in the west began to change color. Juh sat nearby staring at the clouds, but he had not drunk any mescal that day because I was drinking. I decided the night would be better spent sleeping next to Chee-hash-kish. I motioned to Juh that I was leaving for the camp. He nodded, picked up his rifle, and came with me. On the way back we stopped often and talked with others about their trades. It was dark when we wandered through the little brush shelters of the camp. I found Chee-hash-kish sleeping soundly in our blankets. My other wives and children had already returned to the big camp. I stretched out beside Chee-hash-kish and passed out.

I felt the ground tremble as though a herd of horses ran toward us. Chee-hash-kish stirred. I staggered to my feet, my mind stumbling in its clouds, trying to decide if what I had felt was real or a dream. Two shelters away Juh jumped to his feet, his rifle ready, looked all around the edge of the camp, and then stared down the road toward the little canyons of stores lining the streets of Casas Grandes.

Bullets began flying in our direction. One crashed into the sand at my feet, spraying stinging sand against my legs. Juh began firing into the outlines of horses and men in the darkness running toward us. Mounted *Nakai-yi* soldiers and foot soldiers streamed toward the camp from all directions, their rifle thunder echoing from the village's building walls and hills across the road from us.

My rifle was always loaded and ready; I sighted down the barrel and tried to focus on the dark outlines thundering toward us, their shots hitting our people or flashing through brush or shelters near them as they dumbly stared at what was happening. Juh told me to shoot any soldier I could see. In my fuzzy mind, I saw the soldiers in the light of fires they were setting, but they weren't wearing uniforms like those I usually saw around Casas Grandes. They looked familiar, but I couldn't recall where I had seen them before.

Juh and I fired at the soldiers until we were nearly out of bullets and we saw a band of many soldiers on foot running into the camp, some stopping to put a bullet into people already dying, before rejoining the others.

Juh said to me, "Come. We have to go. Now."

We ran across the road and then stayed in the shadows up the hill where most of the others had already run. My clearing mind suddenly thought, *Chee-hash-kish!* I turned and ran back to shelter where we had slept. I had to kill soldiers to reach her, but when I got to our blankets she was gone.

I fought my way back to the road and crept along in the shadows toward the village. Soldiers herded many of our women and children in the street and made them walk tied together with a rope around their necks. I knew they must be headed for the slave market in Ciudad Chihuahua. I saw some of Naiche's relatives in the group, but there was no one else I recognized.

As the light came chasing the night away, I followed the trail of the soldiers I had seen marching with slaves down the road toward Galeana. I found them camped on the trail as the light came in the east. I wanted to kill them all, but I had too few bullets, and there were too many for me to handle alone.

I stared for a long time at the prisoners huddled together and, with some relief, saw Chee-hash-kish comforting a child near the middle of the huddled group. I prayed to *Ussen* for an understanding of how to get her away from the *Nakai-yi* soldiers who watched the group as though the women were deadly warriors, but *Ussen* said nothing to me. I knew if we tried to free the prisoners, the soldiers would kill most of them before we could free any of them. That thought left a bitter taste on my tongue. Ransom was the only way to save their lives.

Using our private signal, I yipped twice like a coyote with a long note on the second call to tell Chee-hash-kish I had seen her, knew she was there, and that I would be back. I slid back through the brush to the camp. All were gone. I knew Juh and the others must have headed for the camp on the *Río* San Miguel. I ran for that camp and came to the trail through the mountains leading to the big camp as the light from the rising sun cast a golden glow in its house behind the far mountains.

I found my wives and children, their faces grim and sad, staring at the fire. When Dohn-say saw me, she forgot her manners and jumped up to run and hug me. She-gha and Shtsha-she also came and hugged me. Chappo stood and nodded upon my arrival as a man should. I told them what had happened.

Chappo asked, "When we will we leave to get Mother back?"

I said, "The only safe way to get her back is to ransom her. That will take time. We'll have to find our own captives to trade for her and others that were taken. I promise you I'll do everything I can to bring her back. While Chee-hash-kish is gone, She-gha will lead the family as number one wife." The others nodded in agreement.

We waited four days for any of the *Nakai-yi* prisoners to escape and return to us, but only one or two returned. Juh decided we had to move southwest toward Sonora to avoid the *Nakai-yi* soldiers. Without the energetic Chee-hash-kish to help with the work and lead the rest of the family, my wives and children were slow to gather our things and move with the rest of the band. I could tell my wives needed help. *Perhaps,* I thought, as we moved over the mountains, *I can find us a slave when we're no longer on the run.*

CHAPTER 24
ZI-YEH

We came to the Great Canyon, to Guaynopa, to the south of Casas Grandes, and after resting a few days, moved on west. Passing through the mountains of Sonora, we crossed the *Río Yaqui* and made our camp on a high ridge where we could watch for *Nakai-yi* soldiers from all directions.

Juh didn't want to leave the mountains for a camp in the foothills and fast rides to the valleys where the great *haciendas* had much wealth and cattle for the taking. Juh said, "Camping in the foothills exposes us to surprise *Nakai-yi* soldier raids."

Several young men had asked to become novitiates and had been given to warriors to council them. The novitiates already included Chappo and Yahnozha, a fearless one I expected to become a great warrior. I had chosen my cousin, whom Chappo often called "brother," Betzinez, as my novitiate. There were several others, including Fun, who had fought as mature warriors at Aliso Creek, and Lot Eyelash, who had also shown much courage fighting the *Nakai-yes* there.

They all were worthy of being warrior candidates, and I was certain they would all become great warriors. I was wrong. My own novitiate, Betzinez, never became a warrior, but that is another story.

Juh and I, as his *segundo,* were at an impasse. I wanted to go raiding in Sonora and take some captives to bargain for Chee-hash-kish and others. I needed to quench the flaming fire taking my spirit by spilling more *Nakai-yi* blood in revenge for the killing of my first family. Juh wanted to return east to the safety of his hiding places in the mountains and, from there, continue to raid in Sonora and Chihuahua, despite its growing number of *Nakai-yi* soldiers.

We talked over what we should do and decided to first take the young men who wanted to be novitiates out with their warrior leaders to support a raid on a village in Sonora. How the novitiates did in a village raid, where we didn't have to worry about fighting soldiers, would tell us how well they might do in the next raid and whether they were ready to watch the camp for *Nakai-yi* attacks, regardless of where we went.

The warriors and novitiates left our mountain camp by the *Río* Yaqui, which was a long day away over rough mountains from the village we wanted to raid. We camped that night without fires on a high ridge above the village while a few warriors slipped down the mountain to scout it. The warriors were back before first light. They said a large number of soldiers were in the village and that they had a big, shoots-many-times gun mounted on wheels (a Gatling gun). Juh and I jerked back at this news.

We had seen and fought against these very powerful guns before. With this gun, one soldier could shoot as many as twenty or thirty men at the same time. We didn't want to fight these soldiers and their shoots-many-times gun with novitiates nearby. We returned to our *Río* Yaqui camp without firing a bullet or arrow or taking anything.

After failing to raid the village, Juh gave much thought to what he wanted to do. We met in council with the warriors and discussed our next move. Juh decided to take his people and return east. I stayed to raid in Sonora with Chihuahua. But before Juh left, I had personal business I needed to settle.

Shtsha-she grew heavy with our first child. She-gha and Dohn-say did more than their share of the work to ease her burden, but there was too much work for a single wife and a nearly grown daughter to do, even when we were not on the move. I needed another wife to help them.

Without appearing to pay them any attention, I watched the women work in camp. One stood out from the others. She was small compared to most of the women in camp, but she was always first to get to work and the last to leave. She was good with an axe. Her piles of wood were always greater than those of the other women as she cut, moved, and piled wood outside her father's *wickiup*. When other women went to the *río* with one jar for water, she took two. When the women gathered juniper berries, her basket always held more than the others. She rarely gathered less of anything than any other woman.

I asked a Nednhi warrior one day as we talked by the fire why the young woman had never married. He smiled and shook his head. "Hmmph. She's good on the eyes. But I think she's too small to do heavy lifting women have to do sometimes. Maybe her babies will be small, too." He shrugged. "I don't know. I already have the woman I want. She's all I can support. Besides, my one woman works me hard to have a child. I don't get enough sleep as it is. I wouldn't think of taking another wife." We both laughed.

I spoke privately with She-gha asking her what she thought about me taking another wife, telling her that I thought Zi-yeh would be a good wife for the family and why.

She-gha smiled. "I have thought since Chee-hash-kish was taken that we needed another woman, even a slave, to help us, and hoped you would see that and find one for us. Zi-yeh is small, but every woman in camp, including me, strains to keep up with her. Yes, I think Zi-yeh is a good choice. You should ask her and give Jelikinne a fine bride gift."

I nodded and smiled, too. "She-gha is a good woman."

A few days later, Jelikinne sat on a blanket in front of his *wickiup* cleaning his rifle, a fine, new lever one he had traded for a pony in Casas Grandes. Nearly every woman in camp, including the three in my family, were in the *Río* Yaqui *bosque* gathering berries. It was a good time to speak privately with him. I carried a blanket on which to sit while I spoke with him.

He looked up from his work when he saw my shadow on his blanket. "*Ho,* Jelikinne. I would speak with you."

"Hmmph, Geronimo. I see you. Spread your blanket, and we'll smoke."

I sat down and pulled out my sack of *tobaho* and cigarette papers. We smoked to the four directions and relaxed while we talked of the trick to wipe us out the *Nakai-yes* had attempted in Casas Grandes, how hard it had been to reach this camp, and how Loco's people had accepted living and raiding with us while living in the mountains. He finished his cigarette first and flipped its remainder in the fire. He waited until I took my last draw and tossed mine in the fire, too.

"What words does Geronimo carry? Speak. I will listen."

I liked Jelikinne, even though he had been ready to put a spear in my chest if I had forced the killing of the child at Ash Flat. I didn't think he held that against me. In war, men often lost their minds and did things they later regretted.

"You know I lost my number one wife, Chee-hash-kish, during the *Nakai-yi* attempt to kill us at Casas Grandes?"

His eyes narrowed, and he nodded, wondering I'm sure, where this talk was leading.

He said, "I know this. I know you treat your women well and will try to get her back. That's a hard thing to do for those taken as slaves."

"Yes, it's a hard thing. I'll work hard to do this. But, with Chee-hash-kish gone, I think my family and I need another wife. I'm Juh's *segundo,* and there is much for my wives to do. I can afford all the wives I want, but I only take those I can care for and truly want. I see your daughter, Zi-yeh, short in statue, not long a woman, but a hard worker. She outworks all the women around her. She always seems happy. I like her very much. Will you allow me to speak with your daughter about marriage? If she accepts me, I'll treat her well. She won't want to leave me and return to your *wickiup,* and I'll offer a good bride gift for her."

A breeze sighed through the tops of nearby pines and junipers. Down the hillside were the yells and screams of children playing, and, above, crows squawked at a nearby hawk. Jelikinne sat up straight, cocked his head to one side, and studied my face.

"You know I would have killed you at Ash Flat?"

I nodded but said nothing.

"It was a bad thing you wanted to do, but I understand the rage that sometimes fills a man's mind. I see you treat your family well. I believe you speak with a straight tongue. You're a leader by nature and are a powerful, respected *di-yen.* Yes, I'll permit Zi-yeh to speak with you. I will tell her this. If she accepts you, accepts being the youngest of maybe four wives if you can get Chee-hash-kish back, then I will talk with you about a bride gift."

Two suns later, I found Zi-yeh alone on a ridge picking juniper berries. When I appeared out of the shadows of the trees, her fingers flew to her lips in surprise. I held up my hands, palms out, to her. "I mean you no harm, Zi-yeh. I wish only to talk with you. You father has given me permission. Perhaps he has told you this. May we sit here and talk?"

She looked to one side and nodded. "You're the great *di-yen* and warrior, Geronimo. I know you. My father has spoken to me and says I have permission, and it is my choice whether to listen to you. Speak. I will listen."

I sat down on a large, flat stone and motioned for her to join me. She hesitated, as a deer does when coming out of the shadows, and then she sat down near me.

When she was still, her eyes watching mine, I said, "I'm Juh's *segundo*. I have three wives, a son near your age, and a daughter four harvests younger. In Casas Grandes, the *Nakai-yes* took my fine wife, Chee-hash-kish, for a slave. I must somehow ransom her back, but it may take a long time. I have another wife, Shtsha-she, who has grown big with a child in her belly and moves slow and careful. That leaves only my other wife, She-gha, and Dohn-say, my daughter, to take care of us all. We need another wife. I've watched how hard you work. You're small in stature, and some men say they don't want a small wife. I want the best wife, regardless of her size. I think, among the unmarried women in our camp, you're the best, and we would be honored to have you in my family. I ask that you accept me as your husband."

As I spoke, Zi-yeh's eyes never left my face, and she listened to every word I had to say.

She looked at her hands folded together on her lap, took a deep breath, and sighing said, "So I will be third wife in the lodge of Geronimo?"

I nodded. "Yes."

"If you can get Chee-hash-kish back, then I would be fourth wife in your lodge?"

Again, I said yes.

She bowed her head in thought. "Do you beat your women?"

"No. Not much. These with me now, I don't think I've ever beaten or whipped. They work hard and are always respectful."

"Would your other wives accept me?"

"I think they'll be happy you're there to help them."

"Will you lie in the blankets with me often? Will the others resent me if you do?"

I was a little surprised, but pleased, at her directness.

"Yes, it's a man's duty to give his wife her children. In the beginning, I'll want you many times until our child grows in your belly. Then I will leave you alone for a while to let the child grow and, after its birth, gain strength outside your body. But I will always support you with our children. I think when a child grows in your belly, my other wives, She-gha and Shtsha-she, will be happy for you and help you all they can."

"Will you be gentle in the blankets?"

"I am a *di-yen*. I know how to make a woman comfortable in the blankets with her husband. Men who have wives complaining about their treatment in the blankets have asked me how to make their wives happy. Their wives complain no more."

She looked again at her hands folded in her lap and thought a little while. "The thought of marrying a man of your rank and age has never been in my mind. I know most men think I'm too small to be a good wife, but I am not, and you see me clearly. I'll think on this. Meet me here at the same time in four suns, and I'll give you an answer."

This meeting had gone well. Perhaps better than I expected. I liked that Zi-yeh wanted to think her answer through and was direct in her questions and answers. "*Enjuh.* I will meet you here in four suns, and I hope you will give me the answer I seek. Thank you for listening to me, daughter of Jelikinne."

She smiled and nodded. I left her in peace and disappeared into the long shadows.

I spoke with Zi-yeh in the shadows of the trees on that ridge again in four days. She smiled and appeared happy when she saw me come out of the shadows. *"Nish'ii'*, Geronimo." She walked over and sat where we had talked four days earlier. I sat down beside her. There was no breeze shaking the trees and brush, no clouds changing the light, and no sounds of animals or children playing. It was like all the world was waiting and listening to us.

Zi-yeh smiled and said, "Since we spoke, I've talked with my father and thought much about your wanting to marry me. You're a great warrior and powerful *di-yen*. Any woman would want you as first wife, but those who would be third or fourth wives, I think not so much."

I felt sadness and thought, *This young woman I want will not accept me.*

"I am young and have much to learn. We live a hard life here. Life for women was easier on the reservation. Many women die in the Blue Mountains. Many become slaves. Many second and third wives are now first wives. I pray to *Ussen* that you can find and again claim Chee-hash-kish, but I hear no answer. I have asked *Ussen* for wisdom in deciding whether or not to take you for a husband. The answer that fills my heart says I must accept you as my husband and that one day I will be first wife."

"*Hi yeh!* Zi-yeh fills me with a glad heart. I'll offer Jelikinne a fine bridal gift. You will be my wife. Of this, I'm very glad."

I stood, and she, too, was on her feet. I hugged her. She didn't resist me, but her eyes were wide with surprise. I think this was the first time she had been next to a man in that way who was not in her family.

I held her by the shoulders and looked in her face. "Today I'll speak with your father. We will decide the best time for you come to my family. I am very happy you've chosen me, Zi-yeh."

Zi-yeh smiled. "We'll have many good years together, Husband. I will serve our family well."

CHAPTER 25
THE BEST OF TIMES

I smoked with Jelikinne and told him Zi-yeh had agreed to be my wife. He made a little smile and said, "Zi-yeh has chosen a great and powerful warrior and *di-yen*. She has chosen well. She will give you strong children for which we will both be proud."

I answered, "Zi-yeh is a woman of great price, one of much value to her father and family. I offer her father a well-deserved bride gift of eight ponies, and four fine Navajo blankets. Does her father think this is an acceptable gift?"

Jelikinne showed no sign of acceptance on his face, but his eyes sparkled, and soon he smiled and said, "It is a good gift for Zi-yeh. I will miss my fine, hardworking daughter. Soon my family will celebrate a feast for you." We smoked again and thanked *Ussen* for good women and good gifts.

Zi-yeh came to my family, welcomed by the smiling faces of my wives and children and by my happy heart. I thanked *Ussen* for her, and I know the other women were grateful she had joined them. It was as if she had always been part of the family. We enjoyed each other in the blankets after I taught her things a young, unmarried woman would not know. I saw that she smiled often in our lodge and was happy.

Soon after she came to me, the warriors held a council to decide where we would raid in the Season of Large Fruit. After we smoked to the four directions, Juh spoke first.

"I speak to my warriors as a brother and a chief. I don't like this place where we camp. It's too exposed if the *Nakai-yes*

211

decide to attack us. It's better to be on top of a mountain, where we can defend ourselves and there are clear lines of sight so we can see them coming. I know Geronimo wants to raid in Sonora and take more *Nakai-yi* blood for the murder of his family. Geronimo is a great war chief and *di-yen* and will take many horses, cattle, and plunder on his raids in Sonora. But I say it is dangerous to raid where he wants in Sonora."

I saw the Chiricahua and Chihenne warriors begin looking sideways at each other, some wrinkling their brows and crossing their arms, and others slowly nodding. The Nednhi warriors, who had always ridden under Juh's chieftainship, relaxed and began to roll another cigarette as Juh continued. Many Chiricahua and Chihenne warriors and their war leaders cocked their heads to one side, listening carefully to what Juh had to say.

"The *Nakai-yes* have lost much to the Apaches. Their *jefes* will not stop coming after us until we leave or they have killed us. It's not much better in Chihuahua, but the strongholds I claim there are much stronger than our camps here in Sonora that are accessible to anyone who can find them. They are barely defensible. We know the Chihuahuan country trails better than the ones in Sonora, and that makes it easier to escape when *Nakai-yi* soldiers follow or search for us. Some of you—Chato, Loco, Geronimo, and others—have family the *Nakai-yes* have taken for slaves in Chihuahua. You warriors want to do everything you can to free your wives, sons, daughters, and other relatives. Camps and strongholds in Chihuahua provide the best places to do this. I go to a Chihuahua stronghold from which to raid."

Nednhi warriors nodded and mumbled, *"Enjuh."* Many of the Chiricahuas and Chihennes who had listened carefully to Juh's words slowly nodded. Frowns deepened on some of the faces of the Chiricahuas and Chihennes. All eyes turned to me as Juh stood frowning and watching me with his arms crossed. I stood to speak.

"Juh is a mighty *di-yen* and warrior. All he says about Chihuahua and Sonora are true. But I think there are other things that need to be considered."

I held up a finger, as if I were counting, to make a point. "First, the military in Sonora has fewer and poorer soldiers than most of the *Nakai-yi* outposts in Chihuahua. The Chihuahuan *jefes* speak many lies to us, take our people slaves, and are quick to try to kill us. I think there is some secret treaty between the Blue Coats and the *jefes* in Chihuahua that allows the Blue Coats to come unhindered into the land of the *Nakai-yes* to attack us with the Loco people as they did at Enmedio."

There were nods and grunts by the warriors. Now the Nednhis were looking at each other and frowning.

I held up two fingers. "Second, because the military is so weak in Sonora, it is easier to raid toward the west than it is in the east in Chihuahua. We have raided the *Nakai-yes* in the San Bernardino Valley so hard and so often that many have left. Their once fertile fields stand covered with brush and weeds. Even the dogs they left starve. We should go easier on them. Then they stay in their fields and work more so that on our next raid we will have supplies to gather, even if we leave them a little to live on through the Ghost Face to plant more in the spring for us.

"I say we need to raid farther west and south beyond the village of Nácori Chico, maybe as far as Ures."

Amid the grunts and nods, this time there were a few laughs.

"I don't believe it's easier to evade any *Nakai-yes* chasing us in Chihuahua than it is in Sonora, or that we are less safe in guarded camps in the high mountains than on a flattop mountain in Chihuahua. It has always been so with Apache camps. You all are tested warriors and know how to think. I leave it to you to decide."

The Chiricahuas and Chihennes nodded. Juh continued to scowl at me, and his Nednhis all had blank looks on their faces as they tried to digest this argument between Juh and me about where to raid.

"I want the *Nakai-yes* to think we've left the country. They'll relax and maybe show us where our people are slaves. We have friends in Ciudad Chihuahua who will be watchful for our women and children. They know them. They'll tell us where they've been taken, and they'll be easier to take back when the *Nakai-yes* don't think we're nearby."

Juh was shaking his head like he didn't believe or agree with anything I said.

"I see that Juh and I have a difference of opinion. Let us part as friends. Those who stay with me will make our camps near the *Río* Bavispe and move the camp as we need. We'll raid in Sonora. Let Juh and his followers go on to the strongholds in Chihuahua and raid as he pleases there. Maybe we meet again in the Season of Earth Is Reddish Brown."

There were grunts of approval among the warriors. Juh gave me a final scowl. shook his head, and then strode from the circle, his Nednhis behind him. Chato, Loco, Nana, Naiche, Bonito, and their followers all went with Juh. Chihuahua, and Kaytennae remained with me to discuss what to do next.

The next morning, Juh and his followers, maybe five hundred in all, including women and children, with about eighty warriors, left the camp and rode east for Chihuahua. Juh and I were still friends, although we had decided to go our separate ways. If we joined forces again, I would be honored to be Juh's *segundo*.

Before he left, I went to his lodge and we smoked, talked of what we would do until the Season of Earth Is Reddish Brown, and had a little drink from a bottle of White Eye whiskey. I had found it and saved it while the White Eyes held us at San Carlos. Juh still wanted to have a treaty with the *Nakai-yes* that gave us the Nednhi land around the Carcay Mountains and would let them trade without fear in Casas Grandes or Janos.

I told him I hoped he got what he wanted but warned that it was always dangerous dealing with *Nakai-yes,* and that he should never trust them. He grinned and nodded while he assured me that he well knew their habits.

Those who stayed in my camp, maybe a hundred, counting women and children and thirty warriors, planned two raids in Sonora. We decided to cast our eyes on mule packtrains and fat little villages as far west and south as Ures in one raid. In another raid to the northwest, we would go as far north as where the *Río* Bavispe turns from flowing north to south. We hid our women and children high in a camp on a flattop mountain in the great bend of the *Río* Bavispe.

These raids were good times. They reminded me of the raiding days with Cochise, Victorio, and Mangas Coloradas. On the raid toward Ures, we took a few well-provisioned packtrains and many cattle, horses, and mules. We loaded our plunder on pack mules and drove the livestock over the mountains to our big camp.

The women, children, and old ones slaughtered the cattle and dried the meat. While we raided far away, the women and children baked mescal and collected nuts and berries. The nearly grown boys who knew how to use weapons did their time guarding the trails to the camp. We took them on a couple of easy raids as novitiates. We lived Apache life as *Ussen* intended. As in the long-ago days, no Blue Coats attacked us, and no White Eye reservation agents cheated us.

A moon after we began raiding, Shtsha-she had our first child, a girl, with an easy birth. I was very happy. On the fourth day after her birth, we had the blessing ceremony for placing her on her *tsach* (cradleboard) made for her by a grandmother, who did beautiful work with the wood she directed me to bring her for making it.

Many of the raids yielded fine American lever rifles that shot many times without reloading and made a mighty warrior good with a rifle appear as many men against *Nakai-yi* soldiers, whose guns had to be reloaded with a new cartridge after being fired only once. Fun learned to do this very fast with his single-shot trapdoor rifle while holding his cartridges between his fingers. He was almost as fast as a man with a lever gun. But very few who had the trapdoor rifles knew how to do this.

A new rifle or pistol taken in a raid requires the warrior to get as much ammunition from the owner as he can. It's too easy to waste ammunition with a lever gun by firing a bullet on a whim at a challenging target. Warriors who did this soon learned they had a fine rifle but no bullets.

With the coming of the Season of Large Fruit, the men complained of running out of ammunition. We held a council to discuss where to find more. We decided we had to go where *Nakai-yes* had big *ranchos* and where miners and Americans were. We would do what we could south of the border and then raid north into the land the White Eyes called Arizona, staying close to the border. It was a good time to raid in Blue Coat country. A time of many rains kept the Blue Coat scouts from tracking us well. The tanks and springs all running over with water and the moon full in three days and staying bright for seven or eight more made it easy to travel at night without much chance of scouts seeing us. We took no novitiates. We had to travel fast, and there were many more Blue Coats north of the border than *Nakai-yi* soldiers south of it.

We rode west across the *Río* Bavispe toward an old settlement, Turicachi. There were mines in that place with miners needing supplies and freighters to haul them. These freighters were easy to ambush and destroy. We hid behind brush and boulders on both sides of a canyon road to ambush a supply wagon and a few cattle escorted by two Americans and two *Nakai-yes*. One American we killed, and we wounded the other in the gunfire, but, somehow, the two *Nakai-yes* managed to duck our bullets, grab the wounded man, and ride away in a cloud of dust like the twisting wind.

One warrior ran to the middle of the road, threw up his rifle, and aimed to take at least one of the *Nakai-yes,* but the *hombre* had his old revolver in his hand and, almost without looking, turned and fired behind him in the direction of the warrior. The warrior staggered backwards and flopped into the trail dust. The *Nakai-yi*s shot hit him in the center of his heart. He was on the ghost pony before he hit the ground. It was the luckiest shot I had ever seen, or else *Ussen* had decided to call the warrior to the Happy Place without warning. We all stared in disbelief at the warrior with the bright, dark red hole in the center of his chest as the *Nakai-yes* and American disappeared up the road north.

The warriors were quick to cut the horses from the harness and fill sacks with supplies as they plundered the wagon. They also found on the wagon two lever guns and a wooden box filled with cartridges that fit our American lever guns. *Hi yeh!* I thought, *This will be a fine time raiding.*

We rode up the wagon road toward Agua Prieta and then stopped in the *bosque* of the *río* to eat, rest a little, and decide where to raid next. Chihuahua and I talked it over. He agreed to take nine warriors with the wooden box of ammunition, the cattle, and sacks of plunder east across the *Río* Bavispe and cache it near the place the *Nakai-yes* called Pilares, where the women and young men guarding our mountain camp could come down and get it when they saw his smoke.

After leaving the plunder and cattle, Chihuahua would ride

west, cross the *Río* Bavispe, and raid along the road between the village of Bacanuchi and the mine at Cananea, before riding north toward the border where we would meet west of Naco.

I would take the other fifteen men, with Kaytennae as my *segundo,* ride fast, cross the *Río* San Pedro, and head for Cocóspera far to the west, where there were *ranchos grandes* that I expected to have much American ammunition, since they were near the border. They should also have many easy-to-take cattle, horses, and mules. From Cocóspera, we would attack *ranchos* on the way to the border to meet Chihuahua and his warriors. I thought the best and easiest place to raid on the north side of the border was in the Sonoita Valley, if we could do our raids quickly and leave before the Blue Coats came after us.

We rode hard and fast the rest of that day and nearly all night. The men slept in their saddles when they could. The moon was falling into the southern mountains when we found a *Nakai-yi rancho* near Cocóspera with many cattle and horses. We took the horses and cattle easily just as gray light began appearing behind the mountains to the east. It was close to dawn, and two *Nakai-yi* men who worked at the *rancho* were already up. One was just pulling up his pants' shoulder straps after leaving the little *casa* where the *Nakai-yes* and White Eyes do their personal business.

Like a ghost, Kaytennae came out of the dawn shadows. His shot hit the *Nakai-yi* in the head, and he fell backwards into the little *casa* doorway. When the other *Nakai-yi* heard the shot, he ran out the door of the *rancho casa* into three bullets shot by other warriors watching for him.

We ran over the body, through the door to scramble through the house, and took all the guns and ammunition we could find. In the pastures around the house, we found enough horses for every man to have two or three to ride when the one he was on grew tired and slowed.

We found another ranch worked by two men, a woman, and several children just south of the border. The woman in her garden saw us coming and screamed a warning to run for the *casa* to a small boy and an older girl working at the corral and two men in the barn.

We were too fast for them. They died quickly. I thought for a moment to keep the children, but they looked soft, and we were traveling fast. Better to kill them. We took much plunder from the *casa* and all the horses we could find. The *rancho* had a good supply of ammunition and some good rifles and revolvers. We took it all before riding on.

From the top of a high hill, I saw a cloud of dust made by running horses coming south toward the border. I watched it with my glasses. Soon I saw a column of Blue Coats, Apache scouts leading them. It was hard hiding our trail from scouts, and I didn't want to spend the sun worried about Blue Coats interfering with our raids. We turned south. I didn't think the Blue Coats would come far into the land of the *Nakai-yes* before they turned back.

Riding southeast we met and exchanged shots with a few *Nakai-yi* soldiers before we rode on. They were easy to outrun and not eager to follow us. As the shadows grew long, we came to a *rancho casa grande*. Yellow light glowed through the windows and, using my soldier glasses, I saw old ones eating with a family that had five children. They were enjoying their meal, laughing, talking, and taking food from large bowls. I understood their good time together, the old ones enjoying their children and grandchildren. But then my memories came as I watched the *Nakai-yes*.

I remembered seeing our women and children slaughtered by *Nakai-yi* soldiers at Aliso Creek. I remembered the *Nakai-yi* soldiers killing or taking slaves after the people drank too much mescal at Casas Grandes. I saw the face of my wife, Chee-hash-kish, sitting in some stinking guardhouse or prison waiting for sale to a *hacendado*. I remembered Alope, my children, and my mother lying in a drying pool of black blood. I called the warriors to me and told them what I saw and then remembered. It was time to make the *Nakai-yes* pay for their murders and taking slaves. I chose four young men, not long warriors, to take our revenge while the rest of us watched.

The chosen ones burst through the door and into the place where the *Nakai-yes* were eating. The woman and a child screamed. Many shots filled the room. In the light falling from a blood-red and purple sky, the smoke from the young warrior's rifles twisted and curled out the open door and into the still, suddenly silent night air. We heard another shot or two before whoops of celebration.

After I reminded them of what the *Nakai-yes* had done to our people, I was sure the young men would take their revenge and dare their ghosts to come as they used their knives to mangle the bodies. The *Nakai-yes* would remember how we repaid them for what they had done to us. I smiled. My warriors had done well this day.

Before we rested, we rode a while into the bright, moonlit darkness toward the place where we would meet Chihuahua and his warriors. Along the way, we raided another *rancho* or two for horses and mules and ambushed riders to take their weapons and ammunition. Chihuahua and his warriors appeared like ghosts from around the water tank where we agreed we would meet. The warriors spoke in low voices, joking and happy to see each other, reminding me of a whispering wind.

While the warriors rested, Chihuahua and I sat together in the cold night air, blankets around our legs, and rolled a cigarette. His band of warriors had done well in finding rifles and ammunition and a few horses and mules, and they had killed many *Nakai-yes*. By not traveling fast, we saved most of the horses and mules we had taken, which had now become a good-sized herd. He was glad to hear of what we had taken in our raids, and we both agreed that we had plenty of ammunition for many suns. We left our meeting place as gray light filled the eastern sky. It had been a good raid for showing the *Nakai-yes* our anger over what they had done to us.

CHAPTER 26
RETURN TO THE GREAT CANYON

Nakai-yi soldiers from a village we passed chased us for a while, but we easily outran them. The next dawn, we came to Baca-nuchi after riding through the day and night. We saw a *hacienda* shining in the bright glow of sunlight high on a mesa above the valley *río*. We knew such a *rancho grande* must belong to a *Nakai-yi jefe*. Chihuahua and I led the attack that killed them all at the *hacienda,* even the many *hombres* who hid from us. From them, we took many rifles and much ammunition. But the *jefe* of the place we could not find.

Four suns passed before we came to the camp of our families and enjoyed the good things we had taken during our long ride across Sonora. She-gha, Zi-yeh, and Shtsha-she, with our baby, met me with laughing faces and songs of triumph. Dohn-say, who helped them, looked even more beautiful and sang happily with them. Chappo, although I had only been gone ten suns, looked more like a grown man. He had done a grown man's work, helping guard the camp, while we were gone. I was proud of him.

We rested for seven suns. I decided to move south up the east branch of the *Río* Bavispe, but Chihuahua wanted to move to the west into the mountains that stretched toward the south between the east and west sides of the *Río* Bavispe.

Before we left our camp, *Ussen* spoke to me as I sat warming myself and staring into the low, orange and yellow flames of the fire outside our *wickiup*. He warned me that Mexican soldiers were coming from Bacanuchi, the town where we had attacked the *hacienda* of the *Nakai-yi jefe. Ussen* showed me the soldiers would come up the canyon trail we used to reach our camp and attack us in the early morning in three days. I told all this to Chihuahua and the warriors, and we decided to wait for the *Nakai-yes* and make them pay for coming to attack us.

The next sun, our people moved down the trail to the east side of the *Río* Bavispe flowing north. We camped hidden in a cane thicket by the sparking water where the children could play and swim and the women could bathe in privacy. The warriors returned to the boulder and brush-filled trail leading up from the west side of the *Río* Bavispe to our camp. Out of sight behind boulders and up high on brush-covered ridges, we made our ambush ready.

Early on the morning of the third sun, we were waiting when the *Nakai-yi* soldiers came, just as my vision had shown me. We killed a few from our hiding places, but then they ran back down the trail toward the *río,* their *jefes* right behind them with pistols drawn and firing at any and every shadow but hitting nothing. We waited for another attack, but they crossed the *río* and didn't come back.

Chihuahua and I talked. The soldiers coming had made him change his mind and decide his people were safer if they stayed with mine. We decided to go to the place where we liked to camp on the west side of the Great Canyon.

Two days after the women built their *wickiups* the warriors, Chihuahua, and I smoked in the shade under junipers on top of cliffs looking down and across the Great Canyon. Now that we had taken enough ammunition to last us through the year, we spoke of things the camp needed and where to raid next. I sat with my back to the canyon with the warriors circled in front of Chihuahua and me. It was a fine time, perhaps two hands before the evening meal. The air was warm and sleepy and filled with the sharp smell of pines and the sound of birds calling in the brush. We planned more dancing and singing that evening to celebrate our great raid in Sonora.

I was speaking on where and what we should raid. Kaytennae sat opposite me. I saw him frown and lean to one side, as if to look over my shoulder toward the other side of the Great Canyon. He had the best far-seeing eyes of any warrior I knew. He said, "Grandfather, I mean no disrespect interrupting you, but there are people who make a camp on the other side of the canyon from us."

I turned and looked across the canyon. I saw the tiny figures making a camp, but I could not see clearly enough to know if they were Apaches or *Nakai-yes*. I used my soldier glasses and recognized a tipi Juh had bought for Ishton a few harvests earlier.

I said to the council, "The people camping on the far side of the canyon are Juh's band." There were many nods and grunts of *"Enjuh."* I said, "I think we ought to wait on deciding about where to raid until we meet and speak with Juh and his warriors. Soon we see them?" They all agreed. We wanted to visit the great chief and *di-yen* and his people.

That night as we danced, some could hear drums from the far side of the Great Canyon when our drums stopped to begin a new dance. I had no doubt they heard ours. Soon we ought to cross the canyon and camp with Juh and his people. It had been four or five moons since we had last been with them. We were not far apart as ravens fly, but to go down our side of the canyon and back up the other side with women and children was a much longer path. I sent a couple of warriors to scout the path I thought would work, and they returned saying it was a long trail, but all our people could manage it in a sun, even the young ones, if they were careful and took their time.

We left the next day at sunrise and rode into the canyon

down a steep wash lined with boulders and big junipers we had to work around. In the steepest places, warriors helped the women and children down. It took some coaxing for a few of the horses and mules, but we reached the canyon bottom before the time of shortest shadows and moved south along the *río* until we came to a wash on the east side of the Great Canyon. This wash was not as steep as the one we had come down, but it was longer. There were many boulders we climbed over or passed around.

Again, the warriors helped the women and children and led the horses and mules up the steepest climbs, but they all made it. I led the people out of the wash to the top of the canyon's east side two hands on the horizon before the sun disappeared into the mountains. As we came out of the trees on top of the ridge, Juh strode forward from a crowd of his people, smiling and spreading his arms, welcoming us to join him and his people in their camp.

It was a happy time for us visiting people we had not seen for months and exchanging gifts and memories of our times together. Juh's band had watched us come and had made a great feast for us. We danced a long time that night. The moon was half full and spread good light.

The next sun, while our women and children set up lodges, Juh and I smoked and spoke of what had happened after we parted. I told him of our last raid and how well it went. He crossed his arms and nodded, saying several times, *"Enjuh, Enjuh."* Then he told me of a battle he had with *Nakai-yi* soldiers.

"We took horses and cattle from a *rancho grande,* but there were many soldiers in a village nearby. They came after us. We tried to hide and ambush them. But they were smart and, for two suns, we ran and fought, ran and fought, ran and fought. We killed a few soldiers but not enough to make them stop. One or two of our warriors had wounds that slowed them down, but they all lived to fight on.

"We were running low on ammunition. Many warriors thought we should leave the fight for another day when we had more bullets, but I led the warriors up a steep mountain, zigzagging and leaving a trail even a child could follow. When we got to the top, I told the warriors to roll a line of boulders parallel to the side of the trail. The boulders were heavy, and it took much grunting and sweating to get them in place.

"The soldiers came on slowly, watching carefully for an ambush. When most of the soldiers were on the part of the trail near the top before the last switchback, we rolled the boulders down on them." Juh laughed and clapped his hands. "I never knew *Nakai-yes*'s eyes could get so big. They screamed and tried to get out of the way. But it was too late. Those stones smashed over trees and brush and, along with a few trees the boulders pushed over, rolled down on the soldiers, crushing all of them. When we came down from the mountain, we killed those who managed to survive, took all their guns and ammunition, and walked away ready to fight again. We lost no warriors that day. It was a good day to kill *Nakai-yes*."

I laughed with Juh and thought, *This man is a great chief. I learn much from him.*

A moon after we moved our camp to that of Juh's, the warriors had grown restless. Hunting was easy, our women eager in the blankets, and our children enjoyed their games. Juh and I held a council with the warrior leaders to decide where and when to raid next. Some wanted to move south where we rarely went; others, north to give the Blue Coats another taste of our medicine. Then Nana stood, groaning with his lame foot and stiff knees. We all listened to his words coming from his chest in his deep, whispery, old man's voice.

"Brothers! Hear me. I and my little band barely escaped the

Nakai-yes killing, scalping, or enslaving us when Terrazas and his *segundo*, Juan Mata Ortiz, found Victorio nearly out of ammunition at Tres Castillos and wiped out our people. The next harvest, I took more than a moon's time of revenge riding on a long raid against the *Nakai-yes* and White Eyes, but I want more satisfaction, more *Nakai-yi* blood.

"The *Nakai-yes* betrayed many at Casas Grandes. They gave you mescal, watched you get drunk, then killed many and took many slaves. Juh has raided in Chihuahua since then, killing many soldiers, and leaving many *ranchos* and villages burning. Still, we have not paid the full debt we owe the *Nakai-yes* for our betrayal in Casas Grandes. Still we have not saved any enslaved at Casas Grandes. We know soldiers from Galeana attacked us at Casas Grandes. I hear stories that Juan Mata Ortiz lives on a *rancho* in Galeana near those soldiers. I think we can attack and wipe out the soldiers in Galeana. Maybe then we settle my hot blood that cries for Victorio's full revenge. Maybe you also want some revenge for what those soldiers did to us in Casas Grandes. That is all I have to say."

Nana grunted with effort when he sat down. The warriors were silent and still as if on a deer hunt. All followed Nana with their eyes and then looked at Juh and me. Wind sighed again through the tops of the junipers around us. Children played and called to each other while their mothers talked and used their sharp knives as they cut and dried meat. High above us, a great, black bird soared and called to the sun. Juh's eyes were bright as he slowly nodded for me to speak. I stood and looked at each warrior and leader.

"Warriors! Leaders! Fearless men! Hear me. Nana speaks with a fine memory and the wisdom of a grandfather. Most of you lost someone in your family in the attack in Casas Grandes. Payment lingers for the deaths and slavery of our loved ones in that attack. Nana still wants the blood of the *jefe* and his *segundo* who wiped out Victorio. I want my wife Chee-hash-kish out of slavery, but I have not yet taken anyone I can trade for her, and my knife hungers for the throats of those who took her. I know my chief, Juh, hungers to settle accounts for what they did to us. I know he'll agree if we decide to go to Galeana. We go to make right a great wrong against us. There is no dishonor if you choose not to attack Galeana. If you choose not to do this, then move to the big trees to your left so we can judge if there are enough men to make the attack with the warriors who want to fight the Galeana soldiers."

I looked at each warrior, each leader. No one moved toward the big trees. I knew then many soldiers at Galeana must surely die. We would avenge Victorio and the killing and enslavement of our families. If *Ussen* made it so, then perhaps this *Nakai-yi*, Juan Mata Ortiz, would be ours also. Nana's debt paid in full. There was a big smile on Juh's face.

I said, "*Enjuh*. At last we'll have our justice. The war leaders and chiefs will decide how we attack Galeana soldiers. Tell your women and children we start east for the mountains above Galeana in two days. Be ready."

As if in one voice the council shouted with lifted arms and glittering eyes, *"Hi yeh! Hi yeh! Hi yeh!"*

Chapter 27
A Blood for Blood Debt Is Settled

We left the Great Canyon camp and rode east two days after the council decided to attack Galeana soldiers. On the way, we danced in our night camps and ate good meals. My women were eager for me, and I enjoyed them all. Even Shtsha-she, a new mother only a few moons, wanted me to come to her. Our baby grew strong in her fine *tsach,* and we all enjoyed playing with and teaching her.

In eight suns, we were in the camp we had made three harvests past when Juh and I had attacked the wagon train carrying beans through Chocolate Pass. Our camp was in a good place with springs and a big tank for water, a good source of firewood and, most importantly, a clear look at Galeana in the distance. We sent scouts to study ranches around the town.

The moon, while not yet full, still gave enough light for Juh and me to ride the road between Galeana and Chocolate Pass to learn how best to attack the soldiers. I saw and remembered the brush-lined wash that ran by the road as it approached Chocolate Pass. As I studied the wash and thought how to use it, Juh rode on toward the pass. I soon turned my attention from the wash to follow Juh through the pass. I stared bewildered toward the pass in the dim moonlight. Juh had disappeared. I had not studied the wash long enough that he could have ridden out of sight, even if it was dark.

I trotted my pony down the road, studying both sides to make sure I hadn't somehow missed seeing Juh. After I rode the distance of a long rifle shot, Juh appeared so suddenly beside me, I thought a night spirit had come to attack me. "Wah! Juh is that you? Where were you hiding?"

He laughed. His words made little clouds in the cool, night air as he said, "Yes, Brother. It's me. There is a large low place beside us. Every warrior in our camp could sit mounted there and not be seen from the road until the rider was nearly on top of them."

I looked around us, but there was not enough light to tell if there was a low place nearby. I looked to the other side of the road, and a short distance off was a hill covered with rocks and brush, casting black shadows in the soft white light of the moon. The air was cold. It made me tremble and hunch my shoulders up under my jacket, but it didn't seem to bother Juh. He jerked his head toward our camp, and we rode off the road and into the shadows of the mountains.

After we heard what the scouts told us about ranches around Galeana and the soldiers in the town, Juh crossed his arms and nodded. We held council. He told us his plan. Even old Nana thought it a good one.

We sharpened our knives, oiled our rifles, and, after a good meal with our families, danced for war. Well before the sun came the next day, we rode down to the *llano* and across to the road from Galeana toward Chocolate Pass and Casas Grandes. The men who hid in the wash left their ponies, held by novitiates, out of sight behind a hill near the road. The brush and weeds in the wash made it easy for them to string out down the wash and hide so only the sharpest of eyes, knowing they were there, would see them. Juh led the rest of the warriors into the low place I had missed when I rode past him three nights before.

Juh and I picked a few men, the bravest in battle, to ride with the scouts who had watched Galeana. For two days they took horses from *ranchos* around the edges of Galeana but no one came out to chase them. On the third day they raided horses from the *rancho* of Juan Mata Ortiz along the *río* that passed to the west of Galeana.

On the third try I stayed with the men in the wash. We watched the glow of golden light grow behind the mountains off to our right. The men sent to Galeana wouldn't be driving back horses they had taken from Juan Mata Ortiz with the Ortiz and the *Nakai-yi caballero* soldiers chasing them until the sun was near the time of shortest shadows.

We wrapped in our blankets in the cold morning air, watched the sun come, and ate from our sacks of dried meat pounded together with nuts, berries, and mescal. The warriors were in good spirits and laughed and joked with each other. It would be a good day to make the *Nakai-yes* pay for what they had done to us and our families in Casas Grandes. Every warrior picked a place to hide near the road and hid under his blanket as the sun floated higher in the brilliant, blue sky toward the time of shortest shadows. We waited.

A freight wagon passed by driven by a wrinkled old man wearing a great floppy hat and a dirty white shirt. The load wasn't heavy. The mules pulling the wagon trotted along with little effort. I thought the mules worth having but kept the men still and in their places. We were after bigger game.

Not long after the wagon passed, two *vaqueros,* laughing and joking, rode by us. They had fine *pistolas* in holsters on their sides and long rifles in tooled leather scabbards hanging under big *Nakai-yi* saddles decorated with silver *conchas.* I thought their showing that much of their wealth to the world meant they were good *pistoleros,* their weapons alone worth the taking. The *conchas* on the saddle would make good belt ornaments, and the saddles would trade for much whiskey in Casas Grandes.

But we waited. *Riders pass by.* They were lucky men not to die that day. I watched them ride down the road toward Galeana with my Blue Coat glasses until they disappeared.

I saw a little dust cloud toward Galeana before I put the glasses away. I watched for a time and saw it growing larger. *Ha! Maybe now they come.* I made a signal for a warrior to listen to the ground. He drove his knife deep into the earth and then put his ear to the end of the handle. Soon he raised his head and nodded. I reminded the warriors of our plan.

"Ha! Brothers! The *Nakai-yes* come. Remember, we let them pass as they chase those who have taken their ponies. Shoot when I tell you but not before. Soon we'll have our revenge."

We heard the hoofbeats coming toward us and the occasional snap of revolver fire, but no thunder from long rifles. I laughed. Our men were shooting the pistols. The *Nakai-yi* solders didn't shoot at them for fear of killing the horses we had stolen. The sound of the running horses grew louder, and we heard the war yells of our brothers driving them. I climbed up behind a bush with my glasses to look down the road. The warriors drove a nice herd of ponies of all colors, reds and browns, blacks and pintos, even a couple of palominos. More warriors, their hair streaming back in the wind, followed them, their revolver shots and war cries drawing the soldiers on. They thundered past us. Just as their dust began to settle the *Nakai-yi* soldiers galloped past, stirring it again. Their leader in his uniform, slapping the rear of his pony with the flat of his drawn saber, looked familiar. It might be Juan Mata Ortiz. I knew Nana would be glad he came with us for this fight.

As the warriors rumbled past, Juh and his men, waiting in the low place, charged up on to the road and began firing at the *Nakai-yi* soldiers. The bullets raised little geysers of dust around the charging soldiers. Their *jefe* jerked his mount to a stop, made a circling motion with his raised arm, and rode back the way he and his soldiers had come. My men appeared, as if by magic, out of the wash, firing as the *Nakai-yes* retreated toward them. The *Nakai-yi jefe* raced off the road charging toward the protection of the rock and juniper-covered hill not far away.

The *Nakai-yes,* beating their horses into exhaustion, made the top of the hill, jumped off, and, with their *jefe* yelling and pointing, began moving rocks to make a wall they could hide behind to shoot.

Juh led the warriors to the foot of hill and saw what the *Nakai-yes* were doing. He directed Kaytennae, Chato, and two or three other sharpshooters to take a position near a lone cedar tree at the base of the hill and to use their skill to keep the *Nakai-yes* undercover while the warriors divided into two groups, one moving toward the front of the soldier wall, and another group, led by Bonito, moving up the hill from the back side. They pushed rocks at least the size of their heads in front of them as they crawled forward. Juh, Nana, and I stayed at the cedar with the sharpshooters.

There wasn't much rifle fire from either side as the warriors crawled up the hill and the sharpshooters kept the *Nakai-yi* soldiers huddling below the top of their wall. I looked back over my shoulder and saw dead soldiers and horses scattered along the way we had come, already cooking in the hot, afternoon sun.

A scream of anger came from the back side of the hill, and suddenly the warriors were pouring over the wall of rocks the *Nakai-yi* soldiers had built. There was no gunfire, just fighting hand to hand with our war clubs and knives and soldiers with their long knives, men grunting and swearing and killing as they wrestled and swung the knives in long, swooping arcs or stabbed at each other, fighting for their lives.

A horse charged out of the fighting and down the hill toward Galeana. A *Nakai-yi* soldier was on him, whipping him to make the exhausted animal run for its life. Kaytennae swung his rifle to take down the horse and then the soldier, but I yelled, "No! Let him go. He'll bring back others, and we'll have more to kill!"

It wasn't long before Bonito stood on the rocks shaking his arms above his head and giving the victory yell. Juh, the others, and I jumped on our ponies and rode to the top. Soldiers, their bodies stabbed or their heads crushed, laid scattered across the top of the hill. An older *Nakai-yi* soldier, wearing symbols of a *jefe,* surrounded by warriors, their knives ready, still lived, his gray hair matted with blood and his arm cut and bleeding. No sound came from his lips, and the hatred in his eyes glowed.

Bonito, his eyes bright with excitement, ran to our horses yelling, "Nana! Nana! We have a gift for you! Come and see."

Nana groaned, "*Enjuh.* I would see this gift," as he swung off his horse, staggered a little as he got his balance, and limped forward to follow Bonito. Juh and I dismounted and followed them.

Bonito, grinning and motioning toward him, led Nana to stand before the *Nakai-yi jefe* the warriors surrounded. Nana stared in silence at the man for the time it takes for a long sigh, raised his hands, and said, "Ho! *Ussen* blesses us. It is Juan Mata Ortiz. I have waited two harvests to find him and his *jefe,* Terrazas. They are the *jefes* who wiped out Victorio and lied that the Tarahumara coward Mauricio Corredor killed him with a rifle, when Kaytennae will tell you Victorio stabbed himself in the heart after he had no more bullets. They are *jefes* who sold our people into slavery and carried scalps of the dead tied to long poles through the streets of Ciudad Chihuahua. These are the men who tried to kill you after getting you drunk on mescal in Casas Grandes."

Nana turned to look at Juh, watching with his arms crossed and slowly nodding. "Yes, Grandfather, I know this Juan Mata

Ortiz. He is the soldier *jefe* in Galeana."

Nana shrugged his shoulders. "He is your prisoner. Your men took him. Do with him as you wish. I have said all I will say."

Our warriors gathered behind us. Juh turned to them. "The only way to destroy evil is by fire. Scoop out a place here. Gather brush and fill it. Stretch this one out over it and tie his hands and feet to the corners. Hurry. Soon more come for us to kill."

The warriors scrambled, some to dig, some to gather brush. Nana nodded. *"Enjuh."*

I never saw fear in the eyes of Mata Ortiz. He spat on the ground when Nana finished speaking. It was good to have such enemies and to destroy them with fire. Some warriors did as Juh said; others stripped the soldier bodies of guns and ammunition. A warrior made a little fire big enough to light a torch while others tied Mata Ortiz over the brush piled in the scooped-out place.

Juh lighted a torch and handed it to Nana. "Light the fire, and burn this evil, Grandfather."

Nana took the fire from Juh and hobbled toward Mata Ortiz. He stood between Mata Ortiz's feet. "You show courage, *Jefe*. Perhaps you will enjoy the fire eating your man parts." He thrust the flames between Mata Ortiz's legs at his crotch and into the brush. The brush caught and burned quickly, as did the pants Ortiz wore. Mata Ortiz, his head back, his face twisted in agony, his mouth wide, lips stretched over his teeth, was a strong man, a good enemy. He made no sound as the flames spread and the stink of burning flesh filled the air, rising high in the black smoke coming from his body.

Juh motioned for us to mount. We had more *Nakai-yes* to kill. He stopped to look at Mata Ortiz, his skin and meat over his bones turning to black char as his reflexes jerked his arms and feet to be free of the fire. *"Adios,* Mata Ortiz. You are evil but a brave warrior."

We rode down the wagon trail toward Galeana. Behind us, the black smoke of Mata Ortiz rose straight up in a feather-like plume, high in the hot, still air. I used my soldier glasses and saw the dust of many horses coming out of Galeana. We rode on. Soon I could see the black specks of horses in front of the dust cloud and then the soldier horses clearly.

Juh stopped and motioned for our warriors to spread out. The soldier horses came on, hurrying, their riders anxious to destroy those who had killed their brothers. A good rifle shot away, they stopped. Their leaders pointed toward us. Too far away for us to understand them, we heard yelled commands.

The soldiers dismounted and began to dig, the sand flying out of their trench like that of a desert rat hurrying to dig a hiding hole from a snake. The shadows grew long. We sat our ponies and watched the soldiers work. Soon the sun fell into the mountains, and the light grew dim. When it grew dark, we rode away.

We returned to our women and children, but we had no victory dance. A few suns earlier, *Ussen* had warned a *di-yen* named She-neah that he would die if he fought that day. He fought, despite *Ussen*'s warning. He died, shot in the middle of his forehead. It was a sad but sweet time. We lost a good *di-yen* but wiped out twenty-two *Nakai-yi* soldiers counting the burning of Mata Ortiz.

Our women fed us and put medicine on our wounds. As we rested, a rider came with word that soldiers from Casas Grandes were coming to attack us. It was all right. Chihuahua and I wanted to return to our camping grounds high in the mountains near the headwaters of the *Río* Bavispe. Juh returned to his

Guaynopa stronghold on the rim of the Great Canyon. We expected to gather again in the next Season of Little Eagles.

CHAPTER 28
JUH'S DISASTER

Chihuahua and I camped at the headwaters of the *Río* Bavispe. Our people had good water, plenty of firewood, and plentiful game in the big meadows and under the tall pines. We rested with our women and children and trained our sons in the customs of raiding and the warpath and how they should act as novitiates.

My wives kept me happy. They worked well together; our fire never went out; they kept food in the pot; and all but Zi-yeh were eager for me in the blankets. I was glad I never had to beat them. Zi-yeh told me with shining eyes that our first child grew in her belly. *Enjuh!* But it seemed such a short time we were under the blankets before we made a child. Time flew like a hawk diving on a rabbit. I knew I grew old, but I didn't feel old. I just moved slower than I did when I first became a warrior.

As we rested, I often went to a cliff edge high above the camp to listen for *Ussen*'s voice and watch over the camp. Memories of my life with Chee-hash-kish filled my mind. I remembered our first days under the blanket and how she eased my sorrow for having lost Alope and our children. I thought of the birth times of Chappo and Dohn-say and how proud I was of such strong, handsome children. She taught them well while I was off raiding and warring. They would be a credit to our people.

As I took other wives, she was their natural leader. There was never any nasty infighting among my women. Chee-hash-kish led by example, and every woman knew her place in our family and was happy with it. Now my fine wife was a slave to some *Nakai-yi* dog. How I wished I could kill them all, but that was *Ussen*'s choice, not mine.

I counseled with Chihuahua and my war leaders and decided it was time to raid and give the novitiates a chance to see what warriors see and help them while we could before snow filled the trails and passes along the steep cliffs. We left the women and children with plenty of meat and the old men to watch the camp and crossed the *Río* Bavispe west and north into Sonora to the roads for packtrains on the way to Ures. There were many packtrains to choose from, but we waited to take only the ones that seemed to be the richest.

We slipped around the towns, stealing cattle and horses, being so careful none of the *Nakai-yes* saw us to raise the alarm. At last, a packtrain came heavy with trading post supplies such as blankets, pots and pans, cloth, axes, and knives that would be very useful in our camps, and we took it, killing all the *Nakai-yes* with it. We never unloaded the packs, only looked to see what was there, before we headed back to our camp just as the first snows came. It was a fine raid, and all the novitiates did well.

I was proud of Chappo and Fun. The women were very happy with the packtrain supplies, and the cattle we had taken gave us enough meat to easily live through three or four moons during Ghost Face Season when snow filled the trails and passes.

When the Ghost Face winds didn't howl often and snow began turning to water early in the Season of Little Eagles, we left our Bugatseka camp at the headwaters of the *Río* Bavispe and moved over the mountains to camp on the edge of the Great Canyon. The child in Zi-yeh's belly had grown large, ready to be born, but it waited until we camped in comfort on the rim of the Great Canyon. Zi-yeh, even as small as she was, delivered a boy,

strong and healthy, in less than a night and had it at her breast
before bright shafts of sunlight flew through the tops of the tall
pine trees standing guard over our camp. I was proud of my
new son and named him Fenton to remember a friend who sold
and gave us supplies near the border when the Blue Coats
weren't looking.

One day near the end of Ghost Face, I sat in the sun studying
the bottom and *arroyos* down the sides into the canyon far below
me when I saw Juh's band moving toward the camp. Juh toward
the back, where warriors stayed to defend their people, rode
slow and stiff, bouncing on his saddle rather than riding with
his usual smooth, fluid rhythm. He usually arrived at this camp
before us or within a few days of our coming to the Great
Canyon, but nearly a moon had passed before his band came to
join us. Most of the warriors rode farther back than normal
from Juh and the band was much smaller than the last time we
had seen them. The faces of Naiche, Chato, and Kaytennae
were grim and sour, and many shuffled, dragging their feet, or
limped as though they had wounds. I looked among the women
but didn't see Juh's favorite wife, my sister, Ishton, or all of
Chato's and Naiche's families.

Children in our camp saw Juh coming and ran to tell their
mothers, who came from the camp with smiling faces that soon
turned to questioning frown wrinkles twisted across their
foreheads as they moved to meet their friends. We were all glad
to see our brothers and sisters in Juh's band come to us, but
sorrow settled over the camp like a gray day with falling mist
that wouldn't go away.

After our first welcome, Juh disappeared into his camp before
coming to my fire as the glow of the rising moon began to light
the black, velvet sky painted across one side with a milk *río* of
points of light. I welcomed him, and we smoked a cigarette to

the four directions. He sat staring at the low yellow, orange, and blue flames for a while before he said, "I will be chief no more. I haven't protected my people. They come to you, asking that you lead them. I don't blame them."

I said, "Brother, you're the greatest chief of the Chiricahuas, and the Chihenne people followed you to live in the strongholds you have in Chihuahua. I see many in your band are missing, including my sister, your wife. Tell me what has happened."

A wolf howled and *googés* (whip-poor-wills) near the edge of the canyon called as Juh said, "We took much from the *Nakai-yes* in raids across Chihuahua during the Seasons of Large Fruit and Earth Is Reddish Brown—cattle and horses, cloth, clothes, food—many things our women needed and wanted. We were moving toward a place I picked for winter camp when we took four loaded burros from an old man leading them. When we looked at their load, the burros were packing many jugs of mescal, a good treasure, at a good time to find."

I grinned and smacked my lips, wishing I had some of that good mescal now.

"I made the warriors wait until we camped for the winter before they drank it. As much raiding as we had done in those late seasons, I expected the *Nakai-yes* in Chihuahua to come after us, and I knew the first place they would look was the stronghold at Guaynopa. I moved our camp about a day's ride west of Guaynopa and hid in a big *arroyo* between the forks of a stream that emptied into the *Río* Sátachi."

"Hmmph. A smart move."

Juh shook his head. "Maybe so, but it didn't do us any good. We drank too much of that mescal. I knew the *Nakai-yes* were looking for us, and we doubled our guards. I even had my slave boys on watch. About a moon after we made camp, one morning in the deep dark before dawn, *Nakai-yes* moving up the trail narrowly missed stepping on one of my slave boys on watch with some Chihenne warriors. Most of the *Nakai-yes* were Tara-humara. They saw him and could tell he was a *Nakai-yi*. They motioned for him to join them, but he took off running down the path to the camp chased by a *Nakai-yi* on horseback. The boy ran into our tipi screaming, "*Nakai-yes* attack! *Nakai-yes* attack!"

"I told my son Delzhinne to stay and protect the women and children. I grabbed my rifle and cartridges and, with my second son Daklegon, ran to fight the *Nakai-yes*. They charged into the camp from two directions firing their rifles and setting fires to all that would burn. Some of the women, already up to gather their morning firewood, were the first to fall. With the *Nakai-yes* in the village, we had to be careful where we fired to avoid hitting our own people. Light from the sun came and helped us, but much smoke was in the air. It was a hard fight, and we couldn't drive the *Nakai-yes* away, and then more came up to attack us from behind."

I knew the answer before I asked the question, and sorrow like a big ball of thorns was in my throat. I croaked, "My sister Ishton? What happened to her?"

Juh puffed his cheeks and stared at the fire, water on the edge of his eyes. "My sons Daklugie and Delzhinne told me the story. Ishton was in the tipi with our new baby girl as Daklugie, my youngest son, and my recently married daughter, Jacali, scrambled to gather food and ammunition for a run to the *arroyo*. Delzhinne, on his knees, fired at *Nakai-yes*, their horses nearly to the door of our tipi. Jacali's husband dashed into the tipi telling everyone to take the baby and run for the little stream in the *arroyo*. Ishton was lifting the baby's *tsach* when a bullet hit it. It never made a sound dying on its cradleboard and the bullet passed on through Ishton.

"Ishton laid the *tsach* down and grabbed the empty rifle Delzhinne had dropped. Fast and furious, she was loading it when another bullet knocked her back. Then Jacali, ready to run, her arms filled with blankets and food, fell, hit in the knee. Delzhinne and Jacali's husband stood at the door of the tipi, taking careful aim and hitting and diverting many riders close to the tipi.

"Suddenly, the firing stopped, and the *Nakai-yes* pulled back to organize a second charge. Ishton told the others to run for the *arroyo* before the *Nakai-yes* came back. Delzhinne squatted down to pick her up, but she told him she was dying and that he must help the others. He argued with her. He wanted to save her, but she wouldn't let him. She told him and Jacali's husband to take Jacali and hide her in the *arroyo*, so they lifted Jacali in a blanket to run for the *arroyo* when a bullet smashed into her husband and killed him. Delzhinne picked up Jacali, tore the blanket from her dead husband's hands, and, with Daklugie, ran. In the *arroyo*, they waded upstream from the camp and hid her in a brush thicket with a little food and her knife. She vowed the *Nakai-yes* would never take her alive. I have brave children, Geronimo."

My heart knotted in grief over the death of my sister. There was nothing Juh could have done. Still, I couldn't help thinking, *How could you let this happen?*

I shook my head in despair and sorrow. *All our children are brave, Juh. When will our suffering end?*

"The *Nakai-yes* charged three more times, burnt all our lodges, after taking anything they thought was valuable, and rode up and down the sides of the *arroyo* shooting into the brush. We were nearly out of ammunition and had to wait a while to get some from a nearby cache. The *Nakai-yes* scalped twelve men, women, and children, took thirty-three women and children captive including Chato's wife and two of his children, and rescued a slave girl who called herself Clemente García.

"With more ammunition, the surviving men and I attacked

the retreating *Nakai-yes* when they were a short distance from our camp. We killed maybe four, wounded that many, and took back a mule and ten horses, but I lost two of my best warriors. *Ussen* has turned his power away from me."

Juh stared at the fire for a time, shook his head, and looked up at the stars and swallowed before he looked at me and said, "It was a very bad day, Geronimo. We had to live on stored food in the middle of Ghost Face as we moved south. The old and wounded rode the only horses and mules we had. We moved out of the mountains, traveling in the open only at night and having fires only when we could hide the light. Always, we headed here for this camp in the Great Canyon.

"On the way, the men often argued, even wrestled over what happened in the attack. Now that we're here, only my family and a friend or two will stay with me. The rest think you're the best to lead them. You're certainly the oldest and wisest war leader after me, but I have no heart, no stomach, to lead the people. I think too often of my lost family. I think you must lead the people. That is all I have to say."

Juh stared into the fire for a long time. I saw the rippling of his jaw muscles as he clenched his teeth. I thought, *Yes, Juh. The people no longer want to stay with you. I must lead them now.*

I said, "Let us smoke another cigarette and talk together about what this means for the people. You must soon tell your story, as you told me, to all chiefs and leaders at one time so there is no dispute about what happened."

CHAPTER 29
RAIDS IN THE SEASON OF LITTLE EAGLES

During the last days of Ghost Face, the war leaders and chiefs met and smoked many times to discuss where to raid. We decided to make two raids at the same time. I and Chihuahua would go south and west into Sonora down around Ures and its surrounding ranches with eighty men and novitiates to take cattle and horses, food supplies, and any goods for the camp we could find.

Chato and Bonito would lead a group of twenty-six hardened warriors, fast movers, across the border to look for ammunition, rifles, and pistols, ambushing packtrains headed for the forts, raiding miners' camps, and slipping up to San Carlos to learn the latest news. The Chato and Bonito band included Naiche, Cathla, Shoie, Dutchy, Beneactiney, Atelnietze, Mangas, and Tzoe, all strong, well-known warriors. The other warriors with them were not as well known among the people, but the warriors all knew who they were and how well they could fight. The women and children we would leave in camps at Bugatseka high in the mountains near the headwaters of the *Río* Bavispe protected by fourteen Chihennes, survivors from Victorio's band led by Loco.

By the time the warm winds began to blow at the beginning of the Season of Little Eagles, we had made ready our weapons, cleaning and oiling our rifles, straightening and cleaning arrows, sharpening our knives, making new moccasins, including spares, and making good, strong rawhide ropes the *Nakai-yes* called *reatas*.

Our women gave us roots from the yucca to wash our hair. It was important to be clean and strong when a man went raiding or on the warpath. It is important that a man always stays clean and strong for whatever he is to face.

All, except Juh, left together as one group. During the Ghost Face, all the people, except for Juh's sons and Loco's people, looked to me to lead them, especially after Juh refused to speak up at council meetings and remained sad and unapproachable. As the Season of Little Eagles approached and warm winds began to blow, making the snow melt in the high passes, Juh left the camp with his three sons, a warrior, and four women and children, but he left Jacali with us. Her wounded leg left her crippled, and she needed the care of women experienced in healing bad wounds. Juh led them north toward the Blue Mountains where the *Río* Yaqui flowed. I was sad to see him go, but every man must choose what is best for him and his family.

Before splitting into separate raiding parties, we camped south of Huachinera for a last meal together before exposing ourselves to the guns and long knives of the *Nakai-yes* and White Eyes. The next day, after we crossed the *Río* Bavispe, Chato and Bonito led their warriors northwest toward the border. All the warriors following Chihuahua and me were on foot. We followed the trail we often used between Tepache and Moctezuma, ambushed a packtrain, and took a few supplies, but there didn't seem to be much movement on the roads.

Chihuahua and I talked it over and decided to steal enough horses to mount every man and then attack every ranch and village we found. We raided many places southwest of Ures and left tall columns of smoke and many bodies scattered across ranches and villages we came to. Yahnozha, a novitiate with us, who in two or three harvests would be my best warrior, told me he counted 110 *Nakai-yes* and White Eyes we had killed. It was a very good raid.

We gathered a great herd of cattle, mules, and horses and drove it east across the *río* into the mountains above Huachinera and headed for our camps in the Bugatseka. We had loads of blankets, clothes, cloth, and many glass bottles of good American whiskey. We drank the whiskey and became very drunk while the novitiates stood guard over the camp, but the next morning, with pounding heads, we moved on.

Chato and his men returned to our camps at Bugatseka two days before Chihuahua and I returned. We moved slowly across the mountains because we had a much bigger herd than Chato, mostly cattle, but both groups had taken what we wanted and needed: cattle and horses, guns and ammunition, and provisions of all kinds. Chato and Bonito lost three men: Tzoe, who returned to San Carlos; Beneactiney, Tzoe's close friend, who was killed in a raid on a camp cooking wood (a charcoal camp); and a lesser known warrior. Chihuahua and I had lost one warrior. For the distance we covered, the plunder we took, and the novitiates gaining raid experience, it had been a very good raid.

Chato and Bonito had also taken a little White Eye boy of maybe six or seven harvests whom we could use for trading with the White Eyes. He had red hair the women liked to touch and rub, and they wanted to keep him. He didn't talk much, but he didn't cry or make noise either. Naiche had his woman, Hah-o-zinne, keep the boy after two warriors argued over who had a right to him.

Because he didn't talk, Naiche thought he was weak-minded. I studied his sad eyes and had seen them before in White Eye children we kept after they had seen their parents die. Some disappeared inside themselves forever; others came back. Naiche and his woman would have to wait and see if this one came back. As long as he was quiet, Naiche's woman wanted him.

The warriors in both bands rested, and then we met in council under tall pine trees near a spring on a saddle between two mountains. We told our raiding stories, while the women, boys, and old people slaughtered cattle and dried meat. That night, we planned a victory dance even though we had lost Tzoe, who had not ridden the ghost pony, Beneactiney, and the lesser known warrior.

The warriors sat on the pine straw in the shade, and I prayed to *Ussen*, thanking him for letting us do our work and asking that he receive as great and powerful warriors Beneactiney and the other warrior riding the ghost pony to the Happy Place. We smoked, and then I asked Chato to tell the story of the raid he led.

Chato stood and spoke as though he were a great chief. Chato was a fine, smart warrior, but none liked him because he was arrogant and wanted all to know how strong and powerful his medicine was.

He said, "We slipped across the border, using the night, and moved quietly into the hills near the village the White Eyes call 'Tombstone.' We found and raided a camp cooking wood for the White Eyes to burn (charcoal) for hot fires. We killed three, uhmm, maybe four, White Eyes there and took their weapons and supplies. Farther down the trail, we found another such camp and killed one man we saw tending cooking fires for wood. We hid in the corral and called for those in a tent to come out, but there was no answer. We shot into their tent in case there was someone there, but there was no return fire. Beneactiney and Tzoe charged the tent to take the supplies that might be there. But a White Eye was hiding in the brush behind the tent and shot once, killing Beneactiney."

It was hard on everyone to lose a warrior, especially one as strong as Beneactiney. All the warriors listening to Chato were still and stone-faced as he continued telling of killing three miners and then a handful of White Eyes and stealing fresh horses. I knew Tzoe and Beneactiney had been as close as brothers.

I said, "Why did Tzoe leave us?"

Chato shook his head. "He had a very heavy heart after his good friend went to the Happy Place. It is less than a harvest since he lost two wives and a child and was wounded at Aliso Creek. We rode on, intending to learn what we could by slipping onto the reservation.

"When we camped for the night on the great mountain to the east of San Carlos, I sent Cathla and Dutchy to learn if Merejildo Grijalva would act as a go-between in case we ever decided to surrender."

I made a face. Chato looked at the ground, but then he lifted his chin in defiance and said, "You always say we must be prepared for anything. Maybe Grijalva we need, maybe not."

I waved my hand for Chato to go on. I just hated to think we might ever surrender again to the Blue Coats, when we were safe from them in the land of *Nakai-yes*. We could always hold our own with the *Nakai-yes*.

Chato went on with his story. "Tzoe sat by himself high up the mountain watching the reservation as the sun disappeared. That night he came to me and said his medicine told him he needed to return to San Carlos. His family survivors needed support. Bonito and I talked it over and agreed that, if he wanted to go, that was what Tzoe should do. Who were we to argue with *Ussen* or some other spirit guiding Tzoe? We gave him a few cartridges for his rifle, some food, and a pony so he could slip into San Carlos unnoticed. We have not seen or heard from Tzoe since he left us. He must have gotten back to his people."

"*Hi yeh!* We might have a good spy at San Carlos. We can hear the news whenever we need it, providing he's not caught. Tell us more of what happened to you."

"We decided to turn north up the San Simon Valley and then back east and raid where the Blue Coats would not expect to see us. We crossed the little pass in the Burro Mountains and stopped at the White Eye wagon road. That's where we found the boy with his parents eating in the shade while their wagon team rested. His parents tried to run and fight, but we killed them both. Two warriors claimed the boy and were ready to fight over him, but Bonito took the boy and kept him in front of his saddle and tied to his body. He didn't want the boy. But he took him to stop the fighting between those who claimed they wanted him. When he finally offered to give the boy to one or the other, they still couldn't agree on who should have him, so Naiche took him. We returned with a good herd of stock, many cartridges, some good weapons, and things for the camp—gifts we will give at the dance."

All the warriors and I said, *"Enjuh."* It had been a good raid. Chato and Bonito had done well. Then I spoke of our raids in Sonora south and west of Ures after we took horses for the warriors. We took a great heard of cattle, horses, mules, and much ammunition and other supplies. We would live well in the next Ghost Face. All the warriors voiced their good hearts to hear all this, and we looked forward to the dance we would hold that night.

CHAPTER 30
VISION OF DISASTER

The People danced all night celebrating the success of our raids in the yellow light of a great, roaring, snapping fire. The warriors drank all the whiskey we had captured except for a bottle or two I managed to hide for when I needed its medicine. Warriors who became very drunk fell into a deep asleep and made no trouble. Our plunder supplied many fine gifts and made all the people ready to sing and dance. Young women with shining, black hair smiled and laughed after the young men with whom they danced gave them special gifts. The elders closely watched the couples coming and going from the dance. I think few young women, if any, lost their virtue that night. Young men acknowledged for their success and bravery danced by the fire, enacting their bravery and how they killed enemies. They danced for recognition from all the people but especially from the warriors and the eligible, young women. I smiled to see every family given warm clothes, blankets, and pots. Some women were given long rolls of cloth and shared them with other women to make new clothes for all in their families.

We had many people in our camps, and the warriors had to raid often to keep them fed, with enough left over to save for the coming Seasons of Ghost Face and Little Eagles. A few days after the dance, fifteen warriors crossed the mountains to the west side of the *Río* Bavispe, after it turned south, and took a herd of about one hundred fifty cattle on a *rancho* near Oputo. When they returned, we butchered the cattle on the same day.

Days of plenty are always good days, but, a few days later, women were cooking some of the meat, and a field of grass caught on fire. We all worked to put it out. No harm was done, except the fire made a tall plume of smoke that reached high toward the clouds. *Nakai-yi* soldiers, seeing such a plume from far away, might learn where we camped. The council decided the villages needed to move to a place on a high ridge to the northwest where we could watch our old camp for invaders.

We left a few warriors to watch the trail to the old camping spot. Little did we know there were some already marching toward us. In two suns, one of the warriors watching the old camp trail ran to tell us *Nakai-yi* soldiers were coming and would be at the camp by the time of shortest shadows the next sun. The chiefs decided to use one of Juh's favorite tricks and lure the soldiers up a canyon side, ambush them near the top, and roll boulders down on them.

It was a good plan, and we killed several. There weren't enough boulders to wipe them out, and they regrouped and fired many wasted bullets at us before they retreated. The shadows were long, and I had no desire for the warriors to waste hard-earned ammunition on retreating *Nakai-yes*. They would not risk coming back. We let them go. Even so, we moved the camp again a few days later, so it would be harder to find, and we had better lookout places to watch for approaching raiders.

The day after we ambushed the *Nakai-yes,* for reasons I couldn't explain, I had a feeling that great evil was waiting for us over the next ridge. I questioned warriors who hunted in the mountains around us, but they had seen nothing to give alarm. None of the other leaders had seen or heard anything, either. I prayed to *Ussen* from a high place, but *Ussen* didn't speak to me. At the evening meal, my women and children drove the bad feeling away with the happy time we had together that gave me great comfort.

That night, *Ussen* spoke to me in a dream and at last, I understood my sense of evil waiting for us. I dreamed I led a raid on a great hacienda *casa*. My warriors and I stopped out of rifle range in a field spread out in front of the *casa's* double doors wide enough to let a big covered wagon pass through.

I studied the *casa* with my soldier glasses, trying to decide how best to attack it. One of the big double doors cracked open, and a woman slipped outside. She was too far away for me recognize, but from the easy grace with which she moved and her black hair hanging freely to her shoulders, I knew she was Apache. She came toward us a little distance and motioned us toward her.

My warriors looked at me and shook their heads, as if saying no. They thought she might lead us into a death trap. I, too, thought this for a moment, but decided Apache women would rather die than betray their men. I kicked my pony's sides, and he walked toward her as she continued to motion us to come. I scanned the wall behind her and saw no gun ports, no guns pointing at us anywhere, no sign of any other human. The only sound came from a little wind stirring the grass and brush in the light of a bright, cold day.

The woman wore a clean, white dress, and something about the way she moved stirred my memory. I felt my heart open when I recognized Chee-hash-kish. She said nothing as she continued to motion me forward, but my pony stopped and went no farther. I was ready to whack it with the barrel of my rifle, but, in the space of a breath, she vanished like an early morning *río* mist behind the great doors that closed with the sound of bolt locks sliding into place. The walls and doors of the great *casa* stood between us, and I saw her no more. When I turned back to my warriors, they, too, had vanished. I awoke deep in the night, saw through the door of our *wickiup* the bright, white, full moon floating like a white gourd in a great *río* of stars filling the darkness above the mountains to the south. I heard the night breeze rustle through the tops of the great, tall, pine trees, smelled the smoke from a dying fire, and knew that *Ussen* was telling me to find Chee-hash-kish and free her.

The next day, I met with the chiefs and leaders and told them of the vision that said to free our people held as slaves. Again, we decided on two raids. Chihuahua and his brother Ulzana would take about twenty warriors into Sonora to look for horses and cattle. I took about thirty of the best warriors, including Chato, Naiche, Bonito, Kaytennae, Zele, and Jelikinne, on a raid into Chihuahua looking for captives to trade for Chee-hash-kish and others taken into slavery during the attack at Casas Grandes.

We came down out of the mountains and took a few cattle, to provide us meat, that were probably not missed until long after we had faded back into the Blue Mountains. We would take them all if we returned that way, but our first purpose was to find captives.

We had rawhide boots on our ponies so their tracks in the trail dust left round holes that few *Nakai-yes* would understand were Apache pony tracks. We added to the confusion when we walked on our heels in the road dust, which also left round holes. Our warriors laughed when they thought of the slow-witted *Nakai-yes* trying to decide what animal could have left those tracks.

We crossed the road south of Galeana and north of Buenaventura and rode east across the *llano* and then through a low mountain pass until we crossed another road and a few low hills to reach the *Río* Carmen Valley and then followed it northeast, always looking for useful captives. We stayed out of sight and saw a few old ones with their burros and peasants working in the fields, but we left them alone. No one would swap a strong Apache slave like Chee-hash-kish for some broken-down old man or woman, or even a young field worker. We needed soldiers or *hacendados* with big *casas* who would swap valuable slaves to get their family members back. Oh, yes; I knew how that worked. I had seen many trades for slaves in my years among the *Nakai-yes.*

I planned to travel northeast until we found the iron wagon road where there should be many *Nakai-yi* women and soldiers who came to wait on the iron wagon. These would be worth taking. Even if the *Nakai-yes* wouldn't bargain for a soldier because he wasn't a *nant'an,* we could test their courage in good ways before they died.

We were close enough to the iron wagon road to see the black smoke plumes from the iron wagons when we found what we were looking for—a group of four women, one who even had a baby at her breast, accompanied by two soldiers, walking toward the iron wagon road—these I thought we could use to bargain for our families.

It was near sundown when we quietly came out of the brush to surround them on the road. The women froze, their faces twisted in fear, and two or three covered their mouths, giving low groans. The soldiers started to bring their guns up, but never fired. Our arrows flew straight to their hearts. The warriors cut their throats and stripped their rifles, pistols, and ammunition in less than a breath's time.

I slid off my pony and raised my hand in a peace sign to keep the women quiet. I spoke good *Nakai-yi,* a language I had learned from my mother from the time I was on a *tsach.* I said to the women, "Stay quiet, and you and that baby will live. We mean you no harm. We want to bargain you for our women and children taken as slaves more than a harvest ago." I pointed toward an old woman, her hair gray, nearly white and plaited, lying long down the middle of her back to her waist, her face holding many deep valleys, but her eyes were bright and alert. "You go on to the iron road casa. Tell the *nant'an* there that Geronimo will be back in fifteen suns to bargain these women, the baby, and others we take for the ones enslaved by the Galeana soldiers in Casas Grandes last harvest. Do you understand my words?"

She stared at me a moment and slowly nodded.

I motioned up the road toward the iron wagon road. "You go now. Do not forget my words. That is all I have to say."

The old woman softly spoke words I didn't hear to the others and then started off down the road toward the iron wagon road.

A woman who seemed to be their leader stepped apart from them while the old woman hobbled away into the growing darkness. "You are the great Geronimo? The one all Chihuahua fears?"

"I am Geronimo."

"What will you do with us?"

"We will take more captives and then keep you all in the Blue Mountains at Bugatseka until a swap is made, all our people for all of you. In Bugatseka, you will help our women until it is time to speak with those who have our women and children, and then we come back to the place called Hacienda Carmen."

"Bugatseka? Where is this place? I have never heard of Bugatseka."

"The *Nakai-yes* call the land there *Mesa Tres Ríos*. Mount behind a warrior. Don't be afraid. They will not harm you. We travel fast. When we find a *rancho* with good horses, we take them and leave these worn out ones behind. If we catch enough replacements, we give you your own mounts or maybe one or two or three to share. We go."

We crossed the road south of Galeana that night and, near

the gray light of morning, we rested by a large water tank in a canyon in the mountains nearby. We let women bathe without disturbing their modesty and then offered them something to eat, but they refused the food. We decided to camp there while the warriors found places on the roads from Galeana to set up ambushes to take more captives. Cattle were the last things we wanted. Once we started taking cattle, we knew we would have to ride for the mountains, because the military in Galeana would be quick to ride against us. I laughed. They were still sore because of our ambushes last harvest, killing all those soldiers, the capture of Juan Mata Ortiz and how we roasted him good over a fire.

The warriors, watching both roads to Galeana, came back that afternoon but had taken no more captives. They had found a few cows near the canyon where we camped and drove them to us for meat while we waited. That sun, I had stayed in camp to watch the women and to make medicine and pray to *Ussen* but had received no guidance. The women stayed close together and made no attempt to run.

When the men returned, the novitiates, who had slaughtered three cows and, with the women helping, cooked meat while smoke from the fire would be hard to see, gave us a good evening meal. My helper, a cousin named Betzinez, who had spent much time in my *wickiup* with my son Chappo, brought me a nice piece of meat cooked just the way I liked it. The camp was quiet as the shadows grew long, and the men, hungry from the long day, ate, cutting good bites of roast with their sharp knives to satisfy their hunger. The women still wouldn't eat. It seemed they would rather starve than take anything we offered them.

I said to them, "You must eat. You need your strength. The way is long and hard." But they shook their heads and refused the meat we offered them.

I was cutting a bite from my roast when a vision filled my eyes. I saw Blue Coats and many scouts in a Bugatseka village destroying food supplies and taking prisoners. *Nant'an Lpah,* on his mule, was watching them. The powerful vision paralyzed me for a moment and, shaken by what I saw, my knife fell from my hand. Struggling to be free of the vision's hold on me, I called out, "Brothers! People we left at our base camp are now in the hands of Blue Coats! What shall we do?"

The meat I was eating seemed to turn sour in my stomach and was hard to keep down. Every man in camp stopped eating and stared at me, their eyes glowing, unbelieving. They did not doubt the vision I had, but they questioned how it could be.

Naiche was on his feet in the blink of an eye. "We must go now. Forget the other captives. What good are they if Nant'an Lpah has our people? How can this be, Geronimo? Didn't the Blue Coats agree with the *Nakai-yes* not to come across the border? How did they know where to find us? Who has betrayed us?"

I held up the palm of my hand. "Patience, my chief. We'll learn answers to all your questions soon enough. You're right. We must go now as soon as it's dark."

Naiche nodded and sat back down while all the men muttered *"Enjuh,"* but said little as they finished their meat and made their ponies ready.

We rode all night. A few warriors split off from us to take a large herd we planned to drive to Bugatseka. We met them and rested just before dawn in a canyon leading into the mountains.

We ate meat left over from the day before. Still the women wouldn't eat. I told them, "You must eat. You need your strength. We'll travel fast, and it will be hard on you. Eat!" Je-likinne, Zi-yeh's father, saw the hard time I had convincing the women to eat. He came strutting up to them like a *nant'an.*

Jelikinne paced back and forth in front of them, pointed a finger at them, and said, "You foolish women, eat or die! If you want to live, you must eat. We won't have time to look after you, and there is a long way to go. Now eat!"

The women looked at each other, fear spilling from their eyes. The one who had spoken up before said, "*Sí,* we eat. Give us some meat, and we will eat now." Jelikinne turned his back on them, looked at me, and smiled before he walked away.

I met with the leaders and decided the trail to use with all the cattle we had. Our horses were becoming tired and wouldn't last if they had to carry a double load. The women would have to run and walk as we got into the mountains driving the cattle. We knew the women would slow us down. They weren't strong and capable like Apache women, but the cattle would slow us down anyway and leave a broad trail, making it easy for the women to follow us if they fell behind.

The trail through the mountains was long and hard. We lost many cattle on the way but kept enough to make driving them back worthwhile. Our families rendezvoused with us the day before we were to reach the main camp. They had not seen or heard of any Blue Coats attacking any camps and, although they didn't doubt my vision, they wondered how such a thing was possible.

That night I had another vision in which a man on a high hill to our left called to us to wait for him. I recognized the place in my vision as where we would be the next day halfway between the time of shortest shadows and when the sun fell into the mountains. I warned my leaders of this vision, and again they wondered what it might all mean.

The next day, at the time I said it would happen, a man on high hill called for us to wait while he came down to give us news. We gathered in council to hear him tell us that *Nant'an*

Lpah had taken Chato's and Bonito's camp and held many of the women and some of the men prisoners in his camp. Jaws dropped on many of the men. They would not claim my vision was false, but thought it might have another meaning besides the one I had chosen. We left our women and children, our captives, and our cattle and climbed a high ridge above Nant'an Lpah's camp at Bugatseka.

CHAPTER 31
SURRENDER TO NANT'AN LPAH

The high ridge above the camp where Nant'an Lpah camped and held our people was steep and held many stone ledges and huge boulders among the tall trees growing up the sides of the ridge. From the boulders and ledges near the top were clear lines of sight into the camp. We came to the ridge deep in the night and climbed to its top. In the dark hours before dawn, I directed the men to climb out on the ledges and tops of boulders with their rifles and watch the camp, but not to shoot at all. There were too many of the People who might die in an exchange of gunfire. I wanted the warriors seen and Nant'an Lpah and his scouts to know we watched them.

Dawn's gray light was coming, and, as brightness grew, we saw in the shadows scouts hiding behind log barricades, and many sticks stuck in the open ground from which waved strips of white cloth. I understood this meant Nant'an Lpah didn't want to fight. Many scouts and the people far below saw us and pointed toward us while they talked to people nearby.

We called down to them asking them to come speak with us. But we were too far away for them to understand what we said. A woman walked from under the trees, crossed the open ground, and approached the ridge. My "sister," Nah-thla-tla, the mother of Betzinez, found a path and began to climb. A hard climb, it took her a while to get to the top where we waited. She reached the top and passed into the trees out of sight from those below. I met her by a fire in the shade of a great pine tree.

261

She surveyed the bare places under the trees where many of the warriors sat, but didn't see her son, my novitiate, Betzinez, and frowned.

I said, "He is holding the horses at the bottom on the back side of the ridge, my sister. He has done well on this raid and taken good care of me. Tell us what has happened."

As the cooking fires grew and the people ate far below us, the good smells of roasting meat rose and filled our bellies with hunger as the men gathered around her.

My sister told us how the scouts had surprised everyone in Chato's camp while the women and old men were drying and smoking fresh meat. They had killed Chihuahua's aunt and, after taking prisoners and what they wanted from the Ghost Face supplies and other things we had, destroyed everything else.

She said, "The one we call Nant'an Lpah, his scouts and soldiers call him 'General Crook,' would not let the scouts mistreat the prisoners, and when Chihuahua had wanted his best horse, saddle, and bridle back, Nant'an Lpah made the scouts give them back. Chihuahua spoke with Nant'an Lpah, and when Nant'an Lpah told him he wanted to be friends and that the attack on Chato's village was a mistake, Chihuahua, very angry, said he thought Nant'an Lpah was lying because friends didn't murder their friends' old relatives, but he rode out to gather his people and bring them in."

Golden shafts of sunlight were passing through the tops of the trees, and birds were in full song, flitting from branch to branch. It seemed a very peaceful morning to be so close to bloodshed and much dying.

My sister sighed. "They ask below what you want. What shall I tell them?"

I crossed my arms and looked at my warriors. We all had questions and believed the scouts had answers. Most of all we wanted to know how they had found us and why they were here. "Tell them below we want to talk with some scouts. That's all, just talk. You have my word we won't harm them."

She nodded. "I'll tell them this. Don't get my son killed, Geronimo."

After she reached Nant'an Lpah's camp, Blue Coats and scouts swarmed around her. Soon a White Mountain scout with a red bandana around his hair came out from the trees and followed the same path up the ridge my sister had used. We tried speaking with him, but he had something wrong with his speech. He stuttered and slurred his words. We didn't understand him and sent him back, telling him to send other scouts who spoke plainly. He grunted, nodded he understood, and started back down the ridge.

Two Cibecue scouts climbed up to talk with us. One Cibecue named Haskehagola, which means "Angry, He Starts Fights," a brother-in-law of Chato, went off to sit under the trees with Chato and his men. The other, named Dastine, which means "Crouched and Ready," was related to Jelikinne. When the scouts reached us, they didn't seem afraid, and I thought this a good thing. Jelikinne and Dastine sat in the shade under some tall trees surrounded by warriors who wanted to hear their words. I sat with Chato and Haskehagola and listened.

Chato was angry. It was his village the scouts had attacked and destroyed and his people they had taken prisoner. His eyes showed he wanted to fight, but he kept calm and said in a whispering voice, hard to hear, "Ho, Haskehagola. Tell us why Nant'an Lpah and all these scouts have come into the Blue Mountains after us. Speak. We listen."

Haskehagola looked at each of us, crossed his arms, and said in clear voice, "Nant'an Lpah comes in a good way to escort you back to San Carlos. He does not want to fight you. The raid north of the border late in the Season of Little Eagles made the White Eyes very angry. The raiders took a child and killed its mother and father. The White Eyes want to come south to fight you in the land of *Nakai-yes*. If they do, the *Nakai-yes* will fight them. Many on both sides will die, and the Apaches will still be in their high mountain camps. Nant'an Lpah knows this. He knows the agents at San Carlos cheated and treated you badly. He wants you to come back so he can fix things. He doesn't want *Nakai-yes* and White Eyes to die fighting each other. He doesn't want any of you to die fighting the Blue Coats."

Chato had led the raid north that took the White Eye child. It was what warriors did. He shook his head and said with a sneer, "This is war. Stealing one child brings the Blue Coats here? This is hard to believe."

"His parents that you killed, they were great White Eye *jefes*. Is the boy still alive?"

Before Chato could answer, I said, "He still lived when we left for our last raid." I pointed at him. "Now tell us how you found this place, or I will send you to the land below us so fast you'll think you're a bird—until you land—then you'll turn into food for wolves."

Haskehagola had darker skin than most Apaches, but then his skin color came close to a White Eye's as we all stared at him, many with hands on our knives. He held up his hand palm out and shook his head. "Nant'an Lpah doesn't want this known. He fears if you learn who led us here, you'll kill him. No one knows for sure except Nant'an Lpah and his chiefs. The scouts believe they know who it is. That is all I have to say."

My eyes narrowed and I grew angry; some told me later they turned red. I pulled my pistol and pointed it at his head. "Tell me, or you die now. I'll soon find it out from someone else." I pulled the hammer back, ready to fire.

Again, Haskehagola held up his hand, palm out, and shook

his head. "There is no need for this. I tell you what I think."

I let the hammer down and holstered the pistol. "Speak."

"There's a powerful warrior, who once rode with Chato, but he left Chato and returned to San Carlos to help his family."

I glanced at Chato, whose scowl told me the same thing I was thinking.

"Teniente Davis and his scouts caught him. They believed his story about returning to San Carlos from the camps here to support his family at San Carlos. He had lost his family, two wives, sisters of Chato, and a daughter, because of the killings at Aliso Creek, and he carried wounds from that fight. He thought it best that all the Apaches go back to San Carlos. He agreed to show Nant'an Lpah the Chiricahua camps. Of that, I am almost certain. I believe Tzoe led Nant'an Lpah here."

Chato stared at Haskehagola. I crossed my arms and shook my head. The scouts kept a promise they made to Nant'an Lpah, but Tzoe had betrayed us. One day he would pay.

We let Haskehagola go and told him we would think on his words. After he started down the trail, I told the men they should decide what they wanted to do and that the leaders should speak with Nant'an Lpah and hear his own words. We all left the ridge to watch the camp from the trees and brush around it and look for an opportunity to talk to scouts and the people to learn all we could.

Nant'an Lpah's camp with the scouts and prisoners stood on a little knoll, and, all around in the open spaces down the sides, much tall, yellow grass grew. We saw Nant'an Lpah hunting birds in the grass with a shotgun. The leaders decided to speak with him. We surrounded him and waited as he collected the birds he shot and came closer and closer to us.

He never heard or saw us. I felt my hand clenching for the handle of my knife, but I never used it or even threatened to after Chato suddenly rose up beside him and jerked the shotgun from his hands, snarling, "You shot toward us. You want war," while Naiche took his bag of birds.

A breeze wafted over the top of the yellow grass, making it ripple like waves on water, and, not far below us, a little stream burbled and fell over rocks and flowed toward the headwaters of the *Río* Bavispe. Nant'an Lpah looked at each of us and shook his head. "I hunt only birds for my supper." He smiled. "I couldn't be shooting at you. Who can see an Apache when he hides?"

I didn't like Nant'an Lpah. He didn't speak the way a man ought to speak who offers respect. My thumb slid toward the hammer of my rifle. We heard the voice of the liar Mickey Free as he came running down the hill yelling, "No shoot! No shoot!" and waving his hands palm out to show he was unarmed.

We all relaxed a little, and Nant'an Lpah said, "Mickey Free speaks true when he tells me your words and you mine. Let's get out of this sun and sit in the shade down yonder by that little creek where we can speak together as friends."

Chato first looked at me for assent, but I looked off down the valley, still uncertain whether to kill Nant'an Lpah or not. But when Chato looked at the other leaders, they nodded they would accept Nant'an Lpah's offer. I followed them to the shade with little to say. What could I say? The scouts had destroyed much of our winter supplies. We would go hungry in the coming Season of Ghost Face and Season of Little Eagles. Nant'an Lpah's scouts held many, mostly women and children, prisoner. They might die if we fought Nant'an Lpah in this place.

After we rolled cigarettes and smoked by the burbling water, we told Nant'an Lpah our complaints about our treatment at San Carlos. We spoke of crooked agents cheating us of our supplies, of the shaking sickness, and how many had died. We said we wanted to live far from the places of shaking sickness at San

Carlos and our old enemies. We said we would surrender and live in peace at San Carlos if he fixed the bad things that drove us away. Nant'an Lpah sat flipping stones in the creek as he listened to what we said.

Then he spoke. "I understand your words. I've heard these things from other bands on the reservation. I've already decided that San Carlos will have a new agent. I have in mind a good chief, a special agent, to keep the peace, distribute supplies due you, and keep you out of the way of bad White Eyes who try to take advantage of you. He waits only for our return. I'll let you choose any land on San Carlos not already taken. It will be good land, the kind you want. It will be far from places of the shaking sickness and good for growing things you like to eat. But all this is up to you. I don't care if you surrender or not. If you don't, then much blood will flow on both sides. I'll hunt you for fifty years if that's what takes. I'll hunt and kill every one of you. It's your choice to make as grown Apache men."

We sat with crossed arms and narrowed eyes, watching him and listening to everything he said. When he finished speaking, and Mickey Free finished interpreting his words, he looked at each leader, including me. They all nodded and said, *"Enjuh."* They had agreed to return to San Carlos for the promises Nant'an Lpah made us.

I wanted to think about this. I said, "I'll think about Nant'an Lpah's words and speak with him at sunrise."

Nant'an Lpah nodded and said, "As you choose, Geronimo. I'll still be here in the morning if you choose to speak with me. I don't care what you do."

The leaders had decided there would be no fighting with the Blue Coats. That was a good thing. But I thought, *We won't fight the Blue Coats here, but those who have betrayed us will pay a price.*

CHAPTER 32
GATHERING THE PEOPLE

The morning after the leaders spoke with Nant'an Lpah, I smoked and spoke with him alone, using an interpreter I thought spoke true, not Mickey Free. We sat under the tall pines and felt the cold morning air prickle our skin as the bright shafts of yellow morning light like thrown spears flew through the branches and down into the *bosque* brush by the water where we heard children playing and women laughing.

I said, "Nant'an Lpah, this is a thing of great Power you do. *Ussen* must help you. The People are ready to return to San Carlos. You've come into the land claimed by the *Nakai-yes,* come into the high Blue Mountains. Some of our own people show you the way here, and your scouts, even some from our own bands, don't hesitate to kill us and destroy the food we have saved for the Ghost Face and Little Eagles Seasons."

Nant'an Lpah blew the cloud off his coffee to cool it. "Geronimo speaks true. I think you know that the Mexican army will decide they have to come here, too. These mountains will no longer protect you from the Mexicans as they once did."

"I've always wanted to be at peace. The White Eyes at San Carlos didn't treat us with respect and give us our due. They drove us away."

Nant'an Lpah nodded. "I know this is true."

"The *Nakai-yes* have no honor. They make war on our women and children as if they were strong warriors. They run away when they see real warriors." I grinned. "I don't need rifles and ammunition for *Nakai-yes*. We kill them with rocks. They've taken my people, even my favorite wife, Chee-hash-kish, and made them slaves. I've taken some of them to exchange for our people and was looking for more when my Power told me you had come.

"I can't fight one great army of scouts, Americans, and *Nakai-yes*. There's no place for us to hide that you won't find us. We're sick at heart that our own people betray us. You must have great Power for other men to follow you this way. You're a great chief. Yours is the face of a god. If we can't make peace, my warriors and I will surely die in these mountains fighting to the last man. Fighting like Victorio. Fighting until we have no more arrows or bullets. Then we will have to stick a knife in our hearts."

Nant'an Lpah took a long swallow from his cup of coffee and nodded.

"Geronimo sees clearly. I don't care if you choose to stay and not return. I'll come back to fight you, maybe even with the help of the *Nakai-yes,* although we won't need them. It's your choice. There's no place to hide anymore. If you decide to come back to San Carlos, come back in a good way. If you want to come back, my soldiers will protect you from Mexicans, and the scouts will help you hunt on the way. The People won't go hungry. At San Carlos, they'll have fair treatment and be treated as they deserve, treated as we all want."

Even with the long gray hair on his face divided below his chin and making two points, Nant'an Lpah spoke with a straight tongue, and his face showed no trace of lies. *Maybe,* I thought, *now there will be peace.*

"When will Nant'an Lpah leave Bugatseka? The women need at least three days to cook mescal. We can eat it on the way. I've sent young men out to find and bring in my people. They even make smoke telling them they should come in."

"Good. The quicker they come, the better off we'll be. I want your People well supplied with all the food they need. It will take all of us working together to cross the border without hunger."

Naiche, Chato, and a strong warrior named Tcha-nol-haye came to Nant'an Lpah's tent to eat a morning meal he had invited them to have with him and to make plans for the People's return. Crook urged them to hurry their people in. Already, Chihuahua had sent out his messengers, and the camp grew as more and more of his people came in.

During the next three days many more came into Nant'an Lpah's camp, including Kaytennae, who came with his people, mostly young warriors. He had thirty-eight in his band, all well-armed. Even the little boys had revolvers, lances made with old cavalry long knives, and bows and arrows. They brought cattle with them. Nant'an Lpah told them to slaughter the cattle for meat on the return trail, and they did this. Old Nana came in with seventeen, and then Loco came with a few and told Nant'an Lpah he had started back before Nant'an Lpah began the long march into the mountains. Others, Loco said, had returned to the reservation after becoming separated at the Aliso Creek fight.

Not many of my people nor those of Naiche, Chato, or some of Chihuahua's came in. The returning messengers said the people saw the smoke, feared a scout trick, and stayed in their camps. We moved Nant'an Lpah's camp down the Bavispe a short way to make it easier for the women to collect and cook mescal. We danced a victory dance in the night and then a social dance that let the scouts dance with our women.

I thought of a way to wipe out the scouts using the dance as a cover, and the council talked about it. But my father-in-law, Jelikinne, said some of the scouts were his relatives, and he wouldn't hear of it. It never happened. I think the chief of scouts, Al Sieber, somehow learned of our plans and called the dance off that night.

The women we captured and planned to use in a swap for captives walked far behind us in our rush to return to our camp. They came into Nant'an Lpah's camp, limping out of the trees and brush, scratched and bruised, their dresses nearly torn to pieces and not much better than rags. The soldiers found them and, after learning their story, gave them clothes and boots, fed them, and promised to return them to their families. We meant the women no harm. We wanted to get our people back, but Nant'an Lpah wouldn't let us keep and use them that way. I tried several more times to get our captives back after Nant'an Lpah left for San Carlos but failed.

We made ready for the trail back to San Carlos. Nant'an Lpah told the leaders he planned to follow the trail on the east side of the mountains to avoid the *Nakai-yes* seeing him twice and maybe attacking. The other leaders and I asked him to wait another week so we could bring in the rest of our people.

We understood when he told us he didn't have enough supplies to wait even one more day. He agreed to let Chato, Naiche, Chihuahua, Mangas, and me stay behind and search for our people and meet him at the border. If we were not in time to meet him, we said we would avoid attacks by soldiers and White Eyes by working our way alone through the mountains to San Carlos.

In the suns and moons that followed, we found our people. I also saw this time as a chance to collect a herd of cattle to develop for the Chiricahuas at San Carlos. As we collected the cattle, the *Nakai-yes* tried to attack us in our camps, but we watched for them and either moved out of their way or ambushed them. They paid in blood for thinking they could successfully attack us.

We made a raid for cattle at the place the *Nakai-yes* call Nácori Chico. Cochise had attacked this place several times without success. Since the leaders and our warriors were all together, we decided to try our luck against the village where Cochise had failed. An early *Nakai-yi* riser happened to see us, so we lost the element of surprise. We had a good fight with soldiers in the town, who charged us. It appeared they had reinforcements left in the town, and we retreated. We were a long way from the soldiers. And although many shots fell short, one did not. Jelikinne was climbing up a rock to higher ground when a lucky *Nakai-yi* shot hit him in the head and killed him. We all grieved for Jelikinne, and fifteen of us went on a revenge raid. Jelikinne was a good man. I knew my wife Zi-yeh, his daughter, would grieve for him a long time.

Two moons after Jelikinne rode the ghost pony, *Ussen* took my brother-in-law, Juh, who was at Casas Grandes with his little group of Nednhi and Mangas and his people. When I returned to San Carlos near the end of Ghost Face, I visited with Daklugie to learn what had happened to Juh. My heart was sad to hear it. Daklugie told me that he and his brothers were riding on a trail above the *río* behind their father when he breathed hard, grabbed at his chest, and fell in the *río*. The brothers quickly pulled him out of the water but couldn't get him up on the bank. The older two rode for help from the warriors in front of them, and left Daklugie to keep his head out of the water. The returning warriors were able to get him up on the bank, covered in a blanket and under a shelter, but he rode the ghost pony that night.

They buried Juh there by the *río,* and Daklugie and his brothers joined Mangas's band. Daklugie returned to San Carlos with Mangas in the Season of Earth Is Reddish Brown. He heard later that *Nakai-yi* horse soldiers caught his brothers, strong young men, and sent them in chains to Ciudad Mexico to work as prisoners in a mine. We never saw them again.

Naiche had told me while we were still in the Blue Mountains that Juh had gotten drunk one day in camp. He mounted a wild horse that jumped while on a high bank and threw him forward into the *río* when it was low, not deep enough to drown him, but they found him with his head lying in the water dead. Kaytennae and Zelle both said Juh, drunk, killed himself when he ran his horse off a high bank to prove his Power. I don't think my nephew lied about sitting on the bank holding his father's head above water or that Juh was drunk. I think the other stories are what the others put together from hearing those who knew Juh and had helped pull him from the *río*.

I continued to gather my people, most of them women and children, through the Seasons of Large Fruit and Earth Is Reddish Brown. They slowly came out of hiding places even I didn't know, which were hard to see and find around Bugatseka, and gathered in our camp.

As the camp filled with my people, I and a few warriors continued to take cattle, saving the best and strongest bulls and cows for a herd when we returned to San Carlos, and living off the rest. The women worked hard to gather and cook mescal, more juniper berries and nuts, all of which would let us live well long into the Ghost Face. Near the end of the Season of Large Leaves, we had taken enough cattle to return to San Carlos, and all my people had come back to Bugatseka. But I decided to stay and take more cattle until our camps began to run out of food.

I thought often of the risks I took in returning to San Carlos. I believed Nant'an Lpah when he said things would be better than when we left and that we could have our pick of land on the reservation. Still I thought of how Clum had tricked and captured me at Ojo Caliente, and I had spent nearly four moons as his prisoner, three of those moons in the dark San Carlos guardhouse where I'd vowed never to return.

I decided I'd rather stay free and hungry in the Blue Mountains than chained and full of regrets in the guardhouse when Naiche and his band decided to return to San Carlos at the beginning of the Season of Earth Is Reddish Brown. I spoke with my son, Chappo, as we sat bathing in sage smoke one evening.

"Chappo, Naiche and his band leave in two suns for San Carlos. He'll meet Blue Coats at the place the White Eyes call Silver Springs on the border at *Río* San Bernardino. The Blue Coats will travel with him to San Carlos to prevent other White Eyes from attacking his band. Most of the way to Silver Springs, in the land the *Nakai-yes* claim, they can stay safe in the mountains, but the band must cross open *llano* for half a day before they reach the Blue Coats. There is always a chance *Nakai-yi* soldiers will attack them, but Naiche doesn't think this will happen, and even if it does, he knows how to handle them."

Chappo's face filled with questions as he studied my face while I spoke, but his eyes flashed in anticipation. He said, "Yes, Father, I know Naiche's plan to return to San Carlos in two suns. When do you plan to return?"

"Our band's women have baked enough mescal and collected enough berries and nuts, and we have enough cattle to stay here maybe into the Season of Little Eagles. I'm slow to return until I'm certain Nant'an Lpah speaks with a straight tongue and his man, this Captain Crawford, will not try to surprise and keep me shackled in the guardhouse the way Clum did. I had rather die fighting than spend another sun there.

"Chappo, you go with Naiche. Watch this Captain Crawford who rules San Carlos. Learn if he is a fair man. Learn if he plans to put me in the guardhouse. When you know these things, return and tell me what you think. Then I will decide what to do."

Chappo, always serious, nodded and said, "My father is wise in the ways of the Blue Coats and White Eyes. I'll go with Naiche, watch Crawford, and tell you what I see."

"Hmmph. A fine son and a bath in sage smoke makes life good."

Chappo found his way back to us through the cold passes and over the mountains early in the Season of Ghost Face. He was no longer a young warrior. He walked and spoke like a tested warrior and told me Captain Crawford understood us and spoke straight. He seemed to be fighting the White Eye agent for what was right. Still, I was slow to return. I didn't like San Carlos. I wanted to live on Eagle Creek in the mountains.

Maybe, I thought, *I can talk Nant'an Lpah into letting the People live there.*

My wives warned me that our food supplies would be gone in about a moon. Chato and his people had already left for San Carlos, driving the herd of horses and mules he had taken in his raids. He had wanted to leave as soon as he had found all his people, but then he wouldn't leave as long as my warriors and I continued to raid. He wanted more horses and mules, too.

His village began to run low on supplies about half a moon before mine, and they began to make their way out of the mountains toward the border. Although it gave me a sour stomach, I, too, led my people out of the mountains toward the border. At least I wouldn't have to meet Blue Coats like all the other leaders. I would stay in the mountains with the herd of fine cattle until they were on reservation land.

CHAPTER 33
RETURN TO SAN CARLOS

We didn't travel fast with our cattle. I wanted them fat and at a good weight when we reached San Carlos. Maybe we would sell some for supplies but keep most for our herd. As we neared the border from the valley of the *Río* San Bernardino, our cattle followed a good distance back of the line of our women and children, protection in case of attack from behind. The land was dry, the cattle raising much dust, but the air was cool, and it was a good time for the women and children to walk and run. The warriors were in front of our band and I saw dust streamers from two riders approaching us. I used my soldier glasses to study them, two Apaches wearing blue coats and red headbands like they wore when they invaded our camps in Bugatseka. Scouts.

We stopped and waited for them. One wore a blue coat with three yellow stripes on the sleeves. His pony walked up to us slowly and stopped. The scout looked White Mountain and spoke loudly, so we could easily hear him. "Teniente Davis has been sent by Captain Crawford, the agent at San Carlos, to ride with you back to the reservation. He waits at the border for you with his scouts and a few Blue Coats to protect you from other White Eyes and doesn't wish to surprise you with his presence close by. Come!"

I nodded we understood, but my blood grew hot. There was no need to escort us like prisoners to the reservation. I had given my word I would come in peace. Now the Blue Coats were treating me like I had lied. I wondered if this was a trick to put me in the guardhouse again. As the scouts rode away, we rode on, but I told my men to be ready for a fight. I couldn't understand why the White Eyes and Blue Coats couldn't keep their word.

I rode up to Teniente Davis, my blood hot, ready to fight. I let my pony's shoulder push against his mule, and I said in Spanish, "Why are you here? Why is there a need for you to ride with us? I've made peace with the Americans. Why would you attack me?"

Teniente Davis was a strongly built young man, stout like Juh in his younger days, but not fat. His eyes showed no fear. He stood out for the Blue Coats like a good subchief for my people. He nodded, understanding my Spanish, and he spoke it well, too.

"We mean you no disrespect or harm. There are bad Americans as well as bad Indians. If we have to pass near a town, some bad Americans, full of whiskey, might try to cause trouble. My scouts are American soldiers. If an American killed one of them, Americans will hang that man, and those who might make trouble know it. Our being here protects you and your people from those bad Americans who might attack you."

His words were straight and made sense. I respected them. I took a deep breath, and my anger blew away across my lips. I nodded I understood, shook hands with him, and said, "You and me, Teniente, we are brothers."

He smiled, made a hand wave parallel to the ground, and then pointed toward the big dust cloud behind us. "What makes the dust cloud following you?"

"Cattle."

Teniente's jaw dropped a little. "How many are there?"

"I counted three hundred fifty, some taken from *ranchos* down the *río* but most near the border. We drive them hard to run from *vaqueros* who might try to follow and attack us. The trail is long and dry. We need to stay here three days to rest the cattle on this grass and water before we move on to San Carlos."

Teniente Davis shook his head. "That's not possible. If the White Eye ranchers or Mexican *hacendados* learn we're here, they might join together to attack us. We must leave no later than the next sun falling into the mountains and keep moving."

I did not want to leave with the next late sun. My cattle needed rest, plenty of water, and a good graze, or they would lose their fat and not bring much money if sold at San Carlos, but I understood the need to get away from the border. Rather than risk losing them in a battle with White Eye settlers or *hacendado vaqueros,* I agreed to only one day of rest for the cattle.

Teniente Davis led us on a trail where the cattle could get water and a little grass on the way, but he traveled far too fast for the animals to keep their fat. I complained about this every night at his tent. Teniente said he understood, but he always gave me a reason we couldn't slow down. We needed to hurry to get around enemies, or we had to get the cattle to water before we stopped in the evening. I was not satisfied with these excuses, but I understood he wanted to keep us safe and didn't argue with him much.

The cattle were losing weight. He made us drive them in a run nearly all day as we hurried across the country. We would soon come to the Sulphur Springs *rancho.* The water at Sulphur Springs was good, and there was plenty for the herd and good grass out away from the dusty *llano.* My people had camped there often in the long-ago days.

One night, I went to Teniente Davis's tent. I said, "Tomorrow we come to Sulphur Springs." I held up three fingers. "Three suns before we move again. Cattle losing weight. They need weight at San Carlos. Water and grass good there. You go on if you choose. Anyplace you can go, you go. I don't care. We stay. We won't move for three days. Cattle get fat again."

Teniente Davis crossed his arms and stared at me. He cocked his head to one side and said, "Last spring, you saw Nant'an Lpah with American soldiers in Mexico to bring your people back to San Carlos?"

I nodded, "I see him. I remember those days."

"Well, then, you must know the Mexicans have the same right to come into the United States. They can still come after you. We're still too near the border to risk stopping."

I knew my face was showing my hatred for Mexicans. "*Nakai-yes!* You worry about *Nakai-yes*? My women can crush all the *Nakai-yes* in Chihuahua."

"But the Mexicans have plenty of cartridges, and yours are nearly gone. There are few in your cartridge belts."

I raised my fist and shook it. "We don't fight *Nakai-yes* with cartridges. Cartridges too hard to find. Cost too much when we buy. We save cartridges to fight the Blue Coats. We fight *Nakai-yes* with rocks."

Teniente Davis smiled and nodded. "All right, Geronimo. We'll stop for a day and see how the cattle look."

I was not happy with one sun's extra grazing time. I would take more, but nodded I understood.

We stopped near the *rancho casa* at Sulphur Springs, but only White Eye *vaqueros* stayed there to look after the *hacendado's* cattle. The *rancho casa*, built with *adobe* bricks, had a wall about chest high around it that included enough land to surround the *casa*, a garden, tents for *vaqueros*, and the springs. A small gate on the north side of the wall was within three long strides of the *casa*. Teniente's packers camped fifty long strides from the small gate, and his scouts a little beyond them. Teniente put up his tent between the packers and the wall next to where the Blue Coat who cooked for them all set up his fire. Two of my families camped against the wall on either side of the small gate, and several camped out of the wind on the east side. Others, including my family, camped on the *llano* close to water.

After watering the cattle, the ponies, and the mules, we left the ponies and mules to graze a long rifle shot from the house. Beyond the horses and mules, three warriors watched the cattle herd to stop them mixing with those of the *rancho*. I had no desire to take American cattle and have *vaqueros* chasing us to San Carlos. The *llano* was very flat with scattered brush no higher than a man's waist, and good grazing land compared to the very dusty land near the *rancho casa*.

Far out over the *llano* toward the mountains on the horizon, we saw the same mountains where Juh and I had lived in our time on Cochise's reservation. The cattle and ponies raised a low cloud of dust as they wandered the *llano* looking for their grass. The sun falling into the mountains left a cloudy sky filled with fiery orange, purple, red, and near-black colors. It was a time of rest and peace. I was glad to have it.

While I ate a meal with my family, I saw two White Eyes come out of the little gate in front of the *rancho casa* and go to the tent of the teniente. They stood outside it and talked for a while and then, laughing and waving their hands at him, walked away back toward the small gate, but the teniente wasn't laughing. He looked angry. As the dusk deepened, I heard one of the scouts who was guarding the camp call to the teniente that a rider was coming, and I saw his dust plume. The light from the cook's fire showed a Blue Coat dismounting at the teniente's tent. They greeted each other without dignity. They were like long-lost brothers, laughing and slapping each other on the back, as White Eyes do when they find a friend that they have not seen in a long time.

They were finishing their meal when the two White Eyes came out of the little gate and spoke again to the teniente and his friend. They sat and talked with the two Blue Coats and then shared a bottle Teniente's friend had brought. I could tell it was White Eye whiskey, and my body wished I had some to warm it through the night. The two White Eyes seemed to drink most of the whiskey and then left.

Watching all this activity around the teniente's camp, I decided we should be ready to fight and run back to Mexico if the teniente had lied, or if the White Eyes and his friend were somehow after us. I told my warriors to be ready to ride or fight and that their women should be ready to head south. We picked the springs in Guadalupe Canyon as the place to rendezvous if we had to go.

When the moon was two hands from being at the top of its path across the sky, a Tonto scout sergeant appeared at my fire and said the teniente wanted to speak to me. My five or six best warriors and I took our rifles, strapped on our loaded cartridge belts and revolvers, and went to answer the teniente's call.

When we walked into the teniente cook's circle of firelight, the teniente and the new Blue Coat were sitting in chairs, warming their hands at the fire and speaking in low, muffled words as though they were planning something. Scattered in the darkness behind them, I saw maybe half his scouts squatting and watching, their rifles ready, but they were at ease.

I stood across the fire from the Blue Coats and said, "Ho, Teniente Davis. You say come; I come. Speak. We listen."

"Ho, Geronimo. I have news. The Big Chief councilors from far to the east sent the two men you saw me talking to late this afternoon. They say to me that when anyone buys cattle in the United States, they have to pay the Big Chief for them, and these men are here to collect the money. They say the charge on your cattle is about a thousand dollars, which they demand I pay here or take the cattle to Tucson for sale. I said I wouldn't do either one of those things. They say they will take the cattle and send them to Tucson using the *rancho vaqueros*. I know you won't agree to this. To avoid trouble, we must start for San Carlos *pronto* and get so far up the road by morning that chasing us is useless. My brother Blue Coat who came in when the sun fell will go with you. I'll stay here to lead the councilmen down the wrong trail if they try to follow. Will you do this?"

Our cattle needed rest and grass. Now the White Eyes were trying to steal them. I felt my ears grow warm as the flames of my anger became a hot fire. My lips twitched as I searched for words and stared at the teniente. I shifted my rifle from my right arm to my left, ready to shoot. I could tell Teniente Davis's friend held a pistola inside his jacket.

"No! I won't do this. I came back to San Carlos on the word of Nant'an Lpah that I would find peace. Instead, I find only trouble and threats, I've had my fill. If these chiefs think they can take my cattle away, let them try it tomorrow. I'm going back to my blankets and, Teniente, I hold you to your promise of a short stay right where we are. Why did you send this man to wake me up about a useless little talk that means nothing?"

The teniente's first sergeant looked at me. He was a Tonto Apache, a band that hated all the Chiricahuas.

He said in the Apache tongue, "Don't be a fool, Geronimo. The teniente offers you a way to keep your cattle."

"But they won't be worth anything to a buyer if they have no fat and grazing is poor at San Carlos if we keep them."

"They can get fat again on the good grass in and around the Fort Apache canyons."

"Hmmph. This is useless talk from weak people."

"If you hurt or kill these men from the Big Chief councilors, every Apache here and on the reservation will suffer, and you'll still lose your cattle. The People who have suffered will come after you, including me and my brother scouts. *Ussen* will leave you. Your family will die when the Apaches and the Blue Coats come after you together. Your band, your women, and your children will all disappear, all riding the ghost pony, because you had to have fat cattle. The plan of Teniente Davis and his friend Teniente Blake is not useless talk. It can save your people and the herd. Think again, or see it all lost."

I looked around at my warriors, who all stared at their moccasins, and then at the scouts out in the flickering darkness, eager for a fight.

Smiling a little, Teniente Davis said, "I think maybe you're afraid your people aren't smart enough to get away without these Big Chief council men and *vaqueros* on the ranch knowing it."

I knew what the teniente was doing, but his teasing still made me angry. "Ha! My People could leave you standing where you are, and you wouldn't know they were gone."

The teniente grinned. "Wouldn't it be a great joke on these men from the Big Chief if they woke up in the morning and found all the Apaches and all their cattle and ponies had disappeared?"

The image of the White Eye fools in the ranch *casa* waking up to find all the Apaches and their animals had disappeared made me want to laugh, but I kept a solemn face. I looked at my warriors and none shook their heads against going.

"We leave *pronto*. You follow as before?"

"I'll catch up with you. I have to stay here to convince the Big Chief men they have no chance of finding or catching you. My friend, Teniente Blake, will go with you until I can catch up."

"*Enjuh*. We go."

The People covered their mouths to keep their laughter from waking the White Eye councilors. No dogs barked. No children cried. We tied the little ones' feet together across the bellies of ponies; small children, we tied to adults. Then we started slowly because of the cattle. After we were out of hearing, we put boys with lances to prod the cattle to move faster, and we all moved fast. When the sun came, *pesh-klitso* outlining the mountains and casting long shafts of light into the canyons and valleys, we had traveled north far from that spring.

For the next two days, Teniente Blake led us northwest as though we were running after a raid. All my people enjoyed the game of disappearing while the White Eyes slept. Now those White Eyes would know better than to try to steal our cattle.

We were less than a day from the southern reservation boundary when we stopped to rest for the night. There was still enough light to see a rider's streamer of dust approaching us. My soldier glasses told me the rider was Teniente Davis. His mule came to a stop at Teniente Blake's tent. There was much laughing, back slapping, and shaking hands again, as they motioned me and my warriors over to them.

Teniente Davis said, "The White Eye councilmen couldn't believe you had gone. Neither they nor the *vaqueros* sleeping behind the wall heard you leave. They even climbed up on the roof in their long johns and bare feet to use their soldier glasses to look for your dust in the distance, but they saw none. They had no idea where you might have gone. They didn't even try to follow you. They told me it was a very good trick and to go to hell. After they put on their clothes, they shook my hand and left. You won, Geronimo. They'll bother you no more."

I smiled and nodded. *"Enjuh."*

Now, I thought, *maybe my herd brings a good price at San Carlos after they fatten for a moon or two.*

CHAPTER 34
SENT TO TURKEY CREEK

The *Río* Gila was running full and fast from melting snows in the mountains. It was a challenge to get the cattle and people across. Teniente Davis expected we would have to camp for maybe ten days until the flow slowed, so he went down to a place with a talking wire and sent his thoughts to General Crook.

But my people had crossed the *Río* Gila many times. We knew how to handle fast water, and we knew the wide places or eddies where it would slow down enough to cross. The People went across first, and none fell or even slipped as the water pushed against them. Next came the cattle. They followed the lead cow into the flow and easily trotted out, wet and shining. The People dried out by fires. I planned to stay here for a while before going on to the reservation. We butchered some beef and ate well.

Two days after we crossed the *Río* Gila, Bonito and McIntosh, once Nant'an Lpah's chief of scouts and who had been with him many harvests and married to an Apache woman, came with the new agent, Captain Crawford. Teniente Davis was glad to see Crawford. He had told me Crawford was strong and honest.

I thought, *Maybe so. We'll see.* McIntosh and Bonito, I knew, and was glad to see them.

Crawford and I shook hands, and then we sat by the teniente's fire and smoked to the four directions. Teniente Davis told the story of my escaping from the White Eye councilmen

286

with the cattle. McIntosh laughed hard, and Bonito grinned. Then we were ready to discuss Crawford's business.

Captain Crawford said, "Geronimo, I want you to understand that the reservation is owned by your people, but the Americans are responsible for the agents who oversee it to protect you and give your people their supplies. The agents must follow American laws when they deal with businesses and other countries. The Americans have given the army the job of helping all the Apaches living there and enforcing all laws of the United States with businesses and its agreements with other countries. You and your people will be part of the reservation, and, as your agent, I'm under the same rules and laws as the rest of the United States."

I kept still and watched Crawford's eyes. I knew what he must be leading up to. I nodded I understood what he said.

"Unless the army is at war, it cannot just take property when it wants to. You stole the cattle you brought to San Carlos from Mexicans near the border. It is against our laws to deal in stolen property. General Crook says the cattle either have to be sent back to Mexico or sold to the reservation and the money sent back to their first owners."

Even though I expected him to say this, my anger roared in my ears and made my blood race. This was not right. I said in a voice that showed my anger, "These are not White Eye cattle! We took them from the Mexicans during our wars. I don't intend to kill all these animals. We want to keep them and raise up a great herd on our range. And what about our horses and mules? We took many of them from Mexicans. Must we return them, too? Captain Crawford, give us justice. Give us what we have worked hard for."

Crawford's eyes never left my face during my angry talk. When I finished, he nodded. "I understand your anger. If I had not known the rules, I would let you keep the cattle. But I must

287

follow the rules that General Crook, my chief, says we keep. San Carlos must buy the cattle for meat and the money paid by the agents given to the Mexicans who first owned them. Even though you stole many of your horses and mules, General Crook says you can keep your mounts and pack animals."

I clenched my teeth and snarled, "So we ride easy while we starve. This is not fair. Not just."

Crawford said, "I understand, Geronimo, but that's the way it must be."

I thought, *One day, Crawford, I'll take many more cattle, be gone, and never come back.*

I was bitter about losing the cattle and would have left the area then, but the people wanted to stay. They were tired of the hard living in Mexico. I told Crawford I would think on the release of the cattle overnight and tell him if I accepted his terms.

Bonito, now a scout but a once powerful warrior, stayed with me and the people and with the council. We talked long into the night. We decided the cattle were not worth losing everything over, but we would make clear to Crook where we wanted to live on the reservation.

We drove the cattle into the agent's corral and had another council meeting with Captain Crawford in the place where he sat behind a big table. He told us he was very happy we decided to give up the cattle. It was best for us that we did.

I said, "The council has met and asks that you send Nant'an Lpah the words I give you."

Crawford motioned to a man with paper and little spears for making word tracks to come close and told him to write what I said.

"I have come here with the understanding that everything I asked for would be granted me. I met . . ." I said, "Crawford, should I call him Nant'an Lpah or General Crook for these tracks on paper?" Crawford scratched his chin, thought a moment, and then said, "To avoid confusion by any others who read the tracks, I would use General Crook." I nodded I understood. "I met General Crook when he was in the Sierra Madre and remember everything he told me. When I saw General Crook, I told him I thought he was a god, and that I didn't believe he was an American. Americans wouldn't come into the Sierra Madre. I was astonished to see him there and thought he was so powerful that he could command the sun and moon; everything. As soon as I saw him, I thought I would leave the mountains and come to live in peace on the reservation. Now I am glad to be here. It's better to live here than among the rocks and thorns in the mountains south of the border.

"I was a long time coming. I'm poor and wanted to get some cattle and horses to bring here. I didn't think I would have friends here to give me those things. All the Apache scouts with General Crook told me that they went to bed early and got up late and had nothing to fear. Here, all the Apaches have nothing to excite them. All this is good for me. I like it. All sent to me said that everybody here is good to the Indians and only keeps them from doing harm.

"I want everything done straight, so everything done before may be forgotten. All made new so we begin again. Before, everything here was wrong with the Indians and the people. Now it is straight. I want to keep it that way. I will never again think like I thought before. Now I think Americans on the reservation want me to live here. I have all I need and don't have to run around in the mountains cooking meat on sticks before the fire.

"My people and me are like wild mules and must be taught little by little until we are all tamed. I believe we have good treatment while we learn to live in a good way. I feel like I'm in a big hole, covered to my chest, while I am at San Carlos. I have surrendered everything, and I will obey orders given me without thinking of resisting them. In the future, if someone says something bad about me, I want to know quickly who is telling bad things about me. I want to fix it quickly.

"Here San Carlos, land is not good. There is no grass, no good water, and some sickness. I want to live where there is lots of water, lots of good land, and lots of wild animals for hunting. I know where there is such a place. Where will we live here? Will we have enough land to stay all together? I want the line around the reservation rubbed out. Now there is no war. There should be no line, except the one that crosses *Río* San Bernardino, the line that divides the Americans from the Mexicans.

"We take great interest in good land and want to farm and live like white men. I think Eagle Creek will be good for us. Now that we are here and you, Crawford, have us in your power, you can do with us as you please and ought to let us do what we want to do. We all have the same things as white men— hands, legs, arms, eyes—just as white men. We are surprised when we ask for and are not given the same things as white men. Nant'an Lpah promised us a legal peace. We expect to get land we want on account of making this peace. I beg you, Captain Crawford, as if you were my father, and ask you to give me what I ask for.

"Write this paper well with good tracks so General Crook will give us this land. All the Indians around me here listened to what I have said and are very anxious to get this land. They want General Crook to know this, so he will give it to them. Around Camp Apache, there is no game, and there is not enough farmland to grow what we need. We want to plant melons, squashes, corn, everything, but if we go to Camp Apache, we will starve to death there, and even after we've worked hard to make the ground good, it will be taken from us after one or two crops. There is no mescal to bake around Camp Apache.

"I want to live on Eagle Creek. If the Blue Coats think I will steal anything, then send soldiers there to watch me. I thought everything I wanted to do in this country, I would do. I am amazed if I can't live on Eagle Creek. When the general was in the Sierra Madre, the interpreter told us that we could live on Eagle Creek or on the creeks that come out of the Mogollon Mountains. If we can't go to Eagle Creek, then we want to go Ash Creek on Ash Flat and see how the country is there.

"We want all our captives here. They are in Mexico. We believe General Crook can get them for us. We believe he can do anything.

"I have heard of a little white boy the general asked about, but I have never seen him.

"We Chiricahuas want to choose a place apart from the unfriendly tribes on the reservation. If these Indians come here after I leave and talk about me, Captain Crawford, I don't want you to believe them. We're going to look for some land to farm, and we don't want any of these Indians around us. We want them to leave us alone, and we want to live where we have a store, so we can buy what we want in the way of blankets and other supplies. We only want a little one just for ourselves. This is all I have to say."

When the man finished making tracks of what I had said on paper, he gave the paper to Crawford, who read the tracks back to me and asked if it was right.

I said, "Yes, that is what I said."

Crawford said he would send it to General Crook and wait for his answer, which should come soon. I was satisfied, and the meeting ended.

Soon Crook answered. We could not have our own store—I

didn't much care—McIntosh had told me he wanted to run ours if we asked for and received it. Soon Crawford sent McIntosh away for stealing our supplies and causing trouble. Crook said the great white chiefs could not wipe out the reservation boundaries. We could not go to Eagle Creek. The White Eyes on Eagle Creek wouldn't move. Our leaders looked over Ash Creek and then Turkey Creek. Most thought Turkey Creek was best, but I was against it because we could not get mescal for baking there. Crook and Crawford decided the best place for us was Turkey Creek, a quarter of a sun's easy ride from Fort Apache.

Crook put Teniente Davis in charge of us. Many of us wanted Crawford, but he was in charge of all the Indians on the entire reservation and too busy to watch over us every day. Teniente Davis got us all to Turkey Creek across the Río Black in flood and set up his tent under tall trees next to a much bigger tent where he stored enough supplies that would last us a moon before more came from Fort Apache.

He needed some of our men to help him keep order as scout police. He made Chato his first sergeant in charge of all the police scouts, which I thought was good. That way he could control the warriors who still wanted to run and help us out with the Blue Coats when we needed it. But as I learned, that was a big mistake in my thinking.

Chato came to think that, because he was the leader of the police, he had to do exactly as the teniente told him and not use his judgment to help us when he could. He wouldn't even give us a few extra cartridges for hunting. Those we had, we had to get from Teniente Davis, who only gave us two or three at a time.

I told Perico he ought to join the police to give me a good ear to hear what was happening among the people. Teniente Davis made Perico second sergeant. Chappo insisted the job he wanted was Teniente's "striker," his servant, his pay five dollars a moon more than a scout policeman. I laughed to see him do as little as possible for the teniente, just saddling his mule, smoking his cigarettes, and watching the cook, Sam Bowman. Bowman and Mickey Free were the teniente's interpreters. I didn't like Mickey Free as an interpreter. He either often lied about what we said or didn't understand us. He made trouble. I liked Bowman. He spoke straight for us.

CHAPTER 35
LIFE AT TURKEY CREEK

My women and children and the people who followed me made camps near Naiche and his people, who camped a hand against the horizon walk away from the tent of Teniente Davis. Kaytennae camped on a high ridge where he could watch the teniente's camp. Chihuahua, Mangas, Loco, and Bonito camped close to the teniente's tents.

Kaytennae told me those leaders often spoke with Teniente Davis. Kaytennae believed Teniente Davis learned about things, such as our *tulapai* making and parties to get drunk, from his spies in the camps. Kaytennae thought the spies were Chato and Mickey Free, but I learned later they were people we didn't know from San Carlos.

From the start, there were seeds of trouble among us. Chato had lost out to Kaytennae to become Nana's *segundo*. He was often so rude around his elders and in council meetings that few liked or wanted to associate with him. Chato resented people calling him a spy in whispers behind his back and looked for opportunities to show his power over Kaytennae.

I didn't think Chato was a spy, but I didn't like the way he treated us, either. And I didn't trust Mickey Free. He had started the Cochise war with his capture by Coyoteros, a tribe of Apaches living north of the Chihennes. He was Teniente Davis's interpreter, but he often told it wrong in White Eye words, either lying or not understanding our words. We asked Teniente Davis many times to use Bowman as his interpreter. Bowman spoke our language better than Mickey Free, but Davis said no. The army paid Mickey Free to interpret our words, and he would earn his money.

We arrived at Turkey Creek too late in the season to plant and harvest large crops, but we did plant family gardens of corn, melons, beans, potatoes, and a few other green things. I hoped the corn produced before the frosts came. It would make much good *tulapai* during the Ghost Face.

My women did a good job working in our garden next to the creek. Mostly I watched them work. No Apache man wants to be a farmer. Sometimes I helped them because I knew the days were coming when we would have to grow our own food rather than taking it from ranches and farms to the south. I knew how to grow corn, melons, and beans, but my women had to show me how to plant and cultivate the greens and potatoes.

Maybe, I thought, *next harvest we'll have enough left over to sell some to the White Eyes and Blue Coats at the fort.*

A moon passed, and Teniente Davis sent word he wanted to have a council meeting with the elders and leaders in front of his tent in three suns. We gathered as he had asked, smoked to the four directions, and I prayed to *Ussen* before I said, "Speak Teniente Davis. We listen."

He looked around the circle at each of us and then said, "General Crook has rules for all who live on reservations for which he is the big chief. I want to tell them to you, although I know some of you must know them already because you made your camps at San Carlos before, but maybe you need to hear them again."

We knew most of Nant'an Lpah's rules already. Agents explained them to me and my leaders after Lyman Hart let us out of the guardhouse at San Carlos. Two of those rules I didn't think were right. One was about wife beating, which I didn't do anyway and had forgotten, and the other was about making and drinking *tulapai*, which everyone, including me, ignored.

Teniente Davis explained the rule about wife beating. The rule said we couldn't beat our wives if they displeased us and, if we did, we served time in the calaboose. That rule made us all angry, and the chiefs ignored Teniente Davis as they talked about this among themselves, and others shook their heads, frowning. He waited patiently while the chiefs settled down. Finally Naiche, tall and quiet, crossed his arms and spoke like a chief.

He said. "Teniente, this is not right. We speak a long time with Nant'an Lpah about returning to this place and making war no more. We agree to do this. We do not lie. When we talked, he said nothing about how we must live. Since the time of the grandfathers we make *tulapai*, what you call *tizwin*. Since *Ussen* makes us men and responsible for our families, when our women don't behave, it's up to us to make them do right. Sometimes that means we have to beat them. If we beat them more than they deserve, then their families make things right for them by straightening us out. This rule against making our wives behave cannot stand."

Teniente Davis made a face and shook his head. Then he explained the rule against making and drinking *tizwin*. *Tizwin* made us drunk and got us into trouble. Agents finding *tizwin* in any form would destroy it. Those making *tizwin* could expect time in the calaboose.

Chihuahua, who liked his *tulapai* as often as he could get it, stood and, shaking his fist, dark clouds of anger coloring his face, said, "Naiche speaks true words. We live now in peace. When we agreed to come back to San Carlos, that's what we agreed to do. We didn't agree to stop beating our wives or making *tulapai*. This is not right."

Naiche and Chihuahua spoke well for us all. We, every man,

agreed with them. I said nothing and watched the teniente. He listened patiently, repeated the rules, and then said the council was over. Most men didn't beat their wives much since their families protected them if they were in danger from their men. We went on ignoring the rule against *tulapai* making, and made sure Chato or Mickey Free didn't catch us.

The *tulapai* we made became stronger and tasted better when five of our women, who had been slaves in Mexico, escaped and returned to us. Among them was a wife of Mangas. Her name was Huera, and she had learned many secrets in Mexico, especially in how to make fine *tulapai*. She also knew how to keep her ears open and heard all the latest gossip among the women, even more so than my own women, and among the scouts who came to have an occasional cup of her *tulapai*. In the moons ahead, she told Mangas and me much over our cups of her *tulapai*.

Making and drinking *tulapai* sent Kaytennae in chains to a place the White Eyes called Alcatraz in the big water to the west. Kaytennae worried me. He was angry and snarling about life at Turkey Creek. He wanted to raid and make war in Mexico and spoke in the dark of night with the warriors about leaving Turkey Creek for Mexico at the right time. I worried that if he left too soon, or left fighting the scouts, the Blue Coats would make the rest of us suffer and probably kill him.

A few days after the council meeting, Teniente Davis went hunting for a turkey for his supper. He knew many fat, young turkeys flocked near the ridge where Kaytennae had his camp. Kaytennae and his men, drinking *tulapai* that day, saw the teniente coming up the ridge with his shotgun. They thought he came for them and made plans to kill him when he reached the ridge top and then run for Mexico, taking as many of the rest of us as they could.

A turkey saved us all. One called from near the creek as the teniente climbed up the ridge. Teniente turned back, found, and took the turkey near the creek. His spies soon told him that Kaytennae planned to kill him at the top of the ridge and then run for Mexico. Teniente had had enough of Kaytennae's threats and snarling language. He was dangerous.

Teniente had Kaytennae arrested by four troops of cavalry the next morning and taken to San Carlos where Nana said he had a trial. The agent, Captain Crawford, serving as judge, heard the evidence against him and sent him to the Alcatraz place on the big water for five harvests. I was glad to hear he was no longer around to make trouble for us. We might have some peace after all.

The eyes of Kaytennae's wife, Guyan, and those of his young, adopted son filled with water when they saw him led away. They thought he would suffer a long time at the hands of the Blue Coats. But Nana prayed to *Ussen* and had a dream that he would come back and be strong again. They knew Nana had true visions and had eye water no more as they waited for *Ussen*'s blessing to come true.

Nant'an Lpah thought Kaytennae might become a good leader for the People after he saw the White Eye towns by the big water and, after a few moons, asked Chato, others, and me if Kaytennae should return early from his stay at this place called Alcatraz. The others said, yes, he should return early.

Chato and I said no. I believed Kaytennae needed to learn all the White Eye secrets he could before he came back to us and to learn to think more for the People than himself. Chato hated Kaytennae and wanted him out of our camps for as long as Nant'an Lpah would keep him there. Nant'an Lpah let Kaytennae return after three harvests. He came to talk with us after we left Fort Apache, fought with the scouts in Mexico, and then agreed to talk with Nant'an Lpah about surrender. He had learned many White Eye secrets, even how to read their tracks on paper, and he did what the White Eyes told him.

Perhaps, I thought, *Kaytennae learned too much from the White Eyes at the place called Alcatraz.*

In the Season of Earth Is Reddish Brown, the high places in the mountains where we lived by Turkey Creek grew cold and, one day or two, we even had a little snow. Every morning there was thin ice on the creek edges. We moved down the mountain to camp near Fort Apache where the cold and wind were not so hard on us. I worked making good hunting arrows and a good bow while sitting with my family as the women worked on clothes or baskets. Sometimes I played monte and smoked and drank *tulapai* with my friends. The Ghost Face was a good time to visit, tell stories, and train children to survive in battle or on raids.

Huera often invited me to have a drink of her latest batch of *tulapai.* She lived in her own *wickiup* as a wife of Mangas. But Mangas stayed most of the time in the *wickiup* of his number one wife, Dilthcleyih, a daughter of Cochise. Mangas and his wives had many children to look after, three of their own, plus my nephew Daklugie, a son of Juh; and Istee, a son of Victorio. Huera took care of Daklugie, Istee, and sometimes Mangas's son, who the White Eyes later named Frank at the place called Carlisle School.

One day I visited Daklugie. He wanted to live with me and my family, but I said no, even though I would have enjoyed having him with me. I wanted him to live long enough to have a family of his own, but I knew that growing up in my *wickiup* much increased his chances of dying in a battle than if he lived with peaceful Mangas.

After this visit with Daklugie, Huera asked me if I wanted to sample her latest *tulapai* brew, and naturally I said yes. When I sat down in her *wickiup,* she told the boys she wanted to speak with me privately.

She said, "Geronimo, I have heard some things I think you should know."

I lighted a cigarette and smoked with her before I said, "Speak, Huera. I will listen."

"I hear stories from the women married to scouts who tell them what they hear during their duties among the people. Many times, what I hear from these women soon happens. Less than a moon before Teniente Davis took Kaytennae, they said Chato laughs often. They said soon many Blue Coats will take Kaytennae. They spoke true, Geronimo. Not just silly woman stories."

I remember hearing the creek burble nearby and the wind shaking the tops of the tall pine trees, making a swishing noise and the good smell of her cooking pot with the taste of fine *tulapai* on my tongue as I listened to Huera.

"Yes, the women spoke true that time, Huera. Why do you tell me this?"

"I tell you this because now they speak about you, and I have heard the same thing from a scout or two who have sampled my *tulapai* even as you do now."

I raised an eyebrow at this. "What do they say about me?"

"Chato is telling the teniente that you and Mangas, especially you, are bad men. The teniente wants to lock you up. Women say the Blue Coats will soon come to take you both to the guardhouse. Coyote waits."

What Huera told me made no sense. I hadn't done anything except drink a little *tulapai,* and even the police did that. I didn't believe what she said, but even as the words came out of her mouth, my guts clenched. I wouldn't go back to the guardhouse.

"I don't believe those stories. I haven't done anything. Teniente has no reason to arrest me."

Huera shook her head. "The Blue Coats will find one. You wait and see. Then it will be too late. You don't believe me? You talk to Nodiskey. You know Nodiskey the Coyotero chief who's married a Chiricahua woman and lives with us. He will tell you."

"Hmmph. You're a good woman, Huera. Thank you for this warning. I'll talk to Nodiskey and listen to what he has to say."

After my drink with Huera, a few suns passed, and I went to visit Nodiskey. Even down out of the mountains, it was cold and windy that day. We sat in his *wickiup* wrapped in our blankets, hearing the wind shake the grass and brush and drinking his coffee from an old battered pot that had seen many suns traveling. His women left to visit and work on their sewing. He and I smoked a cigarette to the four directions. He flipped the last of the ash into the fire, looked at me from under the blanket over the top of his head, and nodded he was ready to talk.

He said, "Ho, Geronimo, how can I help you on this cold day?"

"Mangas's wife, Huera, the master *tulapai* maker, has told me stories she has heard from women of the scouts and from a few scouts when they come for a taste of her *tulapai*. I don't believe the stories she has heard. She says I should talk to you about them to learn if she lies. If she is lying, then Mangas should cure her of this bad character with a good, strong stick."

Nodiskey played innocent and, cutting his eyes toward me, shrugged. "Of what stories do you speak that we should worry about women's gossip?"

"She heard that Chato and Mickey Free are telling Teniente Davis I'm a bad Indian and that soon he will come with many soldiers like he did for Kaytennae, and put and keep me in the guardhouse."

Nodiskey stared into the little fire between us. As a big gust of wind shook the trees and *wickiup,* he pulled his blanket tighter, and said, "They will arrest you."

I shook my head, "How do you know this?"

"I hear the scouts talking. I even heard Chato tell another scout you didn't deserve anyone's trust, and that you were a bad Indian. He said he would make sure Teniente didn't let you get away with anything. First chance they see, they'll put you in the guardhouse and keep you there. That's what Chato says to a young scout who thinks you're a great warrior."

I thought, *Nodiskey has found a good source of peyote buttons and chews too many.*

I spoke slowly to keep the anger out of my voice. "They won't arrest me. I do nothing wrong. I haven't even thought about killing anybody, horse or man, American or Indian. Chato was my *segundo* many times in Mexico. He wouldn't lie about me."

Nodiskey shook his head. "I only know what I heard, Geronimo. I hope Chato and the others were just talking big and thinking they know something they don't. But if it's true, you'll be in the guardhouse soon."

"Hmmph. Nodiskey is a brother. I thank you for telling me this, but I don't believe it. No one will put me in that stinking guardhouse again."

The rest of the Ghost Face, I watched Chato and Teniente closely, but I never saw any reason to leave when my women kept me warm and with plenty to eat, and I enjoyed my little son, Fenton, and spoke often with my grown children.

CHAPTER 36
TROUBLE COMES

During the Seasons of the Ghost Face and Little Eagles, the women worked on leather, mostly moccasins, and baskets, and getting together and sharing seeds for crops planted after the wind the White Eyes called chinook blew across the mountains and began melting snow in the mountain passes. Men played cards, told the young the stories of Coyote and of grandfather times, smoked around fires, and talked of past battles and good raids. The Ghost Face and the early Season of Little Eagles passed in solitude. Two or three times in a moon, I took my family to the Fort Apache trading post. We had a good time visiting with our friends who also came there to talk around the big, iron stove that made the room almost too hot.

Outside, under the covered porches and marching ground, the soldiers thought they would make fun of us and asked the children to point out leaders such as Naiche, Chihuahua, Mangas, or me. Then, when we looked in their direction, they would make a quick hand slash across their throats.

We learned later it was supposed to be funny. But many of us, including the leaders, thought the soldiers were trying to warn us that the Blue Coats were planning to kill us. This made us suspicious of the Blue Coat chiefs, and we watched for any sign they might try to take us. If we saw such signs, whether the sun was bright and hot or snow was falling, we would leave for Mexico. After my talks with Huera and Nodiskey, I began to think it was best that Mangas and I disappear from the reservation anyway. I doubted the Blue Coats could ever catch us again like Nant'an Lpah had at our camps in Bugatseka.

The chinook winds came. We moved our camps back to Turkey Creek. The previous harvest, the White Eyes had bought us tools that horses pulled to break up dirt so the women could plant their seeds in family places and crops in big, clear meadows. The harness for the horses to pull the tools was too big for our ponies. We had to learn many adjustments in how to handle our ponies and train them to pull the tools. I didn't learn how to use the tool they called a plow. I learned to drive one of their freight wagons. That was enough training for me.

I asked Betzinez, who had agreed to be my acolyte when we were raiding in Mexico before Nant'an Lpah came, to use a plow on land my women wanted to plant with their seeds and the land I wanted to plant in barley. It was a good year for crops, and my women's seeds and my barley grew well as the warm days in the Season of Many Leaves came to stay.

But trouble came, and I never saw any food come from the seeds we planted.

A woman brought our trouble. One of the older warriors with much fighting experience had not been married long to a young woman. After a *tulapai* drink, barely able to stand as he staggered up to his *wickiup,* he told her to raise her skirt and get on her knees. She good-naturedly laughed at him and said that in his condition, he wouldn't be able to do what he wanted, even if she let him try. Wanting to show his authority, he beat her with a big stick. He said he didn't remember much about what happened after that. But his new woman went to Teniente Davis's tent that evening. Perico, who was there, said she had many bruises and stripes on her shoulders. Her hair was stiff from still drying blood, and her left arm, broken in two places. Teniente Davis, very angry, put her on a wagon and had Chappo drive her to the Blue Coat *di-yen* at the fort.

As soon as the wagon left, Teniente Davis, Chato, Perico, and two other scouts went to arrest her man. They found him splattered with blood and passed out on the floor of their *wickiup* with a blood-covered piece of firewood in his hand. The scouts handcuffed him, tied him on a horse to keep him from falling off, and carried him to the calaboose at Fort Apache. Still drunk, he only complained when they woke him up.

Chappo brought the beaten woman back to Teniente Davis. The *di-yen* had many bandages and salves on her back and had a splint on her arm to hold it straight so the bones would grow back together straight while she did her work. She told the teniente she was sorry she had bothered him, and that she needed to return to her *wickiup* and fix her man something to eat. She looked confused and then angry when the teniente explained that her man was in the calaboose for beating her, and there he would stay for half a moon.

She begged the teniente to let her man go, but he said no. He said it was against Nant'an Lpah's rules for men to beat their women. She was free to go back to her *wickiup*. She made a low, moaning wail with her free right arm hiding her eyes as she trudged down the sandy trail back to her *wickiup*.

Perico told me several of the chiefs, including Naiche, Chihuahua, and Loco, went to Teniente's tent and said he must let the woman-beating man go, that the Blue Coats must not and could not interfere in family business. Teniente shook his head and told each one no. The man had broken the Nant'an Lpah rule against wife beating. He had to stay in the calaboose for half a moon for breaking the rule. They tried to reason with the teniente, but he said he would not change his mind.

A day or two after this, Teniente went to the calaboose and spoke with the woman's man. Before a half moon passed, Teniente arrested another man, who had held the *tulapai* party when the woman's man got drunk. Now all chiefs were angry, especially Chihuahua, who so liked *tulapai* he was willing to fight over it, and Mangas, whose wife Huera made the best *tulapai* in the camp and received so many presents for making it that Mangas was becoming a rich man. They demanded Teniente release the man who made and served the *tulapai*. Again, Teniente said no.

When I heard this, I thought, *Now Ussen will make things right for all the indignities we have suffered being here.*

Chihuahua and Mangas called a council meeting. They wanted to discuss what we should do about our people being locked up for things they had every right to do. Chihuahua told what had happened with the teniente putting our men in the calaboose and said wife beating and *tulapai* making were our rights. As at the first meeting with Teniente, after he repeated Nant'an Lpah rules, Chihuahua said that, when we surrendered, we didn't agree to those rules. He asked what the council thought about getting rid of the bad rules. Many were angry and, without thinking, said we should break into the calaboose and free those Teniente put there. But all knew that would mean war and much blood, mostly ours.

Each of us had our say. I said little except that the rules were bad and that we needed to do something about freeing the men in the calaboose.

Chihuahua said, "This is what I think we should do. We make a big pot of *tulapai*, good fine *tulapai*. Have Huera do it, don't you agree, Mangas?" He looked at Mangas, who grinned and nodded. "When it's ready, we'll have a big drink. All of us will drink it one evening; most of us will get a little drunk, and many, plenty drunk. Then we go see Teniente the next morning and tell him we've all been drinking. Will he, can he, throw us all in the calaboose? No, he won't. I don't think he'll even try. This will show him how bad this rule is. He'll have to ignore it.

Who stands with me on this?"

We all stood. He ended the council with, "When Mangas tells us that Huera has the *tulapai* ready, then we'll all have a good drink one night, and the next morning challenge Teniente."

We all said, *"Enjuh."* There were many laughs as we looked forward to putting the teniente in a box of his own making. Far off in the distance, I heard a coyote howl. We all knew Coyote waits.

In half a moon, Mangas let it be known Huera had a fine new batch of *tulapai* and invited us to her hidden place in the brush one night for a drink. It was good *tulapai,* very good *tulapai.* That night even Loco drank enough to have a hangover the next morning, but Chihuahua was still drunk when we went and waited outside Teniente's tent as the sky began turning to dawn's gray light and burning *pesh-klitso* on the edge of the mountains. Birds in the brush began singing and calling to their neighbors. We stood calm and quiet in the cool, awakening morning, waiting for the teniente to leave the land of sleeping.

As the light grew brighter, Teniente's canvas door to his tent opened, and he stepped outside. He looked surprised when he saw all the chiefs and subchiefs and about thirty warriors quietly standing there around his door. He nodded and smiled when he first saw us, but frowned when he looked around, didn't see any women and children, and began to understand this was serious business. Some of the warriors had brought their rifles. The chiefs and subchiefs had only their knives, and a few wore their pistolas.

Loco said, "Teniente, we come for a talk."

Teniente nodded. *"Enjuh.* Let me make water, and then we talk."

He walked off into the brush and soon returned. The chiefs, all except Chato and the scouts who stayed outside; Mickey

Free, the bad interpreter Teniente insisted on using; and I followed him into his tent. Chappo was making Teniente his morning coffee on a little iron stove, the kind that Blue Coat chiefs use. Teniente sat down in his chair facing us and turned the lantern light up while we squatted in a half circle around him. He said to Loco, "Speak. I will listen."

Loco stood. I could tell his head hurt from the *tulapai*. He cleared his throat and said, "Hmmph. Teniente, we don't like these rules Nant'an Lpah makes for us. They are bad rules. They must be changed."

Chihuahua was still a little drunk but angry, loud, and forceful. He jumped to his feet and said, "What I have to say can be said in a few words. Then Loco can talk the rest of the day if he wishes. We agreed on a peace with the Americans, *Nakai-yes*, and other Indian tribes. Peace says nothing about how we live. We're not children taught how to live with our women and what to eat and drink. All our lives we eat or drink what seems good to us. White Eyes drink wine and whiskey, even officers and soldiers at the posts. We can drink what we want, too. Treatment of our wives is our own business. We don't treat them badly when they behave. When a woman doesn't behave, her husband has a right to punish her. We have done everything we promised to do when we had our talk with Nant'an Lpah in Mexico. We have kept the peace. We harm nobody. Now we're being punished for things we have a right to do so long as they don't harm others."

Teniente Davis shook his head and said, "Nant'an Lpah had good reasons for no *tizwin* making and drinking. A drunk Indian doesn't know what he's doing. He might kill someone from another band, causing a war between bands on the reservation or even a breakout. You don't think I know, but a drunk Chiricahua, not more than a moon ago, tried to kill his wife. He stabbed her in the shoulder before others could stop him.

"Wife beating is not allowed, either. I had to send a young woman to our *di-yen* because her husband beat her and broke her arm in two places and left many bruised and bloody places on her. I had her husband put in the calaboose for half a moon for that beating. It's only right that we—"

Teniente Davis's talk about the rule against wife beating made Nana so angry he stood up with a dark scowl on his face, spoke a few words, hard to hear in that whispery old man's voice of his, and walked away from the council. All eyes were on him, and men were wondering if they should go, too. Mickey Free didn't want to tell Teniente Davis what Nana said, but he insisted on hearing it.

Mickey Free squeezed his bad eye shut and said, "Nana say, 'Tell Teniente *Enchau* (stout chief) that he can't advise me how to treat my women. He is only a boy. I killed men before he was born.' "

Teniente made a face like he had eaten some bad meat and was sick.

The chiefs nodded their heads and said, "Hmmph." We all knew Nana spoke straight words. Chihuahua, still drunk from too much *tulapai* the night before, staggered a little as he moved up a step closer to Teniente.

He said, as he swung his arm toward all of us, "We all drank *tulapai* last night, all of us in here, those outside, and many more except the scouts. What are you going to do about it? Are you going to put us all in the calaboose? You have no jail big enough to hold us all."

Teniente crossed his arms and looked at each of us. He said, "What to do about this is too serious for me to decide. I was only doing what Nant'an Lpah told me to do, which is for your own good. I'll send him a message on the talking wire and ask what to do. As soon as he tells me, I'll tell you."

Again, we all nodded and grunted our assent, and left Teniente's tent. We would wait and see. Nant'an Lpah should send his answer over the talking wire by the time of shortest shadows.

No answer from Nant'an Lpah came by the time the sun disappeared. We had another council around a fire at a hidden place that night. All worried because the talking wire still had no words from Nant'an Lpah. At my turn to speak, I said, "There's much arguing among the White Eye chiefs over who is in charge of the reservation. Captain Crawford has left San Carlos. Bad White Eyes who cheat us, return. Maybe, Nant'an Lpah has left, too. Maybe that is why he doesn't answer Teniente. Maybe he is no longer here to protect us from the bad White Eyes or other Blue Coats. Maybe his big chief sends him someplace else."

Every face had a frown. Many voices asked what should we do without Nant'an Lpah to protect us.

Naiche said, "What do you think we should do, Geronimo?"

"I think we should wait. Until we understand what has happened to Nant'an Lpah, we won't know the right path to take. If he is gone, maybe we should go, too. Maybe he still decides what to do with us. Some say he will send us away to a bad place. Nodiskey says this, but we don't know if this is true. If he takes too long to answer the talking wire, either he is gone or maybe he is coming here to punish us and send us to a bad place. If we think this, then we ought to leave. We ought to prepare for that anyway."

Mangas said, "Geronimo speaks wise words. We wait, but I tell my women maybe we leave in a sun or two. The talking wire is not broken. Nant'an Lpah should have answered Teniente long time before this. I think he will come to punish us in a bad way."

Naiche crossed his arms and said, "I won't leave even if

Nant'an Lpah comes here. I don't believe he'll want to move us. It was too hard to get us here in the first place. This is a good place. We ought to stay here awhile and see what happens."

Chihuahua, whose taste for *tulapai* had pushed us to this talk in the first place, nodded. "Hmmph. Naiche speaks wise words. I stay, too."

I looked at them. "Then think of what Teniente and Crawford did to Kaytennae. Do you want to spend the rest of your lives at the place the White Eyes call Alcatraz if Nant'an Lpah comes to punish us? The more who go out, the harder it will be for the White Eyes to catch us and put us in the guardhouse. We scatter, and they have to chase us everywhere. That makes them weaker when they find us. Maybe we go. Maybe not. But we should all go out together."

Nana nodded. "I know Loco and the scouts won't go, but I'll go as Geronimo suggests, even if I have to leave my family behind for a while."

I said, "All we can do is wait and be ready to do what we have to do."

CHAPTER 37
ESCAPE FROM TURKEY CREEK

That night I called my women and children to come sit with me around the fire. They studied me with dark, wide eyes as I smoked a cigarette to the four directions and then gave it to my wives and my beautiful grown daughter. I wanted them all to understand this was serious business. My women waited calmly for me to speak, probably already knowing what I would say.

I said, "I met and smoked with the chiefs and leading men to talk about what we should do if no talking wire message comes from Nant'an Lpah, or if he comes himself to take us far away to a dark place like they did with Kaytennae. Mangas, Nana, and I will leave before we let this happen to our families.

"Naiche and Chihuahua say they will stay. If no talking wire word comes from Nant'an Lpah to Teniente, then we will leave Turkey Creek and return to Mexico. I won't risk the Blue Coats throwing me in the dark, stinking guardhouse at San Carlos or the place the White Eyes call Alcatraz by the big water like they did with Kaytennae.

"Huera, who sells her *tulapai* to the scouts and listens to them talk, and Nodiskey, who heads a village, think the Blue Coats will come to arrest me, even though I have done nothing to deserve arrest. If there is no talking wire message from Nant'an Lpah in the next sun, and *Ussen* does not tell me to stay on Turkey Creek, then those three warnings are enough for me. We will go. Be ready."

The orange and yellow light from our little fire cast twisting shadows on the face of my women and children. They said nothing, only nodded they understood. They remembered well how hard and how good life was in the Bugatseka camps in the Sierra Madre. If we escaped, it would be hard and dangerous to run with the Blue Coats and scouts after us, but it would be worth it. They would be ready.

I lay with Zi-yeh under the blankets and then went to Shegha. Both were near to weaning our youngest children and wanted another child. It was a good thing to feel them close to me and the heat of their desire.

Shtsha-she seemed on the edge of a bad sickness. If Shtsha-she had been stronger, I would have lain with her, too, but she needed to rest and regain her strength. I planned to make a healing ceremony for her at the next sunrise.

When the sun glowed bright and blinding on the mountaintops to the east and the smooth black sky turned to the color of blue stone, I prayed to *Ussen* for the day and then began the ceremony for the healing of Shtsha-she. When the ceremony finished, she told me she felt better and was ready to work, but I told her to rest. Soon we would see if the medicine had enough power to make her well.

The sun crept across the sky, passing one hand over the other, but still the talking wire did not speak. As we waited, it was becoming clear that either Teniente or Nant'an Lpah planned a hard punishment for us. Maybe a new Nant'an had replaced Nant'an Lpah and would not treat us fairly. Maybe the new Nant'an would do something even worse than what Crawford did to Kaytennae.

The more I thought about what a traitor Chato had become, the lies Mickey Free had told, and how Teniente Davis ignored me, the more certain I became that, regardless of what they did to anyone else, I would be the most severely punished. I was determined not to let them do me that way.

I sent a runner to find my brothers, Perico and Fun, and my son Chappo. They all worked as scouts for the teniente. The runner told them I wanted to meet that day at my *wickiup*. Fun and Perico appeared in front of my *wickiup* before the time of shortest shadows. I motioned them to sit, and we smoked.

I said, "Still the talking wire is silent?" They nodded. "I have given much thought to this. Teniente and Chato blame me for all this uncertainty, although it is Chihuahua who had the big idea to challenge the teniente. I think Nant'an Lpah and Teniente Davis plan to send many of us to join Kaytennae in the place of bars and shackles the White Eyes call Alcatraz on the big water. I have spoken privately to you often that we must leave this place and return to Mexico. Later today, we will have a council, and I will try to convince our men to go out with us. You will help us all as we run for Mexico if you kill Chato and Teniente Davis and then join us after we leave. The scouts, with their leaders dead, will desert the army and join us. By the time the Blue Coats have more scouts to track and fight us, we will be deep in Mexico. Brothers, will you do this for the People and help us get free?"

Fun first looked at Perico, who nodded, and then me. "Brother, it will be done."

"*Enjuh!* Listen carefully. We'll leave two hands after the time of shortest shadows. You must wait around with the other scouts until after we are gone. That way suspicions won't grow that we have all gone because you are not there. After Teniente learns the People have gone, he will call all the scouts to his tent to give them ammunition and to hear his instructions for tracking us.

"Raise your rifles then and kill him and Chato. Call for all the scouts to come with you, and take all the ammunition in the rations tent. You must move fast after you strike. You move too slowly, they catch you. Bring all the scouts who desert with you. They will be a great help to us. Meet us at our usual place in the Mogollon Mountains to the east."

Again, they nodded and left to return to Fort Apache. They were good men.

Mangas and I called a council for late in the afternoon. All the men wanted to talk about our punishment for us breaking Nant'an Lpah's rules. The men came to council, and so did most of the women and older children, who sat in the brush around us to listen. By the time we met, there was little to say. Teniente told us several times the talking wire had not spoken. We must be patient. Naiche and Chihuahua said they would be patient. I said I had heard many stories of what might happen from Mangas's wife, Huera. Pointing to her in the circle of women and children, I said, "Huera, stand and tell us all what you know, what you hear from the scouts who drink your good *tulapai*."

Huera smoothed the hair from her face and stood waist high above the brush as the light was falling, leaving her in light and dark shadow. With burning, narrowed eyes, she looked around at us all and said, "Teniente knows I made the *tulapai* we all drank. I know he will put me in the calaboose when he comes with his scouts. I call on my husband and all men who like to drink *tulapai* against the rules of Nant'an Lpah to leave and live free in Sonora. We have lived there before. We can live there again. Will you submit like a woman to a man for the arrest and punishment Teniente and Nant'an Lpah will dole out to you? No! You are men. If you're warriors, then you'll go on the warpath. Nant'an Lpah must catch you first before punishing you. Go! Make them work to find you. Punish them because they follow you!"

Before I could say more, Nodiskey stood and repeated the

rumors he had heard that Nant'an Lpah had ordered Teniente to arrest me and Mangas. Now, after we had all become drunk, he would surely do it. The Chiricahuas needed to leave.

Mangas said he was leaving. He had seen the army murder his father. Naiche and Chihuahua listened but said again, as they had at last council, they would stay. I knew *Ussen* was telling us we must go. But after the council, we had only about fifteen men who were willing to leave the reservation. We needed more. We needed Naiche and Chihuahua to go with us.

That night, I lay under the blankets with Shtsha-she. She was still weak, and I stayed there only to comfort her. I dreamed a dream in which the People, like a great stream, ran shoulder to shoulder through the wilderness. The Blue Coats rode hard but could not catch them. When I opened my eyes to the gray light of a new day and heard the birds in the brush start to call and the women chopping wood for their fires, I knew *Ussen* had spoken to me in that dream. Seeing the People like a great *río* must mean there would be enough of us to leave for Mexico. I told my wives *Ussen* had spoken. We would leave the next sun when the sun was two hands off the horizon. They said they would be ready.

After I prayed for the day and ate a morning meal, I went to the *wickiups* of Nana and then Mangas and told them of my dream and when my family and I would leave. They said they would leave then, too.

Nana said, "We must cut the talking wire a few times where it passes through the trees and then tie the ends back together with a piece of rawhide *reata*. Using rawhide ties will make the places of the breaks hard to find and give us more time to leave without more Blue Coats knowing we are gone."

I nodded. "Hmmph. Nana speaks wise words. I'll tell Chappo to do this soon after we leave."

Mangas agreed to bring all the ammunition we had been storing and hiding. That, with the ammunition Fun and Perico took after killing Teniente and Chato, would be enough for a long while in Mexico.

I gathered the horses and mules I planned to use when we ran. Naiche and Chihuahua rode up to speak with me, and I was glad to see them.

Naiche said, "You don't need to do this, Geronimo. Teniente and Nant'an Lpah won't put us in guardhouse. Maybe he only takes our corn supplies so we can no longer make *tulapai*, but he is a just man. The punishment will fit our crime."

All the time Naiche spoke, Chihuahua stared down the canyon and nodded his head but said nothing.

I said, "I think you speak true, Naiche. But I learned a short time ago that my brothers in the scouts decided to leave and killed Teniente and Chato. Now they run, and half the scouts with them. Soon the Blue Coats will come after us. I'm innocent of their blood, but now the Blue Coats will think all Apaches are responsible. They will be after our blood. Now we have no choice but to run."

Naiche's jaw dropped, and Chihuahua's eyes grew round with surprise. Chihuahua said, "Now we have no choice. You're right. The Blue Coats will send us to Alcatraz. Kaytennae will have much company." His jaw muscles rippled as he clenched his teeth, looked skyward, filled his cheeks with air, and blew. "My people and I will come with you, Geronimo. We follow you at sundown. There is no moon tonight. We will be slow, but we come."

Naiche stared off down the creek and shook his head. "You're right, Chihuahua. Now we must go. My people and I will come with you, Geronimo."

"Ho. It's a good thing for the great chiefs Chihuahua and

Naiche to join us and leave this place. I'll leave two hands after the time of shortest shadows. Follow my trail when you can. I'll cross the Río Black and take a short rest in the mountains to the south while we watch for those pursuing us. Then we'll head south for the border."

Naiche and Chihuahua turned their ponies to ride for their camps and gather their people. I smiled as I heard a coyote yip up the canyon, and I thought, *Yes. Coyote waits.*

We were few when we headed into the mountains as the sun rode toward the west. Eight men were in my band, four with Nana, and five with Mangas. When Naiche and Chihuahua joined us, the number of men we had doubled. There were also eight adolescent boys, who, while not warriors, were able to use rifles and pistols as well as their bows and arrows. Among us all, there were ninety-two women and children we had to protect.

We crossed the Río Black Canyon and rode hard across the *llano* to the mountains to the south, where we made our camps for the People to rest and could watch back toward Fort Apache to learn when the Blue Coats were coming. Naiche and Chihuahua's bands were not far behind us and also made their camps on the same crest where we camped.

We had not camped long when Fun and Perico came to my fire, their mouths turned down and their eyes red from little sleep. They looked in bad spirits.

I said, "Scouts! You have joined us. *Enjuh.* Are there others?"

Fun puffed his cheeks and shook his head. "Only Atelnietze came with us. Teniente called us to his tent when the shadows were walking into the darkness. He told Chato and Dutchy to make us ground the butts of our rifles and to shoot any man who didn't. There was no chance to shoot either Chato or Teniente. It was dark when Teniente went into the supply tent to get extra cartridges for the scouts, and we slipped away, but we couldn't kill them—too risky."

I heard coyotes yipping again and smiled. They had warned me twice that day, and I had not listened. Coyote waits. I drank a cup of good, hot coffee with my brothers as the sun was filling the mountains beyond the *llano*. I heard feet running and turned to see Dohn-say coming through the brush. She had gone to visit women in Chihuahua's camp, hoping, I was sure, to see Dahkeya, the young man she wanted for her husband.

Puffing in the cold air and red in the face, she said, "Father! Father! You must leave now. Atelnietze told Chihuahua that the scouts didn't kill Teniente and Chato. Chihuahua has great anger. He says you lied when you told Naiche and him that the scouts had killed them. Otherwise, he would not have left with you. He, Ulzana, and Atelnietze have their rifles. He says he's coming to kill you."

I knew Chihuahua meant business. I had seen him kill men when they crossed him. He was not a man you trifled with. I didn't even think about challenging him. I thought Teniente and Chato were dead when I told Chihuahua and Naiche the news, but that didn't make any difference now. I sent Fun to Mangas's camp with the word that we had to leave fast, go east rather than south, and that I was already moving. Naiche had camped with Mangas, his uncle, and went with him. The women scrambled, and we were quickly moving east.

Later I learned that when Chihuahua got to my camp and found we were gone, he stomped his foot in frustration, then sat down by the fire we had just left to think. He decided, as I had guessed, to move farther north into the Mogollon Mountains to stay out of sight for a while and then to curve back into Fort Apache. But eventually, having to dodge scouts and Blue Coats, Chihuahua turned south and crossed the border in about a moon. Mangas and I worked our way south until we crossed the border about the same time, but to the east of Chihuahua's crossing. Chihuahua wound up on the west branch of the *Río* Bavispe. I made a camp on the southern tip of Bugatseka, and Mangas with his little band went to Juh's stronghold south at Guaynopa. We all needed rest before we began raiding in Mexico once more.

CHAPTER 38
FINDING OUR WIVES

The groups with Nana, Mangas, and I made our camp close to the one Nant'an Lpah's scouts had attacked three harvests earlier in the southern point of Bugatseka. There was good wood, water, and tall grass over large meadows for our animals. Having been on the run for nearly two moons, we all needed rest.

In a few days, the warriors were ready to raid again. We had no dry meat for the coming Ghost Face, and they wanted to increase our horse herd for replacements. Nana, Mangas, and I talked. Nana and Mangas agreed to lead the raids and decided they should take with them the boys who were old enough to become acolytes, ready to begin their warrior training. I stayed in the camp with Chappo and two or three other men to guard the women and children.

Two suns after the warriors left, about a hand after the time of shortest shadows, I sat in the shade of tall pines watching the women work sorting juniper berries from big baskets they had filled and brought back to camp hung on the back of a mule. They had tied the mule to a bush nearby where he would be handy if they wanted to go fill the baskets again.

It was a peaceful time. Insects buzzed in the hot, sleepy air; an occasional breeze off one of the nearby high ridges shook the tops of the tall pines and passed on. The women chatted and shared stories, and the sun's heat felt warm and comforting.

Fenton, my little son by Zi-yeh, was just gaining enough leg strength and balance to go wherever he wanted. We kept a close watch on him. A child that age was easy to lose in the tall grass and brush. He might also fall off the edge of a high bank. Several of the other children laughed and played hide and catch. Chappo, my young warrior son, sat watching his brother and the rest of the camp while I leaned against the rough bark of a pine and smoked after being in prayer to *Ussen*.

Chappo was a good warrior who learned fast and practiced often for accuracy with his weapons. He had named the young woman he wanted for a wife, and I had agreed to talk with her parents about how large a bride gift they wanted for her. Soon enough, there would be children who would call me grandfather.

I was thinking of taking a nap when I saw the mule's ears go up as he looked at one of the ridges. Maybe a wolf or bear was watching the camp. I looked where the mule was watching but saw nothing. Then the mule looked at another place and started stomping its hooves, twisting and pulling against the tie rope like it wanted to run, and making its warning call. I didn't wait to see what disturbed him. I sprang up, and, in two steps, picked up Fenton to carry to Zi-yeh.

As I passed him, I breathed quietly to Chappo, "You may have to jump off the bluff behind us to get away. I go to the women."

Rolling thunder and the swishing whine of bullets suddenly filled the air. My women dropped their berries and started to run with me. I ran on, waving them back and motioning them to get close to the ground. A woman working with them didn't obey and ran into the hail of bullets swarming around us. Bright red spots surrounding dark bullet holes, like some deadly disease, covered her body and arms and threw her backwards to the ground. A boy of nine or ten harvests ran to her. A whining ricochet off a nearby rock hit him in the eye. He fell in mid-step.

I ran with Fenton in my arms through high grass, making quail scatter into the hail of bullets around me. I headed for the brush growing on a steep, sloping bank leading down to a nearly dry stream leaking its water toward the *río*. Fenton laughed and had a good time. I felt the swift snap and tug of bullets flying through my shirt as the bullet cloud grew thicker.

Suddenly the side of my right leg and the flesh near my left shoulder felt burned as if by a red-hot iron. I saw red dribbling down my thigh and my shirtsleeve was black and wet. I kept low and continued to run through the brush with bullets chasing my path, knocking limbs off trees, and sending leaves up and then falling in a spiral in the warm air.

I broke out of the brush and ran to the nearly dry creek strewn with boulders big enough to hide behind. I found a place where we could hide next to a boulder in a little washed-out cave beside it. The shooting had stopped except for the occasional crack and boom echoing off the ridges of a scout's big bore rifle. I heard the scouts calling to each other nearly all the way around the camp as they closed in to take everything we had. One or two passed through the brush I had come from and one looked down the creek bed where Fenton and I hid but then returned back toward the center of our camp.

I waited until it was nearly dark, the shadows long and black and, carrying Fenton, I worked my way toward to the center of the camp. Over seventy scouts were burning all our supplies while they searched through the *wickiups*. They kept the women and most of the children huddled together in a group off to one side, like a herd of cattle. I blew with relief when I saw my women unhurt. I held Fenton close, whispering in his ear to be quiet, that mother was coming soon. I drew as close as I dared to the women sitting quietly, guarded by three or four scouts.

I put Fenton on his feet, pointed toward Zi-yeh, and said in a whisper, "Mother," while I crabbed back in the brush and disappeared.

He saw her, and, holding his arms out, ran toward the group yelling, "Mother! Mother!"

Zi-yeh jumped up, wiping away her eye water with her sleeve, and ran past a scout, who cocked his rifle in warning and then smiled and slowly let the hammer down as he saw the little boy run to her in the dim light. At full dark, but before the moon was out, I crept away to meet those who escaped at the rendezvous point we always chose before making any camp.

We were fortunate that nearly all the men were gone when the attack came. We escaped many losses. Only the boy hit in the eye and the woman who stood up in the first hail of bullets had died, but the scouts took fifteen women and children. At the rendezvous canyon, I first thanked *Ussen* that Chappo survived the jump off the high bluff. He got away with nothing broken and no wounds. My wounds were minor and healing well.

I made medicine to call rain that would wipe our trail to the scouts' eyes. The rain, in great, billowing, black clouds, rolling over the mountains, was quick to come. It hid our trail and gave me time to think about what we should do. Two days later, the raiders met us in the rendezvous canyon.

Nana, Mangas, and I talked over what to do. Mangas decided, after losing Huera to the scouts in the attack, to use Juh's stronghold near the Great Canyon at Guaynopa for his main camp.

Nana decided to camp in the mountains to the northwest of Janos with five men and ten women and disappear until I returned from what I was determined to do, which was to take back the women the scouts had taken from us.

★ ★ ★ ★ ★

With me were my son Chappo; my brother Perico; Dahkeya, who had recently married Dohn-say; Hunlona and Beshe, who had also lost wives during the raid; and four or five women who were determined to help get their sisters and children back.

Nant'an Lpah had many soldiers watching the border where we normally crossed at Guadalupe Canyon, San Bernardino, or through the Animas Valley, but we moved east a hand's hard ride past Laguna Palomas to a wide *arroyo* stretching north across the border where the soldiers rarely went. No one could see us in the *arroyo* unless they were on its edge when we passed. It was easy to cross the border there.

Two moons later, Chihuahua and his brother, Ulzana, used the same place to cross when Ulzana made his great raid for revenge against the scouts and to take back the families who belonged to us.

Our trail made an arc north and then west across the Black Range, the Gila Mountains, and Eagle Creek, until we came to the abandoned camps on Turkey Creek and then approached Fort Apache. I was certain Nant'an Lpah had our women and families at Fort Apache. White Eyes spotted us. We made a little raid to make our pursuers believe that we headed into the Black Range.

We killed nearly everyone in our path, so the White Eyes could get no information about us. We spared one of two brothers. I killed one with a rifle shot and smashed his head with a rock in case the bullet didn't kill him, and I took his shirt and coat.

His younger brother tried to hide from us in the cane and cattails by the creek, but we found and kept him. He was a brave child and looked young enough that we could make him into an Apache. He had a gift for tongues, spoke a little Spanish, and told us his name was Santiago McKinn.

At the time of shortest shadows, we found empty miner cabins in a canyon and took their supplies. But we didn't burn them to avoid giving away our position. We raided a ranch where a woman and her two children got away into the brush. I could have found them easily and killed them, but decided it was best to go on rather than spill their blood and drive the White Eyes to gather in a big band for revenge. We hid most of the day and into the night on a creek coming out of the Black Range.

When the sun came up, I decided it was time for us to head for the *Río* Gila as fast as we could move. In two days, we reached the place I wanted for a base camp. The White Eyes called it Teepee Canyon. It lay northeast of Mogollon peak. The canyon walls were high and rugged. No White Eye would think to look there. We could have fires without anyone seeing their smoke a long way off, and there was plenty of water for drinking and bathing.

We rested for three suns and then moved west, raiding ranches and miner shacks to take horses, mules, and other supplies we needed. In three suns of hard riding, we were ready to approach Fort Apache from down a long canyon that went past East Fork, a small village less than a hand against the sun's ride from Fort Apache. We left Beshe, since he was oldest, and a woman to keep our horses, while we ran down the canyon to the camps near Fort Apache to find and take back our women and children.

We came to the village of East Fork after the moon had begun its fall into the southwestern mountains. An old woman, many of her teeth missing and her hair flying out from her head like she was a ghost, sat in front of her lodge, where she stayed up most of the night guarding her little garden from marauding deer. Even from where she sat in the dark shadows, the smile across her ancient, wrinkled face was easy to see.

I said, "Ho, Grandmother. Now you are our prisoner. Tell us

where our families are, and we'll let you go."

Her soft voice floated like a dream on the cold black air. "I know you. Ho, Geronimo. Only She-gha and your little daughter are near here. I have not seen the others in your family or the families of those with you since you rode away."

My hope for finding them all on this raid fell tumbling, like a flat stone falling through deep water. *Where were they? What had Nant'an Lpah done with them?* "Show me their lodge."

She picked herself up, leaning against her walking stick, and, in bare feet that stirred little puffs of dust in the bright moonlight, she left her lodge, motioning us to follow. We stayed in the shadows of the bright, white moonlight, as we followed her down the hill to the trail toward Fort Apache. Soon we came to a cluster of *wickiups* beside the tumbling, singing creek running toward the *Río* Blanco. She stayed on the trail and pointed to a *wickiup* that sat back from the others near the creek. "Another woman stays with her, a White Mountain."

I motioned for those with me to stay still and ready before I slipped to the blanket over the door, gently pulled it back, and slid inside. The moon was sending bright, white shafts of light scattered across the mats and blankets in the *wickiup*. I saw my daughter sleeping soundly on a blanket on my left. Back in the darkest shadows at the back of the lodge, I could see light glinting on the tips of two blades.

I whispered, "She-gha, I come for you and our daughter."

"Geronimo?"

"Yes, I come. Where are your sisters and our children?"

"I don't know. Maybe Nant'an Lpah sent them to San Carlos."

"Hmmph. Maybe so. The woman with you must come, too. If she makes noise, I will cut her throat."

A deep, throaty voice for a woman said, "I am Bi-yah-neta. I was at Mescalero with She-gha trying to learn if you and your people could hide there. I come with you."

"*Enjuh*. Come."

The Blue Coats swarmed after us, but we took rough trails, hard to follow, and three suns later were in the mountains past Eagle Creek. Perico had a sad face because he had not found his wife Hah-dun-key. She had refused to leave with him when he first left with me for Mexico. He had come back, hoping to find her and convince her that she should be with him, but he had to leave Fort Apache again without her.

Perico admired the courage, willingness to work, and quick mind of Bi-yah-neta. In our little group, he was my *segundo*. The third night after we stopped to rest, he watched Bi-yah-neta work around the fire with She-gha and the other women as we sat and smoked, discussing the best path to cross back into Mexico. We decided to go back into the Black Range and then south, back toward the place we crossed the border. Perico was quiet for a while, and then he nodded toward Bi-yah-neta, who was on the other side of the fire with her back to us.

He said, "I like that woman. Do you want to claim her?"

I smiled and shook my head. "I have one wife with me now and two more waiting for me some place at San Carlos, and soon I will get those, too. The only wife you had refused to come with you to Mexico. I think you need another wife. Maybe you divorce Hah-dun-key, maybe not. I think Bi-yah-neta is a good choice for you. Go. Speak to her. See if she comes with you willingly or if she needs to be trained a little first."

"Geronimo is a good brother."

He pushed himself up and walked over to her and with his head motioned her to follow him. She frowned, stared at him a moment, and then followed him into the dark outside the fire's circle of light. Soon they returned to the fire, and both were smiling.

I said, *"Enjuh."*

It was not proper for She-gha and me to show our feelings for each other, but I whispered good words to her when we thought no one was looking and played with our daughter.

The canyons of the Black Range gave us good cover as we moved south. We were near the southern end of the Black Range when Chappo came running through the trees to me.

In a low voice, almost a whisper, he said, "Father, down the trail there are three Mescalero women and a five- or six-year-old boy gathering piñon nuts. One has a baby on a *tsach,* and one looks young, maybe a woman, but not married, and one, the mother of the boy."

I nodded. "Take them. I don't know why they're not on the reservation, but now they are ours. We will wait here for you."

He rode off with the other men while Beshe and I waited with the women. We dismounted, rested our ponies, and lay back on the pine straw in the shadows of the tall trees. We heard a shot echoing down the canyon, but only one, the kind a hunter might make. Beshe and the women looked to me for what we should do. I shook my head and motioned with my hand for them to stay still.

The riders came up the trail and into the shadows where we rested, their captives holding on behind them. They stopped and let the captives slide to the ground. The boy had apparently run, and one of the warriors had nicked him with the shot we heard. It would leave a good scar, one he could talk about around the night fires when he was old. Dahkeya and Perico herded the three women and boy over to me where I sat watching them.

I said, "You are Mescalero?"

They nodded.

"Why are you here and not on the reservation?"

The women looked at each other, and then the young girl spoke. "The piñon nuts here this year are many, but there are few on the reservation. We came for the harvest on a thirty-sun pass. We came with men who hunt the deer growing fat on the piñons. If they find you with us, they'll fight you. Maybe bring the Blue Coats. Let us go, and we will tell no one."

The young girl had spirit. I liked that. I said, "No, our warriors need women for new wives and young ones to help us. You come with us. Stay with the other women. Share in their work. No harm comes to you. Do you understand?" I stood and looked at each one, and they nodded understanding. I said, "*Enjuh*. We go."

CHAPTER 39
REUNION

My warriors and women, our captives, and I rejoined the others waiting for us in our *rancheria* in one of Juh's old Mexican strongholds about a moon after we left. It was good to have She-gha and our daughter back again, and I lay with She-gha in our *wickiup,* enjoying the warmth and closeness of her body against mine while our daughter drew deep breaths in peaceful sleep as still as a rabbit watching a fox. When we were first alone, She-gha, with water close to her eyes, told me that the woman of a scout had told her that Shtsha-she had gone to the Happy Place before the soldiers bringing them back from Mexico had crossed the border. The same woman had told her she didn't know what had happened to Zi-yeh and Fenton.

I was angry. I asked, "Who killed Shtsha-she and how?" I was already thinking how I would avenge her. But She-gha answered, "The scout's woman says *Ussen* took her. One morning, she never left her blankets. No one knows why. She had no enemies. Two scouts hid her body in some cliffs and said they were sorry she had ridden the ghost pony."

Shtsha-she had been a good wife, as all my women were. I hated to lose her but hoped she had traveled well to the Happy Place.

I had wanted to find all my women at Fort Apache, including my daughter Dohn-say. Perico, for a while a man of many frowns, now smiled and joked often with his new woman, who seemed to be a hard worker. Perico had chosen well. Now I wondered if I should take another wife while we were on the run.

Wise She-gha, who had encouraged me to take Zi-yeh, spoke to me as we rested under the blankets. "You are a great war leader and *di-yen*. You need a wife to replace Shtsha-she to help us, especially in Mexico."

"Hmmph. You see the Mescalero women we brought back from the Black Range. Two already have children. There is the one called Young Girl, Ih-tedda. Who do you think I should take to help us?"

"The women with children will have their children on their minds first and not you. I've watched Ih-tedda. She works hard, even though this is not a camp of her people. I have spoken to her about her life. She has never been with a man. She will be good for you and good for your family. I say take Ih-tedda."

"She-gha is a wise woman. I'll take Ih-tedda."

She-gha smiled and nodded.

I claimed Ih-tedda as my woman, and she came to stay in our *wickiup*. She-gha and other women who had husbands spent several days with her telling her what a woman must do to please her man and what might happen if they didn't make their husbands happy. The night I claimed Ih-tedda as my wife, She-gha took a blanket and our daughter to sleep by another fire. I sat warming myself by our fire. The Season of Earth Is Reddish Brown was fast coming, and the nights were cold.

Ih-tedda walked into the fire's circle of light. She wore a fine fringed shift one of the other women must have lent her. She nodded toward me, "You claim me for your wife. I come."

"*Enjuh*. My Power tells me you will be a good wife. Go in the *wickiup*. I come to you soon."

She stepped around the fire and disappeared behind the blanket over the *wickiup* door. I prayed that *Ussen* would send us children and a peaceful *wickiup,* smoked to the four directions, threw the last bit of *tobaho* in the fire, and went into lie with my new woman. She was awkward with me at first, but I was gentle with her and taught her the ways of a good wife. We slept well side by side that night. I was happy I had claimed her, and she smiled often the next day when She-gha or one of the other women spoke to her.

That afternoon, a runner came to our camp. He said that Chihuahua and Naiche camped in a *rancheria* in the Carcay Mountains that Juh had used. They asked that I come to meet with them. When Chihuahua and Naiche had learned that Teniente Davis and Chato were not dead as I had told them, they had wanted to kill me for drawing them off the reservation with a lie. Now, although I knew Naiche, who had been with Mangas at the time they learned I had seemed to lie, had been angry, he had no doubt cooled his anger and had spoken to Chihuahua. Perhaps I might live through the meeting. We left for the Carcay Mountains that day.

Two days later, we found our brothers in a ridge-top meadow with about twenty *wickiups* in the shade of tall, scattered pines. Their people came out to meet us. It was the first time we had seen them in over five moons and, like us, they were missing many women and children. I swung off my pony as Chihuahua and Naiche came to meet me. I saw no anger in their eyes, and they carried their rifles loosely in the crooks of their arms. Women in the camp led our women and children away to show them the best places to make our *wickiups.* Chihuahua and Naiche came to stand before me.

Chihuahua spoke first. "Ho, Geronimo. Naiche and I have glad hearts to see you and have learned of your raid to get your women back. Our words in council together will be many. Come to my *wickiup,* and we'll drink a little coffee while your women and children make your camp there among the trees with us. There is plenty of water and wood nearby."

"Ho, Naiche and Chihuahua. I'm glad you share your camp with us. Yes, many words in council. I come."

I joined Naiche and Chihuahua at their fire, and we talked for a while about the good days on Turkey Creek and at Fort Apache, while their women gave us cups of good, black coffee. Naiche pulled a small, cloth sack of *tobaho* and papers from a vest pocket, made a cigarette, and we smoked. The war leaders sat in a circle behind us and made their own smoke. After Naiche threw the last bit of *tobaho* into the fire, I said, "Brothers, I've wanted to talk with you since we left Fort Apache. You were angry and would not listen. Now hear my words."

Naiche said, "Speak. We will listen."

"I understand your anger at what I told you about the deaths of Teniente Davis and Chato. It was not true. I believed it was true when I told you. Fun and Perico, members of Teniente's scouts, planned to kill Teniente and Chato before I told you it was true. But Teniente suspected someone in the scouts might try to kill him, just as Kaytennae had the year before, and made them butt their rifles in the sand when they stood before him and told Chato and Dutchy to shoot anyone who did not.

"It was nearly dark when this happened, and when Teniente went in the supply tent for ammunition, Fun and Perico decided trying to kill Teniente and Chato too risky and, with Atelnietze, slipped away to join us. I didn't know this until the next day and, by then, it was too late to tell you differently. We were all on the run and believed Nant'an Lpah was after us to take us all to a bad place. If the Blue Coats catch us now, they will make those who were their scouts dance on air and give the rest of us to a White Eye sheriff who will do the same. I will not dance on air while the White Eyes watch me choke. Nant'an Lpah has our families, but I can tell you that they are not at

Fort Apache. Likely, they are kept at San Carlos with those we had to leave behind when we first escaped, but I don't know this for a fact."

Chihuahua listened to me intently. After I finished speaking, he said. "Naiche and I did want to kill you after Atelnietze told us that Teniente and Chato were alive. But after we smoked on it, we realized you told us they were dead in the time when the sun had fallen halfway to the horizon. Atelnietze told us how Fun and Perico had waited for the chance to kill Teniente and Chato just as the sun was leaving, but that Teniente told Chato and Dutchy to shoot any man who raised a rifle from its butt in the sand. Fun and Perico knew they had no chance of killing Teniente and Chato, so they escaped to join you. You didn't know this. We understand now and have no quarrel with you. Come, join us."

I smiled and nodded. "This I do."

Chihuahua grinned. "Maybe next time I kill you good, you old fox. Chato and his scouts raided my camp and took fifteen of our women and children. We want them back, and we want to punish the men who took them. There were some in our families that we had to leave behind at Fort Apache because we left so quickly. These we want, too."

Chihuahua stared off into the trees for moment, gathering his thoughts. "My brother Ulzana, Naiche, and I have talked about how to do these things. We think we ought to divide into three raiding parties. Ulzana and I will each lead a party of ten or twelve men and acolytes. I will leave first, cross the border, and raid all the way to the Lake Valley *pesh-lickoyee* mines.

"We will take what we can, but the main purpose of my raid is to make the Blue Coats chase us and draw their attention away from Ulzana's path, which goes through the mountains to the west and Fort Apache to look for our families. If they are not at Fort Apache, then they will go to San Carlos. If he can find Chato, Dutchy, scouts, or their relatives, he'll kill them and then return back here.

"The third raid will be here in Mexico. You and Naiche will raid south around Temosachic for cattle, horses, supplies, and revenge. It will be a good revenge raid against Tarahumara who wiped out most of Juh's camp. What do think?"

I listened and thought about the raids. I nodded as the sky turned to blood red and grew a halo of *pesh-klitso* where the sun had fallen into the western mountains. The plan was a good one. But they probably wouldn't find our families at San Carlos without inside help. I told Chihuahua and Naiche this, and they agreed.

We talked a long time about what to do if some part of our plans went wrong and the best places to raid for supplies. When I finally lay down next to Ih-tedda in the *wickiup* she and She-gha had set up, their gentle snores forbade me from calling one of them from their rest.

Ulzana and Chihuahua picked their men for their joint raid and left the *rancheria* within a few suns with twenty warriors and acolytes. They traveled north toward the Boco Grande Mountains, raided the village of Corral de Piedra and the Sabinal mines, and then divided their men.

Ulzana, with eleven warriors, headed for Animas Peak where he would send out scouts to probe the Blue Coat locations for the best place to enter and pass through the mountains to the west as he moved toward Fort Apache.

Chihuahua used the *arroyo* east of Laguna Palomas where I had crossed the border on my raid over a moon earlier and headed for the Black Range, raiding and burning as he went. Naiche, Nana, and I, with about twelve warriors and acolytes and sixty women and children, left on a raid toward Yepómera and on to Temosachic in Chihuahua.

Ulzana lost one adolescent boy on his raid. Sánchez, a White Mountain Carrizo chief, shot the boy in the back while he was a sentinel, cut off his head, and turned it into Crook for money. The Chiricahuas at Fort Apache were near to going to war with the White Mountains over this but settled down. Ulzana and his warriors went to Fort Apache and San Carlos but learned none of our people were there. Ulzana saw Chato working in his field, but somehow Chato sensed there was danger and ran to Fort Apache with his family. Nevertheless, Ulzana and his raiders killed some scout relatives and took a couple of women and a boy captive before they returned to Mexico.

Chihuahua and his raiders took livestock and supplies and hid out in the canyons along the *Río* Animas, raiding ranches, mines, and freight wagons. They took much for supplies we could use in our camps, while they kept the Blue Coats busy until they slipped south into Mexico the same way they had entered the country claimed by the Americans. Chihuahua and his men rode into Casas Grandes to trade the livestock from the United States for mescal, food, and things their women wanted, such as pots, axes, and cloth.

Naiche and I raided around Temosachic, took livestock, burned some ranches, and killed a few Tarahumara, but not nearly enough to claim revenge for Juh. We raided for a moon and then slipped south to the safest, best hidden *rancheria* I knew lying between the *Río*s Aros and Sátachi. We waited for Chihuahua and Ulzana and their raiders to join us there. When they came, the Ghost Face was upon us, and it was very cold during the nights, but my new young wife and experienced Shegha knew how to keep me warm.

Chapter 40
No Place to Hide

There were about eighty of us: twenty-five men, the rest women and children, in the *rancheria* during that Ghost Face after our raids in the Season of Earth Is Reddish Brown in the harvest when we escaped the Fort Apache Reservation. I believed our *rancheria* on a mountain between the *Ríos* Aros and Sátachi was the best hidden and most defensible stronghold our people had in Mexico.

Our *rancheria* rested near the end of the Espinosa del Diablo (Devil's Backbone), where the *Río* Aros makes a big loop. There the *Río* Aros fell in a long stretch of white water, its sound making a soothing rumble over great, white stones that had rolled into its path from the mountains. If the Mexicans or Blue Coats could find us here, then there was no place for us to hide from their attacks and safely rest before our next raid. Up on the ridge near the top was a flat bench where there was enough room to make our *wickiups* and a rope corral for our horses and pack animals. The position let us see the mountains and ridges clearly on the other sides of the Aros, and sentries could give us good warning when enemies approached.

One night, deep in the Season of the Ghost Face, I slept peacefully with She-gha. Fruitful Ih-tedda already carried our first child in her belly, and custom said I must not lie with her again until this child was born and she was ready to make another child.

I lay, barely awake, thinking I might ask She-gha to join me in pleasure again to make her a child, but the mules and pack burros began braying just before dawn. Faster than the flash of a thunder arrow, I was in my moccasins and grabbing my rifle and coat before I ran out into the dark. In the eastern sky, the great milk *río* of stars still glowed in the biting cold air. Three men ran past me to the mule and burro corral. I climbed up on a rock and tried to look over the *rancheria* to see anyone else moving or anything that shouldn't be there.

Sudden flames of fire followed by cracks of thunder came from a low, nearby ridge as bullets fired too high plunged into the ground close to us, some whining as they ricocheted off rocks.

My first impulse was to yell, "Look out for the horses!" I scanned in all directions as the firing into the camp increased, and the people ran from their *wickiups*, their eyes wide and trying to understand what was happening. It was obvious our first need was to get away. We could always get more horses.

I yelled, "Let the horses go, and run for the *río*! There are soldiers and scouts on both sides and above us. Women and children run for the *río*; men follow." Some had made it to the path we used to get to the *río* but firing from scouts drove them back toward the camp.

They looked toward me. I yelled, "Scatter! Go as you can!" Many disappeared off the edge and down the bluff through the brush, following little trails the children had made while playing. Dodging scouts and soldiers pouring more and more bullets into the camp, they slipped to the edge of the freezing cold water and waded across the *río*.

Most of the women and children made it across the *río* and up to the top of a bluff on the other side by the time the sun drove away the fog and mists. We had to leave everything behind: horses, mules, and burros, food supplies, blankets and clothes, rawhide sacks, everything.

Stunned that the Blue Coat scouts had found us, I thought, *How can this happen? How can they find us in the best place to hide in these mountains? Maybe Ussen doesn't want us in Mexico.* From the brush and juniper trees on the far bluff, we watched in anger and sadness during the day as the scouts burned everything we had.

At the time of shortest shadows, I met with Naiche, Chihuahua, Nana, and most of the other war leaders. We had been lucky, considering the strength of the attackers, that there were only a few minor wounds among us. Our only choices were to run or surrender. If we ran, we would go hungry and be cold until we could take food and blankets from our caches. I guessed it would take at least half a moon to gather all we needed raiding, and we would have to raid the rest of the Seasons of the Ghost Face and Little Eagles to keep from starving. Even with that, what would keep the scouts from finding us anywhere? Perhaps we could move farther south.

The easier choice was to surrender and hope that Nant'an Lpah would send us back to the reservation. I wanted us to keep going, but Naiche and Chihuahua had had enough of trying to live in the mountains, and I was ready to rest for a while. Naiche wanted to talk to the leader of the scouts who had attacked us and ask his surrender terms, believing that was the best choice.

He was chief. I didn't argue. My soldier glasses showed it was Captain Crawford who was agent at San Carlos when we accepted Nant'an Lpah's terms to return to the reservation three harvests earlier. Crawford had always been fair with us. Maybe now was the best time to surrender.

I called Lozen, a warrior woman of great Power and sister of Victorio. She had hard, strong eyes with a no-nonsense squint, and her face with its square jaw could easily be the face of a man, but the bulges under her shirt where her breasts lay told a different story. She was in Nana's band, a Chihenne, but she carried no anger against me for what had happened to Loco's people at Aliso Creek.

I said, "Ho, Lozen. Nana says he will accept me speaking with you. Naiche and his leaders ask that you cross back over the *río* and carry a message to Blue Coat Captain Crawford, whose scouts now burn our things in our camp. Say to Crawford that Naiche and his leaders want to meet with him."

Her eyes never blinked as she stared at me and then nodded. "I go now?"

I said, "Go now. You speak good Spanish. Make the interpreters use that tongue. That way you have no misunderstanding of your words or theirs. I watch for you to return."

She wrapped her blanket around her and over a shoulder the way our women wore them and then tied a white strip of cloth to a yucca stalk before working her way down the bluff to the *río*. I watched her and the scouts and soldiers on the far side with my soldier glasses. I saw several scouts watching her but making no threatening moves with their rifles. She pulled up and held her skirt between her knees and held the yucca stalk high as she forded the *río* and started up the other side.

After some banter back and forth with two or three of the scouts, who had surrounded her as she came out of the cold water, they pointed to the top of the bluff and then followed her up the trail to the top where Captain Crawford had his fire and was talking to his officers, packers, and scout sergeants.

I saw Crawford stand and acknowledge her when she appeared at the fire. Lozen spoke to Crawford through a chief of scouts named Horn. Horn spoke Apache, but his Spanish was much better. She told me later that she spoke Spanish, as I had told her, and that Crawford tried not to smile when he glanced at his officers and said he would meet with us at the *río* the next day. He had a pack frame mounted on a mule, and loaded it with food, knowing we would also eat the mule. Handing her the mule's lead rope, he let her return to us with his answer.

Naiche and Chihuahua were glad that Crawford had agreed to sit in council with us. He knew we were all hungry, and they liked his generosity in sending us food. I didn't like the thought of surrendering, but without great suffering by our people, there was no other way to survive the Ghost Face.

I hoped we wouldn't be sorry for doing it. I wanted to die like Victorio, fighting to the last bullet and then stabbing myself in the heart. If I believed a vision from *Ussen,* that would never happen. That night, we ate all we could before lying together as families under pine needles and brush to stay warm, while the sentries kept a close eye on the direction of the bluffs across the *río* and our old camp.

There was a welcoming yell in Apache, "Ho, brothers, welcome!" I thought I was having a dream, but the distinct cracking of fired rifles on the bluffs across the *río* said it was no dream. I told She-gha and the others to stay where they were and, taking my soldier glasses and rifle, crawled through the brush to a sentry who stared at the dark bluffs across the *río.*

I asked, "What do you see?"

"Long column comes. They surround Crawford's camp. Scouts sleep like they're dead. A scout sees part of column and called to them. He thinks they are scouts from another Nant'an Lpah band. The column members already on the bluff fire into Crawford's camp. Crawford's scouts are slow to shoot back." After a time, the firing from each side stopped.

It was foggy as mists rose off the *río,* and the light from the eastern mountains was slow to come. It was hard to see what was going on. Naiche and Chihuahua and a few of the other leaders who had soldier glasses watched with me, but they couldn't see either. We sensed more than saw movements in the rocks on the other side of the *río* from us. Crawford had the fire near where he slept built up for more light and then tied a white cloth to a yucca stalk. He and his chiefs followed the scout chief toward a *Nakai-yi* dressed in military clothes who came toward the light leading his chiefs.

Nana laid down his glasses and was sighting down his rifle's barrel when Naiche pulled it down and shook his head. Nana frowned and nodded. The man, long black hair falling from his hat and advancing toward Crawford, was a Tarahumara Indian. I was quick to understand why Nana wanted to shoot. The *Nakai-yi* officer was Mauricio Corredor. He claimed he had killed Victorio five harvests earlier after leading the *Nakai-yi* chief Joaquin Terrazas to Victorio's camp at Tres Castillos. The *Nakai-yes* were so grateful they gave him a silver, engraved Winchester rifle when he rode into Chihuahua City with Apache scalps on a pole.

Corredor was a liar. Nana told us Victorio had run out of bullets and stabbed himself in the heart to keep the *Nakai-yes* from taking him. That was the way Kaytennae, then Nana's *segundo,* had found him. The chiefs and men following Corredor were all Tarahumara.

Horn opened his arms and, smiling, said something to Corredor, who ignored him and continued on toward Crawford, who was waving the white cloth on the yucca stalk as a sign of peaceful intentions. I saw one of the Tarahumara with Corredor slip behind a small tree and ready his rifle. Behind Crawford and his chiefs, fifty or sixty of his scouts appeared from behind rocks and were busy loading their ammunition belts from a box they had brought from their packtrain supplies. I laughed.

The Tarahumara were there because they were Apache scalp hunters. Corredor had brought them to attack us and take our hair for money. Now they faced scouts who knew what they did and were awake and ready to wipe them out. I thought, *Maybe we won't have to surrender after all. Just kill a few scalp hunters and Corredor and bury Crawford's scouts.*

While Corredor talked to Crawford's officers, the scouts and Tarahumara were shouting insults back and forth about each other's manhood. The scouts said the Tarahumara had no man parts and their babies would look like the dirt women left behind bushes. Tarahumara yelled the scouts were the babies who didn't know where the trigger was on their rifle. The Tarahumara were moving around trying to get on either side of Crawford's scouts and catch them in a cross fire when the shooting started.

Corredor saw what was happening and must have decided trying to take the scouts and Blue Coats would get his Tarahumara killed. He started yelling and waving his hands, "Don't shoot! Don't shoot!"

Crawford turned to his chief, the teniente named Maus, said something, and Maus turned and walked toward the scouts who had just loaded and cocked their rifles. He was shaking his head, saying something as he waved his hands parallel to the ground. Crawford crawled up on a rock about head high and waved his peace cloth again back and forth.

The Tarahumara, who had followed Corredor to the meeting and had slipped behind a tree, stepped out, raised his rifle, and fired. Crawford's head snapped back, and he fell down before sliding off the back side of the big rock. Rifles on both sides roared.

I laughed and laughed as I saw Tarahumaras and a few scouts cut down. The many bullets fired at the Blue Coat chiefs all missed. Corredor tried to find cover behind a big rock, but three scouts were nearby, and the scout Binday rose up and shot Corredor square in the heart. I happened to see it and laughed again. I thought, *Ussen is always good to his people. At last, we settle a debt of revenge against Mauricio Corredor.* I hated to see Crawford killed. We would have trusted him to keep his word if we had talked by the *río* that morning, but no man hit in the head like he was lives long.

The fighting lasted until the Tarahumara realized they couldn't take high ground against the scouts and withdrew to some hills about three hundred yards from where the fighting had been. Horn and Teniente Maus went to the Tarahumara camp. After they returned, there was no more shooting. Then the interpreter Concepcion, a *di-yen*, and three packers with ten mules came bringing food and ammunition for Crawford's scouts from Nant'an Lpah's other band of scouts.

The rest of that sun passed with only the sound of water falling in the *río*. Our women made the best shelters they could with what we had, and the men went hunting to take enough deer to feed us all.

The next day, Teniente Maus went with Concepcion to speak with the Tarahumara and return the six mules they had lost during the fighting the day before. Teniente Maus and the Tarahumara had some kind of argument. Concepcion returned to Crawford's camp. He left Crawford's tent with piece of paper in his hand. Scouts surrounded and appeared to question him.

After he answered, there were yells of anger, and they started stripping down for battle. I laughed, called my acolyte, and told him to run to the scouts and tell them we would help them whip our common enemy. They said they would welcome us to help them wipe out the scalping dogs known as Tarahumara, but there was no fighting. Teniente Maus and the Tarahumara agreed on terms for them leaving, and they left that day, running, as they usually did, and leading their pack animals.

Naiche, the chiefs, and I met in council. With Crawford dead, or nearly dead, the other Blue Coats were likely to march north and forget about us for a while, giving us the opportunity to replenish and restock with small raids until raiding season came. The question Naiche had to settle in his mind was whether we still wanted to surrender, regardless of the loss of Captain Crawford. I argued we should not surrender. We just had to be diligent with sentries and use places for *rancherias* that were unknown and positioned against surprise attack.

Naiche looked at us all and slowly shook his head. "You, Geronimo, said two days ago this was the safest place to hide in the mountains. Yet our own people helped the Blue Coat scouts find it. There is no place to hide from the Blue Coats with the scouts helping. And even the Mexicans, using the Tarahumara, were here a day later, expecting to kill us and take our hair for money the Mexicans would give them. The Tarahumara even wiped out the band of Juh, the best war chief, after Mangas Coloradas and my father, Cochise. We can hide and move around in the land of the *Nakai-yes* and not raid. No one will bother us if we stay. But we can't raid and be men. We would be more like women. Is this what you want?"

He looked at each of us, and we all shook our heads. No, it was not what we wanted. I was proud of Naiche. He had become a good, thoughtful leader.

"You all can do as you please. But I think we should return to Fort Apache if Nant'an Lpah lets us and learn to use White Eye ways of growing fields and even raise cattle. That is what we should do. It is all I have to say."

I said, "*Enjuh.* We'll wait and see what this Teniente Maus does. If he leaves, then let us talk with him and ask to speak with Nant'an Lpah."

Naiche and all the others made the sign of peace. This they would do.

Teniente Maus broke camp the next day in a steady rain and

pointed north toward the village Nácori Chico up a rough canyon trail. Captain Crawford and a wounded scout still lived. Crawford must have had a powerful will to still be breathing. The men took turns carrying Crawford and the scout on their backs. They went no farther that day than a boy could easily run in a hand against the horizon. That night, I sent Lozen again to their camp to ask Teniente Maus for a meeting the next morning. I told her to say that he and whoever came with him must come without their guns.

They came the next morning without their guns. This was a test meeting to make sure Teniente Maus kept his word. I sent Atelnietze and Nat-cul-baye to meet them. We watched from a nearby ridge. Maus came to the meeting with Concepcion, Noche, and four scouts. They frowned when they didn't see the chiefs and me, but Maus nodded he understood when they promised the chiefs and I would come the next day to the same place at the same time.

We watched their camp all that day, and the next morning, watched again and counted scouts, making certain none had gathered at a meeting place for an ambush. Teniente Maus and Concepcion, with Noche and the same four scouts, came again. Naiche, Chihuahua, Nana, and I with fourteen warriors sat waiting for them. I sat in the center of a circle facing Maus and the others. We all had our weapons and our belts filled with ammunition we had taken from our cache with other food supplies.

We studied each other for a time in the morning solitude, and then I said, looking at Maus without blinking, "Why did you come to our camp?"

Maus looked at me and spoke with an honest tongue, "I came to capture or destroy you and your band."

I thought, *Crawford's subchief speaks with a straight tongue, too. Perhaps Ussen smiles at us today.* I stood and walked over and shook Maus's hand with two solid pumps and said, "*Enjuh*. You speak true. I can trust you to report accurately to Nant'an Lpah." Then I spoke of our grievances and why we left Turkey Creek.

Maus sat with his arms crossed, listening to me. When I finished, he said, "I'll tell your words to General Crook, Nant'an Lpah."

"*Enjuh*. Tell Nant'an Lpah we'll meet him in two moons near San Bernardino to discuss surrender terms. As a sign our promise is true, the next sun, we'll send you some of our people to stay with you until we meet with him. I'll send word to No-che if we can't do this."

Concepcion told Maus what I said. Maus smiled. "*Enjuh*. Send your people to me. We will care for them well. Nant'an Lpah will expect to see you in two moons near San Bernardino."

Maus and his men returned to their camp. We went back to ours. The next day we sent nine of our band to the Blue Coats. Nana and my sister, his wife Nah-dos-te; a warrior who was sick; my wife Ih-tedda, with our first child in her belly; my three-year-old daughter; a wife and son of Naiche; and a woman with her son all walked to Teniente Maus's camp.

CHAPTER 41
THE CANYON DE LOS EMBUDOS COUNCIL

We had two moons to gather livestock and other supplies before surrendering to Nant'an Lpah and returning to the Fort Apache Reservation. Food the women had cached for the winter fed us through the days before the men raided for livestock and supplies. Ulzana had not returned from his raid across the border and was many suns later than we expected him. Chihuahua, worried about Ulzana, his brother, took six warriors north across the mountains to look for him. We camped, not far from Bugatseka but closer to the Bavispe, and rested while the women opened more caches of food. The warriors and acolytes went on small raids, and Naiche and I considered where to strike for livestock and supplies to take with us when we moved back to Fort Apache.

I began to wonder what kind of terms Nant'an Lpah would offer us to surrender. *Maybe,* I thought, *the Nakai-yes would offer us better terms. Maybe we can get a better deal from them and just stay in the Sierra Madre.* I had watched Juh try to negotiate with the Chihuahua *jefes* and knew the *Nakai-yes* lied much and offered little. We were lucky to escape from those talks without them murdering us after they tried to get us drunk on mescal. *Still,* I thought, *It might be worth a try to hear what they would offer.*

I asked Lozen and Tah-das-te, wife of Ahnandia, who often carried messages to Blue Coats or Nakai-yes for me, to come and talk with me at my fire. Ghost Face time high in the mountains is cold. We sat down wrapped in heavy blankets by a little fire near the door of my wives' *wickiup*. I made a cigarette with my *tobaho*, lighted it, and we smoked. Their eyes, narrow and expectant, studied me as the cold breeze rippled past the blankets over their heads and shook the covers of my family's *wickiup*.

I said, "You know that in a moon and a half, the chiefs and I speak to Nant'an Lpah about leaving the warpath. Maybe we return to live in peace with the rest of the Chiricahuas at Fort Apache. We need to know that we aren't making the wrong choice. Maybe the Mexicans give us better terms, and we won't have to leave. I was with Juh when he attempted a treaty with them. We had good talks, but something or someone always stood in the way of them being fulfilled."

Tah-das-te held up her hand for me to stop, reached over, and tossed more sticks on the fire. She and Lozen shifted where they sat, so they had the wind full against their backs. I pulled my blanket closer and leaned into the breeze to face them. Tah-das-te nodded, and I continued.

"I want to send two messengers to the *jefe* (prefect) at Bavispe to ask what peace terms the Sonora *jefes* might offer that would let us stay in Mexico. I ask that you go as the messengers and learn this important information for us. If the Bavispe *jefe* answers yes, they want to meet, then come back to us *pronto*. Maybe you find a little mescal for us while you are there? Tah-das-te, I send your husband, Ahnandia, with you until you are close enough to see Bavispe. He waits where he can watch the village with his soldier glasses until you return. I think two suns to reach Bavispe, no more than two suns for the chief to give you an answer, and two suns to return. I think you return in no more than six suns."

Tah-das-te and Lozen looked at each other, made a little smile, and leaned closer to the fire. With dark shadows and yellow firelight dancing across her face and shining eyes, Lozen said, "Our leader asks, we go. We leave for Bavispe with the sunrise, back in no more than six suns. Ahnandia knows he travels with us?"

"I have spoken with Ahnandia. He is ready when you are."

"*Enjuh.* I want to carry my rifle and help Ahnandia if help is needed."

I waved my hand to say she should take it and said, "Just don't take it into Bavispe with you. They might take it away from you, or you might have to use it. Leave it with Ahnandia. He'll wait for you."

They smiled and said together, "*Enjuh*," and then disappeared into the cold blackness to make ready for their ride across the mountains to Bavispe.

Six suns passed, seven . . . eight . . . nine . . . ten. The women and Ahnandia had not returned in ten suns. We watched but saw no marching columns of *Nakai-yes*. I knew something had to be wrong in Bavispe. The Bavispe *jefe* must be torturing them to learn where we were. The *Nakai-yes* might make them tell.

Naiche and I told the camp we had to leave quickly at the next sun. I was very sorry to lose my messengers to the Mexicans. They were good women, and Lozen was a fighter as good as any man and a better shot than most. Before we went back to Fort Apache, I would have my revenge. The *jefe* and his soldiers in Bavispe would bleed and scream roasting over a fire a long time for what they did to our women.

We camped in a canyon hidden in the foothills behind a great mountain north of where the *Río* Bavispe turns and flows south. There we would be close enough to reach in a sun Teniente Maus's camp when we came for the council with Nant'an Lpah.

Naiche and I continued to raid. The land was much warmer than high in the mountains and made the Season of Little Eagles come and go much sooner in the valleys than in the mountains. But winds blew hard and carried much dust in the air. I would not like spending all my days in the low country.

Four suns before I planned to go to Teniente Maus's camp, I stood by She-gha's fire drinking coffee as the light over the eastern mountains grew. Out of the dark, dawn shadows walked Lozen, Tah-das-te, and Ahnandia. For the time of a few breaths, I felt my heart pound. I thought I was seeing ghosts and stared unbelieving at them.

Ahnandia grinned. Lozen said, "Ho, Geronimo, we come." Tah-das-te drew her blanket closer and stepped to the fire pointing at the coffee pot and a nearby cup. I nodded. Always the good wife, she poured coffee and handed it to Ahnandia.

She-gha appeared from behind the *wickiup* door blanket with cups for the women and then disappeared back inside, knowing the messengers and I would talk, but I know she sat close to the blanket door to listen to us. After my messengers had a few swallows of the coffee, I said, "*Ussen* is good. I'm glad to see my brother and sisters. I thought them lost. Tell me your story."

Tah-das-te spoke in her smooth, handsome voice. "We went to the Bavispe *jefe* and gave him your words. He was glad to hear them and said if we waited a few suns he would ask his *jefe*, with the tracks on paper, what he should do and get back his answer. He said we should stay in his *casa* to eat well and rest until his *jefe* answered the paper tracks.

"We said we would return to our own camp and come back to him in a few days. His eyes showed fear. I don't know why. He said he could not let us go until his *jefe* told him what to do. He gave us a comfortable place in his *casa* to wait, sleep, and eat, but only he could open the door and that from the other side of the wall. A man sat outside the door with a big gun made with two barrels across his knees.

"I sat near the door to hear anything the *jefe* or the man with the big gun said. The Bavispe *jefe* came every day at the time of shortest shadows and asked the guard how we were. Through the crack I always saw the guard shrug his shoulders and make a face.

"We were kept in the room for six days. On the sixth day, the *jefe* told the guard that they would let us go. He said the paper from his *jefe* came. The paper told him to arrange a conference and then kill as many of us as he could. They laughed together, and the guard said the joke will be on Geronimo.

"Next day, at the time of shortest shadows, we were taken to the Bavispe *jefe*. He said a letter came from his *jefe* that told him to make a conference and offer generous terms. He asked that we go and give those words to you."

I laughed at this story. We all laughed. The *Nakai-yes* had made fools of themselves again.

Ahnandia said, "I was very glad to see them leave Bavispe. I thought the *Nakai-yes* tortured or maybe killed them. I had decided to leave in a few more suns if they didn't come. I saw them leave Bavispe. Trailers followed them. When they came to me, I gave them horses and led them to the mountains on a trail where we did many double-backs and lost their trailers. When we got back to Bugatseka, all the People were gone. We followed your trail north, even riding at night to follow and find you."

"*Enjuh*. The *Nakai-yes* show again they can't open their mouths without lies flying out. We must never trust them. I'm grateful for you taking the message. Take your rest. In four days, we'll go north to Teniente Maus's camp. Be ready."

We found the camp of Teniente Maus close to the *Río* San Bernardino. It was a hard ride a hand on the horizon west of a high mountain. We sent smoke from that high mountain to announce we were coming. Riding into his camp, Naiche and I spoke to Teniente Maus and said we were ready to see Nant'an Lpah. Where was he?

Maus told us we were safer if we were closer to the border and told us that after we picked a place, he would send for the Nant'an. I was concerned it was a trick to get us close to the border and capture us, but Maus had always spoke straight before. Naiche and I talked privately, and then I told Maus we would go as far north as Canyon de los Embudos.

Maus camped on a little mesa overlooking the canyon, and we camped in a place easy to defend, a long rifle shot away from Maus's camp across an *arroyo* and surrounded by rough ravines.

We were patient. Nant'an Lpah didn't come after three suns. Every sun after that, I asked Maus when the Nant'an was coming. He always answered, "Soon." He said the Nant'an was driving his wagon and bringing our friends to see us.

By that, I hoped he meant Zi-yeh and the rest of my family. We all missed our families. But while we waited, my old friend, Charlie Tribolett, who had sold us supplies and bought things we no longer wanted from raids, sold us some of the whiskey he and his brothers had been selling the scouts. It was strong medicine, and I was glad to get it.

Five or six suns after we camped at Canyon de los Embudos, the Nant'an appeared close to the time of shortest shadows driving his wagon. He came with Nana and his wife, my sister Nah-dos-te; Naiche's mother, Dos-teh-she; and two or three other women I didn't know.

I was surprised and happy to see Kaytennae with the Nant'an. The Blue Coats had planned to keep him at the place by the big water called "Alcatraz" another three harvests. With Kaytennae were Alchesay, the White Mountain chief and scout, other men, and a man named Fly, who made our images with a box he called a "camera" like the man at San Carlos did after we made peace with the Nant'an at Bugatseka.

The Nant'an also brought four interpreters: José Vasquez, Antonio Besias, Jose Montoya, and Concepcion. *Enjuh.* No Mickey Free. I would never use him for this big council.

The White Eyes had a custom of eating at the time of shortest shadows. We Apaches eat when we're hungry. Nant'an Lpah sent most of the others to Teniente Maus's camp while he ate at the camp of the mule packers. I used my soldier glasses and watched him come into the canyon with the others.

When I saw he was eating from the packer pot, I told my warriors to carry their best weapons with plenty of ammunition and to wear the best clothes they had found in the last two moons. Then I sent them down a few at a time to where Nant'an Lpah's people camped near Teniente Maus. Naiche and I were the last ones to walk into the camp. As we walked, I prayed to *Ussen* that we would choose to do the right thing. It was a hard time for us all.

Nant'an Lpah finished eating, talked for a time to the packers he knew, and then motioned us over into the trees where a small stream flowed and shade and shelter kept the sun and wind from making the council uncomfortable. He found a place to sit comfortably on a knee-high ledge. The interpreters, his subchiefs, and his *segundo*, Captain Bourke, who made tracks on paper of all we said, sat down beside him.

I motioned Concepcion to come sit near Naiche and me as our interpreter. Our warriors stood around the rest of us, watching and listening to what was happening.

CHAPTER 42
GERONIMO AND NANT'AN LPAH TALK

Nant'an Lpah had a sour look on his face like a man who had lost a good horse race. He picked up a stick and, like a big cat waving its tail, softly tapped the leaves where we sat. The leaves in the trees were still, as if holding their breath and listening to us.

Nant'an Lpah said, "What have you to say? I've come all the way down from Bowie."

Before I answered, I turned to Naiche and spoke quietly with him so the others couldn't hear. "My chief, are you willing for me to speak for all of us?"

He nodded, "Yes. Speak well, Geronimo. You're our choice to speak for us to Nant'an Lpah."

"Is there anything you want me to say?'

"No. Speak your mind. Use your Power. Speak what *Ussen* wants you to say. We're not afraid if *Ussen* guides us."

"Enjuh."

Crook, wearing his strange, hard hat, stared at the ground listening, his elbows on his knees, and tap, tap, tapping on the leaves as I spoke of why I had left Turkey Creek and Fort Apache. We talked much back and forth. This is what I remember saying.

"I want to talk first of the causes which led me to leave the reservation. I was living quietly and contented, doing and thinking of no harm while at the Sierra Blanca (White Mountains). I was living peaceably with my family, having plenty to eat, sleeping well, taking care of my people, and perfectly contented. I don't know what harm I did to those three men, Chato, Mickey Free, and Teniente Davis. I was living peaceably and satisfied when people began to speak badly of me. I would be glad to know who started those stories."

A breeze blew through the trees and seemed to sigh as a woman sighs when she is sad.

"I hadn't killed a horse or a man, American or Indian. I don't know what the matter was with the people in charge of us. They knew this to be so, and yet they said I was a bad man and the worst man there."

I felt the anger grow in my guts, as I thought of all the lies and false accusations made against me and paused a moment to let my mind cool.

"I didn't leave of my own accord. Sometime before I left, an Indian named Nodiskey had a talk with me. He said, 'They're going to arrest you,' but I paid no attention to him, knowing that I had done no wrong. Then, Huera, the wife of Mangas, told me they were going to seize me and put me and Mangas in the guardhouse. Then I learned from the Americans and the Apache scouts, from Chato and Mickey Free, that the Americans were going to arrest me and hang me, so I left. I want to know now who it was who ordered me arrested. I was praying to the Dawn and the Darkness, to the Sun and the Sky, and to *Ussen* to let me live quietly there with my family."

I waited a few breaths, but Nant'an Lpah, his stick against the leaves still, continued looking at the ground and didn't see or answer me.

"I have several times asked for peace, but trouble has come from agents and interpreters. I don't want what has passed to happen again. The Earth-Mother is listening to me. I hope we always have peace, arranged from now on, that we have no more trouble.

"Whenever we see you coming to us, we think that it is god—you must always come with god. Whenever I have broken out, it has always been on account of bad talk. Very often, there are stories put in the newspapers. The stories say hang me. I don't want that anymore. When a man tries to do right, newspapers ought not to have such stories.

"There are very few of my men left now. They have done some bad things, but I want them all rubbed out and let us never speak of them again. We think of our relations, brothers, brothers-in-law, fathers-in-law, and so forth over on the reservation, and, from this time on, we want to live in peace, just as they are doing, and to behave as they are behaving. Sometimes a man does something. Men go looking for his head. I don't want such things to happen to us. I don't want us killing each other.

"What is the matter that you, Nant'an Lpah, don't speak to me and look with a pleasant face? It would make better feeling. I would be glad if you did. I'd be better satisfied if you would talk to me once in a while. Why don't you look at me and smile at me? I'm the same man. I have the same feet, legs, and hands, and the Sun looks down on me a complete man. I wish you would look and smile at me."

Still Nant'an Lpah sat staring at the ground and didn't face me. The men sitting next to him were watching what he did. I wondered if any of the warriors around us heard me.

"Every day I'm thinking of how I am to talk to you to make you believe what I say. And I think, too, that you're thinking of what to say to me. There is one God looking down on us all. We are all children of the one God. God is listening to me. The Sun, the Darkness, and the Winds are all listening to what we now say.

"I haven't forgotten what you told me, although a long time has passed. I want this peace to be legal and good to you, and you to me, and peace to soon be established. But when you go to the reservation, you put agents and interpreters over us who do bad things. Perhaps they don't mind what you tell them, because I don't believe you would tell them to do bad things to us. I want to have a good man put over me. While living, I want to live well."

Nant'an Lpah slowly shook his head as if he didn't believe my words.

"I know I have to die sometime, but even if the heavens were to fall on me, I want to do what is right. I think I'm a good man but, in the papers all over the world, they say I am a bad man. It is a bad thing to say so about me. I never do wrong without cause.

"To prove to you that I'm telling you the truth, remember I sent you word that I would come from a place far away to speak to you here, and you see us now. Some have come on horseback and some on foot. If I were thinking badly, or if I had done badly, I would never come here. If it had been my fault, would I have come so far to talk to you?

"I'm glad to see Kaytennae. I was afraid I would never see him again. That was one reason, too, why I left. I wanted Kaytennae returned to us to live with his family. Now I believe that all told me is true. I see Kaytennae again as I was told I should." My medicine bag hanging from my neck felt heavy and hot. I held it in my hand and felt water running down my face. I knew it was time for me to stop.

"I have spoken."

Nant'an Lpah looked up and straight at me. I felt my medicine bag grow warmer and more drops of water role down the side of my face.

He said, "I've heard what you said. Your mouth talks too many ways."

I thought, *I don't lie, Nant'an Lpah. Your bad tongue makes me want to leave.*

"It seems very strange to me that more than forty men should be afraid of three, but if you left the reservation for that reason, why did you kill innocent people, sneaking all over the country to do it? What did those innocent people do to you that you should kill them, steal their horses, and slip around in the rocks like coyotes?"

It was war. They were enemies, Nant'an Lpah.

He said, "There is not a week that passes that you don't hear foolish stories in your own camp, but you're no child—you don't have to believe them."

I said, "I want to ask who it was who ordered that I should be arrested."

"Your story about being afraid of arrest is all bosh. There were no orders to arrest you."

I shook my head, "Then maybe the orders come from somebody else. Who is this? I want to know who starts these bad stories and wants to arrest me. Tell me. There's no other captain so great as you. I thought you ought to know about those stories and who started them."

Nant'an Lpah said, "You promised me in the Sierra Madre that peace should last, but you lied about it. When a man has lied to me once, I want some better proof than his own word before I can believe him again. You sent up some of your people to kill Chato and Lieutenant Davis, and then you started the story that they had killed them, and thus you got a great many of your people to go out. Everything you did on the reservation is known. There is no use for you to try to talk nonsense. I'm no child."

Nant'an Lpah shook the little stick he had used to scratch in the leaves at me and frowned. "You lie, Geronimo."

"If you think I'm not telling the truth, then I don't think you came down here in good faith." I threw up my hands. "I want no more of this."

The warriors sitting nearby began to stand, and those on the perimeter of the council began to back away. Naiche shook his head and waved his arm parallel to the ground. The warriors relaxed, and I grew calm. There were other battles still to fight.

Nant'an Lpah said, "All right then, tell me which of your people have been threatened?"

"All of them were. If you don't believe me, I can prove it by all the men, women, and children of the White Mountain Apaches. They wanted to seize me and Mangas."

"Then why did Naiche and Chihuahua go out?"

"Because they were afraid the same thing would happen to them."

"Who made them afraid? What did you tell them to make them afraid?"

"The only thing I told them was that I had heard I was going to be seized and killed, that's all."

"Then why did you send people to kill Chato and Davis?"

"I didn't send anyone to kill them. If it were true, the chiefs here would say so."

"And you reported that they were killed—that is the reason so many went out with you?"

"Hmmph. Look at all the White Mountains here. They can show you I'm innocent. Look over there. There is a White Mountain sergeant, a man like that won't lie."

Nant'an Lpah shook his head.

I said, "Whenever I wanted to talk to Teniente Davis, I spoke by day or by night. I never went to see him in a hidden way. Maybe some of these men know about it. Maybe you ought to ask them."

One of the scouts yelled, "Riders are coming."

It was Chihuahua, Ulzana, and six warriors driving a herd of horses. The White Mountain scouts, who had family members killed by Ulzana and his warriors during his raid before the last Ghost Face, stared hard at Ulzana, some, I think, seeing him for the first time, and I saw thumbs of the White Mountain scouts creeping to their rifle hammers, but the White Mountains held their fire. Another time they would settle their business with Ulzana. Chihuahua and Ulzana herded their horses off to the side and walked to the council. When Chihuahua saw the Nant'an, he smiled and walked over to shake his hand, then Chihuahua and Ulzana walked over to the edge of the council and stood where they could see.

Nant'an Lpah waved his stick at me again like he was pointing at a child, and I felt the heat of anger again growing inside me.

"You're making a great fuss about seeing Kaytennae. Over a year ago, I asked you if you wanted me to bring Kaytennae back, but you said no. It's a good thing for you that we didn't bring Kaytennae back because Kaytennae has more sense now than all the rest of the Chiricahuas put together. You told me the same sort of story in the Sierra Madre, but you lied. What evidence have I of your sincerity? How do I know whether or not you're lying to me? Have I ever lied to you?

"You must make up your minds whether you will stay out on the warpath or surrender unconditionally. If you stay out, I'll keep after you and kill the last one, if it takes fifty years. If you surrender unconditionally, then you and your families will have to go back east to Florida for a time to stay out of the way of the settlers who want revenge for all the killing and robbery you've done to them. You cannot go back to Fort Apache and life with your brothers who never left. That's not right. You'd better think it over tonight and let me know in the morning. I've said all I have to say."

I said, "All right. We'll talk tomorrow. I may want to ask you some questions, too, as you have asked me some."

He started to stand, but the man named Fly with the image catcher box called, "Please wait, General. Let me take some photos of this historic event." Nant'an Lpah sat back down, and no one else moved except when Fly asked us to shift our places a little so the image catcher saw more light. Fly finished catching images and said, "In the morning, I would like to photograph you and your people, Geronimo. May I come to your camp to do this?"

I said, *"Enjuh,"* and the council ended.

CHAPTER 43
SURRENDER

After my talk with Nant'an Lpah, we returned to our camp. I told the warriors to stay ready if the Blue Coats tried anything, but the talks were peaceful. Hungry, we ate at our home fires while we thought over what Nant'an Lpah and I said and argued over at the council. I talked with She-gha and asked what she thought, but she answered only that we always needed to be careful around the White Eyes and Blue Coats. They didn't usually speak straight. Wise woman was my She-gha.

The sun fell into the mountains from a sky of blood-red clouds as the night grew cold. We camped in a depression on top of a cone-shaped hill where, if the Blue Coats came for us, it would be easy to defend ourselves. I went to the fire where Naiche sat with some of our best young warriors. They discussed what Nant'an Lpah and I said that day. They welcomed me and Naiche rolled a cigarette for us to smoke to the four directions that our words might be wise. When we finished, he flipped the last bit in the fire, and looked at us as we hunched over close to the fire trying to stay warm, its flickering yellow light on our faces.

Naiche said, "Geronimo, tell us what you think of what Nant'an Lpah said today in the council."

"Hmmph. I don't like Nant'an Lpah. He doesn't say good words to us. Says bad things about me. Says I lied, when I know I did not."

Naiche smiled on one side of his mouth, "Chihuahua believed

you lied about killing Chato and Teniente Davis to get us to break out with you. He wanted to go back to the reservation after the breakout, but he couldn't. Then we learned that you believed you were speaking the truth when actually Chato and Teniente Davis still lived. We no longer held that story against you. Nant'an Lpah has only the stories he and Teniente Davis learned from those still on the reservation. They don't want you there. Chato and others give the worst side of what happened. Now Nant'an Lpah says we must go away to the East if we surrender. I don't know the places in the East. What will they do to us in the East?"

I answered, "I don't know what they'll do to us. I say we shouldn't surrender until they let us return to Turkey Creek and give us back our families."

Naiche frowned. "Nant'an Lpah says if we don't surrender, he'll hunt us down and kill us if it takes fifty years and, even then, there is nothing that will make him give us our families back. I want my family back. I trust him to do what is right."

From the far side of the hill facing Teniente Maus's camp came sounds of greeting from the boys who served as sentries. We all wondered who had come to our camp from that of the Blue Coats. We looked at each other frowning, and then, as if a ghost appearing out of the darkness, Kaytennae entered our fire's circle of light.

He said, "Ho, brothers. I come to listen to you and see what you think."

Naiche motioned to a place on his left side, the place of honor. "Come sit with us, Kaytennae. It warmed my heart to see you out of chains and free from the place by the big water the Blue Coats call, Alcatraz. Tell us your story. Tell us what you think of today's council."

I thought Kaytennae looked like a man too long away from the light, one who spent too much time in a cave where there was heavy darkness.

He said, "I learned much at Alcatraz. It is on a little land out from the edge of the big water. I couldn't leave there and swim back to the edge of the big water to get away. The White Eyes took the chains off me soon I after I went there. I had to sleep in a calaboose with many, many rooms all made of big square rocks and Blue Coats with guns who watched us all the time. After a while, they took some of us to see the great village on the edge of the big water. The White Eyes are very powerful on the edge of the big water. Many buildings, some with steps that reach high into the sky, many crossing trails, many places to buy supplies and pretty things, and people without number, like the big herds of buffalo in the long-ago days and all in one place. They are so many, and we are so few. To survive, we must somehow learn to make peace with them."

I shook my head, "A good Apache warrior is better than ten or even a hundred White Eyes in a fight."

Kaytennae nodded. "Yes. Geronimo speaks true. But for every Apache warrior, there are thousands, maybe tens of thousands of White Eyes. Besides that, they have much power we don't have. I learned to make tracks on paper and to read them while I was at Alcatraz. These tracks can hold knowledge and understanding of everything the White Eyes know and pass to their children, even beginning in the long-ago times, when the children understand how to read the tracks.

"The White Eyes know how to make the same thing over and over without limit. Everyone can have one. Where do you think our rifles and ammunition come from that we take from them, or iron pots and pans, or warm blankets? Slaves don't make these over and over. Once they did, but not now. Big confusing tools only the White Eyes know how to use make the little tools like our rifles, bullets, and iron pots. If we fight the White Eyes, one day there will be no more Chihennes or Chiricahuas."

In my center, I knew Kaytennae spoke true. I looked around our fire's circle of men and saw only wide eyes and jaws dropped in hard acceptance of his words. There was a long silence, and somewhere off on the *llano* a coyote yipped. I thought, *Coyote waits.*

I said, "Nant'an Lpah says we must give up, go away east, and never return. This I won't do. I would rather my blood and that of my family water the mescal and cactus than for us to go away forever into the sun behind the dawn."

There were grunts and nods of approval around the circle. I could see the fire in the eyes of the young men willing to die rather than leave their country. The older men pulled their blankets closer against the cold and stared at the fire, slowly nodding as if giving up to a truth they had thought but didn't want to speak.

Kaytennae puffed his cheeks and then said, "Maybe Nant'an Lpah will agree to let you return to Turkey Creek in two or three harvests, but you need to leave the country. Not just for punishment but for your own protection. You have killed so many White Eyes and soldiers that those who have ranches and towns here are very angry. They want to kill you on sight or hang you after putting you in jail a little while. You know what I mean, Geronimo. Ten harvests ago, you waited in the guardhouse at San Carlos for the Tucson sheriff to come get you for the White Eyes to hang."

I nodded. I knew very well what Kaytennae was saying. If we did all leave, then the White Eyes would soon come after us wherever we were.

"You can stand being away for two or three harvests rather than watering the *llano* with your blood or having angry White Eyes hang you. I know you all have the strength and courage to do this. Think on it. Maybe he offers that to you, if you agree to peace."

He looked at Naiche, who said, "Kaytennae speaks wise words from his heart. We'll talk about what you have told us."

Alchesay, the White Mountain scout and chief, appeared out of the darkness, and Naiche invited him to join us. He sat down and told us the same things. He said he had spoken to Chihuahua and Ulzana, who were also speaking with their warriors, and that we all had the same worries. Alchesay told us he also believed Nant'an Lpah would keep us in the East no more than two harvests. This he had done with the bands in the northern plains—the Sioux, Cheyenne, and Arapaho. He would be fair and do this for the Apaches.

We talked like this for a long time with Kaytennae and Alchesay, and then went to our blankets, still not convinced to surrender, still wondering whether we would ever get our lives back.

The sun was coming, led by early, gray light, and the smoke from our fires had settled like a morning mist in the bowl where we slept. I left the blankets, went to the top of the hill, and prayed to *Ussen* for courage, strength, and good eyes to see a clear path for our people. I sat by the fire, bathing in the smoke from sage, while She-gha fixed me something to eat. She was a good woman and could run with the best of them, but I wished I had my other women, Zi-yeh and our little son, Fenton, to help her and Ih-tedda, swelling with our first child, back. I would ask Nant'an Lpah to send them to us if we agreed to peace.

When the sun floated up over the mountains bringing long shadows from the east, the *segundo* for Nant'an Lpah, Captain Bourke, brought the man named Fly with the image box and another to help him. Bourke asked if Fly could capture our images that morning while the light was good. I didn't know what good light meant; all light is better than darkness. I had seen these kinds of images before, true representations of what we looked like, better than drawings, and I wanted others—whites and Apaches—to know what we looked like before we decided to fight to the end or surrendered. I agreed for him to capture our images, and we spent much of the morning gathering and standing like he wanted us in small and big groups, on horses, and on our feet.

After Fly captured our images, we went back and talked the rest of the day and into the night about what we should do. Kaytennae and Alchesay came again and said Nant'an Lpah told them he would let us return from the East after two harvests. This is all Chihuahua needed to hear. From the way he talked, I knew he would surrender the next day, and I knew Naiche would follow Chihuahua's lead. If they surrendered, then I knew I, too, must surrender. I wished I had some good whiskey. I wanted to get drunk and forget about the stink of this peace to which we agreed. Maybe Tribolett would sell us some whiskey next sun after we surrendered.

The next morning, by the time the sun was well above the mountains, Chihuahua, Naiche, Cathla, Nana, and I had agreed we would surrender at the time of no shadows. Cathla and I made our faces black with pounded galena and walked with the others to the camp of Teniente Maus and said we wanted to talk.

We gathered under the tall trees with white bark the White Eyes call sycamores. Chihuahua, Naiche, and Nana sat near the Blue Coats, but Cathla and I stayed in better shade under mulberry trees. I studied the trees. We used mulberry wood to make good bows. I would have to remember this place. These mulberry trees had many bows in them. Nant'an Lpah came wearing his hard, white hat, sat down on a ledge again, and said, "Speak. I will listen."

Chihuahua stood in a pool of sunlight and said, "I'm very glad to see you, Nant'an Lpah, and have this talk with you. It is as you say, 'We are always in danger out here.' I hope, from this sun on, we may live better with our families and not do harm to anybody. I'm anxious to behave. I think the sun is looking down on me, and the earth is listening. I'm thinking better. It seems to me that I've seen the one who makes the rain and sends the winds, or he must have sent you to this place. I surrender myself to you because I believe in you, and you don't deceive us. You must be our god. I'm satisfied with all that you do. You must be the one who makes the green pastures, who sends the rain, who commands the winds. You must be the one who sends the fresh fruits that come on the trees. There are many men in the world who are big chiefs and command many people, but you, I think, are the greatest of them all. I want you to be a father to me and treat me as your son. I want you to have pity on me. There is no doubt that all you do is right because all you say is true. I trust in all you say. You don't deceive. All things you tell us are facts. I am now in your hands. I place myself at your disposition to dispose of as you please. I shake your hand. I want to come right into your camp with my family and stay with you. I don't want to stay away at a distance. I want to be right where you are. I have roamed these mountains from water to water. Never have I found the place where I could see my father or mother until today. I see you, my father. I surrender to you now, and I don't want any more bad feeling or bad talk. I'm going over to stay with you in your camp.

"Whenever a man raises anything, even a dog, he thinks well of it and tries to raise it up and treats it well. This is how I want you to feel towards me, and be good to me, and don't let people say bad things about me. Now I surrender to you and go with you. When we're traveling together on the road, I hope you'll talk to me once in a while. I think a great deal of Alchesay and

Kaytennae. They think a great deal of me. I hope someday to be all the same as their brother." Chihuahua shook hands with Alchesay and Kaytennae. Then he said, "How long will it be before I can live with these friends?"

Naiche spoke next and said many of the same things as Chihuahua. Then he said, "When I was free, I gave orders, but now I surrender to you. You order, and I obey. Now that I have surrendered, I'm glad. I'll not have to hide behind rocks and mountains. I'll go across the open *llano*. There may be many men who have bad feelings against us. I go wherever you see fit to send us. Send us where there is no bad talk about us. I surrender to you and hope you will be kind to us."

I spoke next. I said, "Two or three words are enough. We are all friends, all one family, all one band. What the others say, I say also. Once I moved about like the wind. Now I surrender to you, and that is all." I shook Nant'an Lpah's hand two good pumps and then said, "My heart is yours, and I hope yours will be mine. Whatever you tell me is true. We're all satisfied of that. I hope the day will come when my word shall be as strong with you as yours is with me. That is all I have to say now, except a few words. I should like to have my wife and daughter come to meet me at Fort Bowie or Silver Creek."

Nant'an Lpah smiled and nodded. "I will send orders for them to be brought to you with the next courier. Soon they come to you. Pay no attention to any more unfriendly talk. There are some people who can no more control their talk than the wind can."

I said, "I want to ask Kaytennae and Alchesay to say a few words. They have visited with us and helped us decide to do what is right. They have traveled a long way, and I want to hear them speak."

Kaytennae shook his head and said in a croaking, strained voice, "My throat is sore. It hurts to speak, and I can't speak

371

loud this way."

Alchesay stepped out and said to Nant'an Lpah, motioning toward us as the wind rippled through the tops of the sycamores, "They have surrendered. I don't want you to have any bad feelings towards them. They are all good friends now because they are the same people—all one family with me—just like when you kill a deer, all its parts are of one body. No matter where you send them, we hope to hear that you have treated them kindly. I have never told you a lie, nor have you ever told me a lie, and now I tell you that they really want to do what is right and live at peace. I want you to carry away in your pocket all that has been said here today."

Nant'an Lpah stood and silently looked at each one of us gathered there with him. Then he said, "This is a good day. There will be war no more. There will be peace. I'll leave early at sunrise to go to Fort Bowie and use the talking wire to speak with my chief in the East to tell him what we have done here and ask what we must do next. Lieutenant Maus and the scouts will go with the rest of you and protect you from Mexicans here and Americans across the border. May your journey be easy."

Chihuahua said, "I'll send word everyday of where we are and that we are behaving."

Nant'an Lpah answered, "*Enjuh*. Kaytennae can write letters for you." And, with that, he returned to his camp and began giving his instructions to move us to Fort Bowie. Where we went from there, I didn't know.

CHAPTER 44
BREAKAWAY

After our surrender to Nant'an Lpah, every man in our camp wanted some Tribolett whiskey. We all wanted to get drunk. We needed to forget for a while the surrender of our freedom and losing the country we all loved and killed for to keep White Eyes away. The Tribolett brothers had set up a tent a short walk from our camp to sell their whiskey. I went to my *wickiup* and found the paper with faces and tracks painted on it, what the *Nakai-yes* and White Eyes called "money," and went to the whiskey tent. My son Chappo and my brother Fun came with me as the sun fell across the bright, blue sky halfway down its arc toward the nearby mountain.

I pulled back the tent canvas opening and went into the warm gloom and shadows made by an oil lantern hanging on a smooth tent pole. Charlie Tribolett stood alone behind two planks laid across two barrels standing on end. I didn't see his two brothers anywhere around. Behind Charlie stood five or six big baskets holding jugs of brown water, good whiskey. There were more on the wagon out behind the tent. I had traded with Charlie for his whiskey and supplies before. He called the big, basket-covered jugs "five-gallon demijohns." One of Charlie's whiskey demijohns was enough to give all the men and most of the women in camp a good drink and make most of them drunk, which I think they all wanted.

When Charlie, his hat tipped back, scratching the rough gray hair on his face, saw us come in the tent, he grinned, showing his crooked, yellow teeth. Chappo and Fun stood by the door, their rifles in the crooks of their arms.

He said in the language of the *Nakai-yes,* "*Buenas tardes, Señor* Geronimo. I see you. I hear you have told Nant'an Lpah you fight no more and will go where he sends you toward the rising sun."

I waved my hand parallel to the sandy ground and answered, "*Hola,* Charlie Tribolett. I don't see you in three, maybe four, moons. You stay close to the border. I see you have your whiskey here."

Charlie, still grinning like Coyote, nodded. "Yes, sir, I do. Here, let me give you and your boys a taste." He put out four small glasses and filled them from a small, open jug he had on the planks. I motioned Chappo and Fun to come take a glass like I did. Charlie held his glass up like White Eyes do to salute us and tossed its whiskey down his throat. We raised our glasses to him and drank ours. Fire in our mouths! I let the burning water go down my throat and smacked my lips. Fun and Chappo grinned, and I did, too. We said, *"Enjuh!"* and Charlie grinned and nodded.

I smacked my lips again for more, but Charlie just grinned. "How much you fellers want? I got a plenty here." I reached in my pocket and pulled out the roll of money I took in the raids we had made in the last moon. I handed it to Charlie and said, "How much whiskey for this? More than that jug you have here?"

His greedy little pig eyes grew big as he took the roll and looked at each piece of paper with numbers and tracks. With every tooth showing he said, "Yes, sir, it's more than this jug here. I'll give you three of them five-gallon demijohns there fer it. What ya say?"

"Ha. Three big jugs give us all a good drink two, maybe three, times. We take 'em."

I said to Chappo, "Go get others to help you. We take three of the big jugs there. Take 'em to Naiche's *wickiup* and tell him to say to the camp, 'Geronimo gives whiskey to all.' While I wait here for you, Charlie Tribolett and I have another drink from his jug."

Chappo and Fun left carrying a demijohn jug between them. I knew they would come again soon with two others to get the other demijohns. Charlie slid the roll of paper I had given him in his vest pocket and patted it as Fun and Chappo, carrying the big jug basket between them, headed back to our camp. The whiskey trader poured me another glass of whiskey from the little jug by his hand, his smile gone, and his eyes narrowed.

I said, "We no longer see you for a few harvests, Charlie. We go toward the rising sun for a while after we follow Nant'an Lpah to Fort Bowie. We no more give you pesos we take from *Nakai-yes* for your good whiskey. Maybe when we return, you come to Fort Apache and sell us more whiskey when White Eye agents don't look?" I took a little swallow of the whiskey Charlie poured me.

He shook his head. "After you cross that border, Geronimo, I ain't expectin' to see you no more."

"Why you say this, Charlie Tribolett?"

He made a face and then said, "I shouldn't be saying anything to you, but we've been friends and tradin' for a long time. I guess I owe it to you to tell you what I know. Listen close. I'm only going to say this once out loud, so you can hear it. Tell anybody I told you, and I'll swear it's a damned lie. *Comprendes?*"

I nodded and took another little swallow of whiskey.

Charlie said, "See, this here is the way it is, Geronimo. There's a plan that, once you cross the border, they gonna turn you and your boys over to the local people for trials. It's just like you told me old Clum had planned for you when he took you at

Ojo Caliente. Some sheriff is gonna get you, there's gonna be a trial, and then you and most of the others is gonna be dancin' on air hangin' at the end of a short rope. That there is why Nant'an Lpah is headin' north early in the mornin'. He's gonna set things up with whoever is gonna get you on the other side. It ain't right. You surrendered with promises, and they ought to be kept, but from what I hear, it ain't gonna happen."

I thought, *Nant'an Lpah is a liar. I should have known this when he said I was one. He doesn't speak pretty to us. He's a bad man. One day he dies in a bad way. My Power saves us now.*

I finished the whiskey Charlie Tribolett had poured me, sat the glass down with a thump, and said, "I go now, Charlie Tribolett. You're a good *amigo* for telling me this. Maybe we see you sooner than you think."

"Maybe so. *Adios,* Geronimo."

That night before the chiefs and I drank too much whiskey and became drunk. We sat at Naiche's *wickiup,* and I told them what Charlie Tribolett had said, that I believed him, and that I believed we should stay in Mexico until we knew what Nant'an Lpah would do.

Chihuahua shook his head. "You take the word of a White Eye who trades in whiskey? I don't believe him. I trust Nant'an Lpah. He offered to let us return in two years. I believe he will do this. He does what he thinks is best for us. We're going away toward the rising sun to get out of the way of White Eyes who want revenge and more blood. I can live anywhere for two harvests if I have to. What do you think, Naiche?"

"I think until we know what Nant'an Lpah does, it's better to wait on this side of the border. Nant'an Lpah doesn't speak pretty to us like he did before. It's hard to trust him. I think Geronimo is right. We ought to wait and see."

Chihuahua shrugged his shoulders and threw out his hands.

"Do what you need to do. I go with Teniente Maus to Fort Bowie."

Naiche said, "Chihuahua speaks straight. Geronimo brings us good whiskey. Now we drink it. We go to the border with Teniente Maus, but Geronimo and I don't cross until we see Nant'an Lpah's words are true."

There was plenty of whiskey for the men and their women to have a good drink, and we drank more than we should. Some of Ulzana's warriors and a few of mine drank too much and fired their rifles toward the soldier and packer camps and had contests to learn who made the loudest war crimes. We were lucky they hit nothing in the camps to stir up the soldiers.

Later in the night, Cathla and I bet three warriors we could beat them in a race on mules. We took five from the packers' herd and raced north beside the dry bed of the *Rio* San Bernardino. Too drunk, we fell off our mules. They balked when we tried to ride them through a mesquite thicket and sent us laughing and yelling to the dirt. Hitting the sand and dirt didn't hurt us. I didn't try to get up. I rested, lying in the dirt staring at the stars and went to sleep.

Someone kicked my foot. Blinking, I saw the dark outline of Cathla in dawn's soft, gray light. He had splotches of dirt all over his shirt and had also slept in the sand where he landed. He awoke and was sober enough to catch a curious mule watching him nearby. Cathla helped me up on the mule and then swung up behind me.

One of the other warriors racing us had been smart enough to hold his mule's reins when he fell off and, after a little sleep, remounted and found the other two warriors snoring under the mesquite. All three were riding one mule. I was still a little drunk, and they were, too. We were having a good time. By the time the sun brightened the dawn, we heard the clink and clatter of a fast-moving buckboard coming down the dry stretches of the *Río* San Bernardino and a troop of horses following it. Nant'an Lpah was driving the wagon, followed by a Blue Coat escort. He raised his hat as he drove by, and Captain Bourke pulled out of the escort and rode over to us. I slid off the mule and staggered toward him. I thought the mule race was fun and still laughed about it.

Bourke dismounted and frowned as I staggered up and hugged him. He said, a frown making deep wrinkles on his brow, "What are you and your warriors doing way out here away from your camp?"

"We were having a mule race, Captain Bourke, but we were all so drunk we fell off and went to sleep for a while. Now we're all mounted again. Everybody in camp drank a lot last night. Heads will hurt; young men will lose their stomachs. I think we'll be sober pretty soon. I follow with my people in a little while. Don't worry about us."

"All right. I'll join Nant'an Lpah. You get on back to your camp so the mules don't get lost and neither do you."

I gave him a hand wave like the soldiers do their chiefs and headed back to Cathla and our mule. We never did finish that race, but we got back to camp and slept some more.

I spoke the truth to Captain Bourke. Many heads hurt, and the young ones had bad stomachs. The sun was up a long time before we were ready to move north, and we moved no faster than a child might walk. We stopped and camped at the time of no shadows. Teniente Maus wanted to go on, but we all needed sleep. Each family made a little shady place to rest. Soon many snores filled the camp.

The western sky was blood red with touches of black when I sat with Naiche by his fire and talked more about surrendering to

Nant'an Lpah. Naiche said, "I said last night I think you're right. Nant'an Lpah didn't speak good to us this time like he did three harvests ago at Bugatseka. Maybe Tribolett speaks the truth about Nant'an Lpah giving us to White Eye sheriffs who will make a ceremony and hang us. If he doesn't give us to sheriffs, we go to this place he calls 'Florida.' I know nothing of Florida. Maybe it's a place of darkness. I don't like this."

I took a swallow of coffee from my blue speckled cup She-gha carried for me. My head still didn't feel right from all the whiskey I drank the night before, but at least I was thinking clearly.

"You speak true words, Naiche. I won't cross the border. It's too much of a risk. The Blue Coats might take us to the guardhouse to wait for a sheriff. I'd rather use my last bullet and then my knife in my heart like Victorio than dance in the wind in front of laughing White Eyes. I think we can drink a little more whiskey tonight and, next sun, ride up close to the border and camp. From there, we leave when sleep is deep in the night.

"I say we tell this only to family members so Teniente Maus does not learn what we do until after we go. Nant'an Lpah will think we go back to Bugatseka, send Chiricahua scouts under Chato after us." I grinned. "No Bugatseka. We go west past Fronteras, maybe camp on top of Azul Mountains. We can see soldiers and trackers a long way off while we rest up there. What do you think?"

Naiche pulled papers and *tobaho* from his vest pocket and began to make a cigarette. "I think Geronimo is a good war leader. What he says, we do."

"*Enjuh.* Let's smoke, eat, and drink a little whiskey. It may be a long time before we'll have more to drink."

That night we again enjoyed Tribolett whiskey, but not as much as the night before. I told She-gha, Chappo, and Fun what we planned and why. The young men said they were with us. Naiche told his wife Hah-o-zinne and his family men. They, too, wanted to go. Soon word of what we planned had passed from one set of drunken lips to the next.

The next morning, heads hurt, and patience was short. For some, it was hard to see clearly, but we all were ready to move north with Teniente Maus, who kept his distance behind us. We stopped and camped when we were about a finger width above the horizon run (two miles) from the border. Chihuahua kept his people together and camped to the west of us.

When Teniente Maus saw we camped, he rode up to me and said, "Why are you camping now? There's much light left in the day. We could be camping at Silver Springs a good distance north of the border by dark."

I shrugged. "Many heads still hurt from all the whiskey we had the last two nights, and our horses and mules need rest. Be careful of our people. They don't think right and can be dangerous and without much patience when their heads hurt from too much whiskey."

He raised a brow, looked around the camp, and nodded. "All right, Geronimo. Just be ready to ride at sunup. I'll camp up a little north of you."

"*Enjuh,* Teniente."

The packer, Daly, with Teniente Maus, looked first at Chihuahua's camp, then our camp, grinned with one side of his face, shook his head, and rode away talking to Maus. I knew he somehow sensed what Naiche and I planned, and I knew we would have to be very quiet and careful when we left that night.

We took two horses and a mule from the herd and left the rest. More animals would only slow us down in the rough country. As we planned, we headed west toward Agua Prieta and then across the *llano* down the valley toward Fronteras. As we neared

Fronteras, we broke into groups of three or four and scattered in different directions. If Teniente Maus and his scouts were following us, they would never be able to follow us all. I don't think Maus ever saw us, but we watched for him and his scouts as we ran across the mountains to the west of Fronteras toward safety in the Azul Mountains. Even the women and children did well on this run as the warriors began taking livestock and supplies from ranches in our path or nearby. I was proud of my People.

CHAPTER 45
LAST DAYS OF FREEDOM

We rested for half a moon on the top of the Azul Mountains. When we moved, we kept to the mountains and *llano* of northwest Sonora, but after leaving our women and children in a safe place with two or three warriors to look after them, Naiche, the rest of the warriors, and I slipped across the border. Again, we killed all we found to deny the Blue Coats any information they might get from survivors.

One morning at a *rancho casa* north of the border near *Río* Santa Cruz, the warriors shot a woman and killed her baby by swinging its head into a wall, giving a quick death for one so young. I always regretted killing babies. But it was better they died quickly than to suffer from no water and too much sun until found. If they somehow survived, they grew into men and women who stole even more of our freedom and country.

When I rode up, a warrior was about to kill a nearly grown girl. She looked to me like she had not yet had her womanhood ceremony. He had found her hiding under a bed and pulled her out by the ankles screaming and crying. I stopped him from killing her and had her ride behind Chappo. He wasn't happy I made him carry her. She was extra weight for his pony, which slowed him down, and he didn't like having anything to do with White Eye women and children.

I thought she might have been worth White Eye money for her return, or she might make a good woman for one of our men. She didn't need to die before she proved her value. We found two men—I later learned from her—who were her Uncle Peck and his hired man, working cattle near the ranch house. They had no guns. When they saw us watching them from a nearby hill, they tried to get away on their horses. The warriors killed the hired man and shot Peck's horse. When it fell, Peck rolled free and ran, but the warriors easily caught him and brought him back to the top of a hill from where I sat my pony watching. They stood around him in a circle ready to do whatever I said.

Ahnandia, who had learned the White Eye tongue from his friend George Wratten, stepped from the circle and told me Peck's name and then told Peck I was Geronimo. Peck nodded he understood. I saw no fear in his eyes. His wore his shirtsleeves rolled up over the red sleeves of things the White Eyes called "long johns." With his red sleeves, Peck reminded me of my old chief, Red Sleeves—Mangas Coloradas. The man heard and then saw his niece sitting behind Chappo. She yelled that we had murdered his woman and baby, took her, and burned the ranch house. Before he answered, Ahnandia held up his hand, palm out, and said to him, "Speak to her, you die."

Peck raised his chin in defiance but said nothing.

I looked at Peck and understood how he must feel with his family killed and those close to him taken. I said with Ahnandia interpreting, "Your red sleeves make you look like Mangas Coloradas, and you are brave. You're a good man. You live, but you lose your family. Leave his red sleeves. Take everything else on him."

The warriors threw him on the ground and took his clothes and boots. Ahnandia swung up on his pony, pointed back to the smoke column rising from the ranch house hidden behind a hill, and said, "You go back there, we kill you." But I looked over my shoulder and smiled as we rode away. Red Sleeves was walking back toward the burning ranch house.

Two days later, we rode back into the Pinito Mountains east of the *Río* Magdalena in Sonora and gathered our women and children from an a camp at an old abandoned *casa* where we had left them. We had seen a dust plume from horses seeming to come in our direction and sent a warrior to learn what it was. He returned late that evening and said Blue Coats with dark faces were trailing us but without Apache scouts. This sounded strange to me. Nant'an Lpah always sent many scouts with his Blue Coats. Naiche and I discussed this and decided to ride up a nearby canyon, leave easy trail sign, and if the Blue Coats were foolish enough to follow us, wipe them out.

The soldiers with dark faces, who the White Eyes called "Buffalo Soldiers," led by White Eye chiefs, didn't hesitate to follow us into the canyon. We hid and waited with our rifles ready to shoot from behind ledges and boulders on a semicircular cliff. Naiche and I watched the soldiers and their White Eye chiefs come with our soldier glasses.

They came within two long arrow shots when a soldier saw a man peeking around a boulder. The soldier pointed toward us and yelled words I didn't understand. The soldier chief called for the soldiers to dismount and every fourth man to hold the horses while the others formed a line to move against us. Brave, foolish men. They knew we waited, and still they came.

We waited to fire our rifles to make certain we didn't miss. But one of the soldiers shot where he thought he saw a warrior hiding by boulder. The warriors returned fire, killed the soldier next to him, and hit the soldier who fired in the knee but didn't kill him. He was lying in the dust bleeding, holding his leg, and groaning. A White Eye chief ran out, grabbed the soldier under his shoulders, and pulled him to cover behind a boulder. I sent some warriors around one side to grab the soldier horses, but the soldier chief had already sent them back down the canyon where the warriors couldn't reach them.

We fought the soldiers for about a hand against the horizon. Cover was good for both my warriors and the soldiers. No one else suffered wounds on either side. Soldiers hidden behind their cover fired without looking for a certain target. We slipped away with ease unseen and unfollowed.

Nant'an Lpah sent other soldiers, still without scouts, after us. I took the hardest possible trails to wear out the soldiers who followed us. We fought Blue Coat and *Nakai-yi* soldiers often as we roamed northern Sonora. In one fight, *Nakai-yi* soldiers, most of them Tohono O'odam, nearly one hundred fifty, ran when we fired on them from a high hill. They left behind thirty-three of their horses and a good load of supplies, which we took, laughing. Cowards. We even showed them the girl child we took from Red Sleeves and called for them to come take her back, but still they ran.

After we made the *Nakai-yes* run, we rested on a high mountain for a day. Naiche and I smoked and held council that evening.

Naiche said, "Geronimo, the warriors are tired. All we do is hide, fight, run, hide, and fight again. They need a reason to do this. I think something is different with the Blue Coats. With Nant'an Lpah chief, the Blue Coats used many scouts, not just trackers as they do now. What has changed? Has Nant'an Lpah left like he did before? Is there a new Nant'an? Maybe if there is a new Nant'an, then we get a better deal for surrender. I go to Fort Apache, see our people there, and learn all I can about where we stand with the Blue Coats."

I knew all the words Naiche spoke were true, but I didn't like the idea of surrendering again.

"You are chief, Naiche. Do what you want."

"Many Blue Coats ride along the border between Nogales and Palomas. We need to look for a way to get across the border and up to Fort Apache without the Blue Coats knowing we come there. We need enough time to learn what we need to know. The ranch near Nogales where we crossed the line a moon ago might be a good place. Let's send a few warriors there and watch what happens. If we have too hard a time crossing that way, then I want to send Atelnietze with four men east to raid and pull the Blue Coats in that direction while we ride north for Fort Apache. Once we're in the mountains, Atelnietze and his men can meet us."

"Do what you think is best. I, too, would like to know the news from Fort Apache, but I'll return to Sonora and live in our camp on top of the Azul Mountains. I will look for a *Nakai-yi* chief I can trust."

Naiche nodded. "This we will do."

We talked more about places to meet and who to take before we broke council.

After short fights with several different soldier groups as we moved along the border, Naiche decided to send Atelnietze with his four men to raid along the border off toward the east. In five suns, Atelnietze was to meet Naiche in the Dragoon Mountains from where he planned a ride to Fort Apache.

I left Naiche and headed south with Nat-cul-baye; a young warrior, Hunlona; She-gha and Nat-cul-baye's wife, a young boy; and the girl we had taken from the Peck *rancho* who finally told me her name was Trini Verdin. She had light behind her eyes. I liked that.

We had to cross desert country and destroy men who wanted our scalps for money, but soon enough we found our way to our old camp on the top of the Azul Mountains. We had cached enough supplies there that we could rest without moving until

Naiche returned. Nearly a moon later, Hunlona, watching the country with my soldier glasses, saw Naiche leading his people toward our mountain.

Naiche reached our camp as the sun disappeared, casting long shadows across the junipers around our camp. It was good to be together again, and we sat around low fires and feasted on what we had. Children played in the dark and women laughed and whispered their secrets to each other. After eating, Naiche and I smoked and sat by the fire feeling its smoke bathe us in its sweetness and its heat drive away the cold and darkness.

I said, "Tell me of your days in Arizona and what you learned at Fort Apache."

Naiche made a face and slowly shook his head. "It was not what I hoped to find. I left two men with the women and children and joined Atelnietze near the Dragoon Mountains. We rode during the night, making it hard for anyone to see us and, in two suns, camped in a canyon northeast of where the Little and Big *Ríos* Bonito join the *Río* Negro, about an hour's run from Fort Apache. In the early darkness, we left our horses hobbled to graze in grass near the top of the canyon and tied our saddles and supplies in the canyon trees and covered them with branches to hide them before we ran for Fort Apache. Near the Chiricahua camp at Fort Apache, we watched the *wickiups* from the darkness under the trees and looked at everyone near a fire to learn if we knew anyone there.

"I saw my mother, Dos-teh-seh, and crawled into her *wickiup* to speak with her. She told me Nant'an Lpah had already sent our wives and children away to stay with Chihuahua in the place called Florida. It made me angry that he would do that. I saw then that he wasn't interested in bringing us back to make peace but wanted to kill us like Tribolett said. I told my mother we would be watching the camp and not to tell anyone we were nearby."

Far down the side of the mountain, we heard a wolf howl, answered by another closer to us. I thought, *Tonight our brothers join us.*

"I found Kaytennae's *wickiup* and called softly to him. I had my knife ready in case he wanted to fight, but he came out and gave the all-good sign. We had a good talk. I could not see his face well in the dark where we moved off to talk, but he promised to keep silent about me being there, and I believed him."

Naiche, you're foolish. Nant'an Lpah takes him out of Alcatraz to be a scout against us.

"He told me that Nant'an Lpah had been sent away because we left and had not come peacefully across the border as we promised when the other chiefs surrendered."

I laughed and said, *"Enjuh."*

"The new Nant'an is named Miles. Miles thinks Chato should be tribal chief and spoke to the White Eye chief at Fort Apache, saying they should send Chato and other leaders to ask the White Eye big chiefs in the East that the Chiricahuas who stayed on the reservation continue to stay at Fort Apache and Turkey Creek. That made Kaytennae think about killing them both, but he said Miles talked much and did little. He said Nant'an Miles didn't trust scouts except a few for trackers. Now only White Eye Blue Coats chase us. I think that is a good thing. Now they never catch us."

I grinned and nodded. "What else do you learn?"

"I left after talking to Kaytennae. We ran back to our canyon camp, took our horses, and found a safe place to sleep. We took turns watching the Fort Apache *wickiups* of the Chiricahuas who stayed on the reservation. The Blue Coat Fort Apache chief, Wade, was there many times."

"Hmmph. White chiefs must be bargaining with the Chiricahuas about betraying us."

"Late in the sun of the second day, we saw two women leave the Chiricahua camp and walk in our direction. Before the light was gone, I saw that one was Dos-teh-she, and the other was Bonita, the mother of Fun. I waited until the stars were out so the Blue Coats couldn't see us speaking and then walked down to talk with the women but stood in the tree shadows of the moon where they couldn't see me.

"I said, 'Ho, I see you Dos-teh-seh and Bonita. Why do you wander in the dark?' Bonita said, 'Naiche, I would speak with my son who follows you.'

"He is with the horses on top of the canyon. It is too dangerous for you to climb up there in the dark. You must wait to see him. Then Dos-teh-seh said, 'We bring you a message from Nant'an Miles and his subchief Wade. They want you and your people to come in. Nant'an Miles says you will be *justly treated,* whatever that means. I don't trust this Nant'an, my son.'

"I walked out from the tree shadows and made the all-is-good sign to the women. I said to Dos-teh-seh, 'Why do you not trust the Nant'an?' She said, 'First, the Nant'an sent Wade to us asking that the chiefs send a messenger to you. He thinks you are Geronimo, but the chiefs know better. They refused to send anyone with a message. They were afraid to come to you as men meeting men. I know you want peace and rest, regardless of what Geronimo wants, which is to kill, kill, kill. Bonita came with me hoping to see Fun.'

"I said, 'You still haven't said why you distrust this Nant'an.' She replied, 'Before we agreed to bring the Nant'an's message, he offered the Chiricahuas a reward of much silver ($2,500) for the taking of Geronimo, dead or alive, and much less silver ($50) for each warrior. Rather than fight you himself, the Nant'an wants to pay for your murders, using people who would betray you. The Nant'an is a child playing a man's game. No Chiricahua thinks of trying to get this silver the Nant'an offers. They may not like Geronimo, but they won't betray him.' "

The wolves howled again but had moved farther down the mountainside. Naiche told me he didn't trust the Nant'an or know what the Nant'an meant by "treated justly." I didn't trust the new Nant'an, either, but I was glad to learn Nant'an Lpah had gone away. I didn't like him, nor he me.

Next sun, Naiche and I talked more and decided it best to go farther south into the mountains where we camped when the Tarahumara, looking for Apache scalps, killed Blue Coat Crawford. We knew that country and believed it would be easier for us to hide there and raid to the west when we needed supplies.

Early the next sun, we left the Azul Mountains camp and rode for the Madera Mountains about a long sun's ride southwest of where we camped when the Tarahumara killed Crawford. We knew the new Nant'an would send more Blue Coats after us and believed the best way to avoid them was to break into three groups.

Naiche took five men and their women and children to a high mountain to the southwest. I took five men and their women and children and the girl Trini and went east, and Atelnietze took nine warriors with a few women and went northeast. We planned to raid often and hard and confuse the Blue Coats into chasing many false trails for a moon before we gathered again on the flattop mountain in sight of where the *Río* Aros runs into the *Río* Yaqui.

CHAPTER 46
SURRENDER TO LIES

I led my little band north from Agua Fria, staying in the shade from trees along the *río*. It was a land covered by great spans of white rock that reflected the sunlight, as if off a mirror, making the normal glare even more brilliant. Near the time of shortest shadows, we stopped to rest and water our horses and mules.

I developed a strong liking for our little captive girl, Trini Verdin. She proved a worthy captive, and I was glad I didn't let the warrior kill her. She worked hard without complaining, had learned a little of our language, and did as we told her. When we crossed the desert and killed the scalp hunters before going to the Azul Mountains, she made the walk without begging for water or a horse to ride. I now thought that after her womanhood ceremony, I would take her as a wife. I could teach her many things under the blankets.

Trini's light behind her eyes, strength, and willingness to work reminded me of Chee-hash-kish. I missed Chee-hash-kish, but I knew I'd never see her again. *Ussen* showed me this in a dream, and later a trader at Casas Grandes told me he had heard that she had been then sold to a rich family far to the south in Ciudad Mexico. He said there was even a story that she had remarried but the trader said he thought that was just a story. I didn't care. If I ever had a chance, I'd get her back, but I knew *Ussen* always spoke true to me.

Thinking on these things about Trini and remembering the good days with Chee-hash-kish, I thought I heard distant splashes in the *río* and ran to look back toward Agua Fria. *Nakai-yi* militia had just ridden across the *río*. They saw us about the same time I saw them. I yelled to my people, "Run! *Nakai-yes!*"

Trini looked around with wide eyes. I jumped on my pony, extended my hand, and pulled her up behind me as *Nakai-yi* bullets began to fly. My people ran through limbs and leaves flying off the trees as the *Nakai-yi* bullets, like a swarm of angry bees, flew through them. The People ran up a canyon with high, rough walls to find places where they could defend themselves, and I was right behind them. A bullet hit my horse. He pitched forward, throwing Trini and me off. We landed hard in the dirt and sand, but the fall hurt neither of us.

I saw a dark spot among a nest of boulders down the canyon and ran for it yelling "Trini! Come!" But, stunned, she ran stumbling toward the *Nakai-yes* waving her arms and scream-ing, *"Captiva! Captiva!"* She was very lucky they didn't kill her. I hated to lose her. I liked the child, even if she was a White Eye.

The dark spot I saw was a shallow cave that afforded good protection from the initial volleys of bullets. I yelled to the People, "Run for the *Río* Bavispe camp when you can." I moved back far enough in the cave to avoid anyone on the canyon rim seeing me, checked the load in my rifle with the long barrel, and waited for a *Nakai-yi* foolish enough to show himself.

The shadows started to grow toward the east when a *Nakai-yi* appeared on the canyon rim above me looking over the edge for my hiding place. It was an easy shot. I hit him in the center of his head below his left eye. He fell backwards away from the rim. A while later another *Nakai-yi* who had been to his left came into view. I shot him in the ear. Another looked around a thin tree on the canyon. I shot him, too, but don't think I killed him. It was quiet for a time when a sudden rain of bullets began ricocheting off the boulders around the cave. I crawled farther back into the little cave, but one of the ricochets hit me in the meat of my right arm and burned like an iron from a hot fire.

The firing stopped, and I wrapped and tied off a piece of rawhide above the wound to stop the bleeding. I wasn't worried. *Ussen* had already told me I would die a natural death. I crawled forward so I could see the canyon rim, and waited as the shadows grew longer. Again, a man raised above the rim, trying to see in my cave. This one, I hit between the eyes. He had leaned so far over the rim that, when I shot him, he fell off the rim, bounced against a cliff wall, and then landed to the sound of cracking tree branches.

My wound throbbed and hurt, but my arm was still usable. I reloaded and waited as the shadows grew longer, but no more *Nakai-yes* showed themselves. I smiled to myself. I had killed more here than I usually could in a good raid.

As the darkness began filling the canyon, I slipped into the dark shadows and made my way toward the east. In the Teres Mountains, I would meet the People in our safe camp and plan more raids with Naiche and the warriors.

In our camp high on a flattop mountain in the bend of the *Río* Bavispe, I talked with Naiche about new raids. We decided to try our luck attacking one of the mule packtrains that kept Ures provisioned. It had been three harvests since Chihuahua and I had raided Ures packtrains, and they always had a good store of supplies.

We found a sixty-mule packtrain that had supplies we needed and fresh mounts. We packed what we wanted on fifteen mules and cut the throats of the rest. We went southwest toward the village of Nácori Grande and took stock we needed from the nearby horse ranches.

We made four more raids near Cumpas as we returned with

our new horses to our women and children camped on the *Río* Bavispe and rested. Naiche and I had wounds from a fight with Americans near the Santa Rosa mines, but the wounds weren't too bad, just annoying. The next day, we took some stock from around Turicachi. That evening, Naiche, the warriors, and I met in council and decided we needed rest. It was time to tell the *Nakai-yes* we were ready to talk peace and get their usual gift of mescal to get us drunk in peace talks and kill us.

Soon we talked to the *alcalde* from Cuchuta, and he made arrangements for us to talk to the chief of Fronteras, who asked us to wait eight days while he sent word to the chief of Sonora, Torres, about his interest and peace terms. We agreed to wait and returned to our camp in the mountains. I sent two women to Fronteras to collect our mescal and other supplies promised us by the chief at Fronteras. When they returned, we would all have a good drink, our heads would hurt a while, and then we would be ready for another raid, maybe down in the Sierra Madre close to our old camps at Bugatseka.

When the women returned with the mescal and supplies, the whole camp, except for the children, let the fire from the mescal roll down our throats. We had enough to drink for two days, and we wanted a good drink, but after we drank it all, our heads felt like stones in leather-covered war clubs had hit them. The next morning, the ache was not so bad, and pots of coffee that came with the supplies made us feel better.

Near the time of shortest shadows, all the men were sleeping again, most in their family *wickiups,* while their wives and children did their camp work sorting supplies and making ready to travel when we needed. I dozed in the shade near the trail down the mountain while Kanseah, our youngest warrior, used my soldier glasses.

Memories of Trini were floating across my mind when

Kanseah shook me awake. He offered me my soldier glasses and said, "Geronimo, scouts come."

I looked down the trail and, through the wavering, twisting air, saw the tiny figures who ran with a white cloth on a long stick. Kanseah was right. They were scouts. No White Eye could run like that in this heat. I told Kanseah to go to the *wickiups* and bring the warriors, that we needed a council now. Scouts had betrayed us many times. I wanted to kill them all and planned to kill these two when they got close enough. But it didn't happen. The scouts, Kayihtah and Martine, had relatives among us who would not let us kill them. We let them come into our camp and speak to us in council.

Kayihtah and Martine told us they brought Teniente Gatewood with surrender terms from Nant'an Miles. I saw brows lift in interest when the warriors heard this. They were tired of hide, run, fight, hide, fight, and run again. They wanted to see their families, and even I wanted to see my women and children, who were stolen from us last harvest.

Kayihtah and Martine brought Teniente Gatewood with them the next sun to give us Nant'an Miles's terms for our surrender. Teniente Gatewood, respected by us as a strong warrior with a straight tongue, told us if we did not surrender to Nant'an Miles that he would hunt and kill us all, no matter how long it took. If we surrendered, we would see our families in five days. Then big chief Cleveland would send us East to the place called Florida until he decided what to do with us, and we would have our own reservation with all the Chiricahuas in one place.

These terms sounded like the same terms Nant'an Lpah promised five moons earlier. Naiche and the others, wanting to see their families, decided to surrender. I could not fight the White Eyes without these great warriors. I decided to surrender with them. Within two moons, we learned that we had surrendered to lies. Our days of freedom and war, blood and fire, had ended forever.

Now we faced life at the mercy of the White Eye and Blue Coat chiefs. I prayed for *Ussen* to help us. The story of what happened to us when we surrendered to Nant'an Miles and became White Eye prisoners of war is a tale of long harvests spent wandering to places in the east driven by the hands of White Eyes. I have told it to others who will pass it on. One day it will be written in a book that others might know of our journey. The book will be called *The Odyssey of Geronimo, Twenty-Three Years a Prisoner of War*. This is all I have to say.

ADDITIONAL READING

Ball, Eve, *In the Days of Victorio: Recollections of a Warm Springs Apache*, University of Arizona Press, Tucson, AZ, 1970.

Ball, Eve, Lynda A. Sánchez, and Nora Henn, *Indeh: An Apache Odyssey*, University of Oklahoma Press, Norman, OK, 1988.

Barrett, S. M., *Geronimo, His Own Story: The Autobiography of a Great Patriot Warrior*, Meridian, Penguin Books USA, New York, 1996.

Bourke, John G., *An Apache Campaign in the Sierra Madre*, University of Nebraska Press, Lincoln, NE, 1987. Reprinted from the 1886 edition published by Charles Scribner and Sons.

Bourke, John G., *On the Border With Crook*, Charles Scribner's Sons, New York, 1891.

Cozzens, Peter, *The Earth Is Weeping*, Alfred A. Knopf, New York, 2016.

Cremony, John C., *Life Among the Apaches*, University of Nebraska Press, Lincoln, NE, 1983.

de la Garza, Phyllis, *The Apache Kid*, Westernlore Press, Tucson, AZ, 1995.

Debo, Angie, *Geronimo: The Man, His Time, His Place*, University of Oklahoma Press, Norman, OK, 1976.

Delgadillo, Alicia with Miriam A. Perrett, *From Fort Marion to Fort Sill*, University of Nebraska Press, Lincoln, NE, 2013.

Farmer, W. Michael, *Apacheria: True Stories of Apache Culture 1860–1920*, Two Dot, Guilford, CT, 2017.

Farmer, W. Michael, *Geronimo, Prisoner of Lies: Twenty-Three Years as a Prisoner of War, 1886–1909,* Two Dot, Guilford, CT, 2019.

Goodwin, Grenville, *The Social Organization of the Western Apache,* Original Edition Copyright 1942 by the Department of Anthropology, University of Chicago, Century Collection edition by the University of Arizona Press, Tucson, AZ, 2016.

Haley, James L., *Apaches: A History and Culture Portrait,* University of Oklahoma Press, Norman, OK, 1981.

Hutton, Paul Andrew, *The Apache Wars,* Crown Publishing Group, New York, 2016.

Mails, Thomas E., *The People Called Apache,* BDD Illustrated Books, New York, 1993.

Opler, Morris Edward, *An Apache Life-Way, The Economic, Social, and Religious Institutions of the Chiricahua Indians,* University of Nebraska Press, Lincoln, NE, 1996.

Opler, Morris, *Apache Odyssey, A Journey Between Two Worlds,* University of Nebraska Press, Lincoln, NE, 2002.

Robinson, Sherry, *Apache Voices: Their Stories of Survival as Told to Eve Ball,* University of New Mexico Press, Albuquerque, NM, 2003.

Sánchez, Lynda A., *Apache Legends and Lore of Southern New Mexico, From the Sacred Mountain,* The History Press, Charleston, SC, 2014.

Sweeney, Edwin, *From Cochise to Geronimo: The Chiricahua Apaches, 1874–1886,* University of Oklahoma Press, Norman, OK, 2010.

Thrapp, Dan L., *Al Sieber: Chief of Scouts,* University of Oklahoma Press, Norman, OK, 1964.

Thrapp, Dan L., *The Conquest of Apacheria,* University of Oklahoma Press, Norman, OK, 1967.

Utley, Robert M., Geronimo, Yale University Press, New Haven, CT, 2012.

Additional Reading

Worchester, Donald E., *The Apaches: Eagles of the Southwest,* University of Oklahoma Press, Norman, OK, 1992.

ABOUT THE AUTHOR

W. Michael Farmer combines ten-plus years of research into nineteenth-century Apache history and culture with Southwest-living experience to fill his stories with a genuine sense of time and place. A retired PhD physicist, his scientific research has included measurement of atmospheric aerosols with laser-based instruments. He has published a two-volume reference book on atmospheric effects on remote sensing as well as fiction in anthologies and essays. His novels have won numerous awards, including three Will Rogers Gold and two Silver Medallions, New Mexico-Arizona Book Awards for Adventure, Historical Fiction, a Non-Fiction New Mexico Book of the Year, and a Spur Finalist Award for Best First Novel. His book series includes *The Life and Times of Yellow Boy, Mescalero Apache* and *Legends of the Desert.*

The employees of Five Star Publishing hope you have enjoyed this book.

Our Five Star novels explore little-known chapters from America's history, stories told from unique perspectives that will entertain a broad range of readers.

Other Five Star books are available at your local library, bookstore, all major book distributors, and directly from Five Star/Gale.

Connect with Five Star Publishing

Visit us on Facebook:
    https://www.facebook.com/FiveStarCengage

Email:
    FiveStar@cengage.com

For information about titles and placing orders:
    (800) 223-1244
    gale.orders@cengage.com

To share your comments, write to us:
    Five Star Publishing
    Attn: Publisher
    10 Water St., Suite 310
    Waterville, ME 04901